Also by James V. Viscosi

Available Now

Night Watchman
A Flock of Crows is Called a Murder
Long Before Dawn
Television Man
Father's Books

The "Strings" Duology
Shards
Ravels

Anthology Appearances
New Traditions in Terror
edited by Bill Purcell
featuring "The 66th Vampire"

Crossings
edited by Megan Powell
featuring "Draw"

www.jamesviscosi.com

Night Watchman

a novel

by James Viscosi

Prologue

Nicholas Fenton built the Wright Project.

It's become a home to hundreds of people, dozens of families. They're in their new apartments right now, sleeping in their new beds, thankful for windows that aren't broken and a roof that doesn't leak.

In its month or so of existence, the Wright Project has been good for the poor people of Island City.

And Nicholas Fenton built it.

Now he's going to burn it down.

He parks his car two streets away and walks to the Project. A Mercedes stands out in this neighborhood, night or day, and he doesn't want anyone to figure out he's here. Once the fire starts, and people start to die, it won't matter anymore, but for now it does.

The Wright Project, *his* project, cost him a lot of money to build. He hopes the locals appreciate it, but doesn't think they do. Seems like they're always yelling about something, always accusing him of having this ulterior motive, that hidden agenda. Sure, he does, but does that mean *everybody* has to carry on like spoiled children?

Ingrates. They *deserve* to die.

The tenants are still settling into the Project; he's been watching them coming and going all day, every day, for weeks, with trucks and trailers and bags and boxes. He figures the complex has somewhere over five hundred people in it now and he thinks that's enough. He can expect at least four hundred of them to die in the upcoming fire. He doesn't need to wait for it to reach full occupancy. Besides—got to be honest—he's getting impatient. He wants to get this thing done. He wants what's coming to him.

It's a little before two in the morning when he enters the grounds from the northeast. The bustle of the moving-in process is over for the day and the complex is quiet. He doesn't see anybody as he walks down the angled sidewalk leading from the northeast corner to the center of the Project. He walks fast, taking rapid, tight, nervous little steps.

He pauses at the center of the complex, where the five evenly-placed sidewalks come together at a ring of concrete that encircles a small round building made of red brick. The five apartment buildings loom over him, black in the yellow glare of the tall lights. Their dark silhouettes seem to stand in silent condemnation.

Oh, stop being an ass. They're just buildings, and he *built* them, for God's sake. He saunters to the roundhouse, flouting the judgement of the buildings, parading the fact that he doesn't care what they think of him. Piles of concrete and steel, anyway, how smart can they be?

He pats the side of the roundhouse. The bricks are rough and warm. Yes, the little roundhouse loves him, doesn't it? It approves of his plan. It's got more sense than the other five buildings put together. He trots along the wall, feeling the bricks scrape and tug at the skin of his palm. When he reaches the deep hollow of the recessed iron door, he slips into the concealing depression and waits there a moment, making sure nobody's going to come and ask him what he's doing.

He checks his watch. Two o'clock. At two-oh-five he fumbles a ring of heavy keys from his pocket, undoes the padlock on the door, and goes inside. It's stifling hot beneath the corrugated steel roof; the day's heat has been trapped in the windowless, airless chamber, it's soaked into the walls and the steel pipes that make up the guts of the roundhouse, guts that supply the complex with its vital nutrients— electrical boxes, the main water and gas valves, the telephone switchboxes. Utility stuff. It all looks kind of grey and ghastly in the hard light of the single naked bulb above the entrance.

He closes the iron door and slides the interior bolt into place.

Made it. He peels off his jacket and drops it on the concrete floor, then undoes the buttons at the wrists of his dress shirt. Should've worn shorts and a tee shirt but that's no way to dress when you're about to become a minor deity. Still, God, so hot!

On the wall beside the door is an electrical switch, a big one made out of metal bent into a square, with a black light bulb in the middle of it. It's like something from a mad scientist's laboratory. Maybe he should laugh maniacally as he throws it. He grasps the handle and moves the lever from the top set of clips into the bottom. The black bulb begins to glow red—a sinister red, Fenton thinks, bloody. Somebody's idea of a joke, except nobody could know what the switch is really for, he wired it up himself.

He laughs maniacally. Just for fun.

Now he proceeds to the center of the roundhouse, a spot marked by a metal lid in the concrete floor. It looks like a service hatch of some kind but beneath it is more cement; it's really only a marker. If you look at it closely you can tell the hinges are fake, but nobody looks at it closely. Nobody gets into the roundhouse except him. He stands on the marker. A thick black cable ending in a small rocker switch dangles just within his reach. He stretches up, takes the bulb in his right hand, and pushes the switch down with his thumb.

The light above the door dims. A sound like lightning crackles from the big mad scientist switch. The circuit from the lever on the wall is completed. Hidden resistors in the walls of the apartment buildings begin getting juice, heating up. In minutes they will ignite the dry wall, which is sadly deficient in its ability to withstand heat; then the paint will catch fire and the paint will burn like the sun itself.

The completion of the special, secret circuit has the side effect of cutting off power to the electromagnetic catches on the fire doors, causing them all to swing shut. And—*oops!*—they lock. And the smoke detectors and sprinkler activation switches are on the same cut-off circuit. It would be a disastrous design flaw, if it hadn't all been done on purpose.

The fire will be huge and swift and catastrophic and deadly.

He can hardly wait.

Soon people begin to die. Smoke inhalation or burns or crashing into the ground from fifth-floor windows; it doesn't matter how they die so long as they do. Fenton registers each small murder as an electric thrill, a tingle rising up from his feet and sweeping up to his head. Die, he thinks; and die, and die, and die!

Suddenly an explosion outside shakes the little roundhouse. He is startled for a moment, then realizes that he forgot to turn off the gas main. Stupid—how could he have been so stupid! Explosions! They could snuff the fire beneath collapsing walls and ceilings! And now the process has begun, and the black iron wheel that would shut off the gas stands across the roundhouse, far beyond his reach. To turn it off he would—*explosion!*—have to leave the marker, leave the center of the roundhouse; and then the precious, precious energy would be lost, would shoot beyond his reach and vanish!

Shit, shit, shit!

He tries to keep one foot on the iron lid, stretching his legs to reach out for the valve. It remains beyond his trembling fingers, perhaps a foot away. Another explosion roars its fury, the largest one so far. It deafens him, it shakes the brick walls.

Shit!

He steps off the marker. Immediately the power begins to leave him, rushing out like water swirling down a drain. His hands find the wheel, but before they can turn it the roof bursts open above him and a chunk of flaming masonry and drywall comes crashing down. He screams and falls onto his back. The chunk of the Wright Project strikes the gas main and the other pipes and bends them down toward his prostrate form, stopping scant feet from crushing him. He can feel the heat of the debris and scuttles backward. Through the hole in the roof he sees the sky bloodied by fire, bruised by smoke. He hears the screams and the sirens. He feels his power trickling away.

Something hit his head. He's dizzy and injured, blood is running down his face. He crawls back to the center of the roundhouse, stares stupidly at the burning chunk of building that intrudes on his sanctuary. He thinks he should do something about it but can't decide what.

The clump of masonry shifts and slides closer to the floor. The gas main bursts. He has a moment to stare at the ruptured conduit, a second to smell the sulfur.

Then the roundhouse erupts into a geyser straight from hell.

SHADOW KNIGHT

1

One-fifty in the morning. Police officers Nate Watson and Franklin Yaddow respond to a call from Canal Street. They cruise slowly along the pockmarked road. Nate Watson looks out the window, watches the derelict buildings as they pass. It's getting so he can't tell the empty ones from the occupied ones anymore. Buildings are getting so run-down, they could *all* be abandoned and it wouldn't surprise him.

They pass the wide empty lot where the Wright Project used to be. It's become a big campsite for indigents. They get old oil cans as fireplaces and burn any wood they can find; they also burn garbage, old tires, anything that'll hold a flame. Nate watches them standing around the fire, silhouettes holding out their hands to catch the warmth, and he thinks that ten thousand years ago humans were a bunch of grubby vagrants sitting around makeshift fireplaces and after nearly a dozen millennia things are heading that way again.

"This is the place," says Frank. He guides the patrol car over to the curb in front of a decaying tenement. It looks like it might have been habitable once, with rugged sandstone walls and a front stair that spills down to the sidewalk in a graceful arc. The steps used to be white, though now they're stained with piss and paint and the subtle pattern carved into the banister is chipped and broken. The windows are all covered with black bars, iron ones, bolted onto the aging structure with bullet-sized studs. Nate thinks of a person with black iron bars over his eyes, attached to his orbital ridges right around the socket.

Frank parks behind the burned-out shell of a car. It looks like an old Mustang, Nate isn't sure; much of the vehicle is gone, picked clean like a carcass out in the savannah. No one is ever going to bother towing it away, so it makes a good landmark in this part of Island City. Just call it the Mustang Arms, thinks Nate.

Frank radios the dispatcher that they've arrived and they get out of the car, Frank first, then Nate. They lock the doors. Frank pauses, looking up at the darkened tenement, and says, "Lemme tell ya, Nate, I don't like working this part of town."

"Try *living* here, Frank," Nate says.

"No thanks."

Nate sees something in the Mustang and flicks on his flashlight, shining it through the hole where the passenger side window used to be. It's a vagrant, sleeping on the musty remains of the driver's seat. Nate flicks off the light before waking the guy. He wonders if maybe the car belongs to the snoring derelict inside it, if the man had something once, *was* something.

Frank is at the foot of the stairs, gesturing at Nate to follow. He joins his partner and they climb the steps together. The moon goes behind a cloud; the sky is full of them tonight, dark and thick, like floating chunks of concrete. The stairs are marble. Maybe once, years ago, ladies in fur coats came down these steps led by little dogs on leashes and stepped into waiting cabs.

Maybe. Years ago.

Frank pushes open the front door. The hall lights are out. They flick on their flashlights to guide their way. The floor is strewn with crap, newspapers and fast-food wrappers and beer cans, stuff that crunches and crackles as they slog through it. Nate thinks about getting hepatitis shots tomorrow.

He doesn't know, yet, that he has no tomorrow.

The building has elevators. They're in a little nook halfway down the hallway, two doors opening onto the shafts. One door is half-open like a lazy eye; inside it's dark, with no elevator in evidence. The other door is closed. Both doors are riddled with holes. It looks as if somebody stood here one night stabbing the thin metal over and over again with a big screwdriver. The button plate is detached from the wall and hangs down by a tangle of wires. Maybe the guy with the screwdriver got bored with the doors and decided to disassemble the elevator system. Nate thinks of an eyeball plucked from its socket and left dangling by the nerves.

Frank lifts the plate, looks at it, and swears.

"Stairs?" Nate asks.

"Stairs," Frank says.

The stairs are right behind them. They enter the well and start climbing toward the fourth floor. The atmosphere is stale and fetid, like a bathroom that's never been cleaned or aired out. Somewhere below them someone's murmuring something rhythmic, singing or chanting, maybe even humming. Nate finds it hard to imagine someone humming in this environment.

Frank takes the stairs stiffly. Nate has to pause now and again so he doesn't get too far ahead.

"*Doo-be-doo-dah*," sings the voice from below.

They reach the fourth floor. Frank is puffing and flushed and Nate says, "Too many doughnuts, Franklin."

"Nah, too much sex," Frank replies.

Nate pushes open the door. "I stand corrected."

The hallway is cleaner than the one below, and the lights work sporadically. The floor is hardwood, badly in need of tending; the boards are pale and dry and slightly spongy. They go to apartment 412 and Frank knocks at the door. Nate notices a patch of what looks like dried glue on the door, glue and hundreds of small white hairs.

"Who is it?" asks a reedy voice from inside.

"Police," Frank says.

After a moment the door opens a crack. A heavy brass chain hangs parabolically from the jamb. Two suspicious old eyes look at Frank, then at Nate. They narrow. The thin voice asks to see their badges. They both remove their shields and hold them up for Mrs. Barrett to see. The old eyes are blue; they go with a white, almost yellow, face. They inspect the badges, then the door closes and the chain scrapes against its holder. The door opens again, wider this time. The old woman stands to the left. She's too short to look through the fish-eye peephole the city forced the landlord to install. "Sorry," she says. "You can't be too careful. They dress up like police sometimes."

"That's perfectly understandable, ma'am," Frank says as they enter the small apartment. The old woman closes the door behind them. Nate looks around. They're in the living room. It's small and boxlike, with yellow walls turning brown from age. Like being in a room made out of old cheese, thinks Nate, and the smell could be old cheese too but it's probably nothing as palatable as that. Odors drifting in through the old plaster walls, under the door. There's a blue curtain hanging over the window, only partially concealing its unfriendly black bars, visible on the other side of the glass.

A wooden door is half-closed in the wall to his left, mostly concealing the prim little bedroom beyond. He sees part of a low dark dresser, and on it a sepia picture of two people standing arm in arm.

Frank gets out his little notebook. "You're Linda Barrett?"

Nate turns as the woman answers Frank's question. "Yes, I'm her," she says, folding her thin arms as if defying them to tell her she's not. "I called you."

"You said you needed assistance?" Nate asks.

"Yes." The old woman, arms still folded, sinks carefully into a plush chair. Her eyes flick, birdlike, from Nate to Frank and back again.

Frank plops down into her old beige loveseat. "What, ah, what sort of assistance was it you needed?" he asks.

"Well, it's those kids," she says. She lets the statement hang there. *It's those kids.* Surely everyone knows about them.

"What kids would these be?" Nate asks.

The nervous blue eyes flick to him. "Local boys. Teenagers." *Teenagers* is a bad word the way she says it. "They come here—I don't think they even live in this building but the front lock don't work— and they go up on the roof and they do their Black Mass!" Her voice rings with denunciation.

Momentary silence.

"Black mass?" Frank ventures. He doesn't capitalize both words like she does.

"Yes!" Mrs. Barrett points at the ceiling. Her finger doesn't quiver. "They go up there and they chant and they dance and sometimes they even *kill* things!"

"What sort of things?" Nate asks.

"Little things. Defenseless ones. Puppies. Birds. They killed my cat!" The word *cat* comes out as an explosion. "I don't know how she got out but she did and they killed her and later I found her skin stuck to my door. With glue!"

"Have these kids threatened you in any way?" Frank asks.

"They killed my cat," she says. Her voice is haughty now. Clearly she can't believe he would even ask. "They march up and down these hallways pounding on the doors, yelling, cursing. They steal. I don't want to think what they would do if they caught me out there. I stay in here except to go to market now, because of them."

"Are they up there now?" Nate asks.

"Yes," she hisses. "Yes, they came caroling through the hallway forty-five minutes ago. *When I called you*," she adds. "They might still be there. I don't know."

"They armed?"

"Only with knives," she says.

"Would you like us to go up and have a look?" Nate asks. He catches the look Frank gives him and ignores it; the look says *what are you, crazy?* Nate still thinks it's his job to help people like Mrs. Barrett, and he saw the small white hairs stuck to her door with glue.

"That's why I called you," she says.

Frank pushes himself to his feet and closes his little notebook. He says, "Okay, Mrs. Barrett, we'll go up and see if they're still there. We'll tell 'em to find another chapel for their Black Mass." This time he does capitalize both words, egregiously.

Mrs. Barrett rises as well. "You don't believe in it," she says in a whisper, "but be careful. Listen to me! Beware the power of Satan."

"Don't worry, ma'am," Nate says. "We're pure of heart and noble of purpose. Right, Frank?"

"Maybe *you* are," Frank says.

They go back into the hallway. Mrs. Barrett shuts the door behind them and locks it four different ways as they head for the stairs. The air is just as rank on the fourth-floor landing as it was on the first, and doesn't improve much as they climb. "Do you think we need backup?" asks Nate as they ascend the last flight to the rooftop door.

"Nah. For a bunch of kids? They got knives, we got guns."

"But what about the power of Satan?"

Frank points to his groin. "I got the power of Satan right here. Now c'mon, or we'll miss the Black Mass."

They stop at the top landing. Frank eases the door open. It's covered in graffiti, so many different colors and designs it could be made of a hundred different shades of wax all run together. They're on the east side of the roof. They step out onto it. The roof is made of tar and was once covered with pebbles, though now it's mostly bare; the remaining stones grind under their shoes as they take a few cautious paces out of the shed where the stairs come out. An old ventilation unit looms in front of them, big as a truck, silhouetted against a flickering glow that emanates from its far side, delineating the sharpness of its edges, the old pipes sticking out from it, an old air grate curling up from its side like a scorched piece of paper.

There's no chanting going on. No singing either. Maybe they missed the Black Mass after all. Nate looks east. The buildings sort of slope downward in that direction, getting shorter toward the outskirts of town, and beyond them the hills rise up dark and massive into what looks like a gigantic wave about to break over the city and sweep it away.

"Hey, pay attention," Frank whispers. He gestures for Nate to circle the ventilation unit to the right and heads for the left side. He's got his gun out and is pointing it up in the air. His own gun is cold in his hand as Nate creeps along the rooftop.

The big, rusting ventilator comes between them. The night is quiet, like it's listening to him, or *for* him; it's got a surprise planned, something to shock and astound. Nate hears nothing but his heart hammering and wonders why it's racing so. He's done this sort of thing before. Nothing special about this time, nothing *unusual*, is there?

Just the power of Satan.

But hey, he's pure of heart and—

Then he hears Frank shout and knows the surprise is sprung.

Nate races to the edge of the ventilator and looks around the corner. He sees Frank stumbling backwards pointing his gun at a kid, a scrawny shirtless kid swinging an aluminum baseball bat. There are more kids to the right, standing around a star inside a circle done in white paint on the tar. It's dazzlingly bright, brighter than the five black candles that burn at the vertices of the star.

The kid with the bat connects with Frank's hand. Nate hears the *crunch* of bone and the *clang* of metal as Frank's gun flies out of his grip and into the night. He steps out into the candlelight and aims at the rooftop Babe Ruth and shouts, "Freeze!"

The kid ignores him, swinging again at Frank. Frank, wheezing, dodges right into Nate's line of fire. One of the shirtless kids standing around the star, with black hair in a ponytail, reaches out, holding his left hand cupped to the sky as if catching rain. Nate sees this with his peripheral vision but pays no attention; he can see both of Ponytail's hands, he's not holding a weapon. The one with the bat is the problem. "Frank, move!" he shouts.

His partner looks wildly over his shoulder, then spins around and slams up against the ventilator. The metal resonates hollowly under the impact, buckles inward slightly.

Ponytail jerks his fist shut.

And Nate's gun flies from his hand, hits the roof and slides toward the kid as if he has it on a string. Nate is too shocked to do anything but watch his weapon whisper to a stop at Ponytail's feet.

The one with the bat swings it into Frank's stomach. All the air whooshes out of him and he doubles over, coughing. Ponytail kneels and reaches for the gun, never taking his eyes off Nate. He looks about twenty, thinks Nate, twenty and hard as a tombstone.

He's getting the gun. He's picking it up.

Nate charges at him.

He hears metal tearing behind him, like an aluminum can getting squashed only much, much louder. "Nate, help!" Frank shouts, but Nate is bearing down on the star. He can't let the kid get his gun.

"Naaaaaaaaate!" The cry is a wail, a fading wail. Ponytail picks up the gun. The kid with the bat whoops a war cry. The other two haven't moved since the melee began, they could be the statues of saints watching murder in a church.

The barrel of the gun is rising toward him. Behind him someone is running. One of the motionless kids leaps as Nate gets closer, trying to tackle him. Nate catches the kid's arm and jerks it around, pulling the boy in and spinning him around. Now the kid is between Nate and the gun. Ponytail is grinning. His teeth are large and startlingly white. "You gonna die, man," he says. His voice is soft and young.

The kid with the bat is coming. Nate spins his hostage away, sending him at the ponytailed one, and turns to meet the charge. He's too late; the bat is coming at his head, whistling through the air. He twists and takes the blow on his scapula. The skinny kid is stronger than he looks, he knocks Nate to his hands and knees and then flat on his stomach by slamming the bat down across his back. The breath rushes out of Nate, stirring the pebbles near his mouth.

One of the other kids joins in, kicking him in the side. Nate looks toward the ventilation unit. There's a gaping hole in its side, the metal bowed inward. Frank is not there. A scrap of fabric flutters from a jagged tooth of rust.

They should have called for backup.

Then a last, vicious blow to his head sends all that spinning away.

His head is full of fuzz, but he hears the soft voice of the kid with the ponytail say, "Bring him here." Hands grasp his wrists and push him from the side, flipping him over. There's ink in the sky. He feels pebbles roll beneath him as they drag him a short distance and lay him down spread-eagled. Five misty globs of light surround him.

"Take his handcuffs," the quiet voice says. Nate feels a tugging at his waist, then the faint clinking of metal. After a moment icy cold encircles one wrist, then another, and he hears a ratchety clicking as the cold tightens. Now hands fumble with his uniform, undoing the buttons. Someone grabs the neck of his undershirt and lifts it, then cuts it away from him so his chest is exposed to the chilly air.

"What are you gonna do, Billy?"

"I'm gonna cut him," the kid with the ponytail says. You're *Billy*, thinks Nate vaguely. He will remember name and voice. Billy.

Billy straddles him. He can't see him well, his vision is all blurry, and anyway his eyes are drawn to something in his hand, something long and bright and sharp. A knife.

Billy, he thinks, does your mother know you?

The bright thing descends. It pricks Nate's chest, cold as ice. Pain, sharp and jagged, shoots up his neck. Billy works the knife downward, sawing instead of slicing. Nate squirms but his hands are cuffed together around something, and there's a heavy weight on his feet. The pain sears him, radiates in ripples from the furrow Billy creates in his flesh. His blood is hot as it runs off him left and right. At his navel Billy cuts two paths at forty-five degrees. He's done with the knife now, and begins peeling back the skin and meat. Nate can hear it tearing.

"Cool."

"Look at that. Hey, you wanna jump rope?"

Somebody paws at him, he can feel them tugging. Billy curses and slaps the other kid away. The light of the candles is fading, the ink in the sky is getting darker. The voices are fainter. Billy is still lifting the flaps of his flesh, sawing away at some bit of gristle that resists his efforts to pull it apart. "I wanna see his heart, man," one of the kids says. "Open him up some more."

"Man, there's *ribs* around his heart," Billy says. "Don't be a dipshit. I'd have to saw through *bones*."

Let them argue over the bones. He's leaving. There's a cold tide rushing over him, lifting him up, carrying him out of his violated flesh and leaving nothing behind but meat and blood and the internal grotesquerie exposed by Billy's knife. The tide carries him off into the night, into the darkness, and he accepts its embrace, draws it over himself like a blanket.

And sleeps.

2

It takes Billy a moment to realize that his captive has died; he keeps trying to cut through a last bit of gummy cartilage, and succeeds just as Roberto says, "Aw, man, he's dead. You *killed* him, man! I wanted to see his heart."

Billy glances at Roberto, standing there with the bat, and then looks at the cop's face. His eyes are wide and glassy, staring up at the sky; and his guts are steaming where the cold air touches them. Billy stands, closing the bloody blade of his butterfly knife. "Shut up, Berto," he says. "This ain't a fucking operation."

"I wanted—"

Billy lunges at Roberto, knocking him onto his back. "Shut the fuck up!" he shouts. "This ain't pay-per-fucking-view!" Roberto scrambles away, cringing like a whipped dog. Billy doesn't waste any more breath on him. He turns to the youngest one, Joey, who's sixteen. Joey is staring at the cop and is very pale. His freckles look like pennies against his ashen skin. "What's the matter, never seen guts before?" Billy asks.

Joey looks at Billy. "Sure. Sure I have," he says after a moment.

"Yuh," Roberto says.

"Lots of guts," Joey says. "See them all the time."

Roberto rolls his eyes. "Gimme a fucking break. You don't even *got* guts, let alone seen 'em."

Billy grins crookedly. "Okay, Joey, you're so used to guts, you get to stay up here and snuff them candles while we go down to the old lady's apartment."

"What old lady?" Joey asks.

"

"You know," Billy says. "The bitch with the cat. She called the cops. We'll go teach her whose neighborhood this is, right Chaz?"

"Yeah," says the biggest member of their group, still crouched on one of the cop's feet. He stands up, grinning. "We'll teach her."

Joey feels like he's going to puke as he goes around snuffing the candles. Billy doesn't like him to blow them out, he says you have to lick your fingers and squeeze the wick, but that makes Joey's fingers hurt. He snuffs two the right way as Billy, Roberto, and Chaz head for the shed leading down, then blows out the other three. The cop lies there still and quiet in an ocean of blood. He's dead as dead gets but Joey still has the creepiest feeling, like the guy is *watching* him somehow.

Guts. He's never seen guts in his life.

He hurries toward the stairs and leaves the roof door open in his haste. He doesn't like it up here alone in the dark, and he doesn't like the dead body handcuffed to the toilet pipe. He can't quite believe they really killed two cops up here tonight. He's scared they'll catch him, but he also feels proud.

Now he's a *man*.

After Joey leaves, it's quiet on the rooftop. The steam from Nate Watson's cooling body begins to fade. The black candles send curls of smoke into the heedless night air. A bird lands on the roof in a great flutter of feathers, and after a moment hops over to Nate's corpse. It jumps up onto his shoe, sidles up his leg to his waist. It pauses a moment, beady eyes watching for any sign of movement. Then it begins to peck at the ropy tangle of guts.

Suddenly the candles flare back into life. The crow squawks and takes to the air, cawing in distress.

Nate's muscles tense along his body. His limp hands clench into fists. A watery groan escapes his lips. His wrists pull apart and the handcuff chains snap. One shiny, broken link bounces to the rooftop.

Not much time passes.

The stair door clicks shut on the deserted roof.

They make Joey stand guard outside the door. That's okay, he doesn't really feel like participating. He can hear the old lady thumping and grunting inside, trying to scream but she can't because they stuffed her own panties in her mouth, and Joey tries not to listen to her and tries to hum instead and wishes he could be somewhere else, anywhere else.

But he can't leave, because it's not what a *man* would do.

Somebody comes into the hallway from the stairs. Joey looks at him. The light's patchy and he can't see the person very well, but it looks like a guy. Kind of big. "Beat it, man," says Joey, mustering up as much baritone as he can find. "This ain't your floor tonight."

The guy just stands there. Actually starts *moving forward*.

"I said *blow*," Joey says. Funny, he misplaced some of his baritone. "You deaf?"

Keeps coming.

"I got *friends* in here who'll mess you up," Joey says, but then the guy steps into the tepid illumination of one of the ceiling lights and Joey feels his insides turn into water and slosh down into his feet, feels his freckles freeze and fall right off his face.

It's the dead cop from the roof.

"Uh," Joey says. "Uh, uh, *uh!*" He scrabbles at the doorknob with one hand while keeping his eyes on the apparition. The cop raises his left hand. Joey's eyes snap there, focus on the gleaming silver band around his wrist and the little length of chain dangling down from it, and suddenly the chain shoots out fast and sure as an arrow. It snares Joey's ankles, wrapping around them and binding them together, and then the cop yanks the chain and Joey falls onto his face on the filthy hardwood. His head bounces off the floor. The cop reels him in. Joey scrabbles for purchase on the threadbare boards, his nails scraping against the wood as they find small nicks, catch, and come loose again.

He flips himself over onto his back. The cop is a silhouette against the ceiling lights. "Don't kill me, man," Joey says. "I didn't hurt you. I didn't do nothing. Don't kill me."

The chain leaps from his right wrist and entwines itself around Joey's head. It stays tight as it retracts sharply. Joey feels a moment of sharp, burning pain, tastes blood gurgling up from his throat into his mouth and wonders where it's coming from. He sees the floor and wonders how he can have wood against his nose when he's lying on his back. Then the world crusts over with frost, and he stops feeling anything.

Nate releases the chains and draws them back to himself. The kid stares wide-eyed into the floor. He lifts up his wrists and looks at them and then looks at the dead kid again. Then he looks at the door to apartment 412.

Closed.

He opens it.

A voice—*Billy's* voice—says, "I thought you wanted to wait outside."

The other three youths are here; they have the old lady pinned to the floor, one on her hands and the other on her feet, and Billy has his bloody butterfly knife out and is cutting through her slip. None of them are looking at him. They think he's their friend, their friend who he just killed.

For a moment Nate stands motionless. He knows he shouldn't have killed the boy in the hallway and he knows he should give these three a chance to surrender, but he can't force the himself to do it.

He says, "I have to kill you now." It comes out all garbled and drowned, but it gets their attention. They all look up at him. Billy freezes in mid-cut, staring.

"All of you."

"What the *fuck*?" one of the kids says.

Billy stands up, holding the knife in front of him. He motions the other two to rise and they do. "What are you doing here, man?" Billy says as the old woman scuttles away across the floor, futilely trying to hold the front of her dress shut with one hand while ripping a swatch of fabric out of her mouth with the other. "We didn't teach you good on the roof?"

"Billy, man, he's *dead*," hisses one of the other boys. "How's he standing here? Where's Joey?"

"He's not dead," Billy says calmly. To Nate: "You're not dead, my man. You fooled us on the roof, didn't you?"

Not a trace of remorse, not a whisper of fear from Billy. Nate's foggy brain pictures his partner's body in a bloody heap at the bottom of an air shaft. He raises his hands. Billy says, "You wanna fight, that it? Okay." He shows Nate his muscles. "We fight."

The chains fly from his wrists and encircle the necks of Billy's two friends. They gasp and clutch the gleaming, icy bands around their throats. Nate can *feel* them through the chains as if touching them with a second set of hands. They feel slightly warm, soft. They tingle a little bit. The other kid tingled too.

Maybe it's because they're alive.

Let's find out.

He jerks their heads together with a resounding, sodden *crack*. Blood splashes from the impact point as their faces flatten and elongate.

That was it. No more tingle.

He releases them and they slump to the floor. Billy's composure falters, but he keeps the knife out in front of him.

"Son of a bitch," Billy whispers.

"Now you," Nate says.

Billy spits at the floor in front of Nate and when the sputum hits the hardwood it flashes like a strobe. Nate's eyes swim with glare and spots. Through the hazy afterimage of the flare he sees Billy charging him; he feels the sharp blade of the knife enter his guts. The steel is cold. There's no pain. But there's a tingle.

"I killed you before!" Billy shouts. His voice has a rough, panicky edge. It's not soft anymore. "I'll cut you up this time!"

Nate's chains clatter to the floor, entwine Billy's ankles. Billy hesitates and looks down at his feet. Then he looks back at Nate. His face is ashen.

Nate grins.

And yanks Billy's feet apart.

Far, far apart.

Billy wails and topples over backward, his legs bent at nearly one-eighty. Blood gushes out to stain the crotch of his jeans, it gathers in a pool beneath him. Nate stands there a moment looking down at Billy, then grasps the handle of the knife and withdraws it from his stomach. He tosses it at the fallen youth. It lands flat on his chest, the blade pointing up at his chin. "Here," Nate says. "Put yourself out of your misery, if you can." He's got fluid in his lungs and throat; the words are drowned in it, gurgling. He doesn't know if Billy understands what he has just said. He doesn't care.

Mrs. Barrett slowly rises from her hiding place, staring ashen-faced at Nate. He looks at her, nods, and says: "Ma'am."

"*What are you?*" she asks.

Now why would she ask him that?

"I'm Nate Watson," he says.

"*What* are you?"

What is he? He's a man, isn't he?

Isn't he?

He raises his hands and stares at his wrists. A few links of chain dangle from each, the handcuffs glisten in the yellow light of the old floor lamp. He looks at Mrs. Barrett. Then he shuffles out of her apartment. Billy is groaning softly behind him, mumbling "Oh God, Oh God," again and again.

Mrs. Barrett crosses to her doorway but doesn't leave the apartment. She stands there a moment, watching Nate leave, then turns and looks down at Billy. "Does it *hurt?*" she asks him, her voice a hiss.

"Oh, *God!*" he wails.

Mrs. Barrett smiles.

Nate Watson doesn't know where he's going, and he has only the foggiest memory of where he's been. Before Mrs. Barrett's apartment he remembers darkness. He remembers voices. He remembers hands touching him, caressing him, dry and diaphanous as cobwebs but buzzing with electricity. They led him, they carried him, but he doesn't know why or how they brought him back to the roof, to the place where he died.

The place where he died. He has not had a near-death experience, with the tunnel and the guiding light and the spirits of departed friends. Although maybe those hands had been spirits of one sort or another.

Maybe not.

He doesn't think they were his friends.

He stumbles into the stairwell and staggers downward. He puts one foot in front of the other as if walking on level ground and the leading pace always drops an extra five inches or so before landing on the next step, making his descent jerky and awkward. He takes the stairs like a drunk.

He's going to leave the building. Yeah, that's what he'll do. Get out of this dump. But where's he going to go afterwards? Home? What would he say to Ellie? His uniform is drenched in blood; if he unbuttons it his innards will spill out like snakes stuffed into a cupboard. And what about the silver cuffs on his wrists? He knows, somehow, that they won't come off; no key will undo their locks, they're part of him now, them and their chains that elongate and retract and constrict at his will. And what about his eyes? His voice? What about his heart? His heart isn't beating, he isn't breathing, for all he knows he'll start to rot in a couple of days.

Oh. Oh. Oh. He doesn't want to rot. Why'd he have to think of that?

No, he definitely can't go home to Ellie. But he *will* leave this building.

He emerges from the stairwell on the first floor and turns right, shuffling away from the front door. He's just not a front door type of guy anymore. He'll find a side exit into the alley, into the darkness.

Mrs. Barrett waits a long time before she calls an ambulance for the boys. She's pretty sure the two who were sitting on her are dead; the other, the one with the knife and the disgusting, greasy ponytail, is still alive. She hears him groan every so often, or grunt and snuffle like the animal he is. She wants to give the policeman enough time to get away. Obviously the boys did something to him, though she has no idea what; they hurt him, they put the power of Satan into him and he returned it to them tenfold. She doesn't know if she really *needs* to wait—probably the policeman dissolved into dust after he left her sight, ashes to ashes and so forth—but wait she does.

More time for the boy to suffer.

Nate stumbles out the side door of the tenement, into a damp and narrow alley. There's an old concrete landing outside the door and Nate promptly falls off it, landing on something soft and wet beside it. He stares up into the frozen sky.

Sleep.

Yeah, sleep sounds good.

You've done your work. Now sleep.

Yeah, he's done his work. He rescued Mrs. Barrett from those bad, bad boys and now he can sleep. He's earned a rest, hasn't he?

Just close your eyes and let it all slip away.

He closes his eyes. Lets it all slip away. But then blue and red lights flash across Nate's closed eyelids and bring it all back. The lights rouse him. They're familiar.

Police cars.

Nate sits up. His limbs feel stiff and creaky and cold. He feels garbage shifting in plastic bags beneath him. He's in the alley between Mrs. Barrett's building and the one beside it, way up near the rear corner of the tenement, where a high chain-link fence stands as a barrier to vehicle traffic. Beyond the fence is a damp courtyard of asphalt, a tee intersection with another alley. Both alleys are littered with refuse, boxes and mattresses and tottering heaps of dark green bags like the one he's lying in.

He shakes his head, feeling groggy and weak. What just happened? He was so tired . . . was going to sleep. . . .

But he can't sleep now. They'll find him.

He staggers to his feet and goes to the fence. It's ragged and not as sturdy as it looks. Nate at first intends to climb it, but the rickety barricade shudders when he puts his weight on it so he goes through it instead, using his chains to rip an opening large enough for himself. Jagged bits of wire pluck at him as he squeezes through the gap. He doesn't pay any attention to them.

He turns right at the tee, cutting himself off from the police cars. Cutting himself off from the light.

The ambulance men are loading the boys onto stretchers. There's another dead one in the hall; that makes three. Three dead boys. The one with the ponytail simply will not die, to Mrs. Barrett's disappointment, though he is now apparently in shock and has stopped groaning. The ambulance men mutter among themselves as they gently push his legs back together and guide him into a padded, wheeled stretcher. It will be rough getting him down the stairs, but the elevators don't work so they'll have no choice.

The police came too, faster this time; she told them the first two officers had vanished and that improved their response time. Maybe she should say such things when she calls in the future. More of them came too, three cars and ten cops. Eight of them are prowling around the building searching for their fellows. The other two are standing in Mrs. Barrett's small, bloodied living room attempting to learn things from her and not getting very far. One does most of the talking, the other one stands there looking around. The talking one is named Charlie, though she's heard the other policemen calling him Whitey. The other one is named Andy. He looks so young, like Norman's age when he went to fight the Germans and never came back.

"You say the two dead youths were holding you down." Charlie's reading from the little notebook into which he had recorded that fact only a few minutes before.

"Yes," Mrs. Barrett says.

"And the other one was on top of you."

"Yes."

"And then someone kicked the door open and charged in and started killing them. And you didn't see a thing."

"He moved so fast," Mrs. Barrett says. "He was like a blur. And my eyes, they ain't so good no more. I'm *old*, y'know."

The policeman flips the notebook closed. He holds up his hand, two fingers extended. "How many fingers?" he asks.

"C'mon, Charlie, cut it out," Andy says. He takes Charlie's hand and lowers it. To Mrs. Barrett he says, "Sorry."

She shrugs.

Charlie stands there looking at her. She looks back. "Thank you, ma'am," he says finally. "I think that will be all."

Out in the hallway, Andy says, "We gonna bring her downtown?"

"Shit, no," Charlie says. He looks up and down the hallway.

"How come?"

Charlie turns to face him. "Okay, picture this. We bring her downtown and show her to a judge and tell him she's obstructing justice by concealing what she knows about the guy who saved her life by killing three-and-a-half punks. She's this hundred-year-old lady with blue hair and all she does is stand there and shiver because she doesn't have another shirt to put on because the dead kids cut up all her clothes. What does the judge say?"

"Uh. . . ."

"Yeah, uh. This whoever he is, he ain't the one made Nate and Frank disappear." Charlie lets that hang in the air a moment then says, "So c'mon, let's see if anybody found anything, and we'll worry about this mystery man some other time. Like never."

"Yeah. . . ." Andy trails off as one of the other cops appears from the stairwell and hurries toward them. Charlie looks over his shoulder, then turns around to face the newcomer as she stops a few feet away.

"Well?" Charlie says. "What's happening, Randi?"

Randi's out of breath from running up the stairs. "We . . . we just found Frank," she says.

"Shit." Charlie takes a moment to breathe. "Show me where. Andy, you ride with the ambulance and stand guard outside that little fucker's hospital room. They take him to surgery, you stand right next to the doctor. Got it?"

"Got it," Andy says.

"What a rotten fucking night," Charlie says.

3

THE NAME ON HIS CHART is *William Henderson*, but no one ever called him William except his mother and she's been dead twenty years now. Twenty years since the fire. Henderson isn't even really his own name, it was the name of the first of many foster families he went to. He doesn't know what his own last name really was. Maybe if he did, things would've been different somehow, but he doesn't and they weren't and William is somebody gone and forgotten, a potentiality cut off before it could grow.

He's *Billy* and he's a wretched actuality.

They have him flat on his back. His legs are tied down with leather thongs at the ankles, and a thick strap across his chest keeps him from moving or sitting up. His crotch feels like somebody's holding a blowtorch to it. He knows they're going to put him in some kind of body cast but all he wants is more drugs. They shot him up with something but it hardly did a fucking thing except make him dizzy. They don't give a shit about him at all, he could bleed to death on the bed and they would just change the sheets.

It wasn't supposed to be like this. He was supposed to have *power*, man, power to do what he wanted. He wasn't supposed to end up a cripple tied down to a bed. He shifts a little bit—

God!

He grinds his teeth together because if he doesn't he's going to scream and he won't give any of the fuckers the satisfaction. It feels like somebody's shoving a fence post up his ass. Nausea sweeps over him, puke rising in his throat. He chokes it down. His esophagus burns with the acid from his guts. He closes his eyes so tight he sees lights inside the darkness.

"Hello, William," a voice says.

Oh yeah. There's one other person besides his mother who calls him William.

He opens his eyes and sees his visitor. It's a man in early middle age, white, with rust-colored hair and a neatly-trimmed beard. He stands beside the bed looking down at Billy with clinical interest. "I heard you mumbling to that fool God and thought I would come see why." His voice is smoky and harsh and he does not whisper, as if he doesn't care if the cop outside the door hears them talking.

"It hurts." Billy's voice is a hoarse whisper.

"Yes, I imagine it does," the man says. He has taken Billy's folder from its sleeve at the foot of the bed, though Billy didn't see him move, and is leafing through it. "Shattered pelvis, torn ligaments, ruptured colon. . . ." He looks from the chart to Billy. "Nasty thing, a ruptured colon. All sorts of germs get out and swarm around inside you. Being fruitful and multiplying."

"Nicholas . . . help me."

"And why should I?" Nicholas says. "Did you help *me*? Did you follow my directions? Did you do as I said? *Did you?*"

"I did," Billy says. "You know I di—"

"Hah!" Nicholas says. "You're as ignorant as you are crippled."

"What?"

"You spilled blood inside your pentacle, and then you allowed the candles to be extinguished incorrectly. I *told* you the young one couldn't be trusted to follow your instructions, didn't I? But you didn't listen to me. You spilled blood in your pentacle and you left the young one to put out the candles and he did it wrong and created a . . . situation. When the candles went out, the circle was broken and the spirit came back. Back to its blood. Do you know how strong pure blood is, William? Blood without all the *shit* you put into yours? Have you any *idea*?"

Painfully, Billy shakes his head *no*.

"No," Nicholas says, and his voice is calm again. He inspects the back of his hand. "I thought not."

"Help me," Billy says.

"What's in it for me, then?"

"My soul."

At this, Nicholas throws his head back and laughs resonantly. "Your *soul?* If you've nothing to offer but *that* ragged thing, I don't think you and I can do business."

"The man's soul."

"What man?"

"The cop. I'll find him. I'll kill him." Billy's voice is getting stronger the more he uses it, he draws strength from the act of speaking.

"Don't promise what you can't deliver," Nicholas says half-angrily. He delicately returns the chart to its envelope. "His soul is neither yours to give nor mine to take."

"Then what . . . do you want?"

"Do you know what a revenant is, William?"

"You must want something or you wouldn't be here," Billy says.

"A revenant is someone who comes back from the dead. Some are physical, some are . . . projections. There are revenants, and there are *revenants.*" Pause. "You made a *revenant* tonight, William."

"You want me to kill him? I'll kill him."

"So easy, eh?" Nicholas says. He shrugs. "*I* am in no danger from him. Kill him or leave him, I don't care which."

"What—"

"*I want your body!*" Nicholas says. He puts his finger on Billy's wrist. His nail is long and sharp and digs into the flesh. Billy begins to bleed.

"But . . . I *need* it," Billy whimpers.

"And you didn't need your soul?" Nicholas asks. "What use is your body now? You can't walk and your guts are filling up with your own shit." He moves his hand up over Billy's chest, palm pointing down. "But I can fix it. You'll still have the use of your flesh; I just want . . . an interest in it. A stake, if you will, in your corporeity. And the opportunity to give you a few *modifications.* Will you give that to me?"

Billy doesn't consider the offer for long. He can think of no alternative. The pain is deep and strong, and he has no illusions that the doctors will put him together again the way he was. Nicholas can. Nicholas can do things doctors can't.

Nicholas is promising him power. The doctors can't promise anything, and the cops are promising jail.

Slowly, he nods.

"You're a very sensible boy," Nicholas says.

~~~

Outside Billy's room, number 313, officer Andrew Sykes sits in a molded plastic chair commandeered from a waiting room up the hall. He's reading an ancient copy of *Sports Illustrated*, but it's one of the swimsuit issues and this makes it timeless.

Time. Hm. He checks his watch. Twenty minutes until he gets relieved. Thank God. He feels like an exhibit out here in the corridor. He doesn't see why Randi or one of the others couldn't have done this, but no, got a detail nobody wants? Give it to Andy. Thank you Charlie!

Suddenly he hears the prisoner scream—no, not scream, *wail*—just once. The sound startles him and he jumps slightly, then looks around quickly to see if anyone noticed. The hospital denizens bustle back and forth, firmly ignoring him. This is what makes him feel like an exhibit—they *act* like they're ignoring him, but he is sure they are giving him surreptitious glances when he's not looking.

As his heart rate slows he stands, carefully closes the magazine, places it on the chair, and opens the door to 313. He has a clear view straight to the bed.

Empty.

Oh, shit.

The window's open. The curtains rustle in a cold breeze. Through them he sees that the sky is lightening with the approaching dawn. He crosses to the bed. When he gets closer he sees it's not empty after all, there's something in it. Something dark and folded, like a discarded bathrobe. He approaches it carefully. He can't tell for sure what it is, but it looks like . . . *skin*.

He takes his nightstick and prods the puddled mass. It *is* skin, and hair, and the thin blue hospital robe the prisoner had been wearing. He gets his truncheon beneath the thing and lifts it off the bed. It slides out from under the thick chest restraint, slips out of the smaller ankle cuffs, making a whispery fabric sound. It's limp and empty; it could be a Halloween costume, except it quite clearly belongs to the prisoner. The greasy hair, still in a ponytail; the ring in the left ear; hollow eyelids individually lashed; the broad expanse of the chest now collapsed and deflated.

Oh, this isn't even a little bit funny.

He pictures the punk wriggling out of his skin like some kind of
~~~

giant molting insect. The thought makes him want to puke and he shuts it off quickly and spends a moment breathing through his teeth, trying to get his gorge down.

Not gonna work.

He drops his nightstick. The skin puddles up on the bed as Andy stumbles off to the bathroom to vomit. He stays in there for some time, heaving up the remains of his dinner and then attempting to disgorge his stomach in its entirety.

While Andy throws up, the sun creeps to the gap between two buildings across the street. Its first oblique rays find the hospital room and fall on Billy's discarded skin. After a few seconds a pale smoke rises from the derma; after a few more seconds it begins to foam and bubble, decomposing, evaporating.

Gone.

Andy emerges from the bathroom dabbing at his lips with toilet paper. He still has no idea how he is going to explain this, but at least he'll have something to show Captain Weiss. Look, Captain, empty skin! Weird, huh? Unbelievable.

He sniffs the air. Something smells like burned pork rinds.

Then he sees his nightstick lying on the empty bed and stops, holding the soiled tissue inches from his face, staring at the sun beam on the vacant sheets.

Uh oh.

The guy behind the desk at the morgue looks up from a magazine when Andy comes careering through the double doors. "Hey, slow down, you'll fall and break your neck," he says, as something slides out of the sandwich he's eating and plops down on a starlet's pretty face.

"I need to see the bodies," Andy says. He's got a rusty nail taste in his mouth, from running all the way down to the basement and from the most appalling premonition that he's about to find himself in *very* deep shit.

The guy puts down his sandwich and produces a huge vinyl-bound logbook. "Which bodies?" he asks, flipping through the pages.

"The three John Does who came in this morning," Andy says.

Upside down, the names look like they're written in a foreign language. It kind of creeps Andy out, thinking each one came in with a body and stayed behind after the body was gone and all that's left now is a name scratched in a book. . . .

Okay, deep breath, deep breath, calm down.

The morgue guy—his hospital ID says he's *Danny Finch*—runs his finger down the page. "They keep saying they'll get me a computer," he muses, apparently to no one, "but have I a computer? Surely not. Three John Does, yes sir. Oh!" He looks up at Andy. "Those are the ones that detective came to look at."

"Detective?"

"Nick Talcott. He came in twenty minutes ago maybe. Still here, I think. You work with him?"

"I never heard of Nick Talcott," Andy says, drawing his gun.

Danny's eyes get big and round like the hard-boiled egg sticking out of his sandwich.

"Call hospital security," Andy says. He pushes through the metal door beside Danny's desk. It's icy cold. The room is large and bare, with pistachio-colored cinderblock walls on three sides. The fourth wall, the one opposite the door, is metal-faced and contains the drawers.

There's no sign of Detective Nick Talcott.

The ambulance gates in the right wall are closed and barred on this side, the door next to them padlocked for the night. The only other exit is the one he came through. Andy looks at the stainless steel autopsy tables; their surfaces are nicked and scratched from years of pathologists' knives, their original luster dulled from use.

He looks under the tables. No one is there.

The door swishes open behind him and he whirls, gun out, but it's only the morgue guy. He's got his sandwich in one hand and he's chewing nonchalantly, like he's at the park or something. "Called 'em," he says around a mouthful of egg.

"Are you trying to get shot or something? Jesus God," Andy says.

Danny shrugs. "No," he says, as if it were a real question. "The Does are in drawers seven, nine, and ten." He looks around. "Talcott's gone, huh?"

Andy goes to one of the drawers the morgue guy named. He grasps the latch, takes a breath, and slides it open.

Empty as a robbed grave.

"How about that," Danny says.

As dawn breaks over Island City, Nate Watson goes underground. He finds a manhole cover and sends his chain through its holes, threading it like a button, then he lifts it up and slides it away and climbs down the ladder beneath. It takes him to a ledge beside a fast-flowing stream of polluted water. The air is rank but he doesn't notice. The sound of the effluent echoes like a river in the brick-lined tunnel.

He picks a direction and shuffles away from the manhole. The tunnel walls are damp and slick. They meet in an arch overhead. He neither sees nor hears rats even though Island City has been having a problem with them.

Maybe they're avoiding him.

When he is well away from the manhole and its ladder he stops and sits on the ledge, staring off into the darkness. The sound of the water fills his ears. He wonders why he's here, why he came back from wherever Billy's knife had sent him. There must be a reason, he thinks; something as consequential as resurrection surely doesn't just *happen*. He lies down on his back on the damp brick floor. The wound in his torso is icy cold.

Why has he come back?

What has he become?

Got to keep his perspective. He's Nate Watson. He's a police officer, and still new enough to take the idea seriously. He has a wife who wants a baby but they're going to wait until they have more money, a bigger apartment. They're going to wait for Ellie to get promoted to office manager at the travel agency. Only a matter of time, the place would fall apart without her, nobody else even knows how the computer works.

Nate stretches his cold, stiff body, feeling his muscles tense and then relax. His wrists itch beneath the handcuffs. He's lonely for Ellie. She must know by now that he's gone missing. He pictures her sitting on the couch with his picture, crying, hoping he'll turn up all right. Frank Yaddow's wife is probably doing much the same, though they may have found him by now, depending on where that air shaft lets out. Lila Yaddow may have the comfort of finality.

Ellie does not, and will not, unless he brings it himself.

He has to see her again. Tell her what happened. He starts to sit up, then stops. It's daylight up there. He can't go out in the daylight. It'll . . . *do* something to him. Slowly he lies back down on the slimy bricks. Their wetness soaks through his uniform.

Ellie.

He has to tell her he's sorry.

He shuts his eyes against the darkness outside.

The darkness inside remains.

4

Eleanor Watson has always dreaded this night, the night Nate doesn't come home. Except it's a morning, not a night. Somehow that makes it worse. Outside it's still dark but soon the sun will rise over another grey morning, and the pre-winter wind will blow in off the river, and dawn will come and the day will begin without Nate.

He would be home by now. He works nine to five, night to morning, and gets home around six. She gets up early so they have some together time in the mornings. Got to pinch that whenever you can, when you both work and your schedules are at odds. She has coffee ready in the morning, and they sit together at the tiny table in the tiny kitchen, talking, watching the sky lighten from black to whatever shade will dominate the day, blue or white or grey. Sometimes they make love, and the light coming through the blinds sends stripes across their bodies.

She gets up from the kitchen table and pads across the wrinkled linoleum to the living room. Her eyes flit from one piece of empty furniture to another. The old yellow couch from her college days. The *papa san* chair Nate fell in love with, then couldn't find a place for and it ended up jammed in a corner. The antique rocker that belonged to Ellie's grandparents. She was going to rock her and Nate's children to sleep in that chair, when they were small and sick.

She falls into the rocker and sits there pushing on the floor with her foot. Back and forth. Back and forth.

Just her in the rocker.

They caught the four boys who killed Frank; someone really worked them over, killed three of them, they said. Ellie's third dearest wish, at the moment, is that she knew who did it so she could send them a thank-you note. Her second dearest wish is that she had done it herself.

Six o'clock. If she turns on the television now, she'll see the news. She knows Nate and Frank and the dead boys will be the top story, and it won't do her any good to hear an anchor reading about the wreck of her life, but she picks up the remote and switches on the set anyway. Her clock must be a little slow because the broadcast is already in progress. A field reporter is standing in front of the tenement in a tan trenchcoat, and he's describing how police found the four murderers—he calls them *suspects*—violently assaulted. Three dead, one badly injured. He wraps up his monologue and they cut back to the studio, where the pretty morning anchor is looking earnestly into the camera. "And we've just learned of another development in this mysterious case," she says. "Police report that all four suspects have *disappeared* from Marina Hospital. The bodies of the three dead youths—their identities have not been released because of their ages—have apparently vanished from the morgue, and the fourth suspect, William Henderson, twenty-three, disappeared from his hospital room. Police are baffled by—"

Ellie turns of the television.

Disappeared.

How could they have *disappeared?*

She looks around the room and it feels cold as a grave. She's familiar with the routine for guarding suspects in hospitals, there was a cop right outside Henderson's room, there had to be. And there must have been an attendant at the morgue. So what happened? Where'd they go? Did their gang come and rescue them somehow? Steal the bodies? Is it a clerical error, the dead kids filed in the vegetable drawer instead of the morgue? Did they just get up and walk away?

She looks at the door. She imagines the three dead boys shambling through it with their cold hands outstretched and their eyes glassy and stinking gases drifting out their gaping mouths. . . .

Oh, this is just too much. She needs somebody to distract her.

She picks up the phone and calls the station. They put her through to Nate's captain and she asks him if he can send someone to sit with her for a while.

He says he has just the person.

Andy Sykes sits uncomfortably in a chair in the captain's office. Watches the captain put down the phone and resume reading Andy's report about the disappearance of William Henderson. He knows this meeting is not going to go well because the captain's face is furrowing into a scowl and the scowl is deepening the closer he gets to the end of the report. It's like someone is slowly feeding the captain an extra-tart lemon.

He wishes he could disappear like the Henderson kid. Preferably with his skin coming with him, though.

Finally the captain flips back to the first page of the report, regards it briefly, and lays the small stack of papers on his desk. Andy waits for the inevitable upbraiding. But what could he do? Either he reported finding the prisoner's *skin* in a puddle on the bed, in which case he seems a lunatic, or he simply skips that whole aspect of the incident, in which case he seems an incompetent. Andy chose to seem an incompetent. Incompetents get punished but they don't get institutionalized.

"This report don't tell me jack," the captain says thoughtfully. He is an *arbiter elegantiae* critiquing Andy Sykes's contribution to department literature. "It's got holes in it I could see my desk through. You heard a noise. You went inside. The prisoner was gone and the window was open. Okay, that's great. Tell me something that surprises me."

"I can't tell you what I don't know," Andy says.

Lying to his boss. What would his mother say?

"How could the kid open the window with two broken legs?"

"A broken pelvis," Andy says.

"Thank you." The captain glowers. "So, you *do* know something. What sort of noise did you hear?"

"Hard to describe," Andy says.

"Give it a shot," Weiss says.

"Well, it was kind of like . . . a wail."

"A whale?"

"A scream," Andy says. "A real sharp scream. Like somebody stuck him with a pin."

"The kid had a broken pelvis. I doubt a pin would have pushed him over the edge." Weiss sighs. "But I get the idea. So the kid screamed, you went into the room, and he was gone and the window was open."

"Yes," Andy says.

"The fifth floor window."

"Yes."

"But we have no body, which we *would* have if he had jumped or been thrown out the window."

"Yes."

"Just making sure we understand our situation." The captain pats Andy's report. "Okay. Here's what we'll do. I will keep this load of hash and study it for hidden meanings. You will go on to a new assignment."

"Yes, sir," Andy says. He knows this assignment will be something boring at best, demeaning and disgusting at worst. Maybe he'll get lucky and get sent back to the tenement to join Charlie on guard duty. Should've stayed there in the first place.

The captain scribbles an address on a piece of paper and hands it to him; Andy takes it and reads it. "Go to Nate Watson's apartment and keep his wife company," the captain says. "Since you can't seem to keep track of kids with broken pelvises, and our friends at the hospital can't seem to keep track of the corpses in their morgue, we might as well try keeping track of somebody who's alive and well."

Andy is relieved. It could have been worse; this is a reprimand, but a relatively gentle one. The captain must be too shaken over the loss of two men to be truly abominable to him. "Thank you, captain," he says.

"Don't thank me," the captain says. "Just don't you disappear on me too."

The buzzer jolts Ellie out of a fuzzy dream. She sits up under the afghan and looks around the apartment, shaking her head, while her heart slowly returns to a normal pace. Damn buzzer has always been too loud, it sounds like somebody coming at you with a chainsaw. The dream still clings to her mind like gobbets of taffy; it was a dark dream, sinister, a dream about Nate, though now that she has awakened she cannot remember the details. She goes to the intercom and pushes the button to talk and says, "Yes?"

"Ellie? It's Andy Sykes. Captain Weiss sent me."

"Come on up." She buzzes him in. She knows Andy Sykes vaguely, by name; Nate has mentioned him once or twice. It will take him a few minutes to ride up in the old, slow elevator. Normally she would unlock the apartment door and return to whatever she had been doing before the buzzer rang, but not now. Not after what's happened to Nate and Frank. Instead she waits near the door until Andy knocks on her door and looks through the peephole before she lets him in.

"Hi, Ellie," he says, giving her a hug that's meant to be reassuring, a *we're-all-in-this-together* hug. She knows this hug well, having given it several times herself. Now that she's on the receiving end it seems a pitiful, inadequate, tattered thing. "How you holding up?" he asks as she closes the door behind him.

"Okay, I guess," she answers. Andy is younger than she is. He has cropped blonde hair and his skin is faintly reddish, like his mother scrubbed him down with a rough washcloth before sending him off to work.

Must be getting old, she thinks. She's twenty-nine.

Nate would have been thirty-two in three weeks.

No, no, mustn't think *would have been*. He could still be alive out there somewhere.

Out there.

Somewhere.

Suddenly she can't stay in this apartment anymore. She has to get out of here, do something. She knows what. "Andy, will you take me to the building?"

Andy, who has been examining the living room, looks at her blankly. "Take you where?" he asks.

"The building. Where . . . where it happened."

Concern floods his face. He is going to say something for her own well-being. "I don't think that's such a good idea," he says.

"I want to see it," she insists.

"Why would you want to go there? It's a dump in a bad part of town. There's nothing you can do there. We went over it top to bottom. If you go it'll just make you feel worse."

This response is actually rather convenient, because it encapsulates all the objections she had thought he would raise and she can dispense with them as a group. "I want to see where my husband disappeared. Is that unreasonable?"

Let's see him try to argue with *that.*

Like a sensible man, he doesn't.

The car Andy brought from the police station is an old Nova, a behemoth from the depths of the Seventies, gun-metal grey with a dark blue vinyl top. He natters on about nothing as he drives; he points out structural details in buildings and identifies the architects, he tells her who streets are named after, he points out parks and says who donated the land.

It's like riding with a tour guide.

"How do you know so much about Island City?" she asks finally.

"I take an interest," Andy says. He shrugs, as if to ask *doesn't everybody know this stuff?*

They reach the Hunter River Bridge and start across. The bridge is wide and flat and the water beneath it is the same color as the car. The Hunter River flows sedately by, straightened and tamed and marked out with buoys where the navigation channel is. Barges keep the channel dredged out so boats can use it; there's one down there right now, a squat brown thing with all the charm and character of a scab. It's not dredging right now, it's just sitting there. Pretty soon the river will be closed to traffic anyway, it'll freeze over and the barges will go away until spring.

Farther south, where the river widens into Kenkona Lake, she can see sailboats flashing white and blue and red in the morning sun. It's getting late in the season for sailing, though, nearly Halloween. Before long the pleasure craft will be gone too, and the river and the lake will be empty, nothing but water the color of slate, like you could write on it.

Andy's chattering about the history of the Hunter River now. God, doesn't he ever shut up?

Ahead is the Canal District. There's no canal there anymore—they moved it into the Hunter River and turned the original canal into a road—but it's still called the Canal District because that makes it sound colorful and quaint instead of just run-down and grungy.

Andy and Ellie wait for a light at the end of the bridge where it makes a tee with Harbor Road. Andy drums the steering wheel with his hands. Ellie eyes the apartment building across the street. She can almost *see* the roof sagging farther and farther into a U as she watches. It looks like a big one-family house that somebody converted to a multiple dwelling. That's what a lot of the housing in this area is, sumptuous old houses subdivided and partitioned, drawn and quartered.

The light turns green. Andy turns right and they noodle down Harbor Road. On their right is the river, with rows and rows of docks and piers in various states of decrepitude. Old fishing boats are moored here, and rowboats, and beat-up motorboats; no sailboats or yachts bob in these waters. On their left are businesses serving the marina, if it can be called that, bait shops and secondhand nautical supply stores and a big saloon. Ellie envisions men swilling beer in the bars, then staggering across the street to take their boats out onto the river. She remembers last week when an overturned rowboat was found pushed up against one of the bridge pilings; the occupants still have not been found, though divers had been going down into the icy dark water for several days. They're probably at the bottom somewhere, beer still drifting from their gaping mouths.

Oh, very nice, she tells herself. Very compassionate. Bitch.

They pass by a wildly overgrown park ringed by a crumbling cement wall two feet high. Great place to get mugged. To her surprise, Andy doesn't know who donated the land for the park.

Canal Street is a left turn several blocks from the bridge and one block from the park. This is the road that used to be an artificial waterway connecting the interior of the state with the river and, subsequently, the lake, another river, another canal, and ultimately the Erie Canal.

At least, that's what Andy tells her.

The remains of the last lock still stand, crumbling and crusted with moss and lichen, at the riverside. The grey bricks are now blighted by graffiti and broken by age. The city grew up around the old canal, and then it let the waterway die and be forgotten, filled it in and turned it into a road. Like a child turning on its parent, thinks Ellie. Well, now the city's economy is down the tubes, so maybe it's getting what it deserves for being such a rotten offspring.

An apartment building borders the park at the corner of Canal and Harbor, where two small businesses, a seedy diner and a new convenience store, attempt to survive in the hostile environment. The wall of the convenience store is mottled with concrete-colored paint.

Patches over graffiti. They'll be covered again by the end of the week. Ellie doesn't know why they bother.

Except for those two small buildings, Canal Street is residential, tenements and apartment houses. These buildings were actually designed as apartments, squat square brick things with all the personality of a stack of dice. Ellie stares at the buildings as they scroll by. Even in the daylight their broken windows seem like damaged eyes, their decaying architecture screams mortality. A few of them are boarded up, all their windows and doors blocked with plywood, but these don't really seem to be in any worse shape than the ones that are still inhabited. Maybe they've been seized by the city and are awaiting auction. This happens a lot, absentee landlords who don't pay their property taxes, that sort of thing.

"Urban renewal ain't reached here yet," Andy says.

She glances at him. He seems too well-scrubbed to be saying *ain't*. He must be trying to sound like the veterans. Probably going to take up swearing, too. His mother would be appalled.

There are people on the sidewalks, but not many. One catches her attention, a tall young woman with impossibly long legs tottering on stiletto heels as she carries two brown paper bags full of groceries; a small boy follows her, pausing now and again to inspect something on the sidewalk and then darting to catch up. Ellie wonders if the woman is the boy's mother, or if perhaps the child is just hoping something will fall from the teetering pile of brightly-colored boxes in her bags. Ellie watches as the woman passes an elderly man sitting disconsolately on the bedraggled steps of one of the buildings. He is staring across the road as if it were an ocean and his love lost on it. The little boy stares at the man a moment, eliciting no reaction; then he dashes to catch up with the woman again. Two teenagers, too young to be out of school today—a Tuesday—stride up the sidewalk from the opposite direction. They are side by side, talking, laughing, gesturing. The woman with the groceries steps into the rubbish-strewn gutter when she meets the kids, but the boy darts between them like a miniature Odysseus scooting between those two monsters, whatever they were. For a moment Ellie is afraid the youths will take this as a slight and do something to the child, but they ignore him, continuing their conversation. Ellie feels vaguely guilty. Would she have had such a thought in her own neighborhood?

Ellie turns away to look straight ahead. Canal Street is broad and straight, as if it were still important, a river of asphalt running between two banks made of trash. They're heading down a gentle slope right now, but up ahead the street rises again, up, up toward the morning sun.

Andy pulls the Nova over to the curb behind a marked police car. "This is the place," he says, throwing the vehicle into park. "You sure you want to do this?"

Ellie doesn't answer him. She is staring out the window at the decrepit tenement. It is a decaying, dying building, and it has taken her husband and secreted him somewhere in its rotten heart. She gets out of the car. A feral cat dashes out of the dark alley between this building and the next and runs off down the sidewalk, its rump high up in the air. Seconds later two little boys and a little girl come tearing out of the alley, pause in front of her looking left and right, panting. Ellie might as well not exist. They spot the fleeing cat and pursue, holding broken chunks of asphalt.

"The natives are on the hunt," Andy says, watching the chase recede. Ellie climbs the stairs, the stairs Nate climbed last night, and passes through the door he passed through. Andy hurries to catch up with her. "Hey, where you going?" he asks, taking her elbow as if to stop her.

"I want to see the roof," she says.

"No," Andy says. "No. No, you don't."

"That's where he went. I want to see it." She pulls out of Andy's loose grip and walks carefully up the hallway, toward where a broken electric *exit* sign dangles from the ceiling. Andy hesitates a moment, then follows.

"You're just going to—"

"Don't tell me what I'm just going to do," Ellie says. "I want to see the roof."

"It'll just upset you more," Andy says, trailing her into the stairwell.

The building has ten stories. She climbs the stairs without speaking and Andy, for once, is quiet. She comes to yellow police tape strung across the stairwell after the tenth floor, and she ducks under it and keeps going. There, she thinks, now she's a criminal too, she's in her element.

The door to the roof is ajar. The handle is wrapped in a brown paper bag that's taped down tightly. They're protecting it from being wiped or tampered with. She pushes on the battered metal and the door swings outward. She hears Andy arrive behind her, his shoes clicking on the stairs. She doesn't wait for him.

The roof is spongy, and strewn with pebbles that grind under her feet. Several yards away a ventilation unit squats like a huge mechanical beetle, its carapace rent and dented. A uniformed policeman is coming around the ventilator on the right, looking stern and purposeful. He expects to find kids or gawkers, but his expression changes when he sees her. Ellie knows him; his name is Charlie, but everyone calls him Whitey because of his hair, so blonde it could be moonlight. He's got dark circles under his eyes. She wonders how long it's been since he got some rest. "Ellie?" he says as he approaches. "What're you doing here?"

"I wanted to see where it happened," she said.

He looks over her shoulder. "You bring her, Andy? You shouldn't have brought her."

"I practically put a gun to his head," Ellie says. "Where'd it happen, Charlie?"

Charlie says to Andy, "Watch the door," and then he turns and crunches back around the ventilator. Ellie follows. On the other side, the massive unit is guarded by sawhorses with police tape strung between them like a gigantic cat's-cradle. There's a big hole in the fragile sheet metal between the sawhorses. "We figure that's where Frank went down," Charlie says, looking at the hole. His expression is blank. "He got banged up pretty bad falling down the air shaft. The fan down at the bottom's one of them turbo types with all the blades. It wasn't spinning but it still did a job on him."

Ellie really doesn't want to hear this. She looks to the right, at the pentagram made famous by the morning papers. It seems to be drawn in chalky white paint, like the boundary lines of a sports field. The star is a little sloppy but unmistakable, five points connected by lines the way kids draw them, surrounded by a circle passing through all five vertices. At each point a black candle sits in a wax-filled pie tin.

Charlie appears at her elbow. "The candles are suspicious, real greasy; the lab is analyzing samples. Animal fat, we think."

Animal fat. Jesus, these were *kids*.

There are pebbles inside the pentagram. They're stained a dull reddish-brown. Ellie wonders how much blood is in the tar, invisible against the black background. Nate's blood.

"Your pentagram is pretty much a generic symbol," Charlie says, warming up to his topic. "It really don't mean much to find it here. You can see it in a hundred movies. Kids just copied it, is my guess; there ain't no organized cult thing going on. There's a lot of blood inside the star. You can see how the chalk is stained heavily. We figure they had Nate or somebody else in there. Not Frank, they just whacked him around some with a baseball bat and then he fell down the hole."

Ellie imagines Nate on this filthy roof in the frigid night, his life spilling out onto the tar, while around him a bunch of punks watch and laugh. She wishes they weren't dead already, so she could kill them herself.

"Forensics worked the site over last night but they're coming back to go over it again in the daytime. Actually. . . ." Charlie checks his watch. ". . . They ought to be here by ten. You wanna stick around and talk to them? Maybe they can tell you some more."

As if Charlie hasn't told her enough already. She says no, and thanks him. "I'm really sorry, Ellie," he says gravely, giving her the *we're-all-in-this-together* hug. He walks her back to the rooftop shack, where Andy is standing nervously outside the stairwell door. She brushes past him—he's nothing, a dream, a cloud—and slowly walks down the stairs, one foot in front of the other; and the sun shines in through the open door behind her.

"You okay?" Andy asks as they descend the stairs.

She doesn't answer him.

As they're passing through the front door, they meet an old woman shuffling up the steps. She carries a brown paper bag with groceries in it. Ellie suffers a momentary delusion that she has been in this wretched building for fifty years, and the young woman she had seen earlier has aged into an elderly spinster never having put down her burden. She shakes her head slightly to clear it of such nonsense. This is the real world. Come back from fantasyland.

The old woman continues resolutely up the stairs, unaware, it seems, of anything but rising to the next step. Ellie moves out of the way, holding the door open. Andy steps through the opening.

"Thanks," he says, blinking in the sunshine.

The old woman, walking with her head bent, bumps into him. Now she looks up. Her face is frightened until she sees Andy's uniform; then it relaxes and she says, "Excuse me, officer."

"Ma'am," Andy says, stepping out of the way. But the woman doesn't keep going, she stands and stares at him, squinting as if he is difficult to see. Andy gets uncomfortable and shifts from one foot to the other, and finally says, "Is something wrong, ma'am?"

"Oh, no," the old woman says. "I just wanted to see if you were one of the policemen I talked to yesterday, but you're not."

"Actually, ma'am, I am." Andy talks to her like she's his mother, thinks Ellie, deferential as a kid in Sunday school.

"They ate me out of house and home," the old woman says, as if she didn't hear him. She shakes her bag. A blue coffee can and a triangle of newspaper protrude over its lip. "Look, I had to buy more coffee, more cheese, more—"

"Are you the one who called the police last night?" Ellie asks.

The old woman favors her with a suspicious glance. "Who're you?" she asks.

"I'm Ellie Watson. Nate Watson's wife."

"Nate Watson is one of the policemen who disappeared here last night," Andy says.

The old woman's eyes go from rocks to gumdrops. "Oh, honey, I'm so sorry about your husband. My name is Linda, Linda Barrett. Yes, I called the police. I told them—" She raises a finger to the sky. "—beware the power of Satan! But they didn't listen, they didn't believe, and those boys killed them."

"Nate hasn't been found yet," Andy says. "We don't know he's dead."

"Do you want to come up for coffee?" Mrs. Barrett says, the invitation clearly extending only to Ellie. "I can tell you all about what happened, all about the boys."

Ellie looks at the old woman, then at the tenement. She *would* like to talk to Mrs. Barrett, find out more about what may have been the last minutes of Nate's life; but not today. She isn't up to it today. "Maybe tomorrow," she says. "Would tomorrow be all right?"

"I get my hair done tomorrow," Mrs. Barrett says crisply, fingering the wispy strands that cling like cotton candy to her head. "But

Thursday would be nice."

"Thursday," Ellie says.

"Four o'clock would be nice. Do you work? I know how young women are these days, maybe later would be better?"

"I'm not going to work this week," Ellie says. "Four o'clock is fine." She will bring something to eat, she thinks, doughnuts or something; and she will listen to Mrs. Barrett talk about how the neighborhood has decayed and the people with it, and how things were when she was Ellie's age. She will find out what Nate said and did before he went to the roof. She will find out why he died.

If he died, that is. Which hasn't been proven yet.

Mrs. Barrett has said something, Ellie realizes, but she didn't catch what it was; so she nods her head and smiles. Apparently this is a satisfactory response, because the old woman turns and continues into the building, vanishing into the darkness inside the trash-strewn hallway.

When they're back in the car Andy says, "The old lady lives in apartment 412. You might want to know that so you don't have to go knocking door to door."

"Thanks," Ellie says.

"You really want to come back here?"

"She talked to Nate before he disappeared."

"We have records of everything she said. You don't need to talk to her to find out what she knows."

"Yes I do. I want to get it straight from her. I want to know exactly what happened. I can't ask a transcript questions."

"I guess."

"Besides, she's a lonely old lady. Obviously nobody's listened to her in years. It'll make her feel good to have somebody to talk to."

"You're a saint," Andy says. "You need me to drive you down?"

"I'll get a cab." Then she has a thought. "Cabs come here, don't they?"

"Sure," Andy says. "Long as you give 'em a really big tip."

They get back into the car. Andy starts it up, then looks at her and asks, "Home?"

Ellie stares at the receding building. Home? Where's home? "No," she says. "Take me somewhere."

"Huh?"

"Take me somewhere. Anywhere."

"I don't think—"

"You must have somewhere you like to go," Ellie says. "Everybody has somewhere they like to go."

After a moment, Andy says: "Inside or outside?"

"Outside."

"Outside it is," Andy says.

5

THE PLACE ANDY LIKES TO go is nowhere Ellie's ever been before.

It's a hill south of the city, where the land slopes up from the bay in gentle green strokes. The route to this place is tortuous, lefts and rights and lefts on roads Ellie never heard of, roads that—once they get away from the city—look like any minute the cast of *Deliverance* might come tumbling out of the brush and stampede across their path.

He pulls the Nova off at a wide spot, where the shoulder of the road bows outward in a hard-packed crescent. Trees huddle together by the roadside, a phalanx of wood forcing the pavement to turn aside. The dark opening of a path beckons passers-by to explore gloomy sylvan avenues.

"You bring girls here?" Ellie asks as she gets out of the car. Andy grins sheepishly and turns a darker shade of red. Ellie says: "No shit. You do, don't you?"

"Sometimes. C'mon, follow me." He scampers off toward the path. He's like a little kid exploring a favorite terrain. Ellie goes after him. She can't remember the last time she went wandering in a forest. Honeymoon, maybe. With Nate.

She closes her eyes. She inhales. The air up here is cold, smells of old bark and decaying leaves. The place is probably gorgeous in summer and early autumn. Now it's just bare and dead-looking.

"Come *on*, Ellie!" Andy hollers. He sounds like he's forgotten all the things that have happened in the last twelve hours. Ellie wonders again how old he is. Probably not even old enough to remember when there was no MTV.

Opening her eyes, she follows him into the forest. He's gotten quite far ahead of her. She sees him only as a blue splotch ducking in and out of trees. She doesn't worry about losing him, though. Many smaller tracks branch off from the wide one, but the main path is always obvious. It slopes downward slightly and is slick with fallen, damp foliage. She is walking too fast, slips and almost falls, catches herself by throwing her arms around a slender tree. As she pulls herself erect she notices that Andy has doubled back and is standing there grinning at her.

"Careful," he says. "Slippery."

"You don't say."

"You ever been up here before?" Andy offers her an arm, which she takes. He guides her down the path, helping her keep her footing. How can he walk so surely in those patent-leather shoes?

"I don't even know where we are," she says.

"The trail to Knife Point."

"Knife Point? That doesn't sound good."

"It's a promontory," he says. "See, it's where the rest of the hill eroded away but there was a vein of rock that was harder than the rest of it and it stayed. You can see the lake and most of the city from it."

"That sounds nice. We're not trespassing, are we?"

"Hm?" Andy seems distracted, as if listening to the songs of invisible, inaudible birds. "What? Trespassing? Don't think so." He points out a marker hammered into a tree. "State land. Undeveloped."

"They could at least put in stairs or something."

"Don't worry, it's worth the trouble."

After a quarter-mile or so of descent the land slopes upward again. The soil turns rocky, stone protruding through the dirt path like bone where the flesh has rubbed away. Andy probably thinks it looks like sea serpent humps or something. At least the trail is getting less treacherous; she doesn't think she needs a steadying hand anymore. As soon as she pulls away Andy says, "I'm gonna run on ahead." And he really does; he *runs* on ahead, bounding up the rapidly steepening trail like some kind of two-legged mountain goat.

She pauses to rest. There is a wind in the trees that makes them creak faintly. Ellie thinks of her rocking chair. It creaks, too. Groans.

A homey sound, a comforting sound. Up here it's a lonely sound. The trees are whispering about her, the clever ones pointing out the grieving wife to their less observant brethren. She hears a crow, a long way off. *Raw, raw!*

Onward and upward. The path crests the ridge of stone and turns right, running along its spine. She feels rather intrusive, walking on the earth's bones. A stand of pines grows here from the crevices in the rock. The path heads straight through the middle. Beyond that she sees only wide grey sky.

She walks the gauntlet. The trees giggle. She notices a circle scratched into the stone, scratched deep. Somebody put a lot of work into it. It's got four triangles pointing in the cardinal directions, but no lettering for north or south or anything. An unfinished compass. It's obviously been there a long time, it's got moss growing from its edges, where people don't walk.

She steps out onto Knife Point. It juts out from the hillside, narrow and jagged. Serrated. There are no fences or rails to keep her from falling. She could step off the edge of the blade and there would only be clouds to stop her.

Andy appears from somewhere. "It's hazy today," he says. "View's not so good. Wicked cold, too."

He actually uses the word *wicked* when he means *very*. Ellie doesn't know if she should pick on him or pack him a lunch. He leads her out onto the blade. Far off is Island City, a dark stain on the mainland, an assortment of Lego buildings on the island. Three rusty old iron bars stick out a foot or so from the tip of the rock, each angled slightly differently, pointing at the city. Maybe someplace for rappellers to attach their lines. Maybe lightning rods. She sees the wide Hunter River, the four bridges connecting the two parts of the city. Beyond that, lost in a chilly haze, is the lake. The water is as leaden as the sky; maybe it *is* the sky, curving down to cup Island City in a blustery hand, pick it up and carry it into the clouds.

She could jump right from here. She could fly.

Andy stands beside her. "So whaddya think?"

"Wicked," Ellie says.

Nate Watson awakens from some kind of stupor. It isn't sleep and it isn't that strangely seductive trance he nearly fell into last night; it's just inactivity, hibernation, waiting out a hostile climatic condition: daylight. He sits up, for a moment not remembering where he is. He vaguely thinks he has fallen out of bed and is lying on the cold, hard floor, stiff from sleeping there. It's the sound of rushing water that reminds him he's in the storm sewer, far from his bed, far from his wife.

He gets to his feet. His shirt feels rigid, starched. The blood-soaked fabric has dried and become crusted, but it still gives a bit when he pushes on it. He wonders what his body looks like under the shirt. Probably his skin is glued to the uniform by the blood. If he unbuttoned it, it would be like unzipping his own meat, and his guts would come spilling out onto his shoes.

He touches his uniform cautiously. He can't remember buttoning it up or tucking the three flaps of his flesh back together, though he must have done both. He remembers the stairs and the boy in the corridor and everything else after that, but not getting off the roof.

Nate shuffles back to the ladder he came down earlier. Someone has replaced the manhole cover; this amazes him. He had sort of figured it would just lie in the street until it was nothing but a rusty smudge on the pavement. He lifts his right arm and the chain shoots from his wrist, threading the holes in the cover, lifting it and sliding it aside. It's a fifteen-foot climb, at least, and as he makes it Nate wonders how far his chains can stretch, and where they go when they aren't extended. He wonders what's animating him, what keeps his brain operating and his muscles working. It's not his heart, that's for sure, because his heart is still and heavy, it may as well be a slab of steak in his chest. He wonders, again, who brought him back and why.

Questions he can't answer. Questions he shouldn't even *ask*.

Questions that have nothing whatever to do with his purpose tonight, as he emerges from his sanctuary below the slick black streets of Island City, questions to be tucked away in the darker corners of his mind, to be examined—or shoved into still-darker corners—later, when light happens to fall on them again. Tonight has nothing to do with metaphysics.

It has everything to do with his wife.

Billy shambles up Canal Street toward the tenement. He doesn't remember how he got here or where he came from. He doesn't remember anything after he agreed to the deal Nicholas had offered in the hospital room that morning. It's night now; could be the same day, could be weeks since he nodded his acquiescence.

This sort of thing happens when you deal with Nicholas.

What did they do to him? The hideous, fiery pain in his groin is gone, but it has been replaced by a prickly sensation all over his skin, like he's wearing a body suit lined with needles. It hurts when he moves. It hurts when he doesn't move. He thinks he's been fucked over but doesn't know how.

This sort of thing also happens when you deal with Nicholas.

The sidewalk is deserted as he shuffles toward his destination. It's very dark, wilderness dark, because the streetlights don't work and the moon is just a toenail in the sky and the only real light comes from the fire in the oil drum up the way, in the empty, overgrown lot between the old lady's building and the next one.

Where the Wright Project used to be.

Don't think about the Wright Project.

Forcibly not thinking about the Wright Project, Billy plods past where it once stood, past the bums and their bonfire and the knee-length grass still and silent in the windless night. He grunts slightly as he walks. He looks at the homeless people. They don't pay him any attention. He may as well be a ghost; or maybe *they're* ghosts, the spectres of ancient nomads whose spirits still gather around their phantasmal campfire.

He wonders which of them are women. He squints at them, trying to figure it out. Not easy. The multiple layers of clothing they wear conceals their sexes under lumpy, shapeless rags. He sees one or two who have female features but that doesn't mean anything, they could just be pansies who look like women but aren't.

He keeps walking, but now his cock feels engorged, it burns as if it has suddenly filled up with something mildly acidic. The end of it begins to drip onto the sidewalk, the drops sizzling faintly as they hit. Startled, Billy looks down at himself. He's stark fucking naked. He's all shiny, too, like somebody greased him up good for a royal screwing. He has a hard-on fully ten inches long, and thinks: Thank you Nicholas!

But this isn't good. He'll have to find clothes. Can't wander around naked without freezing or getting arrested. He looks again at the homeless people gathered around the fire. Maybe he can get clothes from one of them. He could charge across the broken ground and kick over the oil barrel to create confusion; then he could select a man about his size, isolate him from the rest, and twist his head on his neck like a chicken; then drag the man away to strip him of his clothes.

He likes the idea. He likes the though of wringing a bum's neck, watching him as he dies. Death is cool. But there are too many of them, some might get away, they might even fight back and overpower him. He'll have to find clothes somewhere else. Someone else to kill.

Death is even cooler when you cause it yourself.

Nate walks on the inside of the sidewalk, as far from the street as he can get, and he keeps his hands in his pockets to conceal the silver bracelets around his wrists. The city are quiet anyway; there aren't many other pedestrians, and they ignore him and he ignores them. It's the way it should be, the living and the dead not interacting.

He crosses the bridge over the river. The moon is reflected in the dark water, a shaving of luminous ice rippling below him. There is little traffic over the bridge at night; few people have business in the older part of town between dusk and dawn, and those who do go about it furtively. Somewhere a seagull cries, the sound harsh and lonely.

Nate walks and walks. He leaves the bridge behind. He listens to his shoes. They creak slightly as his feet shift inside the patent leather. The wind gusts and papers blow by, rustling. Urban tumbleweeds. The lighting gets better the farther from the old city he gets. It makes him uncomfortable, but there are more people here too, it is easier to meld and vanish. He draws surreptitious looks, but no challenges, no questions. He doesn't meet anyone he knows.

He stumbles over something and nearly falls. Reflexively he pulls his hands from his pockets, steadies himself on a building.

Behind him a voice screams, "Take it! Take it!"

Nate looks back. He tripped over an old man sitting down against the building. The man is holding up a rusty coffee can, shaking it so it clinks. "Take it, don't kick me anymore!"

"I didn't see you," Nate says. His voice is throaty, but doesn't gurgle like it did yesterday. The fluid must have drained to somewhere. The man peers at him, but his eyes are wrong, they aren't really seeing him. Pedestrians swish by in either direction, oblivious. Nate realizes his cuffs are showing and quickly hides his hands.

"Watch where you're going, then," the man says, pulling the coffee can close to his chest. Nate waits for the old man to ask a question, but he doesn't, so he digs into his pockets and finds some battered bills. Lunch money, snack money, *doughnut dollars* Ellie called them. He drops them into the coffee can. They make a faint sound as they flutter to join the coins.

He won't be needing his doughnut dollars anymore.

The man looks up, his eyes on some point over Nate's left shoulder. "Thank you, sir," he says. "A good man's reach is longer than he knows."

Nate continues on without a word.

He hesitates when he reaches Owl Street. His apartment building is not far now, just a block away. He can't get inside, his keys are in his locker at the police station. Well, he doesn't want to go inside anyway. It seems a sacrilege for him to walk the lighted corridors of his life, now that the shadowy ones of death have opened for him.

But he needs to see her once more.

He keeps walking. Stands in front of his building for a few minutes, just looking at it. He hasn't really *looked* at it in a long time. Somewhere between the time they moved in and now the structure got old and weatherworn. He remembers when they first got their apartment, it seemed like the best and brightest building in the city.

He goes around to the side, the alley between his building and the one next door, the one they can see beneath their window. Here he finds the answer to his problem: the fire escape. He'll climb the fire escape.

He has to see Ellie again, even if only through a glass in the darkness.

When he reaches Mrs. Barrett's tenement, Billy pauses beside the eviscerated Mustang. He bends over and peers through the gap where the passenger window used to be. The interior of the car is all wormy fabric and exposed springs and bare metal, wires and cracked plastic and garbage. A guy sleeps in what's left of the driver's seat, the same guy who's here every day. Billy knows him. He's crazy old Ronnie, or Arnie, depending on which personality is in charge at the moment. Ronnie claims the Mustang used to be his, but Arnie says it wasn't.

Fucking psycho can't even agree with himself.

Billy never paid the guy any real attention before. He didn't have anything Billy wanted. Until now.

Billy reaches in through the open window. His hand closes on Ronnie's right shoulder. He's startled at the strength of his own grip, feels like he could squash rocks if he wanted to. His fingernails meet resistance but he doesn't realize he's dug into the man's flesh until he feels blood well up under his hand. The blood feels scalding hot. Billy's skin seems to soak it up.

Ronnie is coming to some sort of mumbling wakefulness; he looks stoned out of his mind. Obviously blood's not the only stuff flowing through his body. Billy yanks him out of the car, pulling him across the open space where the passenger seat used to be and out through the window. It's surprisingly easy, like there's nothing more to him than his ragged clothes. His eyes are half-open, Billy can see them lolling in their sockets. He opens his right hand wide and puts his open palm over the man's face. His splayed fingers are incredibly long, they arch up over Ronnie's forehead, around to his ears, under his chin all the way to his throat. It's like palming a basketball.

Ronnie opens his mouth. Billy feels the lips moving under his hand, but Ronnie's not saying anything. Then he squeezes hard and Ronnie's skull shatters like a collapsing egg shell and Ronnie will never say anything again.

Easy as crushing a beer can, thinks Billy. Easier.

The body jerks spasmodically, just once. And that's the end of Ronnie. And Arnie, too. Billy carries the guy into the building. He strips the corpse in the stairwell. The dead man was skinnier than he looked; only the outermost layers of his clothing fit onto Billy's frame, and even they're a little bit tight. Billy tosses the unused clothing down the central shaft of the stairwell, and sends the limp, rag doll corpse down after it. He adjusts his stolen clothing: a stained blue shirt and a brown jacket to wear over it and grey trousers that look like Ronnie crawled ten miles through the mud in them. Ronnie had no shoes, just newspapers wrapped around his feet, and he didn't have any underwear but who gives a shit about underwear? The clothes chafe somewhat, increasing the irritated prickly feeling in Billy's limbs; and they cling to the goo that covers him, whatever it is, the weird shiny sticky stuff. He'll need to wash it off later, when he can find someplace to bathe.

He climbs the stairs. The old cement is cold under his bare feet. After a few floors he glances behind him and sees a trail of bloody footprints. They steam slightly, as if hot.

Huh. Where'd those come from?

As he watches, they evaporate in succession, the most distant ones disappearing first. His eyes follow the progression; he feels like he's watching a fuse burn, a fuse leading to a pack of dynamite strapped to his chest. *He* is leaving the footprints, he realizes. He looks at his feet. They are raw, red meat and tendons, the nails are long and black and end in points. He looks at his hands and they're the same way. A glistening sheen covers his bare flesh, like gelatin or Vaseline, somehow holding him together, keeping blood from weeping out of the exposed mantle of his body.

Cool, thinks Billy.

At the top of the stairs, police tape stretches from wall to wall, but someone has pulled it down and trampled it. Billy walks right over it. The door to the roof is ajar. He goes outside and slowly crosses the roof. Pebbles stick to his feet. He rounds the ventilation unit, and stops, looking at the pentacle where he cut the cop. The candles are out, but he sees three shapes there silhouetted against the lights of the rest of Island City. He can tell they're looking at him, though he can't see their faces; he can tell they're *waiting* for him.

He knows who they are.

And he smiles.

Getting onto the fire escape is easy. He sends one of his chains up and tangles it around the bottom of the extendible ladder, then pulls it down to where he can grip it. He climbs up the ladder to the first landing and ascends from there. The spindly black metal rattles and clatters beneath his feet, shivering, as if it will at any moment detach from the building and go crashing to the alley and he'll go with it and get his brains smashed out on the cobbles.

Nate isn't sure this would be a bad thing.

He counts floors until he reaches four. He walks carefully along the narrow balcony, attempting to be quiet, but the rickety metal doesn't cooperate, it creaks and rattles and groans. What if there were a fire here, and all the inhabitants scrambled out their windows onto the fire escape? It shakes so much with just him, it could never handle the weight and the vibrations of hundreds of people in panicked flight. It would surely pull loose from its rusty moorings and collapse. Many people would die. There would be headlines and accusations for a few weeks, then some other event would supersede it and the issue would fade away.

He can't believe they ever thought this was a wonderful building. Everything looked wonderful when they first got married. The future was bright and open and waiting for them and life was grand.

Now he knows that life is just something that happens between two nights, one without a beginning and the other without an end.

He stops. This is their window. An African violet droops on the sill, sad and flowerless. Ellie loves her violets but they never bloom in their apartment; she says the light is wrong, too weak. They're in the shadow of the alley.

Nate crouches down and peers through the glass. The lights are on in the living room. Ellie is on the couch under an afghan. Her eyes are red from crying. Candles—*their* candles, the one they light when they make love—sit on the coffee table that runs in front of the couch, their flames flickering gently as they burn. Ellie is looking at the television. Facing his way. She's covered in TV light; it's blue and it flickers just like the candle flames.

She must be cold, alone under the afghan. She needs someone to keep her warm. That wouldn't be him, though, not anymore. He has no warmth to give anyone.

He shouldn't have come here tonight.

He shouldn't have come here ever.

He should have just ripped his own heart out and replaced it with broken glass.

He'll go, and he won't come back, and he'll do it before she sees him.

But instead of going he leans forward and puts his hands on the glass and kisses it gently, as if it were her.

At that moment Ellie looks at the window.

Her eyes grow wide.

And she cries out, "*Nate!*"

They follow Billy when he comes down from the roof, shuffling along behind him like a chain gang. He stops at the first landing below the roof, because he wants to look at them in the light and let them look at him. They line up in front of him, quiet and attentive.

They know he's their master.

This is an unexpected bonus, a gratuity from Nicholas. This pleases Billy. He's gotten more than he asked for.

They all stand there in silence: Billy with his greasy flayed flesh showing pink and grey in the buzzing fluorescent light; Joey with his head lolling brokenly to the left, bobbing on his neck like it was a spring; Roberto and Chaz side by side, the shattered hemispheres of their skulls facing each other, thick and sticky with dried blood. The three of them look at Billy with eyes like stagnant milk. Only hours ago such a sight would have sent Billy screaming into the night, but not now. He has embraced the obscenity, leapt headlong into the sacrilege, shed the concealing skin that allows others the pretension that they are more than blood-soaked meat.

The moment lasts a minute or so, the seconds measured by the buzzing of the light. Then Billy turns away and pads softly down the stairs. The others follow, feet slapping as they walk.

Billy has a destination in mind, a place where they can stay hidden until they find the man. A place where they have unfinished business.

Apartment 412.

When they get there, Billy doesn't bother with such subtleties as knocking. He just kicks in the door. The deadbolt is driven home but doesn't hold, it rips through the old wood of the door frame leaving behind a thin plate of twisted metal.

Beyond the door, Mrs. Barrett is sitting on the couch watching television. She looks up with wide eyes as they burst into her living room. One hand flies to her mouth, the other to her chest, fluttering like a butterfly over her heart. Joey pushes the door closed with his foot and leans up against it as the others advance on the old woman. "We're back," Billy says, showing her his claws. "Ain't no Night Watchman to save you this time."

Her scream is high, and thin, and interrupted.

6

ELLIE THROWS OFF THE AFGHAN. Wadded tissues cascade from it in a powder blue avalanche, puffy and harmless, boulders light as feathers. Her feet get tangled up in the discarded blanket and she stumbles but catches herself before falling. Jerking herself free, she goes to the window. Her shadow falls on the glass and transforms it from a mirror to a window, but she sees nothing through it. Nothing. Darkness.

She falls to her knees, fingers scrabbling at the locks. When they're undone she shoves the window open. Cold air floods the apartment. She thrusts her head into the current, out into the night, and there's nothing outside her window except the rickety old fire escape, black and barren. She looks left, looks right. The skeletal iron platform clings to the side of the building.

No one is here.

She finds herself crying again, tears leaving icy tracks down her face before dropping from her chin. She sobs her grief out to the night, which responds by throwing snow at her. The flakes are small and hard, little pustules of ice. Ellie suspends her crying and looks up into the amber sky. The snow looks like tracer fire as it drops through the city's cocoon of light. It is not snowing hard—or rather, it will soon snow much, much harder—but it is early for snow, not even November yet.

Ellie shakes the flakes from her hair and slowly pulls her head back inside the warm apartment. Seeing things. She's seeing things. It's not Nathaniel, it's not his ghost. It's in her mind.

Hallucinations. Just what she needs.

Think of Knife Point. Think of the view. The sky above and below. They're all folded up in the sky: her, Nate, Frank, Andy. The kids. The old woman at the tenement. All of them here together.

All of them, prisoners of the sky.

Nate doesn't move until she closes the window; then he carefully lowers himself to the platform outside the third floor. He releases his chains from the bars overhead and retracts them to their normal length. Then he reaches up and carefully brushes his fingers across his face. They come off wet. Some of Ellie's tears landed on him as he hung from the fire escape below their window. Each drop is precious as a diamond, fragile as glass.

His heart would be racing, were it still beating.

The snow bounces off his skin, nestles in his hair. It does not melt. Why should it?

Nate turns away from the building and puts his hands on the flimsy railing. He is thirty feet in the air. If he dives head-first from the fire escape, he should at the very least fracture his skull and break his neck. But will that kill him, or will he rise from a second death as well, even more damaged than he is now?

He thinks of Frank; at least Frank's wife has a body to weep over. Ellie has to cry to the snow.

She needs a body.

He takes a last look at the sky.

Dives over the railing.

Falls.

He could have talked to her.

Vertigo.

Pavement rushing to meet him.

He could have talked to her!

. . . could have . . .

Impact.

Billy drags the old woman by the head. His big fingers are locked around her face, black nails digging into her skin and flesh. Chaz and Roberto have nearly finished cleaning out the refrigerator. There wasn't much in it, just milk and some Tupperware containers filled with food. "Faster," he tells them. "She shit her pants. I want her away."

They don't work any faster when he tells them to.

"Oh, get the fuck out of the way." He shoves them aside and begins tossing stuff over his shoulders. Then he grabs the wire shelves, one in each hand, and rips them both out. He stuffs Mrs. Barrett into the refrigerator, bending her almost in two to do it. The door bumps open after he closes it the first time, but the second time does the trick. He looks at the two of them and says, "Was that so fucking hard?"

He goes out of the kitchen. Chaz and Roberto follow him like puppies. Joey is still leaning up against the door, his head lolling to the left, staring at the doorknob. The prickly feeling in Billy's flesh seems to be increasing. He wonders if he's drying out or something. Nicholas didn't mention that Billy would be coming back skinned. Maybe he'll bring it up next time they talk. Find out what the fuck Nicky boy is up to.

Billy remembers what Nicholas said about the man. *Kill him or leave him, I don't care which.*

Maybe Nicholas doesn't care, but Billy does.

He goes to the middle of the living room. The boys all look at him, even Joey, who puts his hands on his head and turns it so he can look at Billy. They watch expectantly. Waiting for instructions. Waiting for him to tell them what to do.

He says, "You remember the man, the man that killed you?" They gape at him, not answering. Maybe they can't talk anymore. Doesn't matter. "Well, we're gonna find him and his wife and his kids."

Billy rubs his hands together.

"And we're gonna fuck them up."

She knows he's not out there, but still Ellie throws on her thick coat and grabs a flashlight and her purse. Her purse is heavier, by several pounds, than it was this morning. The extra weight consists mostly of steel and lead. Just in case.

It's quiet outside. The snow hisses as it bounces off the buildings and the street and her coat. The flakes diffuse the streetlights, making them into great fuzzy amber globes. The storm is picking up steam. No traffic. No pedestrians. It's three in the morning or so. Normal people are in bed.

So who ever said she was normal?

Nate comes to his senses face-down on the pavement in the alley. He tries to lift his head but can't. His neck muscles won't respond. This is probably, he thinks, because he splintered his spine when he hit the pavement. He decides to try his fingers.

Pause.

Fingers don't work either. He doesn't even try legs. Fingers don't work, legs won't work. But his brain seems to be functioning just fine.

Shit.

The only thing keeping him from kissing the ground is the pulpy remains of his nose. The filthy floor of the alley is almost touching his lips. He could lick it if he wanted to. Which he doesn't.

If he were having a nightmare this is the part where he would want to wake up.

Hey! Wake up!

Pause. Try to wiggle the fingers. No response.

Not a nightmare. He didn't think it was, but it's obligatory to at least try. Well, maybe he can drag himself out of here with his chains. Find his way to a circus. Step right up, kids, see the quadriplegic zombie!

Can he use the chains?

They go *shhhhhhink* across the pavement.

Then, through the numbness, a tingle. It starts near the nape of his neck and quickly works down to his tailbone. The touch is feather light and electric, battery-powered doves fluttering along his spine.

Wiggle the fingers.

Movement!

He turns his head. He feels jagged things in his neck grinding together. Still tingling. He turns left and right, left and right. The motion gets smoother, the jagged things go away.

All the king's horses and all the king's men . . . helpless bureaucrats, every one. He's putting himself together again and he doesn't even know how he's doing it.

He pushes himself to his feet, sways there a moment. He still feels the feather touch, down near his legs. Small hard flakes of snow pelt him like ineffectual bullets. Walking is next. He goes away from the street, farther into the alley, and stops beside a large, battered

Dumpster that stands next to a steel door in the building opposite his. There is a narrow opening between its back and the wall, dark and inviting. A place to hide.

He circles the trash receptacle. On the other side the opening is blocked by a mountain of wooden crates marked with obscure numbers that may have identified their contents, when they *had* contents. Nate tries to lift the lid of the Dumpster but it's chained shut. He wonders if it's going to be emptied soon. He hopes not because he's going to hide behind it.

Getting on his hands and knees, he crawls into the gap between the trash bin and the wall. The air is stale and rancid, it smells like last month's garbage. He pushes his way back to where the crates form a sheltering wall. The wind and snow whip by but can't touch him in his hideaway. The back side of the dumpster is angled outward, nearly meeting the building over Nate's head, leaving only a pencil-thin crack where amber light shines through. He squints up at it for a second, then drops his gaze.

He sees someone coming down the alley.

It's Ellie.

Fucking curtains. Full of holes. When the sun rises, it'll come right through them. Billy lifts and squeezes them, then drops them in disgust and crosses to the bathroom. The others follow him with their eyes but don't move from their positions near the door. He glances at them. "Stop *staring* at me," he says. They keep right on doing it. "Ah, fuck you," he says.

Didn't take long for hero worship to get old.

Billy flicks on the overhead light. The bathroom is a cubicle, the sink nearly protruding into the bathtub's air space. The room is windowless, though. Be a good shelter from the daylight. The hands of the clock in the living room are sweeping toward dawn and Billy doesn't want to get caught by the sun.

Returning to the living room, he orders Joey away from the front door. The deadbolt and knob lock are both ruined, their sockets splintered; and the chain latch has been pulled from the wood, leaving behind four jagged vampire-bite holes. As Joey moves away the door slowly swings inward. Billy picks up a big, frilly chair and shoves it in front of the door.

When he turns away from the door, he discovers Roberto inspecting a newspaper clipping. "What's that?" Billy asks, plodding over. His feet stick weakly to the floor. The prints still smolder, not as much as they were before but enough to scent the living room with acrid smoke.

Roberto shows him the paper.

The clipping is part of a front-page story about the things that went on here that night, about the two cops they murdered. Complete with pictures. Franklin Yaddow, killed in the line of duty. Nathaniel Watson, missing.

Missing. Ha! Not for long.

Billy's wide mouth slowly breaks into a grin. He looks at Roberto and says, "Find me the phone book."

She's coming right for him, oh God, she saw him in the alley! He can see she's carrying a flashlight but she doesn't have it on, she's relying on the street lamp. "Hello?" she calls.

Go inside, thinks Nate. Go back inside.

Instead she switches on the flashlight.

"Nate? Are you there?"

He closes his eyes. *Go away!*

Silence.

Nate opens his eyes. She's standing in the snow. Her hair ripples in the wind. The flashlight is pointing straight down, making a circle on the pavement. "I'm such an idiot," she says softly.

He could still go to her. He shifts carefully, puts his hands on the ground. He can crawl right out to her, she's not even twenty feet away.

The handcuffs glisten on his wrists.

Yeah. Sure. He can crawl out to her. Maybe they can go back up to the apartment and light up some candles. Just as long as she doesn't ask him to take off his shirt.

She switches the flashlight off. Turns her back.

Leaves.

And he's once again alone in the dark.

7

ELLIE GETS UP WITH THE sun. She hasn't been able to sleep anyway, and she's tired of lying in bed. Makes her feel like an invalid. Which she isn't, in the physical sense at least.

She makes a cup of coffee. She has a little brewer that makes the coffee directly in the mug, a present from Nate, because she always used to let the coffee pot get all crusted with old coffee until you couldn't even see through it anymore. Now she lets her coffee cup get that way, but nobody notices.

"Okay," she says, as the coffee maker bubbles and steams. "Let's make a deal. I'll always wash out my cup, and you give me Nate back. What do you think? That sound fair?"

The maker runs dry. The dripping stops a little while after. God doesn't comment on the deal.

She takes her coffee into the living room and settles onto the couch, looking out the window. Her view stops at the ugly wall of the opposing building. They'd just started looking for a new apartment, a bigger one where they would be able to see something other than the side of another building. They'd just started talking about getting their own car. They'd just started talking about kids.

They'd just started a lot of things. Really, they'd just started life. They should have had fifty, sixty more years. She takes a sip of coffee. She'll start today, washing out her cup. Just to show God she was serious.

She saw Nate's face in that window. She knows she did.

She knows she couldn't have.

Ghosts. She doesn't believe in them. Nor apparitions, poltergeists, black magic on rooftops. Hokum.

But what if . . .

The telephone rings, making her jump. She fumbles it into her hand. Maybe this time it'll be her family, she thinks. She left a message on their machine days ago and they haven't called her back. Jesus, you'd think she'd married a Nazi war criminal the way they carried on. "Hello?"

"Ellie? Andy."

He's all breathless enthusiasm. Ellie thinks of a puppy.

"Listen, the captain says I can keep you company again today if you still want me to."

"Thanks, Andy, but—"

"Please don't say no," he says, his voice suddenly a whisper. "If you say no I'll have to go back to Canal Street. With Whitey."

"What does Charlie think of you running around with me while he's stuck on the roof at Canal Street?"

Pause. "I don't suppose he likes it much."

"Maybe Charlie'd like to keep me company today."

"Aw, Ellie . . . you won't have nearly as much fun with Charlie! Listen—I thought we could go down to the lake. Watch the waves. You like waves?"

Waves. Whee. Waves on the lake are like six inches high. "Andy, I don't know what you think, but these aren't just fun little outings for me," she says.

"I'm just trying to take your mind off things."

"No, you're just trying to stay out of the slums."

"Uh . . . two birds, y'know? We both get something out of it. C'mon! Please?" he adds.

God, it's like shooting Lassie. "All right," she says. "Just . . . no climbing."

"No climbing," Andy says seriously.

Ellie almost expects him to say *scout's honor*.

A few hundred feet from his apartment, Nate crouches on the cold pavement in the sheltering darkness of the Dumpster. He has his back up against the crates and is facing the open mouth of his little nook. His line of sight to the street is uninterrupted from this position, and he is watching the day; watching the cars and the buses, watching the people go back and forth on the sidewalk. How secure they all must feel in their cloaks of daylight. What would they do if he emerged from his hiding place like Lazarus from his tomb and went to walk among them? Which beliefs would he destroy, and which would he confirm?

Nate creeps to the edge of his hiding place. The sun is behind him, shining down at an angle, leaving him a little porch of shadow beyond his sanctuary. He slowly stretches out his arm, hesitant, unsure of what he's doing. He is intruding on the daylight, where he does not belong. What punishment will the sun visit on him for such boldness?

Suddenly the door beside the Dumpster bangs open. Nate snatches his hand back as a beefy man emerges from the building. Nate can only see his ponderous midsection, pale round gut protruding from the gap between a stained blue T-shirt and scruffy black pants. The man is whistling some non-tune Nate has never heard before. He scrunches back into the darkness, cursing his timing.

Chains rattle as the custodian unlocks the lid of the trash bin. He throws it open with a *clang*. The Dumpster shakes as he hurls something heavy into it. He interrupts his whistling to sing, in a mock Italian accent, "It's a-fucking *cold* out a-here!"

The guy must not have seen him, thinks Nate. If he knew he had an audience, he wouldn't be acting like such an oaf. But then, as the man heads back inside, he stops at the mouth of Nate's hiding place and says, "I saw your hand, buddy. I gotta go back in and get another load of garbage. I'm also gonna get a broom handle. I'm gonna take that broom handle and stick it up your ass if you're still here when I come out again."

The gut jelly-rolls back into the building, and the door slams shut behind it.

Well isn't this marvelous.

Nate creeps back to the mouth of his shelter, and farther: he goes into the lee of the Dumpster. He goes to the very line between shadow and light, and there he hesitates.

Another inch and he'll be in the sun.

But if the sun harms him, what does that say about what he's become? Is he really so completely lost that he has to skulk in the dark like a vampire?

One way to find out.

He pushes his hand into the light.

The sun is warm on his fingers. He realizes for the first time that his hand is smeared with blood. It must be from when he buttoned up his shirt that night, in that blank stretch of time between the roof and the hallway. He turns his hand over, looks at the familiar creases of his palm. The sun is impossibly bright today, it picks out all the tiny details of his skin. Or maybe he's just forgotten what he looks like in the daytime.

Nate closes his hand into a fist. The sun doesn't seem to be hurting him; the flesh isn't melting from his bones or bursting into flame. Maybe he's not so unwelcome in the daylight as he had feared.

He crawls fully from his shelter, and stands facing the light.

The sun shines on Nate Watson.

He stands there letting its rays sweep over him and through him, through him like he's made of glass, heating him, soothing him. It feels like the tropical sun in the height of summer, not the weakening sun of autumn. He could stay here forever, as long as the sun stays with him.

But the sun won't stay, and neither can he. The man will be returning soon with his broom handle. Nate doesn't know how he will respond. He may kill the man without meaning to.

Suddenly he's struck by the idea of going back to the apartment. Last night that seemed impossible, a sacrilege, but now that he knows he can stand in the sun the concept of returning home seems less abhorrent. Nate walks quickly to the fire escape. He doesn't think Ellie locked the window again after she opened it. If she did, he'll go elsewhere. He won't break into his own apartment and leave a shattered window and shards of glass for Ellie to find. That would be cruel.

There's still sporadic traffic on the sidewalk, though the early morning crowd of work-goers has thinned considerably. Most of them don't even glance into the alley as they pass by, but still Nate waits for a lull before sending his chains up to grab and pull the ladder that gives access to the fire escape.

Except when he finally commands his chains, they don't respond. They just hang there inert.

He tries again, arms raised above his head. Still nothing. He stands there a moment looking foolish before it hits him: *sunlight.* It doesn't harm him but it strips away his control of his chains. It takes away his gifts.

Okay. He'll just do this the old-fashioned way.

He goes back to the Dumpster and picks up two empty crates. Stacked one on top of the other, the crates form a platform from which he can just barely reach the bottom of the ladder. He pulls it down and climbs up it, then hurriedly ascends to the fourth floor.

Maybe if he jumps from the fire escape now, he'll really die. Or maybe he'll just lie in the alley, paralyzed, until nightfall. He decides not to test the matter. Instead he finds his apartment. As he thought, the window is unlocked. He shades his eyes with his hand and looks through the glass. The apartment is quiet and empty. Ellie must be out. He lifts the window and squeezes through the opening, into the familiar confines of the apartment he has shared with Ellie for the last three years. His stiffness impedes his agility; his clumsy foot knocks one of the African violets off the sill. It tumbles down, spilling dirt across the floor. Two of its fleshy leaves snap off.

Nate picks himself up and looks at the mess he just made. Luckily the ceramic pot didn't break, but even if he cleans up the dirt Ellie will notice the broken leaves and wonder what happened. Shit.

He sweeps the potting soil into a pile with the side of his hand, leaving behind a brown streak of dirt in the carpet. He'll have to vacuum this up and turn the plant so the broken leaves face the window and hope Ellie's too distracted to notice. He carries out this plan of action, and when the dirt is cleaned he carries the leaves into the bathroom and flushes them down the toilet, watching the two splotches of green dogfight on their way down.

He goes into the bedroom and retrieves new clothes from the closet. He is not sure yet if he'll actually put them on. He returns to the bathroom and stops in front of the mirror, examining himself. His skin is pale, his lips have a bluish tinge to them. His eyes, wide and somewhat glassy, are underscored with shadows. His face remains clean-shaven, though he hasn't seen a razor in two days; apparently his reanimation hasn't extended to every biological function. Hunger and thirst haven't visited him, thank God, and he hasn't had to go to the bathroom. He wonders what has become of his last meal, eaten just before he and Frank went to Canal Street. Is it still sitting somewhere in his gut, slowly decaying?

What a lovely thought. Thank you, mind.

Nate lifts up his wrists. The handcuffs are no longer handcuffs, they've become seamless silver bands from which the chains simply emerge. Nate takes one chain between his thumb and forefinger and tugs, but it doesn't stretch or elongate, even when he pulls with all his strength. He touches the cuff. It feels hard and cold, thoroughly metallic. He tries to slide the bracelet up his wrist but it's affixed in its position. He may as well try moving his fingers from one hand to another, or maybe slide them up to his elbow.

He drops his arms to his sides and stands there letting the parody in the mirror look at him. He wonders now if he'll have the nerve to do what he's thinking about doing.

Well, hell, he had the nerve to dive off a fire escape.

His fingers tremble as he unfastens the first button of his uniform. The fabric sticks to his skin, welded down by the blood that gushed out on that rooftop. He pulls harder but the bond won't yield; his shirt won't come off without taking part of his flesh with it. He'll have to reliquefy the crusted gore.

He goes to the tub and turns on the water, adjusting the knobs carefully. Then he thinks he might as well just take a cold shower, he can't really feel the warmth anyway, and that makes things easier. He turns up the cold, turns off the hot, and climbs under the stream.

The water splashes over him, soaks into his clothing, cascades down his body. The fabric of his uniform gradually loses its stiffness as the old, dry blood washes away, circling the drain in crimson spirals. He takes a long shower, letting it wash him clean. Wash it all away. The blood. The memories. The murders. Wash it away.

He finally turns off the water and stands, sodden, in the tub. He waits several minutes before getting out, letting himself air dry. Then he walks back to the mirror. His wet clothes squeak and pull. He looks just like he did before, only damp. Nothing was washed away, not really.

He slowly undoes the buttons of his shirt. The uniform peels back easily now, leaving rust-colored smears on his flesh. Opening the third button reveals the beginning of the incision. The flesh to either side of it is puckered up into a lip, as if his torso is split by a gigantic mouth.

It makes him want to puke but he doesn't stop. He unbuttons the entire shirt, then shrugs out of it and stands before the mirror with his upper body bare and glistening. The huge incision is an inverted *Y* in the center of his body, beginning between his nipples and running down to just above his navel before diverging into two spokes running to each side of his pelvis. He can't tell what's holding the wound together, what's keeping it from opening up and letting his guts spill out into the basin of the sink.

He traces the line with his finger. The flesh is hard and cold. Nate thinks of cheese that has begun to go stale, the way it gets stiff and brittle at the edges. Where the three cuts meet the corners of his flesh curl up slightly. He probes at the spot with his finger and it yields. He could push his finger right inside his own abdomen, could go pawing around his own innards the way that kid did up on the roof.

It's irresistible, like biting at chapped lips to make them bleed. He inserts a second finger into the opening, then a third. He pushes in. The flesh yields, making small, sticky sounds. He should stop but can't. Cold blood oozes out around his probing digits.

He ends up with three of his fingers inside his own guts up to their second knuckles. He wonders what he's touching in there, if it's anything important. Then he thinks, no, he doesn't *have* anything important anymore. His heart isn't beating, what good could any of his other organs be doing him?

Suddenly his fingers are caught in a grip like iron.

Nate yelps and jerks his fingers out of his abdomen, but *something comes with them*, a hand and an arm behind it. The limb erupts from Nate's guts covered in blood and ooze; its fingers are locked around his own, its nails are dark as graphite. Nate staggers back from the mirror, staring at the apparition he sees reflected in it. Then he hears a scream, high and sharp, and he wheels to his right, and there's Ellie in the doorway, holding her purse in front of her like a shield.

The extruding arm flails, blood flies from it like fléchettes, spattering the walls and Ellie's dress. The arm is followed by a head, a head like a skinned tomato, but with a wide mouth filled with black teeth; and the mouth is screaming too, screaming like Ellie, and the black teeth are sharp and bloody and breath like rot billows up into Nate's face.

And then he sits up in the darkness behind the Dumpster.

All a dream.
"Son of a bitch," Nate says.

8

THE BATHROOM IS CROWDED WITH all four of them in there, but it's the only refuge in Mrs. Barrett's tiny apartment; the other rooms all have windows to admit the sun, except the kitchen, which has no door. Joey, Roberto, and Chaz are in the bathtub, sitting side by side by side, their milky eyes staring straight ahead. None of them have moved since dawn. They might as well have croaked again. Billy wonders if they are able to do anything at all when it's daylight outside or if that somehow cuts them off from their animator. He envisions Nicholas somewhere, somewhere Billy can't quite imagine, manipulating his three dead friends like a puppeteer.

Cool, thinks Billy.

Mrs. Barrett has a heavy old rotary phone. Billy brought it into the bathroom with him, and he sits on the toilet with the phone book on his lap. The book is open to a page that reads *Waterman-Weaver*. There aren't that many Watsons listed, only about a hundred, and of them only five have a first name that starts with *N*. Three of the Watsons have a black line through the names.

Billy looks at the book as he calls the next number. He uses his long black nail to dial. He listens to the phone ring. After five, a machine picks up and identifies itself as Nancy and asks him to leave a message. After the beep Billy says, "Hi, Nancy. I don't know what you look like but I'd love to fuck you." He hangs up, then scratches the name off with his fingernail, leaving a black line on the paper. The next number is also a dud, it belongs to some people named Norman and Lucy. He leaves them a message offering to do things with their corpses.

The motherfucker has an unlisted number.

Wait, isn't there someplace you can call to get numbers? Yeah . . . he goes looking through the phone book. There it is, it's called *Directory Assistance*. He dials it and tells the operator what he wants. She says she finds no listing. He says the *F* word so many times in one sentence that the operator hangs up on him.

Billy snarls and hurls the phone book at the bathroom door. It flies in a confusion of fluttering pages like an ungainly yellow bird, slams into the door and cracks it down the middle. Luckily it doesn't split enough to let the sunlight in. Billy goes to the door and runs his fingers over the crack. The door is hollow, just two sheets of plywood on a frame. He could easily have broken it. He needs to learn to control his anger and his strength, to be more careful how he uses it.

He'll use it against the Night Watchman. He'll take those chains and tie them in knots.

Billy goes to the sink. It's a column-style basin with twin chrome spigots for hot and cold water. Above the sink is a mirror, so old that in places the reflective backing has worn away. These spots look like lesions. Billy examines himself in the mirror. One of the lesions is right in his forehead, as if some invading growth is spreading across the glistening meat of his face. He tilts his reflection off the worn spot in the mirror.

But the spot moves with it.

Billy is startled, and reaches up to probe the mark on his forehead. It's smooth and dry but itches furiously when he touches it.

What is it?

Billy picks at the thing, digging at it with his nails. Pain sparkles from the spot, blood dribbles down the skinless crest of his superorbital ridge. He manages to get under the growth and he tears it off like a price tag. He sweeps it down to look at it more closely. It hangs limp and bloody from his fingernails. He turns it this way and that, examining it from each side. He shakes it and drops of blood fly from it, speckling the yellowed enamel of the sink.

As far as he can tell, it's *skin*.

Billy turns on the cold water and rinses the little piece of skin beneath the stream. His fingertips get wet. The water dissolves the clear layer of grease or jelly that holds him together and the white stream turns crimson. Billy howls and yanks his fingers away. Blood weeps from the exposed tissue, patters from his thumb and first two fingers. He jams them into his armpit and squeezes them tight. Awkwardly, he turns the water off with his other hand. There is a red-streaked pool in the sink; it drains slowly, its exit route partially blocked by something. Billy stares into the basin, watching the bloody water swirl around the drain. When the last of it has vanished Billy sees that the blockage is the little piece of skin he picked off his forehead.

The piece of skin has a fringe of fine black hair around it. As he watches, the little hairs begin to squirm.

He feels like he's gonna puke.

He turns and sits down on the toilet and stares at the crack in the door and wonders what the fuck Nicholas is doing to him.

Andy's driving a big old Charger today. It fits his mood. He's full of enthusiasm for their trip to the lake, regaling Ellie with stories about how his parents used to take him there, how he used to ride the kiddie rides and play with the kiddie amusements.

Ellie thinks that this could not have been that long ago.

Andy eases the Charger into a spot near the beach that edges this section of the lake. Artificial, of course, the sand trucked in from a quarry up in the hills. Andy knows this because Andy knows everything about Island City. The parking lot is deserted, the only other vehicle a beat-up Volkswagen at the other end, surrounded by seagulls as if it's a giant lump of carrion. Sand creeps across the pavement, blown over from the beach. Ellie can see it whipping off a sculpted dune that rises above the grassy ridge around the lot. It rises in clouds from other, unseen, dunes, even from the shore itself, cresting over the knoll and then raining down on the lot.

Andy steps out into this sandstorm. "C'mon," he says. "The rides are closed but the arcade should be open."

The arcade. Well, maybe she can find a video game where you get to shoot bad guys and watch them bleed. She can pretend they're the kids who killed Nate. Therapy.

She gets out. As soon as she stands up from the shelter of the door, the wind grabs her and pushes her off-balance. She stumbles back a pace as the door slams closed. "God, Andy! Is there a gale warning today?"

"Winter," he says. "It always gets a little windy at the beach." He isn't even looking at her, he's eyeing the wooden ladder that climbs over the steep artificial ridge. Like he thinks the treasure of the Sierra Madre is on the other side. "See the roof? That's the arcade." He points at a black slate peak that is just barely visible above the ridge, like a lurking beast that thinks it's hidden but isn't quite. "It's got a wall on the side facing the beach so the wind won't be so bad there."

They climb the wooden ladder. It creaks beneath them. The lake comes into view, vast and grey. The wind hits full-blast, whipping Ellie's long coat out behind her. She fumbles the flaps back down and ties her belt tighter and stares at the lake. Far off to the left, the high hills Andy took her to yesterday rise to mottled heights, curving around the far side of the lake before vanishing from sight. The arcade partially blocks her view to the right, but she can see, beyond it, the beach looping back on itself, following a spit of land out into the lake to create a breakwater. Winter storms get pretty bad sometimes, creating oceanic waves and shoving big chunks of ice up to the beach. The breakwater is supposed to prevent this but doesn't.

She looks back at the hills. She wonders where Knife Point is. Andy seems to read her mind because he points up into them. "Knife Point is that grey mark right there," he says, though she can't make out what he means. "It's easier to see in summer, because it sticks out from the leaves." He pauses. "Sometimes people have parties up there at night. Bonfires. You can see them from the beach."

Ellie thinks of the bums standing around the oil drum. That bonfire has a different purpose than ones lit on Knife Point.

They go to the arcade, following the right branch of the boardwalk as it winds along the crest of the ridge. The left branch zigzags down to the beach and is half-buried in the sand. The boardwalk ends at the near edge of the structure. Beyond it are the rides, a rickety-looking Ferris wheel dominating. The amusements look skeletal, as if a herd of huge, misshapen creatures crawled from the lake and died on its shore.

The enter the arcade. It's long and narrow, lined with benches that face the lake. That wall consists mainly of thick windows. The roof is supported by colonnades with peaked arches between them. No video games are in evidence.

Andy sees her face and smiles. "Different kind of arcade," he says.

"I like it. It's quieter."

They sit at one of the benches, in the lee of the wall. The wind mutters loudly as it smacks into the obstacle. They look out at the lake.

"Knife Point used to belong to some business guy," Andy says suddenly. Ellie has concluded that silence makes Andy uncomfortable.

"Yeah?"

"Yeah. I just thought of it, because, remember, you said you were afraid we might be trespassing."

"Uh-huh." Being with Andy is a rather exhausting experience. Even when he's sitting still, he conveys the impression that he's about to jump to his feet and do a hundred jumping jacks. Ellie wonders where he gets his energy, and if she can get some too.

"Anyway, this business guy . . . I can't think of his name, I knew it once though . . . he did put up all these *No Trespassing* signs and told everybody he was going to develop the land up there. He had this idea he would build right on the hillside."

Ellie glances up at the hills and tries to picture them covered with hotels and resorts and ten-million-dollar homes. "I'm glad he changed his mind," she says.

"Oh, he didn't change his mind. He got killed. In a fire. The Wright Project fire. His estate got its butt sued off by the survivors, and they ended up with the land and donated it to the state."

"The Wright Project?"

"Yeah. He built it." Suddenly Andy snaps his fingers. "*That's* his name."

"Wright?"

"Fenton. Nicholas Fenton. He was involved in a lot of construction around Canal Street, Cross Street . . . the old parts of the city. I kept running into his name so I looked him up in city records once." Andy leans back. "Yep. Old Nick Fenton. He cut all kinds of corners with the Wright Project. He was practically begging for it to burn down, is what the investigators said. Just didn't expect to go with it."

"What a nice story," Ellie says.

"Yeah," Andy says vaguely, looking out at the lake. Then he looks back up at the hills. Like he's already losing interest in what they're doing and plotting their next adventure. Ellie wonders if she should get out her book, or just sit and wait until he grabs her hand and drags her off to some other slice of his childhood.

After five minutes she decides to chance it.

Big mistake.

When the sun vanishes, Nate crawls out of his sanctuary and stands in the enveloping darkness. He doesn't belong here, so close to his old home, his wife. His is an unnatural existence, it brings with it dangers and implications he can't fathom; but if his dream was anything, it was a warning, a warning that he should stay away from Ellie. What would the thing inside him have done to her when it had finished ripping itself loose from his guts?

Nate doesn't know. He's just glad he woke up when he did.

He stumbles up the alley, back to the bright sidewalks of Island City; and he puts his hands back into his pockets and tips his head toward the pavement, assuming the posture of the invisible. He walks away from his building, from his wife, without looking back. He will not repeat the mistake of Lot's wife, who cast a final, fatal glance at what she was leaving behind.

Billy is alone in Mrs. Barrett's apartment. He has sent the others out into the streets to search for some trace of Nate Watson, some hint to the man's whereabouts. Billy figures Watson can't have gone far, not if he's in the same kind of shape as Joey and the others; and Billy thinks they're all about identical, these things that were dragged back from the dead. He sees it in their eyes; they all have the same eyes, like the white underbelly of a dead fish.

Nicholas called Watson a *revenant* but Billy has no idea what that means. He should have Joey find a dictionary and look it up for him. He wonders if Joey, Chaz, and Roberto are revenants too. "Rev-en-*ants*," he says, just to hear it. He thinks it's a cool word.

He has the television on. It's an old lady's TV, one of those huge ones in the fake wooden case, with knobs and dials instead of a remote and in black and white, too. The news is on. Billy has the sound turned down and is watching for a picture of Watson or the other guy. Maybe they'll do an interview with the family, he thinks, or show a picture of the building where he lived. He hopes they'll do that. Then he would know where to send his boys.

He hears voices outside, in the hallway. Women. Young ones. They're talking and laughing loudly, their voices slurred. Probably stoned or something.

Billy wonders if he can still get stoned.

He gets up from the couch. His dick is humming again, filling up. He can feel it shifting in his stolen pants. He moves quickly to the door and opens it, sticking his raw, peeled head out into the corridor; but the women are gone, ducked into an apartment or something. The hallway is deserted.

Frustrated, Billy steps out and yanks the old lady's door shut. It won't stay closed, he broke the latches when he kicked it in yesterday. He could just leave it open but then somebody might wander in and open the refrigerator and find the old lady, and that wouldn't be good. That would cause problems. He goes back inside and closes the door. His cock feels like a tent pole. Maybe he should just jerk off.

No. Can't do that. That's not what he wants.

He shoves the chair back in front of the door and then goes to the window. He can't stay inside, he has to go out in search of . . . something. He throws the window open and kicks at the bars. The brick is old and decrepit, it only takes three really solid hits for them to let go of the bars and leave the window wide open. An autumn breeze comes in, smelling of musty old furniture that has gotten wet and never dried and burning rubber from the vagrants' fires and exhaust. Underlying all this is a trace of dead fish and contaminated water.

Billy breathes the air in deep, holds it, expels it. A long time ago, he thinks, the air here smelled like grass and trees and the river. Where the buildings protrude like islands from rivers and lakes of cracked and crumbling asphalt, green fields once rolled off to the horizons and forests grew and streams laughed and the stars flashed like expensive baubles in the sky.

For a moment—just a moment, and a short one—something inside Billy stirs from the deep strata of muck at the bottom of his soul. Like poison water rising from the depths of a lake, an inexplicable feeling of loss bubbles up, inexplicable because he suddenly misses something he never knew, something that hasn't existed for a century or more, something he never thought or cared about before now.

Cheated.

Robbed.

It should have been his.

He should have had green fields.

He should have had forests.

He should have had stars!

He'll extract payment for their loss from anybody he finds.

Billy puts a clawed hand on the window sill and jumps out into the darkness.

Nate steps off the bridge, the same one he crossed last night when he thought he could somehow go home again. But in the opposite direction this time. Not toward home. Away from it.

Because now he knows better. Home, where he was safe, where he was loved—that place isn't there anymore. Or it's there, but he can't reach it. He's separated from it by something much wider than the river and impossible to cross.

He turns right on Harbor Road. His destination is the apartment building where he died. He's going to go back, have a look around. See if there's any clue there, a hint of what happened to him and why. In the marina, boats sigh and creak in the icy water. He slows down, listening to their lament, and finally stops and turns and hooks his fingers on the chain link fence and just *listens.*

Listens to the vessels cry.

The marina consists of six or seven weatherbeaten docks, their uneven wooden surfaces spattered with the chalky white droppings of river gulls. At the end of each dock is a single light, insufficient to do more than cast the moored boats in a ghostly pallor. Battered sailboats rock gently beside rowboats partially filled with filthy water. Moldering old yachts bob in a morass of their own spilled fuel and flaked paint. At the largest dock a few small, decrepit houseboats float beside an ancient fishing trawler.

Nate wonders if the trawler sails anymore, if it goes out into the lake. It looks like it maybe even used to go out to sea. He thinks about the ocean, its cold and peaceful depths. He could lose himself in the ocean, could fall into the water and let it draw him down into its silent pockets, down where he could never be found or brought to light.

On impulse he scales the fence. It's an easy climb. The chain link rattles as he clambers over it, but nobody seems to hear, nobody comes out. He drops to the gravel path on the other side and goes to the big dock. There's a bigger light on a tall pole nearby, but it's turned off.

Nate takes a step onto the old planking. It's damp from melted snow and it creaks under his weight, the boards sagging slightly beneath him. The houseboats bob insensately. He hurries past them and stops in front of the fishing boat at the end of the dock.

It looks even worse close up. Battered and patched. Nate wonders what war it went through. If it were his, he wouldn't take it out to sea; he wouldn't even chance untying it from the dock.

He hears something behind him. On the dock.

Creaking.

Footsteps.

There's nowhere to go, nowhere to hide, so he'll play it cool, yeah, he'll survey the river like it belongs to him and he's inspecting it for ducks. That's the rule, known by punks and perps everywhere: always act like you should be wherever you are.

The footsteps stop. They're close.

A voice like congealed soup says, "Night watchman."

Great. The marina has a night watchman. Nate turns to look at the guard. He's only a yard or two away. He opens his mouth to say something and freezes before anything comes out.

He knows the face.

He broke the face.

The face Nate broke grins and whispers, "I thought that was you, night watchman."

9

B ILLY LANDS LIKE A CAT despite the forty-foot drop. He looks left and right quickly, sniffs the air. Garbage and smoke, and . . . perfume.

His cock seems to be on fire. It leads him to the right, toward the sidewalk. Across the empty lot the fire burns in the oil drum, a beacon for the homeless and the decrepit. Even the drum is shabby, it's riddled with holes that glow fiery orange like hell's eyes. Sparks curl incandescently upward; if you could catch onto them you could ride them into the sky.

Billy doesn't want to ride into the sky. He just wants to stick his dick in something.

He hears voices from the sidewalk. A man and a woman. They're arguing about something. The woman's voice is threatening, the man's is petulant. Sounds like she caught him doing something she doesn't like, caught him messing around or at least thinks she has. She is demanding he stop *lying* to her, he is saying she has to *understand* what it's like for a man.

You tell her, brother.

He can see them now. They're standing near the old man's Mustang. They're probably standing in his blood. The woman is tall and the heels of her shoes are long and narrow and she's wearing a tight little skirt that barely covers her tight little ass. The man is bigger than Billy but somehow foppish, with a shiny leather jacket and a chain that gleams in the streetlight. Guy could get killed for a chain like that, for a jacket like that.

Billy decides to steal them when he's done, make that look like the motive for the attack. Make the rape look like an afterthought.

The man sees Billy coming now and says something to the woman, something Billy can't hear. She begins to turn just as Billy enters the cone of light. He feels it on his flayed flesh like a shower of tiny splinters. "Jesus!" the guy says, and the woman makes a shocked little hiccuping gasp. Billy lunges, one arm grabbing the woman's throat, the other the man's. He lets his nails bite into the guy's flesh, crushes and then removes his larynx. Blood spurts from the dude's throat in a boiling shower as Billy yanks the woman back into the shadows. He lets the guy fall where he was, twitching and gurgling as his heart pumps away, idiotically emptying the body of blood.

The woman is struggling feebly, crying, whining. Hysterical bitch. Billy doesn't care. He takes her some distance from the sidewalk then throws her face-down to the lumpy grass. His cock salutes her, though he can't remember unzipping his pants to free it. She is sobbing and pleading but that doesn't slow him down, not for a second. He thrusts in from behind and comes immediately, feeling hot liquid spurt from him into her. There's no pleasure in it, no rush of relaxation; there is only release, and the placation of the urge.

Slowly he stands. His penis is limp and shriveled now and he stuffs it back into his pants. The woman is screaming and screaming, like he poured acid on her or something. He runs back to the street and quickly strips the guy. The jacket is ruined, covered in blood. He puts it on anyway. He takes the chain and stuffs it into his pocket. He hears the woman gagging and sobbing behind him. "C'mon, baby, it wasn't that bad, you liked it a little," he says loudly. "Hold still, I'll show you how good it can be."

The noises stop immediately. Billy grins.

Now this is *power*.

His loot gathered, he runs up the sidewalk, away from the field and the canal. He runs for several minutes before he realizes he's still carrying part of the guy's throat, stuck to his hand like a wad of gum. He hurls the bloody mass of tissue across the street.

Let a dog find it.

Nate and the boy are face to face on the dock. The side of the kid's head glistens in the moonlight as if the slick of blood from his shattered skull is still being fed. Otherwise it would have dried by now, thinks Nate. It would be crusted over like his own wound. For a dizzy second he thinks maybe the boy is still alive, still bleeding; or maybe the intervening time between the boy's death and now has all been a dream, a long dark ghastly nightmare. Maybe *this* is a dream. Like the thing that came out of his guts.

The breeze off the river ripples Nate's hair. The dock creaks in the cold. The water laps at the pilings and the shore. And the youth smiles vacuously, an idiot smile. He turns away and shuffles toward the riverbank.

"Hey," Nate calls.

Why is his voice shaking?

"Hey, come back."

The kid keeps going. Nate stares after him. His mind shudders with the implications of this meeting. But why should he believe only *he* can come back from the dead? If him, why not one of the boys he killed?

Hell. Why not all of them?

Billy is following the railroad tracks east when he suddenly feels a tugging at the corner of his mind. It is gentle but insistent, claiming his attention like soft music in the morning. He has no idea what to expect as he responds to the call. Maybe Nicholas is trying to communicate, though Nicholas usually just shows up. But when he lets the whisper in he learns it comes from a source he didn't expect, one he didn't know was capable of sending this kind of message.

It's from one of his boys.

It says, *The man is on the dock*, and then falls silent.

The wind kicks up, fluttering the pages of a discarded magazine, the sound of a bird taking flight.

The man is on the dock.

The man.

One of his boys has found the man.

Billy does an about-face and lopes back the way he came.

Nate stands on the dock staring at the shadows where the dead teenager disappeared. For some reason he's shivering, even though he can't feel hot and cold anymore, not really. He opens his mouth to call the kid one more time, but when all that comes out is a squeaky little choke he shuts it again.

Gotta get a grip.

He should've *known* there was more to this scenario than himself. Something sinister is moving in the shadows of Island City. He's part of it somehow, but he's by no means the prime mover or even a major player. He senses this clearly. Whoever is behind what's happening is through with Nate now. All done. Except Nate refused to lie down and sleep when offered the opportunity, just after he killed the boys. No, he had to get up and keep going, and now he's stuck on this midnight merry-go-round with no way off.

He could almost wrap his chains around the worm of corruption that burrows beneath the dirt and asphalt, the worm whose child now lies coiled in his own guts. But his chains are physical, they're limited, they can't fight this enemy.

The enemy has a name.

Dread.

Nate has lost the boy in the darkness, can't tell if he's still lurking nearby or if his shuffling feet have carried him away. He suspects the kid is still here, skulking beyond the reach of the light. Waiting. Their meeting is neither accidental nor over.

The kid was *searching* for him.

He wonders if there are others searching for him, too.

Nate walks slowly up the dock toward shore. He listens to the oily water lapping against the pilings and the groaning of the ships; those are the only sounds in a night that has become unnaturally quiet.

Headlights approach from one of the roads that tees with River Street, igniting the darkness. The beams sweep in an arc as the vehicle makes a right turn, cutting a brief swath of illumination through the night. Nate freezes as the light engulfs and dazzles him; the moment of sight shows him not one but *three* figures skulking on the river bank near the dock.

Three.

The three boys he killed at Mrs. Barrett's apartment.

"What do you want?" he says to the night. "Why won't you stay dead?"

In the quiet that crashes down after his outburst he hears the chain-link fence rattle. Someone is climbing it. Nate takes a step back toward the end of the dock. The old, weak wood shifts under his weight and moans in protest. He stands still and listens. The fence continues to rattle in a feeble squeal of violation. Then it stops, and there is a soft, heavy sound, an impact. Nate stands motionless as footsteps crunch gently on the crumbling sidewalk and approach the dock.

For one last moment the night is quiet again.

"It *is* you," a soft voice from the darkness says.

Nate opens his mouth, but nothing comes out of it and he closes it again. He *knows* this voice, it's imprinted in his brain, its pattern burned into his mind. It could be no one else, on this cold dark night in the decrepit marina, where the dead have gathered like shipmates back from separate voyages.

Billy.

"What do *you* want?" Nate asks.

There is no reply for a second, then Billy explodes, "*I want your ass!*"

The kid has changed. His voice is deep, a boom, a roar. It slams into Nate and he falls back before it, staggering farther out onto the dock. He can't see Billy or his companions; he is nearer the light than they are, it conceals them behind a veil of illumination. He could send his chains into the darkness, but then what would he do with them?

He hears the dock creaking.

"Shit," Billy mutters.

It creaks again.

Suddenly a beam of light knifes out from the darkness and catches Billy in its illumination. A flashlight, someone's coming out with a flashlight and they're shining it at Billy and he can see quite clearly that Billy is the thing from his dream. He's coated in blood, slick, he must have been rolling in it. It glistens in the light. Skin grows patchily on his exposed body parts, mottled and dusky; fine filaments of black hair grow like cilia from the leading edges of the epidermal islands.

"What the fuck are *you* supposed to be?" a voice says. It comes from the source of the beam.

"Who the fuck wants to know?" Billy says mildly, not taking his eyes off of Nate.

"The guy who's gonna blow your head off if you try anything funny." There's a loud *click* like a gun being cocked, but it isn't, it's a switch being thrown. The light on top of the tall pole flares into life, dousing the marina in illumination.

Nate's heart turns into a lump of ice.

The three dead boys all bear the marks of the wounds that killed them, two fractured skulls and a broken neck. The kid with the broken neck is holding his head steady with his hands, his palms splayed on either side of his face. The other two have smashed-up heads like half-deflated volleyballs.

Billy glances over at the light pole. Nate notices that his feet are bare and bloody and the dock smokes where they step, the viscous vapor dribbling across the old wood and spilling over the edge with almost fluid consistency.

A man dressed in black sweats and a grey sweatshirt stands at the pole, one hand still on the switch. His breath snorts out in foggy puffs. He carries a rifle.

"What the fuck's this shit?" the guy says. "Do you think this is fucking Halloween?"

"Every day is fucking Halloween," Billy says.

The man holds his rifle one-handed like it's a large handgun. "Not here it ain't. Get outta here, you freaks."

Nate moves his gaze between the man and the boys. Of *course* the guy thinks these are costumes or disguises. Everybody knows there's no such thing as zombies, no such thing as monsters. But what the guy believes could kill him.

"Be careful, man," Nate says. His voice sounds dry, two pieces of sandpaper rubbing together. "This is for real."

"No, *this* is for real." The man wiggles his gun. "And the hole it'll make in you is for fucking real. Back off, punk." The added warning is for the kid Nate first saw, one of the broken-skull ones.

"So shoot me," the kid says.

Billy looks back at Nate. "This should be fun," he says.

Crack!

The report itself is sharp enough to cut you. A hole bursts into existence in the kid's back. He grins and keeps going, lifting his arms in the classic zombie pose. He moans theatrically. But the man seems to take the boy's groan as a sign of injury, and rather than backing off he fires again. This time the kid's left shoulder erupts in a shower of meat and bone. His left arm drops to his side and hangs like a pendulum.

The grin vanishes. The kid charges. The other broken-skulled kid goes that way too. Billy says to Nate, "What you gonna do, man?"

They're more than thirty feet away. Nate doesn't know if his chains will reach that far. And even if they will, what's he going to do? If he uses his chains to help the man, he'll leave himself open to whatever Billy does.

And Billy just stands there, tensed, fully prepared to do *something*.

Finally realizing his peril, the rifle guy backs off a step and then turns to run. Too late: the kid falls on him and knocks him down. His fist rises and falls. The sound of each impact is soft and fleshy.

Nate flings his chains at Billy's throat and arm. If he can't kill the punk, he can at least pull him off the dock and then help the fallen guard. But Billy's ready for this. His hands move in a blur and snatch the chains from the air and hold them tight. Nate *feels* the kid's flesh through his chains, soft and slippery. He tries to retract but this only jerks him forward; Billy's rooted like a tree. The kid yanks the chains and Nate loses his balance and falls face-down on the rough wood.

As the other two punks beat the life out of the guard, Billy begins hauling Nate in like a fish. He bounces along the dock, closer and closer to the kid, who stands on the cement bulwark. "Gonna fuck you up, man," Billy says.

But he's letting the chains puddle up on the surface of the dock. He didn't learn the first time. Nate surreptitiously guides his tendrils off the edges to either side. He probes around and finds two cylinders beneath the pier.

Pilings.

He is almost within the kid's reach. He can see Billy's black toes, can see blood vessels pulsing beneath a glistening sheen of transparent slime.

Hurry.

He entwines the pilings. They are spongy, rotten. This dock should probably be condemned, torn down.

Maybe he can save the city the trouble.

He yanks on the timbers. Every scrap of strength he can muster, he sends into his chains. They must do what would be impossible for human muscles. They must break the timbers that hold up the dock.

"You're *mine*," Billy says.

The supports groan loudly.

They do not break.

Billy reaches down with one taloned hand, holding both chains in the other. Nate releases his hold on the right piling and rolls to the left. He feels the kid's claws snatch at his uniform, snag, tear free. Billy rotates into view, his skinned visage snarling, showing teeth like jagged chips of basalt. Then Nate is off the edge of the dock, and falling. He feels a momentary jerk as he swings briefly on the end of his chains. His feet and legs splash into the water. The kid growls and lets go of the chains and Nate falls completely into the river. The icy darkness envelops him, hides him. Quickly he retracts his chains to prevent Billy or one of the others from grabbing them again.

Before he goes under he hears the kid say, "You lose, Night Watchman."

Billy's ink spot eyes stay on the frothy, bubbling spot where Nate disappeared. He watches the two chains skitter into the water. To his right Chaz and Roberto are still pummeling the guard, though the impacts of their fists and feet have lost their initial solidity and taken on kind of a slushy quality.

The guard is not the one Billy came to kill.

"He's gone," Joey whispers in his strangled voice.

"He ain't gone far," Billy growls. He kneels and grasps the edges of the dock, one hand on each side. The structure is narrow and his arms are long, but still he can barely grip both sides at once. He digs his nails into the soft wood. When his hold is solid, he lifts with his legs and back and twists with his arms. He feels his muscles tighten up, strong as bridge cables. The dock moans again, unused to all the abuse it's taken, and this time it breaks. The boards nearest Billy rip up from the left and he guides them over to the thinning field of bubbles where the Watchman went down.

The wood crashes into the water in a shower of nails and crossbeams and rotted timber. Water leaps skyward. Some of it splashes on Billy's hands and face. He doesn't flinch. He expected it this time.

The damage to its structural integrity is more than the dock can withstand. It collapses sinuously, undulating and writhing like a dying snake. Pilings topple over, planks plunge into the river in raft-sized chunks. Billy steps back from the water's edge, blood dribbling from his hands and running down his face. The dock is in ruins, reduced to a few standing timbers and several forlorn pilings jutting from the rippling surface of the river. Most of the boats have lost their mooring and have begun to drift slowly downriver. They will collide with the vessels tied up at the next dock down. The water is choked with debris and loose ships.

There is no sign of the man.

Billy calls Chaz and 'Berto off the guy. They've already made a mash out of him, he looks more like a bloody cigar than a man. "We gotta blow," Billy says. He picks up the rifle, holds it a minute, points it at the outboard engine of one of the rowboats and fires. There's a metallic *ping* and a second later the motor explodes. The rowboat starts to burn.

He laughs and throws the gun into the water. Who needs a rifle?

Still laughing, he goes to the fence. The others trail after him. Billy vaults the barrier and waits on the other side as they slowly begin to scale it. Their movements are slow and unsteady, as if they don't really remember how to climb. He should get impatient with them, but he doesn't. He's feeling too good.

He has beaten the night watchman.

10

As Nate completes the retraction of his chains he hears something from the direction of the dock, a creaking sound carried and amplified by the water. He looks that way but he can't see a thing through the ink. His flailing feet kick against the bottom of the river; it's rocky, he can feel the small round stones through his battered shoes. He kicks something hard, a discarded anchor or a motor maybe. The creak builds to a crescendo, a wooden scream, and he realizes it's the dock.

Suddenly something massive crashes into the water only a few feet from his head. The shockwave of water pushes him backwards and his foot somehow wedges itself beneath the heavy object he just kicked. Nate's leg twists around as a section of the dock rolls over onto him and pushes him toward the river bed. He feels no pain in his leg, only pressure, like a branch being bent to the point of snapping.

The hunk of dock presses him down, down. He struggles to get out from under it but the angle of his leg makes it impossible to move more than a few inches in any direction. More debris is falling around him. The dock didn't just collapse; *the kid tore it apart with his bare hands.*

His leg feels like it's about to splinter.

His back feels like it's about to break.

Then the dry old wood's buoyancy kicks in and it reverses direction, heading back toward the surface. The pressure on his leg eases. He pulls his foot free. Chunks of waterlogged pier drift by, floating mid-level in the water. Pieces of the dock bounce of him like slow-motion bullets. He stays submerged, where the kid can't see him.

He doesn't want to face Billy again.

Last night he tried to kill himself; now he cowers and hides, fearing for his life. No, not even anything so precious as his life: his *existence*. Because that's all it is now. His life ended on the rooftop of the apartment building. It ended when he turned his back on Ellie and came back here to the Canal District. To the place he was killed.

Death has turned him into a coward.

Billy leads his boys home. They cross Harbor Road and enter the overgrown jungle of the little park on the corner of Bayshore and Harbor. The park has a name and somewhere in the mass of rapacious foliage there's a statue of the man who donated the land, but he and his name are both forgotten and his little patch of nature has become a wilderness where humans serve as predator and quarry.

He's been through the park many times before, with his boys.

So how come he never noticed before that the place *breathed?*

It does, he can feel the pull of its breath. *In, out, in, out. In* is a tremendous pull, a terrific attraction drawing his steps at an angle toward a thicket of gnarled trees and dead brambles. *Out* is a fetid, cloyingly earthy breeze washing over him, air stripped of something — energy, life—by the breather.

In.

Out.

Billy lets the *ins* lead the way. He stumbles through the bracken, shoving them aside. Some are thorny and cut him. The pain is prickly and arousing. His penis rises and falls with the breaths, like he's getting a blowjob from an invisible head.

The boys stumble along behind him, crashing like elephants along the path he's making.

Then the brambles give way and he finds himself at the edge of a small clearing formed by blacktop that is still mostly intact despite the neglect of the years. Across the clearing is the statue, the statue of the man who made the park.

Billy recognizes the statue.

It's Nicholas.

He walks forward.

In.

Out.

He stops within a foot of the statue, staring up at it. His penis is fully erect, and throbbing. Suddenly a hand reaches around from behind him and grabs it.

Joey's hand.

"What—" Billy has only a second to gasp the beginning of a question and then he's spurting up at the statue, painting it with his seed. The stuff is brilliant white in the darkness, and it keeps coming and coming.

Finally his pulsing member quiets, goes limp.

Then the semen starts to move, oozing up the statue's rocky surface.

Like white worms.

Crawling into Nicholas's open mouth.

Billy turns away, feeling sick to his stomach. Feeling used. Feeling raped. Chaz, Roberto, and Joey stand nearby watching. "Fucking *zombies*!" Billy shouts. "Fucking *freaks*!"

That's why Nicholas brought them back. Not to serve Billy. To help complete some ritual of his own.

"Fucking freaks," Billy says. His heart begins to slow. The three of them stand there with their faintly luminous eyes the color of sea foam. Watching.

Smiling.

"Get away from me!" Billy cries, turning and plunging into the underbrush. He crashes through and hears them following. They won't leave him alone.

He bursts from the park onto Cross Street, turns right and stumbles as fast as his wobbly legs will carry him. Unwilling or not, the orgasm has left him weak, drained, like he's let a portion of his power go with his semen. He reaches the tee with Canal Street and takes a look toward Mrs. Barrett's building. There's a single cop car in front of it, lights flashing. Billy can see two cops talking to the foxy bitch he raped earlier. Shit. He looks behind him. Chaz is just staggering out of the park.

He bolts across the street and into the narrow, rancid alley between the all-night diner and an apartment building. The twists and turns of the alley take him to the edge of the wide, rocky field that used to be the Wright Project.

The Wright Project.

Memories flood back to Billy. Memories of dormitory-like low-income tenements built back in the early seventies. Fire swept through the projects twenty years ago, burned all five buildings to the ground. Since then a sign has stood in the northwest corner of the field. It's still there now. It says *Future Site of Wright Project II.*

The vast empty field has been the future site of Wright Project II for longer than Wright Project I stood.

The grass has grown higher as the lettering has faded. The sign is metal, or the homeless who dwell in the overgrown space would have ripped it down and burned it, flames consuming the future as they did the past.

Billy has vague memories of the fire; he lived here, once, long ago.

It began with a bad smell, acrid, like burning insulation. Young Billy awoke with the odor in his nostrils and his eyes. The smell was frightening: it was dangerous, it promised worse things to come if you only waited a bit. Billy stumbled out of bed and plodded from his cell-like bedroom to the living room. He was crying and not even Mr. Knob, his wooden-headed doll, could comfort him.

Crying because it smelled bad. He was such a baby.

His mother and one of her friends were sleeping on the threadbare couch. The TV was on, showing snow. Billy put Mr. Knob on the table and tried to wake his mother but she didn't stir, didn't even mumble. There were needles in the ashtray.

Billy went to the door. The keyhole was level with his eyes. The chain was undone. He grasped the knob; it was slightly warm in his hand. When he opened the door smoke rolled in like fog. The smoke was black and heavy and it stung, so he held his breath to keep the smoke outside himself as he went into the hallway. He heard the fire burning to his left, could see it as an orange glow. He looked up at the ceiling and could hardly see it through the smoke. He knew vaguely that there were *things* on the ceiling that were supposed to make noise when they smelled smoke, but they must have been sleeping.

Other tenants rushed by him as he stood stupefied in the hallway, one hand on the door and the other dangling by his side. One of them plowed into him and knocked him over and kept going. Billy fell down. His hand was jerked off the knob and the door swung closed, the lock engaging with a faint *click.*

He got up and tried to open the door, but the knob wouldn't turn. He pounded on it with his small fist, screaming for his mother, but she didn't let him in. Then somebody picked him up and carried him, screaming, away from the door. Away from the fire. Away from his mother. Billy screamed and kicked and struggled but it didn't do any good, the guy carrying him wouldn't let go, and eventually he blacked out from smoke inhalation or exhaustion or fright.

When he woke up he was outside, across the street from the complex, and fires were sweeping through the squat buildings like the entire place had been picked up and transported to hell. Now he knows the swiftness of the fire was due to the shoddy construction of the Wright Project: the kind of paint they used, the kind of drywall, the lack of fire barriers. But back then, when he was small and the flames roared so high they licked at God's heels, it seemed almost supernatural, as if the Wright Project had been targeted for cosmic retribution.

They never found his mother's body; they never found a lot of bodies, the fire was so hot it burned them right up. Billy doesn't even know what her name was. He was only three, she was *mommy*.

He closes his eyes.

Mommy.

When he opens his eyes again, the boys have arrived. They stand knowingly mute and observant, watching him from a short distance up the alley. He hasn't got the stamina to run from them anymore.

"Come on, you fuckheads," Billy says.

Together they circle the edge of the lot, crouched in the tall, brittle grass. The cops don't see them, and the homeless people aren't paying any attention, they never do, talking to shadows, staring into their barrel. The cops don't bother asking the bums questions because the bums never see anything.

As they creep toward Mrs. Barrett's building an ambulance pulls up in front of the tenement, its lights going off like flashbulbs. Four white coats get out of it. One talks to the cop while the other three kneel down around the dead guy. Billy motions for the fuckheads to stop and sits there on his haunches, watching. They're going to want the woman to get in the ambulance. They're going to want to take her to the hospital.

That can't be allowed. He'll charge across the lot and rip the ambulance to pieces if that's what it takes to keep her from going with them. Can't have doctors poking and prodding her, looking inside her. Nobody looks inside her.

Is that him thinking, or Nicholas thinking for him?

The first cop and the fourth paramedic are talking to the woman now, but she steps away from them shaking her head. They're urging her to go to the hospital but she's refusing. Maybe she's an illegal, maybe she has tracks up and down her arms and doesn't want them to see. The other three white coats are loading the corpse onto a stretcher. The cop puts his hand on the foxy bitch's shoulder and talks at her earnestly.

The second cop looks at the police car, then climbs into the front seat and picks up the radio mike.

The paramedics shove the stiff into the ambulance. The bitch looks at him, then at the cop, and her shoulders sag and she goes around to the back of the ambulance, and—*shit!*—gets in.

"Follow me," Billy whispers. If they're gonna trail him everywhere, he might as well use them. He moves fast through the grass toward the alley between Mrs. Barrett's building and the building behind it, on Sutton Street. He keeps his eyes on the ambulance.

The second cop gets out of the car. He gestures up the street, toward the river. Somebody must have finally called the pigs about the fight in the marina. Now they have a dilemma: they got a murder here and mayhem there, and which one will they get in trouble for not investigating? The two pigs talk face to face, their arms flailing around. Must be Italians or Jews, the way they talk with their hands. Billy bets they end up going to the marina.

The pigs talk to the fourth paramedic, then get in their car and roll out toward the marina. Billy pauses at the mouth of the alley just long enough to see the ambulance driver get back into the vehicle, then he runs up the alley and hangs a left at the tee.

Got to hurry.

Got to stop the meat wagon.

He *knew* the pigs would go to the marina. *Knew* it. Somebody will come back in the morning to check out the crime scene, or maybe they won't; one more murder on Canal Street is hardly worth their time if the victim isn't a cop or the fucking mayor. A familiar scorn for the law rises in Billy: the cops will come to accuse them and arrest them but not to protect them or find their killers. Like when the Night Watchman murdered his boys. The pigs didn't give a shit, they probably wanted to hand the guy a medal and a box of doughnuts.

He squeezes through the hole in the chain link, puts on a burst of speed, jumps out into Canal Street right in front of the ambulance.

He can see the driver get all surprised, his eyes going wide as the headlights on the vehicle. He slams on his brakes and swerves left. Billy jumps up onto the running board on the passenger side and yanks the door open and climbs inside and smashes the guy's head with one hand while grabbing the wheel with the other. He stomps on the brake and puts the ambulance into park.

The guy's white shirt turns red as blood pours out of his pulped skull.

"What the hell's going on?" demands a voice from the back of the ambulance. It's open through to the rear but there's a white curtain hanging down to separate the driver from the rest of the vehicle.

Billy pushes through the curtain. The woman is lying on a cot and a paramedic is next to her, talking to her. Two others are examining the stiff.

The foxy bitch screams. The paramedics stare.

Six seconds later the inside of the ambulance is covered in blood and the foxy bitch isn't screaming anymore because she's got gauze stuffed in her mouth.

Billy opens the back doors of the ambulance. The fuckheads are standing there staring at him. Good boys. He picks up the foxy bitch and sets her on her feet and says in her ear, "No doctors. No hospitals. You go back to your apartment and stay there or I'll give you to them."

She stares at the dead boys.

"You understand?"

She nods once, quickly. Tears run down her cheeks, streaked with her mascara. Billy doesn't care. He gives her a little push out the doors and the fuckheads catch her and steady her on her feet. "Walk her home, boys," Billy says. "I'll ditch the ambulance. Meet me back at our place."

Keeping their cold hands on the woman, the boys shuffle away.

Billy shuts the doors, goes back up in front. The ambulance is still running. He pulls the stiff out of the driver's seat, settles in, and drives the meat wagon away.

The water is quiet, and has been for a long time, before Nate surfaces. He's facing the dock, or what's left of it; all that remains are several of the pilings and a few planks that managed to stay secured to them, so that now they look like ribs on the wormy carcass of some behemoth. The boats have drifted away, coming to rest up against the next dock down, tangled in with the other vessels, crowding each other to suckle at the dock.

He awkwardly swims to shore; he has never been very good in the water, especially when he's fully clothed, waterlogged, and still stiff from his recent death. As he nears the sea wall he sees that its side is constructed of old brick and mortar, with concrete slathered on top of it like frosting. There are many gaps where the mortar has softened and sloughed away. He could use them as fingerholds, but instead he wraps his chains around the fence that tops the wall and hauls himself out of the river that way.

He comes out only a few feet from the body of the man who intervened in his encounter with Billy. The corpse has been pummelled into unrecognizability by the zombie thugs. He stands up, staring at the guard's carcass. He looks left, then right, then back at the guy. He looks like he was caught in an elephant stampede.

Nate's wet clothes stiffen in the icy air.

He notices that there's smoke drifting up from the pile of boats. Something's burning.

He reaches out and turns off the light on the big pole. The lever is hard to move but he manages it and the illumination goes away, leaving a faint orange glow from the middle of the jam of vessels.

Shutting the big lamp also lets him see flashing red and white lights spinning off his surroundings.

Nate drops into a crouch and whirls to face the street. A prowl car is creeping up Harbor Road, its lights blazing like the eyes of a demon. As Nate watches, the driver flips on the vehicle's spotlight and begins playing it over the wreckage of the marina.

The beam sweeps toward him.

Nate doesn't move.

The police are coming, cops from his own precinct, people he knows, people he worked with. His *friends*.

Not anymore.

Just before the spotlight reaches him, he turns and jumps off the sea wall. In the seconds that he hangs above the water he hears a voice boom through a bullhorn. It shouts a garbled warning, an order to halt, as if Nate could somehow suspend himself in mid-air indefinitely and await the arrival of the police.

He drops into the inky water. The river draws its obscuring veil over his head. He clumsily kicks away from shore, out of the small backwater which forms the marina. He lets the current take him and carry him off.

Just another bit of rubbish swept away by the flow.

11

Coming back from the old boat launch where he drove the ambulance into the river, Billy pauses on the sidewalk in front of the tenement. The cops didn't even bother to put up any of that stupid yellow tape they think keeps people away from crime scenes.

Fucking cops. Don't give a shit about the people who live around here.

He glances over his shoulder, at the building across the street. Abandoned hotel. Maybe he can find a place in there where he won't have to worry about running into other occupants. He knows the rumors about the old hotel, sure—the place is supposed to be haunted by a demon made of fire and the ghosts of some people who got murdered in the lobby—but who gives a shit for rumors? Not him; not anymore. He's got Nicholas looking out for him. Nicholas *needs* him for something, yes he does. So maybe tomorrow night he'll find a new place to hide. In the hotel.

Yeah. Tomorrow.

After he gets rid of the fuckheads.

Nate surfaces facing downstream, away from the marina and toward the old, decaying lock that used to form the terminus of the canal. He kicks for it, seeing as he does an orange glow on the tips of the small waves. He looks back toward the boats. A spit of the riverbank blocks his view, but over the hump of land he sees a pale and weary caricature of sunrise.

The small fire he left behind has grown.

He reaches the lock and kicks his way between the walls. They're made of grey stone, held together with masonry that has grown black and foul. The water that finds its way between the walls is trapped there and becomes stagnant and oily and thickly weeded. The water is slushy, the weeds dead and clinging. He pushes into them. His feet slip on the muddy bottom. The weeds pluck at him like little fingers, beseechingly, as if hoping he can transform them into orchids and lilies. They float in a slick and soggy mass, a mattress of plant corpses. He bulls through and reaches the riverbank and climbs up it.

At the top of the bank he's still between the walls of the lock. About two feet of grey stone protrudes from the ground. He crawls forward, keeping low, and at the end of the wall looks up toward the marina. One of the houseboats is on fire, making the glow. The police car is parked on the street, lights flashing. He can't see the cops.

Across the street from the marina, kitty-corner to it, is an overgrown park. He never noticed it before—more accurately, he never paid attention to it before—even though it's been there plain as day. He probably wouldn't be paying attention to it now, either, except that the plants are moving, the barren limbs and branches thrashing as if a hurricane is blowing through them.

There isn't a hurricane.

But deep inside the park, something is answering the fire with a glow of its own.

It's the end of another day with Andy. Ellie feels like she's been grabbed and dragged along by a tornado. Just when she'd thought they were going to spend a quiet afternoon at the beach—after she'd gotten out the paperback she was working on, a light mystery, nothing *dense*, nothing *sad*—Andy said, out of the blue, looking at her book, "You wanna go to the library?"

They had exceeded his allotted sit-still time.

Off to the library, then. And while Ellie sat trying to read her mystery, Andy was scuttling around the stacks and the archives and the microfiche hunting up information about Knife Point and the Wright Project. Because, he said, she was interested. Because she had said she was glad the developed who wanted to build on Knife Point had changed his mind.

Andy obviously has a more than passing interest in the hills, Knife

Point in particular. Turns out his parents had taken him camping there. The developer had aimed at creating a super-expensive subdivision on the green slopes of Andy's childhood, the bastard.

Thanks to him, she now knows more than anybody ever needed to know about Nicholas Fenton. Whenever he found out new, juicy tidbits, Andy relayed them to her in a stage whisper that echoed all around the paper-scented halls of the library. So she knows that the guy's full name was Nicholas Jeremiah Fenton. She knows he wasn't originally from Island City, moving in when he was in his twenties. She knows he had reputed, and unproven, ties to organized crime. She knows he was a real estate baron, particularly in the Canal Street area. She knows he donated land down by Harbor Road as a park. She knows he built the Wright Project.

Of course she remembers how the Wright Project burned down. Or up. Like a gigantic Roman candle. She had not remembered that Fenton was inside at the time. They never found his body—they found very few bodies, in the ashes that were left of the place—but his car was parked nearby, and he never resurfaced after the fire, and after fifteen years somebody finally got around to pronouncing him dead.

The survivors of the fire were not numerous, but they were soon rich. Fenton's estate was divided up between them and their lawyers. Seems Fenton's people had used paint that was only slightly less inflammable than, say, rocket fuel. And had cut other corners as well, specifically fire walls and fire doors and sprinkler systems. And, as it came out, this was all done not only with Fenton's knowledge, but with his approval.

In fact, it had been *his* idea.

Almost like he had *wanted* the place to burn down.

But why would he want that?

Nate darts across the street, staying low. The park is just one block toward the marina, but rather than risk detection he goes up Canal Street one block, turns left on Cross, and comes into the park from the other side.

He nearly changes his mind when he sees it up close.

The trees are shaking violently, shivering convulsively, their trunks shimmying and their upper limbs whipping about like tentacles. The smaller vegetation, the brambles and the underbrush, rattle and hiss. They are backlit by a pale blue-white luminescence coming from the interior. He can't tell its source. It seems to emanate from the trees themselves.

Can't anybody else see this? Can't somebody else take care of it? Shit.

He clambers over the low stone wall. The ground hums under his feet, making his soles tingle. He moves into the park. The air feels sticky, clingy, cloying and fetid. There's a faint sharp odor that gets stronger as he pushes through the animated brambles. They flail at him, whipping at his legs and waist and then shrinking from his hands when he tries to grab them and shove them aside. The trees swing their limbs down, trying to hit him, but whatever force is animating them hasn't made them supple enough to succeed.

They can't stop him from reaching the light.

It's coming from a clearing.

It isn't one of those quiet, peaceful meadows you find out in the forest. It isn't a sward of grass in the midst of a woody thicket. It's an elliptical patch of leprous asphalt fifteen or twenty feet across. The crumbling remains of pebbled concrete benches are scattered around the perimeter. They are all angled to face the life-size statue of a man which stands at the far end of the pavement. Just in case you couldn't tell what you were supposed to be looking at as you sat at your bench feeding the pigeons.

Of course, the way the statue is glowing would make it the center of attention anyway.

It's cocooned in sticky light, a gooey-looking splotch of illumination that envelops it and sends out tenebrous filaments to the surrounding trees and ground. The light hums and pulses in time with—or directing—the vibrations in the earth. Where the tendrils fall, the trees are limned in pale whitish-blue and the pavement is matted with a web of jagged glowing veins.

Like a chrysalis, thinks Nate.

Like something waiting to be born.

The air smells like bleach. The ground throbs. Nate's head begins to ache, the combination of stench and hum gets inside his brain and erodes it.

The statue seems to be *looking* at him.

The trees and bushes seem to be chattering about something.

He's losing his mind.

He sees writing on the base of the statue but can't tell what it says. He creeps closer. The spiderweb of light on the ground is spreading. He avoids the veins, picking his way across the pavement. The trees surrounding the park sway back and forth, back and forth, their barren crowns scraping across the red glow of the marina fire.

He's almost close enough to read the inscription.

Then the light goes strobe on him.

There's a roar as the marina goes up in a fireball. Nate has an instant to perceive the plume of flame rising above the trees and then he is hurled back by the force of the light pulse. Streamers of gelatinous illumination trail along behind him. He hits the pavement ten feet away and tumbles into one of the cement benches, ending up wedged between the seat and the ground, facing the statue.

The glob of light has become a flame, a white nimbus dancing around the statue. As Nate watches it erupts thirty feet into the sky, leaving the statue suddenly unclothed. The amorphous mass hangs motionless a second, then shoots off toward Canal Street.

The trees stop waving. The ground stops humming. But the scent of bleach lingers.

Nate extricates himself from the bench. He is wedged tight, and it takes a while. There are no more explosions from the marina but the glow is brighter now, the entire place must be on fire. He wonders if the police were caught in the blast. He has a sick feeling they were.

He stands up and finds that his legs are unsteady. Perhaps this is because someone has replaced his brain with cotton candy. He staggers to the statue. It is inert now, stripped of its illusion of awareness.

Nate reads the inscription.

Nicholas Fenton.

Nate decides not to go back to the marina. He goes the other direction instead, up Canal Street. A quick walk puts him in front of Mrs. Barrett's building, but he doesn't go inside, he just stands on the sidewalk staring up at the ghostly face of the tenement, with its caged eyes and its decaying carapace.

He can't bring himself to enter.

Come on, Nate. Just up the stairs and through the door. Nothing difficult there. Up the stairs and through the door and *you're in the building where you died.*

Where's Billy?

Where's the glow he saw around the statue?

Are they both in here, waiting for him to join them?

The wind is icy as the moon. His clothes are still wet and are getting stiff, freezing as the temperature plunges. Nate turns away from the building. He can't go inside yet. The scene is too raw, too recent; the situation is too amorphous. He needs time to think about what he's seen. No more blind wandering. The force he's up against —whoever is pulling Billy's strings—has a plan.

Nate needs one too.

So he has to find a place to go, somewhere nearby, where he can keep an eye on what's going on. His gaze falls on the abandoned husk of a building that stands opposite the tenement.

Perfect.

He crosses the street and surveys the decrepit structure. It's so obviously derelict, it must be crawling with homeless people looking for shelter. He ought to fit right in.

The building looks like an old hotel. It has architectural niceties that set it apart from the boxlike apartment buildings surrounding it: little ledges that run between floors, supported by curls of concrete that loop out like nautilus shells; and vertical columns, suggesting pillars, that run up between rows of windows and spread outward at the twelfth story to form a parade of arches that support a weatherbeaten cornice. The cornice is illustrated with what look like scenes from Greek mythology, satyrs and nymphs cavorting through concrete woods, galleons sailing on concrete waves, and in the middle, a wild-haired face looking blankly across at Mrs. Barrett's building.

Not what you would expect to find in this crap-hole part of town. But then, it wasn't always a slum. Even the dump where Mrs. Barrett lives still carries hints of lost splendor. Maybe there was block upon block of shining, hopeful buildings here once. Gone now, anyway. Burned or knocked down to build human hives. Misdirected urban development.

Nate goes in through the hole that was once the front door. He can make out the outline of a sign posted on the wall to the right. It's covered in so many layers of graffiti its original lettering has been obliterated. Presumably it once said *condemned* or *no trespassing* or *abandon all hope ye who enter here.*

He finds himself in a wide, cold lobby. Moonlight filters in through the smashed panes of glass that line the front of the building, then seems to stop in the dead air without reaching the floor.

Nate takes it slowly, one foot in front of the other. The floor is rough and uneven, like somebody pulled up all the carpeting and didn't replace it. Every time one of his shoes touches the floor it makes an entirely too loud scraping sound, even though he treads as lightly as he can.

Not that anybody's listening.

Are they?

Nate shakes his head. Let them hear. Anybody holed up in this place has just as little right to be here as he has.

Damn, it's dark.

He sends his chains out about five feet and uses them as extra hands, skittering back and forth across the floor. Like a cane. *Tap tap.*

The floor is hard and rough and cold.

So it's a surprise when his chains touch something soft, warm, and wet.

A person. Covered in blood. Freshly killed. Or . . .

"Billy," Nate says. Billy, the skinned man. But if it's Billy, it isn't telling. It just lies there letting Nate's chains take a walk up and down it. Definitely a person. Feet, shins, knees, thighs, gut—large gut, not Billy after all—chest, shoulders, neck, head. Lying on its back. No clue where the blood's coming from.

Nate retracts his chains. He kneels down and feels around for the body. His fingers touch floor. And more floor. And more floor.

No corpse.

Maybe he's imagining things.

Yeah. Right. He's been imagining everything since he got killed on the roof. He's died and gone to hell and it looks very much like Island City.

He extends his chains again, probes the floor. He quickly finds the body. It's exactly where it was before, and he's sure he would have felt it with his hands if it was there to feel.

He starts walking. He drag his feet, to make sure he kicks anything that might be lying in his path. Nothing is. But it doesn't take him long to find another body. This one, a woman, is slumped against a pillar, sitting up on the floor, head lolling off to the side. He finds the pillar with his hands. Smooth stone. He slides his hands down it to the floor. No woman.

He does find a chalky gash in the stone, though. A dent. He feels it with his finger. Its diameter is slightly larger than his finger's. He finds another hole a few inches up and to the left and sticks his finger in it.

No doubt about it. This is a bullet hole. But how old is it? For all he knows this pillar's had bullet holes in it for fifty years.

So what about the bodies he felt with his chains? Ghost corpses? The spectres of hotel guests gunned down in the lobby?

As he stands there, he again feels eyes on him. From behind. Watching, probing, evaluating. He turns slowly.

There's a shadow in the doorway. A big, round, bulbous shadow. Like a very fat woman standing in silhouette. There seems to be a red, fiery light behind her, like she's standing in front of a bonfire.

She's *looking* at him.

"Hello?" he calls.

She vanishes and takes the red glow with her.

Nate gawks at the doorway. That was a neat trick. He goes over to the nearest window, or rather, what *used* to be a window. Now it's just a big empty gap. He makes it without using his chains as guides; he doesn't need to find any more bodies that aren't there. They don't do much for his peace of mind.

At the window, he props himself up on the sill and looks out at the street. He keeps his head low, so as not to be seen. Not that there's much going on out there. Street activity around here ends at dusk; the only people out in the dark are the criminals, the trash, the gangs, and they all have better things to do than wander up and down Canal Street at three in the morning.

No fat woman. No red glow. Nothing much at all.

He wonders where Billy and his dead cronies are hiding out. Maybe they're nearby. Maybe they're across the street. Maybe they're *here*, in this very building. Sneaking up behind him. Nate whirls and looks at the vast black smudge of a lobby. Nothing there but invisible corpses.

Nate slides to the floor, leans up against the wall, watches the darkness.

And feels the darkness watching back.

12

Ellie Watson brings a pie to her appointment with Mrs. Barrett. It's banana-apple, her specialty; in her honest moments she'll admit that, more accurately, it's the specialty of her favorite bakery. During the drive to Canal Street she notices the taxi driver sniffing the air and favoring her with furtive glances. Finally he asks what kind of pie it is. She tells him. Banana-apple is a new concept for him and he hints, with a sledgehammer, that he would love to try a piece.

She gives him directions to the bakery.

From the arch of the Hunter River Bridge, Ellie can see the ruins of the marina. It was on the morning news, clips of the fire and the explosions. Apparently a dock gave way and this somehow produced an inferno. She didn't pay much attention to the broadcast. It wasn't about Nate, so who cared? But she had no idea the destruction was so bad. From the bridge, she can see the charred remains of docks and boats, indistinguishable from each other, all jammed together in a mass of flotsam against the southern wall of the marina. Everything that could float was pushed there by the current. Other bits of wreckage protrude from the water: sunken boats, burnt pylons. Here and there a vessel that somehow survived the fire bobs in the water; she can only see three, mixed in with the debris.

"I hear they was a gang fight there last night," the driver says. The way he says it, *gang* and *fight* are one word. "Gangs, they broke the dock and they shot their guns and set something on fire, and *boom!*"

Boom indeed.

"You live round here?" the cabbie asks, glancing back at her. According to the license pasted to the back of the front seat, his name

123

is Harmon Banerjee. The picture on the license makes him look all ears and teeth.

He *is* all ears and teeth, now that she gets a good view of his face.

"No," she says. "Just visiting somebody."

"Oh," Banerjee says. Then: "I used to live on Cross Street. Right across from the park. I could see the boats from my living room window. It was very relaxing to watch them float at night."

Ellie wonders if she's a terrible person for not wanting to know this much about her cab driver. She says, "Well, all I can see from my apartment is the building across the alley."

And her dead husband in the window.

No, she tells herself, she still doesn't know he's dead. He might be alive.

Every time she has this thought it gets weaker. Like an old tea bag.

Banerjee goes on at length about his old apartment. The way the rug in the hallway smelled. How noisy his neighbors were. His shit of a landlord. Ellie listens and nods occasionally.

Harbor Street is closed at the marina. Beyond the barricades are several police cars and a fire truck. Their lights are all flashing, just in case you thought maybe they had all gathered in the middle of the road for no reason. Banerjee takes an alternate route, turning left off the bridge and circling around to get to Canal Street from the other side. Through some doubling back that Ellie discreetly ignores, this involves traveling down Cross Street. Banerjee points out his old window. It is on the fourth floor and does, indeed, directly overlook the park and the marina.

Too bad the park is an overgrown weed patch and the marina, even before the fire, was the sort of place where a pile of garbage bags would be considered a wall to block an eyesore. Now it's just gone. Harmon gazes up at his window and says, "I thank God I am out of that place."

As they approach Mrs. Barrett's building, Ellie notices that the bars have fallen off one of the windows facing the field. She hums a song she learned in high school. *Leprosy . . . I'm only half the man I used to be. . . .*

The cab pulls to the curb in front of Mrs. Barrett's tenement house. Ellie slides her money through the slot in the plexiglas wall between the front and back seats. Banerjee slides back the change.

She leaves some as a tip, takes the rest, and has started across the street when he sticks his head out the window and calls, "You want me to come back for you?"

"Okay," she calls back, surprised. "About two hours, maybe."

"Two hours maybe. Very good. Have a nice visit with your friend!" The taxi driver waves as he pulls away, and Ellie, feeling somewhat foolish, waves back. She has apparently befriended him, simply by letting him talk. She yells, "I'll save you a piece of pie!"

He waves again, and honks.

Grinning what she supposes must be a stupid grin, she climbs the front steps and enters the building.

Nate opens his eyes.

He's lying on his side below the window sill, in the shadow of the wall. Sunlight is inches from his nose. In the daylight, the things he thought he saw and felt last night recede. Phantoms. This is just a big, abandoned lobby, stripped off its pretensions, down to the skin and bone.

And his wife's voice carried right through the wide, broken windows.

He sits up. Ellie, here, in *this* neighborhood? Why? He must be hearing things. The voice must belong to someone who just sounds like her. Why would she come *here*, to the building where he died?

Then he thinks, of course, this is *exactly* what she would do. She'd want to see it, explore it. Now that he considers it he's surprised she hasn't come sooner. But it sounds like she's come alone, and that isn't good.

Maybe she brought his gun.

But he and Frank had guns and look what happened to them.

He lifts his right hand, slides it forward along the floor, stopping when his fingers are just shy of the line of brightness. He remembers the dream—the nightmare—he had behind the Dumpster.

Maybe this is another dream. Maybe he'll see the tomato-head man again. Maybe he'll see something even worse.

Maybe he thinks too much.

Nate pushes his hand out into the light. There is no warmth from it, but, reassuringly, it doesn't make his flesh split and wither or turn to dust. His skin is milky-pale with a bluish tinge and his nails are purple and blood is smeared across the flesh, sticking the small hairs down flat against his skin.

Not a pretty hand. It's a hand of death. The sunlight doesn't destroy, but it reveals and that's horrible enough.

He pulls himself up to the window sill and looks out at the deserted street. Ellie has already gone inside the building. He tries his chains, ordering them to leap out through the window and entangle the streetlight. They hang limp and unresponsive, as if they were nothing but the severed links of a pair of handcuffs.

It's like losing his arms. He reminds himself that three days ago, when he was alive, he had no such peculiar attributes as extensible, retractile chains, and he got along fine without them.

But that was before he'd met Billy.

The interior of the building is as dark and rancid as Ellie remembers. She walks quickly up the hallway to the stairs. She is alone this time, in a place where *alone* is synonymous with *vulnerable*; she tightens her grip on the shoulder strap of her purse. It's not her usual purse, it's her small one, and it contains only her driver's license, a credit card, and enough money for the taxi ride here and back. Just the essentials.

And, of course, her husband's spare gun. The essentials.

The stink in the stairwell is worse than before. The smell of rotting meat has been added to its usual unclean bathroom odor. Someone probably tossed a bag of garbage down the central shaft, thinks Ellie. Combination lavatory and trash disposal all in one. She tries to hold her breath and manages to make it to the fourth floor having inhaled only nine or ten times. Outside the stairwell she pauses a moment, breathing in deeply, holding it, letting it out. Up here the air is almost clean.

Almost.

She goes to Mrs. Barrett's apartment and knocks but gets no answer. After a moment she knocks again and calls the woman's name. Silence. She looks up and down the deserted hallway. It's badly lit, cast in a perpetual half-shadow like an expensive restaurant, though the atmosphere here is more decrepit shithole than *haute couture* and what lighting there is comes not from candles in silver sconces but landlord halos in the ceiling. These circular fluorescent tubes are naked in their steel plates, resembling glowing intestines.

Some are flickering and the rest are out.

Still no response from inside the apartment. Mrs. Barrett must have gone out. Ellie tries the knob and finds it locked, but when she applies pressure to the door it creaks inward slightly then stops. Ellie's eyes go to two patches of clean wood where the lock and deadbolt have broken through the jamb. The exposed interior of the door frame is crumbling and spongy-looking. Dry rot, thinks Ellie. She pushes the door again but now it won't move, there's something in its way. Icy air wafts through the tiny opening.

"Mrs. Barrett?" Ellie says again, putting her mouth close to the crack between door and frame. This, also, elicits no response. Ellie looks at the broken jamb again. Somebody must have forced his way into the apartment, she thinks, and the ancient wood gave up without a fight. There's a piece of furniture or something behind it to keep it closed, and that means someone must still be in the apartment, either the intruder or Mrs. Barrett. Ellie can't think of a reason why a burglar would break into an apartment and then barricade himself inside, so it is probably the old lady; but then why doesn't she answer? Maybe she had a heart attack or something from the shock of the invasion of her apartment.

Yeah . . . maybe. Ellie unzips her shoulder purse and takes out the gun, slips off the safety. Because maybe she's wrong.

She puts her shoulder to the door and pushes. The door begins to move slowly. Whatever is behind it makes a loud—a much, much too loud—scraping sound against the floor. She stops pushing when she has an eight-inch opening.

Ellie squeezes into Mrs. Barrett's apartment. The splintered wood of the jamb plucks at her backside as if trying to stop her from entering. *Turn back, turn back!* She has to half-clamber over the thing blocking the entrance, a big frilly chair; pushing the door caused the chair to begin to rotate and it moved over to partially obstruct the space between the door and the wall. Holding onto the gun with her right hand makes this task more difficult but she is not about to put the weapon down, especially after she sees the sharp crimson stain that mars the white background of the flowered chair.

The apartment appears deserted. The first thing that grabs Ellie's attention is the big living room window. It's wide open and she has a clear view through it. No bars. At least this explains how the apartment can be empty but still have something jammed up against the door: the intruder kicked the bars out and exited through the window.

Forty feet above the ground.

Are we talking about Superman here?

Cold air billows through the window, taking full advantage of this gap in the building's defenses. She looks again at the blood stain on the chair. Mrs. Barrett wouldn't have left the window open if she was able to close it. She is obviously gone, either dead or fled. The apartment is empty. Ellie starts to close the window, then thinks better of it and stops. Don't disturb the scene of a possible crime.

She approaches the bedroom. Ellie calls the old woman's name one more time. Still no answer. She cracks the door and looks around the meagerly-furnished room. The bed is a twin, primly made, waiting for someone to climb into it. Other than the bed, the room contains a beaten dresser and a huge, scarred wardrobe. In the left-hand wall is a narrow closet door with a crack down the middle.

Ellie slowly enters the bedroom. She passes by the dresser. A yellowed doily graces the thing's scuffed surface, and in the middle of the doily a tarnished brass frame surrounds a sepia photograph of a young couple embracing. The man is wearing a military uniform, the woman a bowl-shaped hat from which a flower sprouts. They are cheek to cheek, smiling into a future that has ended here. World War II, thinks Ellie. Did it take Mr. Barrett away?

The knob of the closet door is cold through her gloves. Ellie turns it and pulls the door open, stepping back just in case something falls out, but there's nothing inside except a small assortment of clothes, shoes, handbags. Ellie shuts the door, moves on. More clothes are in the wardrobe. She begins to relax. The place is as deserted as it looks.

There's no phone in the bedroom, but there must be one in the kitchen; there's always one in the kitchen. Ellie crosses the apartment. She wonders if her own dwelling will be like this someday, a museum of things that were, a twin bed and a faded picture standing in mockery of what might have been.

No. She'll shoot herself first.

She enters the kitchen and flicks on the overhead light. It sputters into life after a moment, the harsh fluorescent tube giving everything a greenish cast.

She stops and stares.

Food is piled up in the sink, some wrapped up or in Tupperware, some just loose, as if the refrigerator vomited its contents across the room. Ellie's eyes move from the sink to the fridge. She lifts the phone from its cradle. Receiver in one hand and gun in the other, she goes to the refrigerator. It hums softly. One of those old latch models. She opens it with three fingers of her left hand, the one holding the phone.

The refrigerator door clicks open. She slowly swings it wide.

And there is Mrs. Barrett.

The elderly woman is wadded up like a piece of old gum, arms and legs bent at impossible angles to make her fit into the small opening. The spindly body faces into the fridge but her head is twisted halfway around so it is looking straight at Ellie with eyes like frosted glass. A purple tongue protrudes slightly between blue lips flecked with blood.

Ellie backs up a step, and another, staring at the apparition in the appliance. She drops the telephone. She hears a strange high-pitched whine and realizes it's coming from her own throat. She clamps down on it hard. None of that. None of that.

But she keeps backing away.

She steps on the telephone.

It twists beneath her and throws her off-balance. Arms flailing, she falls over backwards, hits the counter hard with the small of her back. She drops the gun. It hits the floor, and fires. A tiny bloodless hole appears in the middle of Mrs. Barrett's forehead, right between the eyes. *Bang.* Couldn't have hit it better if she were aiming.

Then the back of her head slams into the cabinets opposite the fridge. The world around her flares as if it's all part of a giant flashbulb; and like the afterimage of a flash it fades to purple, then to black.

13

SHE MUST BE GOING TO the roof, thinks Nate. He's moving faster than he has in days, forcing his cold, stiff legs to pump like their muscles still have blood. Into the building. Into the stairwell and up.

He's being foolish. She's likely to see him, and then what will he do? And if he finds her in trouble, he'll be helpless in the daylight, a man armed with nothing.

Not even life.

Ellie becomes conscious of a pain in the back of her head. She groans and shifts position. The movement causes her to slip off the edge of the cabinet and collapse onto her side. The impact on the floor forces a little grunt out of her. Her eyelids flicker, then open. She is eye-level with the old grey and white linoleum, it stretches out before her in a checkerboard plain. Not far away she sees Nate's gun. Its barrel faces away from her, pointing at the refrigerator. She moves her gaze up and the corpse of Mrs. Barrett is staring at her with eyes like marbles.

Jesus.

Ellie pushes herself upright. Her head throbs. She hears the harsh alarm of the telephone from not far away; it's been off the hook too long and has decided there's some sort of problem. She slept right through the semi-pleasant voice that says, "If you would like to make a call, please hang up and dial again," and gone right to the hateful *eh-eh-eh-eh-eh* that follows it.

She rubs her brow. Shadows gather in the living room, joining together, gaining strength.

Gaining strength.

It's getting dark.

She needs to get out of the apartment. Something *bad* is going to happen to her if she doesn't, she knows it is. This sudden flash of fear hits her somewhere in the gut and radiates out from there, stealing up her stomach, sending tendrils into her heart and the base of her brain where the old instincts hide. She can't stand Mrs. Barrett's gaze anymore. With her foot she pushes the refrigerator door closed, but it won't stay shut; the old woman's arm has fallen out of the box and the door bounces off it. The blue flesh shifts as if she's trying to move, trying to beckon Ellie closer.

Still groggy, mind filled with taffy, Ellie gropes for the gun. She can see it there, right in front of her, but for some reason her fingers keep going to the wrong place. A few seconds of failure precede success. The weapon is reassuringly cold and heavy. It does not feel one bullet lighter. She forces herself to stand then closes her eyes as a painful head rush swoops down on her. She steadies herself with a hand on the counter. Can't fall down again. Got to stay on her feet.

Then she hears a noise from across the apartment, a faint creaking, as of a door. Her ribs strain to hold her heart steady in her chest. She opens her eyes just in time to see the bathroom door click shut.

She can't see anyone in the apartment, but the kitchen door reduces her range of vision to a very limited arc. Someone could have slipped out of the bathroom and flattened himself against the inside wall and he would be hidden from her view. Facing the archway leading to the living room, she backs up until she reaches the phone. She is careful this time not to step on it. She doesn't look down as she bends at the knees and picks up the receiver. She shifts her grip on the gun to get a finger free, and using it she punches in the number of the police station. She has trouble hitting the buttons because the phone won't stop shaking.

She listens to the series of clicks as the phone dials. It's got a keypad but it's still rotary, it's older technology masquerading as newer. Each click seems louder than the last, and slower, clickclickClick Click Click CLICK *CLICK* . . . come *on*, thinks Ellie. At last the phone begins to ring. Ellie hides her gun hand behind her back.

Someone appears in the archway, a kid, a teenager. Like the

teenagers who killed Nate. The youth is grinning and staring at her with a vacant, glassy gaze. Drugs, thinks Ellie; but then she notices that the kid's face looks funny, lopsided. The right side of his head is a mass of congealed blood and jagged bits of skull. And his shoulder has a great cleft out of it, showing red meat and shattered bone.

"Hi," the kid says. "Who you calling?" His breath is rank and fetid, the rotten stench of kitchen garbage that has been left sitting too long.

The phone rings and rings. Where *are* they, God damn them? Then at last a gruff voice comes on the line and growls, "Yeah?"

"Help! I need help!" Ellie says. "I'm at—"

"I'll help," the kid says.

"Who the fuck is this?"

She has misdialed. She has not reached the police. With this realization she feels her lungs turn to ice and melt down into her stomach. "Please help me," she says. "Call the police! Tell them—"

"Fuck you." The line goes dead.

The kid is moving towards her, bringing his odor with him. Ellie stands immobile, waiting. "Billy wants you," he whispers. His voice is like snow sweeping off a roof. He reaches out and takes the phone out of her hand, and that's when she sweeps the gun up under the kid's chin and pulls the trigger.

He passes the fourth floor, Mrs. Barrett's floor. He and Frank came through that door and went up to the roof, to their deaths. He takes the stairs two at a time. *I got the power of Satan right here*, said Frank. *They got knives, we got guns.* They had something else too, something that still lingered even after they were all dead, something that reached out for their corpses and brought them back like a strange tide. Something his wife is walking right into.

He crosses the police line. The yellow tape has been pulled down and trampled. It sticks to his right foot but he doesn't slow down to remove it, he just drags it along behind him. The door to the roof is closed. He yanks it open and stumbles out onto the patchy field of crushed stone. His shadow is swallowed up in the bigger shadow of the stairway cover behind him. It points at the ventilator, and beyond it, the altar.

The altar where he died.

"Ellie!" he shouts, stepping forward. An icy wind whips north to south, promising snow later in the afternoon, tomorrow maybe. The sky is the color of old lead except at the horizon, where an angry, infectious red surrounds the sun. Still dragging the yellow tape behind him, Nate stumbles across the roof, hearing the pebbles crunch and grind under his feet. Snow glistens in pockets of shadow, accumulating wherever there's a shelter where the wind can push it.

He has almost forgotten why he came here. He remembers his wife, but that image is being superseded by another one, a darker one. Flashes of the night replay in Nate's mind, little snatches of death. He circled the ventilation unit to the right and he does so again. He crept around the corner and saw—

Frank stumbles around the far side of the ventilator, moving backwards, gun pointing shakily at nothing.

Nate shuts his eyes tight, counts to three, opens them again. Frank is gone. Frank was never there. Tricks and games of his tired, cold mind. Ellie isn't here either. There's no one on the roof except for him. He can see the pentacle from here, partially obscured by snow. Several of the black candles have blown over in the wind. Nate wonders why they didn't take the candles away but then he thinks, what would be the point? The candles have nothing to do with what happened, not in any sense that a court would recognize.

The crime scene is old, it's cold, and it's empty. Off to the west he can see the river, leaden as the sky. It'll be dark soon and Ellie is still in the building somewhere. Nate starts to turn back to the stairwell but freezes as his gaze sweeps over the pentacle.. The long cut in his torso stings him teasingly, reminding him it's there. Images rise again in his mind, rise and sweep him away

He shuts his eyes.

Yes, darkness, he remembers darkness; it followed the pain, swift and clean and cleansing. After that, movement, sliding through a tube made of clouds and cobwebs into a cold dark place. The stars were huge overhead, big as light bulbs, hot and bright, but they didn't give any of that light or heat to him, no. They let him lie there. Stars . . . so many that in places they blurred one into another into another, a mosaic of light; so hot that if the earth came beneath them its forests would burst into flame, its oceans into clouds of steam.

But they warmed and lighted Nate Watson not at all.

And in the blackness that surrounded him there was a presence, darker still. It came to him. It touched him—

And then a sound penetrates the memory, burns a hole through it and sets it aflame.

Gunshot.

It's muffled but unmistakable; he's heard enough of them to know. Shaking off the shreds of the remembrance, Nate makes for the stairwell, forcing his stiff legs to pump faster, faster.

It has suddenly occurred to him where else Ellie might have gone: Mrs. Barrett's apartment.

And Billy might have gone there too.

The sound of the gunshot reverberates in the kitchen. The explosion of hot gases from the end of the barrel is the first thing that does damage to the kid, causing the skin below his chin to burst open in a pattern like a jagged star. A tiny jet of flame follows, singeing his flesh. The scent of burning meat becomes an undercurrent to the sharp odor of gunpowder before the bullet even leaves the pistol. When it does it punches a hole through the kid's bottom jaw. A little puff of smoke comes out of his mouth. The projectile goes through the soft upper palate and into the kid's head, but it doesn't come out.

As the boy takes a shaky step back, she shoves him aside. He falls down, twitching and writhing. She runs past him. His hand closes on her ankle and she falls face-down on the cold linoleum. "Billy wasss you," the youth says, his voice slurred by the holes in his mouth.

Before she can stop herself, Ellie shrieks. He can still *talk*? She just sent a .22 slug bouncing around the inside of his skull and he can still focus on her, still grab her? What *is* this?

She jerks her foot free. His grip isn't strong enough to hold her. She flips onto her back and retreats from him on her hands and feet, the way she used to do in gym class in high school a million years ago. *The crab walk*, they called it. The kid rolls over onto his stomach and gets up on his hands and knees. He's not bleeding at all. He shakes his head as if he's got water in his ear, then he rubs the broken side of his skull. Ellie hears fragments of bone clicking together. They sound like dominoes.

She gets to her feet, turns for the door. She has to get out of here. The shadows have conquered the apartment now, the sun has dropped below the obscuring buildings across the river. She can't afford another minute in this room, in this building. There's a corruption here, she can smell it, feel it, taste it, it sticks to her skin like paste, it fills up her heart and turns her blood to sewage.

She scrambles around the chair. Damn the narrow opening! She should have moved it when she had the chance. Stupid, stupid, stupid—she hasn't done one damn thing right since knocking on the door of the apartment.

Halfway through the opening, she gets stuck on the jagged wood.

A second later, a wet hand grabs her arm, the arm that ends in the hand with the gun. Sharp nails dig into her flesh. Ellie gasps. Her grip on the gun loosens and she feels it ripped from her hand, hears it clatter to the floor and slide away across the faded hardwood.

Then the hand jerks her back into the apartment. The room spins around her as she is whirled around and slammed over the back of the couch. She catches a moment's glimpse of her assailant, and comes away with the impression *red*. He's wearing red makeup, he has red hair, he has a red shirt. Something.

There are two more kids standing in front of her. One has a smashed skull that complements the one in the kitchen; the other can't seem to make his head stay straight on his shoulders. Each one grabs one of her hands, and their grips are much stronger than the other kid's.

"Gonna have some fun, baby," the one behind her says, as he begins fumbling with her pants.

Ellie begins to scream.

14

Nate stumbles down the stairs, faster than his legs can carry him. He vaults the railings where they bend back on themselves, he jumps to the landings from five stairs up, he does *anything* to squeeze any scrap of speed out of his laboring body. The police tape hisses along behind him. It gets caught in the door at the fourth floor landing, tripping him up momentarily. He untangles himself and keeps going. He remembers the number, it's tattooed in blood in his mind.

Four-twelve.

Billy's cock feels like it's ten feet long. He can't wait to sink it into this hot little bitch. She squirms, but she's gonna love it. Her pants give him some trouble, they have some kind of weird double-loop belt thing that he can't figure out. Finally he just slices through it with a jagged fingernail. The slacks come loose. He gets ready to pull them down, to expose the gates of paradise.

She keeps screaming hysterically. "Don't worry," he whispers in her ear. "I'll take care of you."

She stops screaming.

Billy puts his hands on her pants.

But instead of sitting still for it like a good little bitch, she pivots forward on the sofa and jams her foot into his balls. She's wearing winter boots with solid rubber heels, and it's the heel that gets him edge-on. Unbelievable pain shoots up from Billy's crotch and he hears a sudden gush of liquid splash to the floor. Acrid smoke blossoms from the puddle. His crotch suddenly feels cold, icy cold.

He slowly looks down.

Through the smoke he sees his scrotum hanging down, empty and ragged, like a burst balloon. Blood pulses from it in time with his heart. His penis has gone limp and shriveled.

"Fucking *bitch!*" Billy yells. He raises his arm, fingers splayed, talons eager to taste her meat. "I'll give you something you'll remember!"

The door crashes open behind him.

Before he can even turn to look, he hears the rattle of chains and feels cold iron ensnare his wrist.

The Night Watchman has arrived.

Nate jerks the kid's arm back, spins him around and away from Ellie. Billy howls and grabs the chain with his free hand and yanks Nate forward, swinging him on the end of his chain, pulling him right off his feet. Nate goes sliding across the floor in an arc, smashing through a floor lamp and an old rocking chair. Billy keeps swinging him, swings him too far; the chain hits Chaz and Joey and bowls them over. They try to hang on to Ellie, pulling her up over the back of the sofa. Her arms stretch straight. Her feet kick at the couch as she tries get herself over the back of it, tries to get away from Billy.

Nate comes to rest beside the open window. He flings another chain, this time at the two zombie kids holding his wife. He twines the chain around their legs as they struggle to stand up again, then pulls it tight and reels it in. The two of them go down on their faces; one of them lets go. Ellie hangs half-over the back of the couch for a moment, then her wrist pops from the second punk's hand and she slips down behind the sofa. Her eyes sweep over Nate as she falls, and they widen into blue half-dollars. "Nate!" she screams.

"*Nate?*" Billy says. He bends slightly and a second later Ellie reappears squirming in his grip. His red fingers are closed around her neck. "You know this bitch, Night Watchman?"

Nate slowly stands up. Billy's hard obsidian eyes are fixed on him. The two zombies push themselves up onto their hands and knees as Nate releases them from his grip. "C'mon, Night Watchman," Billy says. "Who's the bitch? Wife? Lover? Wife's lover?" He gives Ellie a little shake and she chokes back a shriek. "Who are you, bitch?" Billy breathes in her ear. "Do you fuck the Night Watchman?"

The third zombie appears in the doorway to the kitchen. He clings to the wall of the archway, barely able to stand, shivering and twitching uncontrollably. Nate's eyes flick to the kid, only for a second but long enough to see a ragged hole under his chin, a body-contact entrance wound. Ellie must've plugged him. Good girl.

Billy says, "Well *fuck me* for asking." Without changing his grip he swings Ellie up over the couch and hurls her at Nate. Billy follows after her, vaulting the sofa. He leaves a trail of blood on the yellowed upholstery, the red stuff spilling from his wounded crotch. Nate wishes he could say it was slowing the kid down, but it's not.

Ellie plows into Nate and knocks him over. He lets himself take the full force of the impact, he rolls with it back against the wall, cushioning Ellie with his arms as they hit the floor together.

Billy's coming.

Nate lets go of Ellie and flings his chain at Billy. Billy catches it. "Didn't I teach you last time?" he roars.

He keeps coming.

Nate retracts the chain as fast as he can, using his free hand to swing it toward the half-open window nearby. It pulls back faster than Billy is moving and Billy, startled, is jerked off-balance. Nate guides him in a semicircle and sends him crashing through the glass.

Shouting curses, Billy vanishes.

But he doesn't let go of the chain.

As the kid falls, Nate slides across the floor and slams into the wall beneath the window, legs apart and feet planted on the narrow ledge of the sill. He holds onto the chain with both hands as Billy swings outside the building.

"Joey! 'Berto! Pull me in!" Billy yells. The two kids shuffle over to Nate and, as if he isn't even there, put their hands on the chain and begin hauling it hand-over-hand. Nate tries to grab Joey but the zombies simply step on him and he has no leverage to get himself free. He's got a foot on his left arm and his chest, on his neck and his right arm. Then the third kid appears and practically falls on him, pressing his torso up against Nate's legs. Nate squirms but he's in a position where he can use practically none of his strength.

So he uses his free chain instead.

He sends it around the third kid's body, encircling his head and jerking the kid off him. The zombie's neck *cracks* as Nate flings him aside. Then he rolls up his body, kicks out hard with both legs, one foot for each of the two kids holding him. They both go staggering back.

Then Billy grabs him from behind and spins him around.

The kid is in the window, covered in blood and broken glass. Bits of it stick to his glistening flesh, adhering to his coating of slime. The claws of his left hand are dug into the old wood; the other hand is on Nate's shoulder. Billy drags him closer, opening his mouth to display a row of black, jagged teeth. The maw is inhumanly wide, his jaw must be double-hinged. The kid's breath is foul. Rotting meat fried in bleach.

Then Ellie elbows Nate aside. She's holding the gun. She shoves it into Billy's open mouth before he realizes what's happening, her hand disappearing up to the wrist.

"Fuck you for asking," she says as she pulls the trigger.

Blood pours from Billy's jaws as the bullet punches through the back of his mouth and erupts from the base of his neck. His eyes go wide, then seem to sag in their sockets, to glass over; his fingers loosen on the sill and on Nate's shoulder. Ellie pulls her hand out of his mouth as the kid falls. Nate leans forward to watch Billy's descent. It takes a couple of seconds and ends with a gentle *whump* that is echoed in the apartment behind them. Ellie and Nate both turn. The zombies lie limp and still on the floor, all of them, as if they derived their animation through Billy's existence and its end is theirs as well.

Ellie lays the gun on the window sill. She stands mutely, looking at Nate. He takes a halting step forward, reaches out and clumsily caresses her cheek. She feels scorchingly warm. "Oh, Nate," she says, throwing herself against him. He feels her heat up and down his body. Living heat. "I *knew* you were alive, Nate. I *knew* it!"

How will he tell her he's not alive at all? How?

Then he thinks, to hell with how, and folds her up in his arms.

THE MEAT MACHINE

15

"I KNOW YOU IN THERE, bitch!" the fat man shouts, pounding on the door. "You owe me three hundred! Open the God damn door!" He rains a torrent of blows on the old, scarred wooden surface, but there's no response from inside. Hasn't been for the last two days. Bitch die in there or something? Move out and stiff him on rent?

A door up the way opens and the skinny black lady who lives there sticks her head out. "Why you gotta make all that noise?" she says. "People are trying to sleep!"

"Put a pillow over yer head," he says. Then: "Are *you* all paid up on your rent?"

"You know damn well I am," she snaps, withdrawing and slamming the door.

"Bitch," the landlord says. He reaches into his pocket and takes out a ring of keys. He has gotten in trouble before for going into tenants' apartments without permission, but the bitch is two months behind in her rent so the city can kindly fuck off, thank you very much. He can't remember which master key works in her lock. He has to try three before he finds the one that opens the door. He looks quickly left and right—no one is in the hallway—and pushes into the apartment.

He stops dead one pace in, because he must have the wrong place. This is a slaughterhouse. The walls are caked in blood, like somebody had it in a bucket and tossed it all around. Guts are strewn across the floor. It's as if somebody gave a deranged kid a big fat knife and a corpse to play with.

The fat man's dinner is coming up on him. He covers his mouth with a beefy hand. He can't just puke on the floor. Instinctively he runs for the bathroom. He bulls the door open and then halts as if smacking into a wall. The bathroom is worse than the living room. And . . . and sitting on the toilet . . . the fat man can't hold it in anymore. He whirls and vomits into the sink. His stomach heaves its contents up into the old white basin then tries to follow them itself.

When he can move, he takes one more surreptitious look at the apparition on the commode. It's the woman who lived here, he can tell because her *face*, at least, is intact. Her eyes are wide open and glassy, her mouth frozen in a blood-choked scream. Her abdomen and most of her chest cavity are gone, blown open as if she swallowed a hand grenade. She's a mass of ragged flesh suspended from sticks. The fat man, his shirt stained with puke and bile, backs out of the bathroom. He uses her telephone to call the police. They tell him to wait until they get there and not to touch anything, but he can't stay in this place a second longer. As soon as he hangs up he stumbles out into the hallway and slides down the wall to sit on the floor. His heartbeat is as ragged as his breathing.

In a few minutes a cop approaches, seemingly from nowhere. The fat man squints up at him. The cop is middle-aged, with rust-colored hair and a neatly-trimmed beard that comes to a point below his chin. The fat man struggles to his feet as the man shows him a badge. "That was damn fast," he says.

"I was close by," the cop says, like this is very significant. The landlord doesn't care, he's beyond noticing anything now. He gives the cop his name and phone number and address, and as soon as the officer says he can leave he lumbers off. He's gonna go to Wilson's on Harbor Road and get so shitfaced he forgets his name, let alone what he found in the apartment.

The cop enters the blood-soaked apartment. He closes and locks the door behind him. And then he isn't wearing a uniform anymore, he's wearing a mustard yellow suit nattily tailored and he's looking around with the pleased air of someone surveying the house he just built with his own two hands.

Nicholas bends and drags one long finger through the gore. He looks at it, then sticks it in his mouth and pulls it out clean. He smiles widely.

"Well," he says. "Thank you, William. Now we're making progress."

They decide not to wait for the taxi.

Nate takes Ellie out through the side door, the one he stumbled through three nights ago when he was newly born. This puts them in the alley on the opposite side of the building from Mrs. Barrett's apartment. Nate remembers the lights of the police cars flashing on the walls, remembers the billowing steam of the exhaust. To their left is Canal Street. To their right, the hole he tore in the fence. It hasn't been, and never will be, repaired.

"Nate. . . ." Ellie is standing a few feet away, hands in her pockets, looking at him. "Nate, what was . . . *that?*"

She means Billy. And the kids. "I don't know," he says. "I don't know what they were or where they came from."

"Are they . . . ?"

"The ones who killed me?" Nate nods his head. "Yes."

"The ones who *killed* you." Ellie is turning this concept over in his mind; he can hear the words rotating in her voice. "Nate . . . You're not dead." She moves closer. "You're *here*, with me. You can't be dead."

"There's dead, and there's dead," Nate says.

"What's that mean? That's crap." Ellie, the realist. "There's dead, and there's alive."

"You should know better after what just happened. *I* know better." He starts walking toward the fence and Ellie follows, falling in beside him. After a moment he feels her fingers fumbling with his. He thrusts his hands into his pockets and waits for the questions.

"Nate," Ellie says, haltingly. "Nate, it . . . it *is* you, isn't it?"

"It's me," he says. "But it's not me."

"I don't understand this at all. You're not alive, but you're here. Those kids weren't alive but one of them tried to rape me."

"Billy—the one who tried to rape you—was alive. I think. I didn't kill him, anyway. Just the others."

"It *was* you." She makes a mirthless little laugh. "I remember thinking, *I hope it was Nate who killed them.*"

"I'm not proud of it," he says. He helps her through the jagged hole in the chain link. They make another right. Now they're walking behind the tenement. Ahead of them is the open field, the former site of the Wright Project. Ellie digs at his hand again and this time he lets her take it. Lets her feel how cold it is. She doesn't comment on it.

"Charlie said they thought the kids . . . cut you."

"They did. Want to see?"

"*No*, Nate. Jesus." A momentary silence. "Why are you acting like this?"

"You have to understand what I am now."

"And what's that?"

"I don't know. But not a man."

"You look like a man to me," Ellie says.

Nate and Ellie step out into the rocky field that was once the Wright Project. Canal Street, a hundred yards away, is quiet and deserted. "Stay here," Nate says. Extricating his fingers from hers, he creeps along the side of the building. It's easy to tell which window belonged to Mrs. Barrett, it's the only one without bars on the outside, and when he gets there Nate finds what he's looking for lying broken in the grass.

Billy.

The kid did a slow spin as he fell and ended up face-down with his head pointing at the building. The back of his skull has a jagged hole in it where the bullet broke through, but there's more damage than that: Billy seems to be decomposing. His body is seething, the gleaming, greasy flesh rippling as though small creatures are at play inside him. Already the kid's spine and part of his rib cage are exposed, but they aren't white like normal bones, they're charcoal black to match his nails and his teeth.

Nate turns away from the grotesque thing, starts walking back to where Ellie waits in the shadows. After a few paces he hears a sound like a bubble popping and the stench of decay washes up and over him, but he doesn't turn to see what's happening to the corpse. Thank God he arrived in time to prevent Billy from raping Ellie, because only God knows what would have happened to her once she had Billy's corrupt fluid inside her body.

He stops in mid-step. God isn't the only one who knows. Who was pulling Billy's strings?

He starts walking again, slowly. He thinks about what happened in the park. He remembers the name on the statue. Nicholas Fenton.

"Is he dead?" Ellie asks when Nate returns to her.

"Yes," Nate says. "Dead."

"We're not going to call the police."

"No," he says. "This isn't something for the police."

"Nate, *you're* the police."

He shakes his head. "Not anymore."

They resume walking. The grass crunches under their feet. They cut across the field to Sutton Street, parallel to Canal. Ellie's breath billows out in clouds. He catches her eyeing him surreptitiously, probably looking for similar clouds. She won't find any. She stays close to him, bumping up against him occasionally, but now she keeps her hands in her pockets. As they reach Harbor Road he says, "You can't walk all the way home."

"I will if you are."

"No. We'll call you a taxi."

"Ride with me, then."

"No."

"Nate . . . You've been gone for days. I thought . . . Don't leave me again." The sentence that trails off, *I thought . . .*, says more to him than all the other words she's spoken since they saved each other in the old woman's apartment. He can think of a hundred things to end it with. *I thought . . .* you were dead, I would never see you again, no one would ever find you. And what does she think now? This reunion has given her hope, cruel hope, that he'll come back to her. But he can't. He's no more a man than any corpse that lies cold and stiff on a coroner's slab. The only difference is that he walks around.

They turn right on Harbor Street. Nate leaves her plea hanging in the air. He doesn't know how to answer it yet. He knows he should leave her; there's no future in marriage to a walking corpse.

One catch: he doesn't want to.

To their left, out on the river, a buoy clangs erratically. The sound has a distant, otherworldly quality that persists no matter how close the buoy might be. You could be right next to it and it would still sound a thousand miles away.

They walk. The buoy gets farther away but still sounds the same. As they pass the little park, Nate slows. Ellie says, "What's wrong?"

He doesn't answer her.

The park is *watching* him.

It's the same feeling he had yesterday, when he was in the presence of the statue; and again later that day when he went into the old hotel and felt dark eyes on him. But he'd thought the park was clean now. The light had gone out of it and left it inert.

But apparently something's come back.

"Nate?"

He looks at her. "Do you feel it?"

"Feel what?"

He looks back at the park. "*Eyes.*"

She stares at him without answering.

"Something's in there. . . ." He trails off, staring into the trees. Then, suddenly, he says: "I'll be right back."

And plunges into the park.

"Nate!"

"Don't follow me!" he calls, over his shoulder.

She can't believe it. He's left her standing, alone, on Harbor Street.

At night.

After they just got back from an episode of the *Twilight Zone*.

And then he tells her to stay put?

Not bloody likely.

She jumps the fence and runs in after him.

The trees aren't doing their dance. The underbrush isn't reaching for him with its little fingers. Whatever has taken up residence in the park is too *discreet* for such theatrics.

There are shades meaning behind such deliberation. It *could* be that the new resident just isn't that powerful. But for some reason Nate thinks it's that the thing in the park now is more refined than the raw energy that Nate experienced. It's more sophisticated. It's more *evolved*.

The question is, what has it evolved into?

He isn't being very subtle in his approach to whatever it is he thinks is looking at him. Crashing through the brush. Sounds like he's driving a bulldozer through the park.

What does he think he's going to find, anyway? Ghosts? Goblins? The cast of *The Wizard of Oz*? He's so strange now . . . distracted, abrupt. Hardly himself at all. Of course, he *has* been murdered and risen from the grave. Or at least he thinks he has.

Face it, she thinks. He's right. She was almost raped by three zombies and a skinned man, and she was saved by her undead husband. Something to share with the girls in the office on Monday.

Suddenly, ahead of her, the crashing stops. Ellie freezes, then starts moving again. Slowly. Quietly. Can't let Nate hear her sneaking up behind him. He's a silhouette in the darkness, standing very still on, she realizes, the edge of a paved clearing. Across the pavement is a statue. She can't see any details, except that it seems to have two heads. And Nate is staring at it.

The second head turns, almost imperceptibly.

Ellie freezes again, this time because her blood seems to have turned into slush.

It's *looking* at her.

It *wants* her.

"What are you?" Nate asks.

It's a hunter, thinks Ellie. It's a beast.

"What do you want?"

It wants me. It wants everyone. *It wants to eat us!* The thought shoots like lightning from somewhere deep in Ellie's brain, the old fear of the predator surfacing from the fading evolutionary past.

Danger!

Panic!

"Let's get out of here, Nate!" she hisses.

He looks back at her, surprised. "Ellie—what—"

The second head vanishes.

"Oh, shit," Ellie says. "Oh, shit. It's coming."

Nate wheels around, looks at the statue. Looks back at her. "You saw it?"

"Come on, Nate." She clutches at his hand, pulls him toward her. Starts moving toward the wall. She hears whispery movement through the brush, too faint to be placeable. The beast is on the move.

"What did you see?" Nate asks.

"Nate, for God's sake." Dead trees, dead bushes. Brambles. Where's the damn wall? Which way did they come? She looks for the streetlights. There they are. To the left. She turns that way, pushing through the thicket.

"*What did you see?*"

"I don't know! It was dark!" Why won't he be quiet and just *run*?

"You didn't see the light?"

"What light?"

"I'm the only one who can see the light," he says, musingly.

She's not really listening to him anymore. She can see the low wall through the trees now. Almost there. As if the sidewalk's any safer.

Noise from the right. Like a small animal dashing through the bushes.

"You didn't see its face," Nate says. "It's Fenton."

"What?"

"The thing's face . . . It's not human, not even close . . . but . . . It's *Fenton*!"

A brown blur erupts from the brambles on their left—the *left*, there haven't been any noises from the left at all—and flies at her. It's barely as big as a five-year-old but it hits like a truck. Ellie loses her grip on Nate's hand as the thing bears her down to the park floor. She looks into its void of a face. All she sees are its eyes, flickering like distant candles.

Silver chain wraps around the creature's throat. Nate yanks it off her, swings it up over his head and releases it, sending it flying over the treetops.

"Run!" he says.

"Nate!"

"I'm going after it. You *run!*"

He vanishes into the darkness.

She scrambles to her feet.

Run.

The wall isn't far. She vaults it when she gets there, and crosses to the other side of the street. There's no sidewalk here, just the crusty grass of the riverbank and the twisted chain link fence surrounding the remains of the marina.

Melted by the heat.

The fire.

"*Nicholas* Fenton?" she says, to no one.

16

This is insane. The park isn't this big.

Nate crashes on through the trees. He should have come the other side of the park by now, but all he sees ahead of him is more trees.

No sign of the beast.

He wishes he knew what was going on. How Fenton ties into all this. What the little creature is, and what it's doing.

And where the hell this forest ends.

Maybe chasing the thing after he threw it wasn't such a good idea. Maybe he should kind of turn around and leave. Instead he keeps going.

He pushes through a particularly thick clump of gnarled brown bushes. His foot catches on something and he falls face-down to the ground. He feels asphalt under his fingers. Raising his head, he sees the pedestal that supports the statue. He's somehow come into Fenton's *sit-and-worship-me* tract from the back. He sits up on the pavement.

Sees right over the top of the pedestal.

Statue's gone.

He has a second to contemplate this, and then a cold, metallic hand grabs him around the throat.

A police car turns off the bridge and heads down Harbor Road, toward Canal Street. Finally responding to a call about the gunshots, thinks Ellie. Far too late to help.

The patrol car has its lights on but not its siren, and the flashing blue and white and red strobes are eerily silent, like some monster from a fable stealing toward unsuspecting prey. She turns and looks out across the river so they can't see her face. She wonders if they'll stop when they see her standing there. They don't. Over her shoulder she watches the car go by, follows its progress until it turns left at the next block.

Canal Street. She was right.

Maybe she should've flagged them down, sent them into the park to help Nate. But no, they couldn't help him. Whatever's in the park can't be arrested. It can't be arraigned. It can't be imprisoned. Let them investigate the gunshot and then go back on patrol in blissful ignorance.

But the police aren't going where Ellie thinks they're going.

"Here we are again," Charlie says as he guides the patrol car up to the curb. "I'm getting tired of this fucking street."

"I'm getting tired of this fucking *job*," Andy announces, back on patrol and not loving any of it.

Charlie looks at him and snorts. "Yeah, right," he says. "Your momma know you talk like that?"

After a moment's hesitation Andy says, "No."

Charlie laughs. "That wasn't a real question." Still laughing, he radios in their location. The dispatcher wants to know what's so funny but Charlie doesn't tell him. Then the two of them get out of the vehicle. They stand a moment in the frigid night air, breathing out clouds of ice, looking up at the building in front of them. It's a stubby little tenement five stories high and just one block up from the river. The top two floors probably get an aces view of the waterway, though Andy has no idea what such a view is worth in this neighborhood. Right next door is the all-night diner on the corner of Canal Street and Harbor Road. A little sign in the window says *WE NEVER CLOSE.* "What say we get a cuppa after this one?" Charlie says. "End our shift the right way."

"Coffee's bad for you," Andy says.

"Oh. Yeah. I forgot." Charlie starts laughing again. "Sure have missed you, Andy."

The front door of the apartment building has one of those buzz-to-enter things on it but it obviously doesn't work—half the buttons are missing, that's the first clue—and the door is propped open with a brick. They enter. Charlie says, "A-fucking-1 security system. Where we going again, Andrew?"

Andy pulls out his little notebook and flips through it. "One-oh-one," he says. "Landlord says there's a woman in there who looks like she . . . um, exploded."

"Goodness gracious," Charlie says. "Maybe there's a new kind a crack that makes you blow up."

"Oh, I doubt it," Andy says. He listens for the chuckle and is rewarded. Charlie doesn't get to laugh much, his wife's a drunk and his kids never visit, but it seems to amuse him when Andy acts like he just fell off the turnip truck. The least Andy can do for his partner is make him laugh.

Apartment 101 is a short walk down the hallway, which for some reason starts at the front of the building with apartment 150. The door of their destination is ajar. Motioning for Andy to stay behind him, Charlie raps on it and calls, "Police."

No answer.

Charlie gives the door a little shove and it swings inward.

The apartment is revealed.

Everything looks clean. Nobody is inside.

"Where's the landlord?" Andy says. "They told him to wait."

"Looks like a crank," Charlie says. He walks into the room and says loudly, "Hello! Anybody here?"

Andy heads into the bathroom, where the corpse allegedly can be found. He emerges a few seconds later, shaking his head. "The bathroom is cleaner than mine," he says. "The caller said there was a stiff sitting on the toilet but the only thing stiff in there is the toilet brush."

"And your dick," Charlie says.

"How'd you know about that?" Andy asks.

Charlie guffaws and claps him on the shoulder. "C'mon, let's get that cup of coffee," he says. "They got killer bearclaws at this diner."

"Yeah?"

"Yeah." Charlie leads the way out of the apartment, keeping his hand on Andy's shoulder. "Sure did miss you, kid," he says.

The carpet is old and brown and obscures the bloody footprints they track behind them. Charlie leaves the door of the apartment open but kicks the brick out of the front door and lets it close.

Back inside the building, the door of apartment 101 also swings closed.

And locks.

The statue!

It lifts Nate up by the throat, holds him a moment, then hurls him across the clearing. The pavement seems to stretch ahead of him. He hits it, goes into a roll, ends up in a heap near the edge of the trees.

The brass Fenton lumbers toward him in an awkward run.

He flings a chain at it, entangles its legs. The statue crashes to the ground and breaks into pieces, arms and legs and torso and head.

The pieces rise into the air and begin putting themselves back together.

Nate gets to his feet, feeling wobbly. He backs up a pace. The statue finishes its reassembly and comes at him again. He dodges left, circles back around to the pedestal. The clearing has become impossibly distended, like a stretched-out camera shot in a Hitchcock movie.

Suddenly something lands on Nate's shoulders. Vertigo sweeps over him and leaves him nauseated; it passes in a second and he's still in the clearing but it's back to its normal size and the statue of Fenton is right where it should be.

Illusion.

But the thing on his back is real. He feels its cold, rubbery legs locked around his throat, its arms around the top of its head. It's the beast and it's right on top of him, bathing him in fetid exhalations that seem to soak into his skin and make him light-headed.

He flails at it, beating it with his fists, but its body feels like foam rubber, it just absorbs the blows. The twilit world gets darker still, black crepe crowding the edges of his vision. The thing's breath is knocking him out. His legs wobble, making it a struggle to even stay upright.

Nate turns away from the statue and staggers backward, losing his balance at the last second. The beast realizes what he's doing and jumps clear. Nate slams into the statue. His head bounces off the metal, hard. He hears a sharp *crack.*

That was his skull.

He can barely stand. The creature skulks nearby, a shadow lurking in the embrace of the trees. It'll come at him again. Facing it, Nate backs away. The back of his head hums with the electric tingle of regeneration; his whole body is awash in the buzz, like the creature's influence is being purged from his system.

The flickering little eyes watch him carefully. It does not move toward him. Nate continues to retreat, into the forest. Still groggy. He finally turns to face the direction he's moving. The thing won't make a frontal assault anyway, it'll come at him from the back or the side, so it doesn't really matter which way he looks.

But it doesn't come at him at all.

The park has returned to its real size. Another illusion. He must have been stumbling around in circles while images were projected into his mind. That's a dirty way to operate, Fenton, he thinks.

Maybe this is an illusion, too. Maybe he's really back in the clearing, and this is all a dream, and the thing is really still on his back breathing on him and frying his brain.

Dream on, then.

He reaches the wall and falls over it, landing in a heap on the sidewalk just as a couple of kids go by. He finds himself looking up at them as they look down. "Dude!" one says. His voice sounds like a slowed-down record. Nate's brain feels full of sludge. He opens his mouth but nothing comes out of it.

"You don't go in the park, man," the other kid says. They're about the age of Billy's little playmates. They bend, each taking one of his hands, helping him to his feet. His head spins. They hustle him up the street, following the curve of the sidewalk. Getting away from the park.

"You look like shit, man," the first one says.

"He looks just like I feel," the second one says.

"No, you feel just like he looks." The two of them think this is hilarious, almost choking with giggly mirth.

His feet half-drag along the ground. He can hardly walk. His body tingles furiously as it tries to throw off the creature's poisonous breath. He's too groggy to even wonder if it will succeed.

Footsteps from behind. Nate casts a wild look over his shoulder, suddenly afraid the beast is coming after them, but it's Ellie. She's running toward them, her coat flapping behind her. "Nate!" she cries.

The kids look at her, then back at him. "Hello there, *Nate*," the first one says. They both giggle.

Ellie catches up to them and stops, panting. The kids watch her. One of them starts to pant himself, in a most exaggerated fashion. Ellie makes a little face. "Can I have my husband?" she asks.

"You sure can, honey," the first one says. "Go to your old lady . . . *Nate*." They both dissolve into giggles again as Ellie puts her arm around Nate's shoulder. Then, suddenly, something seems to register on the first kid. "Hey, you're a *cop*." He elbows his friend. "Look, Mal, he's a *cop*."

They stand a moment staring at Nate and Ellie as if they each have three heads, then turn and run up the sidewalk, whooping and wobbling. Nate stares after them.

Ellie shakes her head.

"Stoned as a rock garden," she says. "Come on, let's get out of here." She helps him walk up the sidewalk, away from the monster, away from the park. A few blocks up they come to a ramshackle bar. Nate skulks outside an open window, listening to country tunes drifting out into the night, as Ellie calls the taxi company for a ride. She comes out again after a minute and they continue up the sidewalk to the intersection where the Hunter River Bridge comes into Harbor Street. They stand there a while without speaking.

Then Ellie says, "Ride back with me."

"I can't," Nate says.

"Why not?" she asks.

"I don't want to be seen," Nate says. "Not by anybody sober, anyway. I look too . . . weird."

"You can't *walk* all the way back to our apartment."

"Done it before," Nate says.

She looks at him. "You *were* outside the window." He says nothing. "I *knew* it! Damn it, Nate, how could you do that to me? Why didn't you answer me when I came looking for you?"

"I didn't want you to see me like . . . like this."

She looks away. After a moment she says, "That is so typical."

"*Typical?* It's *typical?*"

"Yes."

"Of what?"

"Men!" She's looking across the water, toward the riverside apartment towers: tall, graceful, expensive dwellings that are separated from mainland Island City by much more than the river. "Do you have any idea how *selfish* that is? You didn't want me to see you like this. What makes you think I'd rather not see you at all? It was just *easier* for you to hide and pretend you weren't there, so that's what you did."

"It wasn't *easy* at all," Nate says. "You think I *wanted* to hide behind that Dumpster? You think I didn't want to come out and go home with you? I stayed away from you for your own good!"

"What the hell does that mean? My own good? How was that for *my own good?*"

"Ellie . . . I'm *dead*. You're acting like I just have a cold. I'm not going to get better, honey. I'm only going to get worse."

Now she looks at him. "Nate . . . stop saying you're dead."

"But I am."

"We'll take you to a doctor—"

"Don't need a doctor." Nate takes her hand and guides her fingers to his wrist. Her skin feels hot as fire. "Do you feel a pulse?"

Her eyes are dull. She shakes her head, black curls bouncing, and then drops her gaze. "Nate. . . ." She trails off, as if she can't think of anything else to say.

He guides her hand up to his chest, letting her feel the crusted uniform and the pinched skin beneath. "This is where they cut me," he says. "I don't know what it looks like under my shirt. I haven't taken it off since . . . since they did it."

She's crying, face glistening in the amber streetlight. He tries, clumsily, to wipe the tears with his thumbs. Her face is scorching. His hands shake. He tells himself it's the lingering effects of his encounter with the little monster.

The monster.

"I need you to do something for me tomorrow."

She takes him by the wrists and kisses his cold hands. "What?"

"Go to the library and find out everything you can about Nicholas Fenton."

She looks at him and then laughs through her tears. "Been there," she says. "Done that. What's next?"

Nate hangs back as Ellie gets into the taxi. Back, in the shadows, where the driver can't see him too well. "Please ride with me, Nate," she calls through the open window. "I'm worried about you."

"I'll be fine," he says. "I just need to think about what happened."

"Okay. Just be careful. Come home."

"I will."

She waves goodbye and rolls up the window as the cab begins to move. He waves back. After the cab leaves the curb, reversing direction with a three-point turn and heading back up the bridge, Nate emerges from the concealing shadows. He looks left, looks right. All clear. He walks quickly across the street, hands in pockets, head down. It's like that second night all over again, when he crept through the city to the threshold of his home before coming to his senses and retreating back to where he belonged. Now he's been invited home; but does that make a difference?

The bridge runs high over the river, reaching fifty feet before leveling off. It's illuminated by sodium globes that shine like a string of pearls catching the light. The pedestrian walk is on the right side of the bridge, fenced in by a mesh of thick iron wire. It could be a cattle run, with blades waiting on the other side.

That's it, Nate. Pick out something upbeat to think about.

Nate didn't notice the high walls or the lights the first two times he crossed the bridge. His mind has cleared since then, his perceptions have sharpened. But it would be delusional for him to think that makes a difference. He's just as dead as he was last night, and the night before, and the night before. His future still covers him like a shroud.

At the middle of the bridge, where it arches up over the channel in a drawbridge that never opens, he stops. The water shimmers below, moonlight reflected on black ink. The river is wide, the river is deep. He stares down at it, thinking about Nicholas Fenton. Feeling very confused. Is the creature in the park somehow related to Billy? The kid tried and failed to rape Ellie, but did he succeed elsewhere? If so, was the little beast the progeny?

But that would mean there's some connection between Billy and Nicholas Fenton, who's been dead for twenty years. Caught in his own inferno, the Wright Project.

Maybe he just *thinks* the little creep looked like Fenton. In the darkness, in the chaos, who could really tell?

The fence behind him rattles suddenly. Like something's climbing up it. Nate whirls, sending his chains out several feet, preparing for an attack—

—but nothing's there.

He stands a moment in the moonlight looking at the black mesh. Metal wires zig and zag together, forming a network of diamond-shaped holes the size of his hand. He can see through them to the vehicle portion of the bridge. There's a gap between the sidewalk and the road, two feet wide maybe, a gap leading straight down to the river.

Long way to fall.

Rattle from behind.

He whirls again. Nothing. Mind's playing tricks on him.

Yeah, right.

Time to be going. Quickly.

He starts walking again, faster. The fences begin an incredible cacophony behind him, shaking and clanking and rattling like some giant is trying to pull them off the bridge. He feels the sidewalk hum beneath his feet, the way the ground in the park hummed before . . . before the explosion. . . .

Finally he spins around again. Just in time to see faint light fade from the interwoven metal fibers.

The rattling stops.

Then, to his right, with a screeching, ripping sound, the fence tears itself open, making a hole big enough for a man to squeeze through.

Or be pushed.

Suddenly the little creature is on the fence to his left, hanging from it like a monkey. He can see it well now, in the rippling light, but its colors are all distorted, nightmare shades that should never have been swirled together. Its arms and legs are absurdly long for its stout, stubby body, and absurdly strong for their spindly length. Nate finds this out when it swings up, plants its feet on his chest, and pushes him out the hole. The jagged ends of the ripped chain link snag on his uniform, tear free. The world tips around him.

Falling.

He flings his chains up at the bridge. They snag the fence and his fall is abruptly halted, nearly jerking his arms out of their sockets in the process. His downward motion is translated into a pendulum swing, back and forth, back and forth, fifteen feet below the bridge and forty feet above the water.

Okay. Now what?

Before he comes up with an answer, the fence bends and sags under his weight, comes unraveled. His chains slide from the twisting steel threads.

His fall resumes.

The wind roars in his ears. The surface of the water flies up to greet him. He wonders if he should expect pain on impact. Slowly spinning, Nate makes one last rotation. Now he's looking back up, toward the bridge. A small dark shape is falling after him. Its flickering eyes reach down to snare him.

Oh, God.

He hits the water.

No pain.

17

THE WATER SEEMS TO SHATTER when he hits it. It splinters around him like it was painted on an eggshell, plunging him into the frigid murk within. He sinks down and down into ink, feeling himself slowly rotate as the current catches him and begins to carry him away.

Ice. A thin layer of brittle ice had formed on the skin of the river and he smashed through it and it'll freeze over again soon and no one will ever know there was a hole.

Arms grab his neck. Thin, spindly, iron-band arms. Something enters the back of his head, something cold, a knife that's been left out in the snow. It cuts down inside of him, down his spine and into his chest where his heart lies dormant in its cavity.

It reaches for something Nate thought he didn't have.

Darkness swirls around him. He feels his flesh slip away.

Falling.

Not from the bridge this time, but from the sky.

Island City is below him, distorted as if seen through a fish-eye lens. The streets and buildings bulge toward him in a convex hump. The sky curves down at the edges, cupping the city in the grip of sullen purple clouds. He can see nearly the entire town: sky meets earth at the Hunter River on his left and the lake on his right. Gloomy, smoky vapors drift sluggishly across the waters—reflections, or long-forgotten ghosts resurfacing? Beyond the bowed horizon a red glow stains the air like the rising sun, disrupting the image of the sky on the Hunter River with a wavering vermillion stripe.

But it's not the rising sun. Because smoke billows from area of the glow, gushing into the mauve sky and lending it an increasingly oppressive pall. Nate can't see the fire itself, but judging from the position of the smoke he guesses it's coming from the area of Canal Street.

The Wright Project fire.

He realizes, suddenly and startlingly, that he is *not* falling. He's floating. Hands are touching him, holding him in mid-air. They're light and deft, like fluttering doves; the sensation is faintly electric, vague tingling spreading from the points of contact. They carry him sideways through the air. The buildings roll by beneath him, approaching slowly, accelerating as they near the apex of the illusory hump, flashing by in an instant as they pass below. The river widens as he approaches.

The fire will soon come into view. Then he'll know for sure.

But before it does, he shoots down at an angle, rocketing to street level, racing between the buildings so fast they become muddy streaks, taking corners with ninety degree turns.

He ends up on the long, straight, broad expanse of Canal Street, roars up it like a missile. Past the empty field where the Wright Project used to be. There's no fire there after all. The old hotel is up on the left and the hands carry him into it. It's very dark inside, gloomy, the contents of the hotel are a blur. He flies through the lobby and into the elevator nook in back, where he catches a glimpse of two yawning black openings—the elevator shafts—and a wide old mirror between.

The hands shove him into the mirror.

There's a momentary resistance, then the stuff gives and he breaks through. Shards of glass and darkness spin off around him, jagged and dangerous. One hits him in the side, down near his pelvis. The fragment burns like ice welded to flame and it doesn't stop at the outside, it passes right through him, carving a line of frozen fire from his left kidney to his right collar bone, where it exits, leaving behind a burning sensation thin and bright as the filament of a light bulb.

The pieces of the broken mirror spin off into shadow. As the fragments pass from his sight they leave rents in the dim light, gnawing fissures through which he can glimpse something else, something beyond, some great patchy backdrop of blues and purples; and once created the fissures spread and widen, join together into a network of interlocking jags that quickly overtakes and supplants the interior of the hotel, becoming a yawning hole in the world through which the hands pull him. The pace increases again, he feels himself rocketing along through twists and loops like he's strapped to the bottom of a stunt plane.

It's too much, after all he's been through today.

He would really like to pass out now.

Unfortunately, he doesn't. But the ride is over quickly, and he feels himself smash through another barrier, and then he spills onto a hard, crusty surface and lies still. The hands vanish. He's alone again, the ride's over. Thank God.

The earth is hot and lumpy under his back. He watches the stars that blaze overhead in such tight formation that the blackness of space is visible only as holes in the brilliance.

He's been here before.

The pattern of the stars is slightly different, but their character is the same: they're huge, like glowing coins, yet somehow their light doesn't illuminate his surroundings. And the darkness that encompasses him is familiar too, though it's as featureless as any other patch of shadow.

This is where he went when Billy killed him.

The memory is foggy. He looks at the stars and lets them lead him back. . . .

It was the hands that brought him, that first time. When he came out of his body on the rooftop they were there, they grabbed him and carried him away, and he thought they were going to take him to heaven or hell but they didn't, they brought him here and left him in the dark. And he lay there, and lay there, and then something came to join him in the darkness, a presence, a being.

It spoke to him. What did it say?

Then it touched him, and its touch seemed to fill him up, and it ran its hands along him and relit the fires of his mind, then the hands picked him up again and brought him back to his body on the rooftop, and as he floated there they closed up the three great flaps of his torso, halted the degradation of his flesh, and then they pushed him down and touched him to his corpse and it seized his spirit and sucked him back in, water to a sponge.

And the Night Watchman was born, simple as that.

A voice brings Nate out of his reverie. Pale and clipped, brittle as glass, it says: "If you wanted oblivion, you had only to ask. It is not so easy to discard what you have been given. There are *ways* of bestowing and *ways* of taking, ways *you* are ignorant of."

The voice seems to be circling him as it speaks. Nate imagines a man eyeing him appraisingly while pacing slowly around him, like a predator surveying potentially dangerous prey.

So if you know ways of taking, thinks Nate, go ahead and try it.

"I know you're tired of your half-life. I know you've tried to end it yourself. You cannot succeed without my help. Say the word, and that help is yours. I have already freed you from your body; if you'll let me, I can send you on to your reward."

Send him on to his reward? What kind of talk is that?

"Who are you?" Nate asks.

The voice says, after a moment: "A friend."

Yeah. Right. Nate bites his tongue on something sarcastic. Whoever the speaker is, he isn't acting out of concern for Nate. *Freed* him from his body. Oh, sure. *Snatched* him is more like it. That little monster that looked like Fenton just ripped him right out of . . . out of. . . .

Could *this* be Fenton he's talking to now?

Impossible. Fenton's dead.

Then again, he's dead himself.

"What do you want from me?" Nate asks.

"Nothing. I only want to—"

"So who do you want something from, then?"

"I only want to—"

"I bet you wish I would listen to your pitch, don't you?"

"It would be—"

"But I won't. Because whatever you're selling, I'm not interested in it."

"I only want to help you," the voice protests. It's starting to sound a little flustered. Obviously, whoever this is, he isn't accustomed to backtalk.

Nate lets the silence stretch on and on.

Finally, the voice asks, "You don't believe me?"

"No, Mr. Fenton," Nate says. "I don't."

"Very good," Fenton says after a moment. "Would you like a prize?"

"I'd like some answers."

"You won't get them," Fenton says.

"Do I have to squeeze them out of you?"

"Oh, I am *so* scared!" Fenton's voice has changed, it sounds like a human voice now—and a petulant one at that, annoyed that Nate saw through his charade. "What are you gonna do, catch me with your little chains?"

Good idea, thinks Nate.

He targets Fenton's voice and shoots. The chains fly a few yards then strike something that feels like a person. Nate hears a surprised little wheeze as he entwines Fenton and constricts, but then Fenton vanishes, he just melts away in the grip of Nate's chains and they clatter to the ground.

Nate tries to sit up but the darkness resists him now, pushes him back down. He tries again and doesn't even get as far as he did the first time. It's like trying to move through thickening rubber cement.

The darkness is congealing on him.

The stars dim as the shadow coalesces. Nate struggles to move in the thickening morass. He's got no leverage, his arms and legs can barely make any headway at all through the coagulating goo. The stuff presses down on his nose and lips, trying to force its way into his mouth. Panic takes over and he starts thrashing, desperate to escape the gelatinous encapsulating mass, but it's too thick, too heavy.

He's being buried alive.

Falling into quicksand.

His thrashing struggles wane, not because he's losing his strength but because the stuff is becoming more and more unyielding, thickening from soup to molasses to glue to concrete.

Finally he gives up and lies still; and the stars go out, one by one.

He's not coming.

Ellie waits for him, and waits, and waits, while the hands of the wall clock sweep inexorably toward dawn. Nate will come by sunrise, she thinks, or he won't come at all; and as the sky outside slowly lightens from coffee to cream she rises from the couch and walks dazedly into the bedroom. Something must have happened to him on the way. He was run over by a car, shot in the head by a thug.

Would being shot in the head kill him? Would anything?

Maybe he just decided not to come home, she thinks.

Maybe he just gave up and jumped into the river.

Maybe the thing from the park got him. Maybe it did something to him. When it was on her back, just for that second, she felt it . . . *probing* her. That's the only word for it. Probing. Looking inside her for something it wanted . . . but maybe it found what it was looking for in Nate instead.

Nate said it looked like Nicholas Fenton. She wishes she'd paid more attention when Andy had gone on his research binge. She'll call him today, she thinks, and find out everything he learned about the developer.

And what about Nate?

She can only hope he's still out there, hiding from the daylight somewhere. He never said as much, but it's obvious that he considers himself a night creature now. A ghost, a vampire, a zombie.

She can imagine what went through his mind as he made his way home: *She'd be better off without me. I'm not alive, I'm dead. How can she be married to a corpse? What kind of a future would she have with me?* Against such thoughts, how flimsy must his promise to return have seemed?

Or maybe it was the little monster.

No. He's still out there. He has to be. But she knows he *doesn't* have to be.

Makes no difference. She'll find him.

And when she does, she'll never let him out of her sight again.

18

Ellie sleeps until three in the afternoon, when the shifting sun finally penetrates the bedroom blinds and lays light down in strips along her face. Her eyes crack open, red and unfocused. The blinds are aglow, a wall of brilliance, as if behind them every star in the sky is blazing. She can imagine angels emerging from that shining curtain, trailing golden hair and strumming harps; or darker things, from colder lights.

She sits up in bed. The air is cold on her bare back and shoulders, it tingles on her chest. Sleep didn't refreshed her; sleep dragged her mind down into an abyss filled with corpses that would not lie still and people who shuffled around with their skin trailing behind them and geysers that fountained blood and innards. She was there looking for Nate, looking but never finding, now and then catching a glimpse of him somewhere far ahead. She was calling for him to wait, begging him to stop, but he just kept going.

She had to fight her way through the corpses and the zombies and the rivers of blood in pursuit of her husband. By the time she woke up, her dream-self was crusted with gore and bone-tired, and now that she's awake she doesn't feel much better.

She has Billy and his zombie buddies to thank for that lovely dream. And Nate. But it's not his fault, they did things to him, they dragged him down to join them in the territories from her dream and she *will* have him back from that fell assembly.

She'll need help. But help from who? A priest, a rabbi? No, she thinks, the big religions won't have anything to offer. She doesn't know much about any of them, but she doesn't think her current situation is covered in their holy books. They're like big corporations, things are their way or no way.

She needs help from a smaller operator.

She'll have to go to the psychics and the mediums, the fortune tellers and the astrologers. She has always considered them fakes and charlatans, but after last night's events many of her beliefs are open to revision. Probably most of them *are* fakes, but maybe . . . maybe. . . .

Okay. Now she has a plan, and simply having it makes her feel a little better. It gives her a reason to get out of bed, get into the shower, get on with things. She's doing something. She's exploring her options. She's launching a crusade.

She's going to go straight into the belly of the beast that swallowed Nate, and she's going to bring him out whole or join him in the darkness.

It isn't until frustration has stilled his thrashing that Nate realizes his oversight: he's been struggling with his arms and legs and body and left his chains unused. But they're small, they'll run into less resistance; and they're stronger than his other limbs. Maybe they can free him where his natural appendages have failed.

The first thing he does is try to move them, just extend them a little bit. It's difficult, but it works: they burrow through the stuff like silver worms.

Okay. Good. He extends them slowly. Burrow, silver earthworms; burrow, burrow, burrow.

They go.

And go.

And go.

And they don't reach the end of the glop.

What if there *is* no end to it? What if it spreads out for miles like an ocean, and he's at its bottom? He could extend his chains forever and not come to the end of the stuff. He could—

He wrenches his mind away from such speculations. If he isn't careful, if he lets his thoughts boil over with the heat of panic and starts thrashing around again, he's only going to get his chains all gummed up and tangled and then he'll *really* be trapped. He waits a minute or two, counting sheep, before letting his chains resume their progress through the muck.

After a few more feet, a few more hours, his patience is rewarded: the ends of his probing tendrils emerge from the goo into open air. But this isn't enough. He needs leverage, he needs something to grab onto to pull himself free. He reaches out farther. His chains scrape along the ground. It feels rocky and uneven, like a barren mountaintop or broken parking lot.

Where *is* he?

He can't stretch his chains much farther. It's becoming more and more of an effort. He never did establish the effective range of his tendrils but it seems like there is one and he's approaching it.

Oh, God, what if there's nothing to grab onto? Nothing to use as an anchor to pull himself free? Wherever he is, it feels flat and drab and featureless, nothing to hold, and that's just not going to do it.

Then his chains stop. He's maxed out.

And there's still nothing to fasten onto.

He thinks he's going to be sick.

No, can't give up. Can't. He sweeps his chains back and forth, back and forth, and he finds something to hold onto, something round and narrow, a cylinder of some kind. Nate wraps his chains around it, interweaving them so they won't slip.

Then he begins to retract.

For a moment he thinks it will be easy, but only for a moment; when the resistance hits he realizes he was simply reeling in the slack, and when that's done the effort shoots from the minimal to the absurd. The chains snap taut and stay that way, and for a moment it seems as if his wrists are going to give out before the jelly.

Then, ever so slightly, his position shifts to the left.

Yes! That's it! His prison is not irresistible after all! He keeps up the pressure, willing his chains to come back to him but not letting go of the object. He moves still further, slowly rotating until he's in line with his chains. It's like moving through taffy, but it's *movement* and that's what's important.

He begins to slide. The rough ground moves beneath his back, the impinging darkness slurps over his eyes, his nose, his lips. It still tries to force his mouth open, like it wants to come *inside* him. He clenches his jaws against it.

It seems to take forever for him to reach the end of it. First his arms come free, then his head. The stuff leaves him clean, with no residue, thank God. He pulls and pulls. If he can just get his shoulders out, the rest will be easy. But the stuff seems to have realized it's losing its prisoner; the resistance increases so much that the tension of his chains lifts him off the ground. He feels his spine stretching, feels his elbows separating. He imagines the top half of his body bursting from the bottom, leaving him still half-trapped. Can he regrow everything below his waist?

Then he pops free and goes rolling across the ground, banging to rest up against the object he was holding onto, his source of leverage. When he gets home he'll build a model of it and assign it a place of honor. He lets his eyes travel upward, to see exactly what it is that allowed him to save himself; and astonishment widens his eyes.

It's a flagpole.

And dangling from its top, the American flag.

Nate uses the pole to haul himself to his feet, staring at the flag. It hangs limp and still, with no breath of wind to stir it; and it's tattered and faintly pathetic in a way Nate has never seen the flag before. Here it's nothing but a sad parody. Here it's a joke.

He looks away from it, back the way he came.

He was right about the ground: it's asphalt, cracked and blackened and calving into thousands of grey, misshapen clots. About ten feet away is his erstwhile prison, a dome of sticky darkness that stands taller than him at its apex. He kicks a chunk of pavement at it. The rock skips and bounces and thuds into the bubble with a faint, muddy *plop*. The entire dome wobbles with the impact. Reflections shake and dance across its surface, reflections of things Nate had somehow failed to notice. Reflections of fire. And . . . buildings.

Nate turns around slowly. He doesn't need to hold onto the pole anymore but he does. If the pole were alive he would be strangling it.

He's in a place that was destroyed twenty years ago.

He's in the Wright Project.

Ellie steps out of the shower. More awake now, that grainy feeling in the eyes washed away, that sour taste in her mouth rinsed and spat out. She towels off in front of the mirror, inspecting herself. Shadows, like fading bruises, underscore her eye sockets, and her throat is a little red where Billy held her. Rotten little bastard. Her arms, her stomach, her back . . . almost everywhere she can be sore, she *is* sore.

Still, she's lucky. Could've been worse. *Lots* worse.

She wraps a towel around her short, wet hair and goes into the bedroom. *Where did you learn to make a turban?* Nate would ask.

When I was in the harem, she'd say.

And then he would take hold of one end of the belt of her robe, slowly pull it out of its loops. *What did you do in the harem?*

And she would show him.

She sits down on the bed.

She'd show him. . . .

Stop it. He's not here.

But if he *was* . . . what would those chains of his feel like?

The telephone rings harshly, makes her jump almost out of her skin. *Got* to put that thing on a lower setting. She rolls over and picks it up.

Bet it's Andy.

"Hello?"

"Hi, Ellie, it's me."

Give that girl a prize.

"How're you doing?" he asks.

"Okay," she says. "Hanging in there."

"That's good."

"Listen, Andy, got a question for you."

"Shoot."

"Did you ever hear about Nicholas Fenton being involved in. . . ." Oh, just say it. ". . . Black magic or anything like that?"

Pause. "Black magic?"

She hears Charlie in the background say, in a falsetto, "Beware the power of Satan!"

It sounds so stupid, echoed back to her in a *what are you talking about* tone of voice. But Andy doesn't know, Andy didn't *see*. "Yeah. You know . . . voodoo or stuff like that."

"Voodoo isn't black magic, and no, I haven't," Andy says. "Is this because of Nate? Because, that pentacle thing, everybody thinks the pentacle is some kind of magic symbol, so they just use it when they're messing around. It doesn't mean anything."

"It's not because of Nate," Ellie says.

"Look, I know there's a lot of stories down around Canal Street about Fenton and his buildings—ghosts in the old hotel, workmen bricked up in the walls, blood poured into the concrete. Personally I think the guy was a scumbag. But all the talk is just urban legends. You know, like the old story about the guy with the hook hand in the graveyard. He was a slumlord, sure, but that's it."

"What about the park?"

"Huh?"

"Any stories about the park?"

"Heck, Ellie." She can't believe he just said *heck*. She hears Charlie guffawing in the background. "There's stories about everything. You get a bunch of people together with nothing to do, they tell stories. Fenton's soul is in the statue. Pieces of Fenton's body are buried in the park. I've had drunks swear up and down that they saw the Wright Project back in the field. Those buildings have been gone for *twenty years*, Ellie." He sighs. "I don't know what you're after here, but Nicholas Fenton couldn't have had anything to do with what happened to Nate. The guy's been dead almost as long as I've been alive."

"I know," Ellie says.

"Listen, you sound really strung out. Do you want me to come over? You have a VCR, right? I'll bring you a video."

"Okay. Later, though. I have errands."

"That's okay, I'm calling from a pay phone anyway, I don't get off for a couple hours yet."

"Okay," Ellie says. "Is seven too late?"

"Seven is okay," he says.

"Okay, see you tonight. Rent something funny." After the formal goodbyes, Ellie hangs up. She lies on her back, looking up at the ceiling.

Urban legends.

Well, she thinks, maybe they *are* just legends.

But everybody knows a legend is just a fact no one can prove.

19

Ellie emerges from yet another mystic's boutique and leans up against the building, eyes closed, panting. She takes a few seconds to regulate her breathing, then opens her eyes and looks at her right hand. One of her knuckles is split and bleeding slightly, and all of them are sore. She never punched anyone in the jaw before and she didn't realize it was going to hurt so much.

She shakes her head. What kind of creep would try to make it with a woman who came for help in finding her missing husband?

When she thinks she has calmed down enough to draw a straight line, she takes a pen and a small notebook out of her purse and crosses Maurice Yacobelli off her list. So far she has been to three mediums, a fortune-teller, and a channeller, and all have been obviously sleazy, clearly fraudulent, or both. Every one! And, damn them, why don't they all open shop in the same part of the city so she doesn't have to hop in and out of dirty cabs driven by smelly men and . . . okay, okay, she thinks; time to count to ten.

One. Two. Three. Four. Smack, right in the jaw.

Oh, hell.

She notices for the first time a bench outside Maurice's establishment and slides down into it. What did she expect, anyway? She knew when she started this mission that ninety-nine percent of them were phonies. But still. . . .

Ellie suddenly notices her face is cold and wet and it's because tears are simply flowing from her eyes and rolling down her cheeks and she didn't even realize she was crying. As she wipes them with her fuzzy wool gloves, a massive dark shape stops in front of her. "I hope you didn't go in there," a big voice says. "That Maurice, he's nothing but a sham man."

Ellie looks up. The shape is a black woman wearing a hugely oversized purple coat and carrying a handbag the size of Ellie's apartment. The woman looks down at her with eyes that seem to say *I've seen a lot of road kill on the highway of life, and that's why I carry a spatula.*

Ellie has no idea where that thought came from but it makes her burst out laughing; then the laugh strangles itself and turns into a sob. More quickly than her frame should allow, the large woman rotates and plops herself onto the bench beside Ellie. It creaks threateningly. "Don't cry, honey," she says. "You bring a problem to Maurice, you leave with that problem and a new one. But maybe Yolanda can help."

Yolanda. Ellie pulls her crumpled list from her pocket and consults it. There are no Yolandas there. The big woman tips her head to get a look at the paper. "Do you . . . are you in . . . Maurice's line of work?" Ellie asks.

"Hell no," Yolanda says. "His line of work is thievery!" She yells the word *thievery*, but there's no response from inside the building. "Yolanda does *real* work. *Real* work. You get that list outta the phone book?"

Ellie nods.

"Mistake number one." Yolanda wiggles to her feet, then extends a hand to Ellie. "Get up and come with me. My place is down the block. We can talk there. I have heat!" She makes this last statement proudly, as if heat to the rest of the city has been shut off and she is somehow smuggling it in.

Ellie allows herself to be pulled off the bench, and she follows Yolanda down the sidewalk to her shop. It's the bottom floor of a little three-story brick building. The front door isn't labeled and there's no marquee hanging from the building; the only indicator that this is a place of business is a little sign that says *CLOSED* in neat block letters.

Yolanda unlocks the shop and ushers Ellie into a small waiting room, rather like a doctor's office except it's devoid of magazines. The floor is polished hardwood with throw rugs scattered around haphazardly. The furniture is red velvet, a couch and several matching chairs and a triangular table shoved into a corner. Illustrations of the zodiac hang from the walls, drawings rendered on purple velvet and bordered with ornate yet cheap-looking frames. "You're an astrologer?" Ellie asks. "You want to know my sign?"

"Not at all, honey," Yolanda says. "Those are just for effect. Window dressing for the customers. They don't like bare walls." Without flipping the sign on the door from *CLOSED* to *OPEN*, Yolanda motions for Ellie to sit and then toddles through a bead-shrouded archway. The hanging strands are iridescent and refractive; their movement sends tiny fragments of rainbow skittering along the walls and dancing across the faces of the zodiac.

It's a good room, thinks Ellie, better than most she's seen today. Clean but not antiseptic, nothing unidentifiable lurking under the chairs or at the fringes of the rug. And it's bright. A couple of the other places had black curtains on the windows to keep out the sun. Maybe the proprietors of those places think people expect their shops to be gloomy; or maybe they just want to make it hard for the people they fleece to pick them out of a police lineup.

Before the beads have stopped shivering Yolanda returns, minus coat and bag. She looks at Ellie and says, "Take off your coat, honey. I told you I had heat." Ellie complies. Yolanda plops herself onto the sofa and waits for Ellie to sit again before speaking. "What's your name, honey?"

"Ellie Watson."

"I of course am Yolanda, as I said. What brings someone such as yourself out in search of a psychic? Yolanda ain't never seen you around before."

Ellie says, "You're the psychic; you tell me."

Yolanda shakes her head vigorously. "Oh, no. Yolanda don't play that game. What's in your head is yours, not mine. Anybody tells you different, you know they fake."

Ellie smiles. "I want help finding my husband."

"He run away?"

"No, he was taken."

"You sure about that?"

"Absolutely."

Yolanda slowly rubs her chin. "He dead, or alive?"

Tricky question. "I don't know."

"Yolanda ain't no missing persons bureau," she says. "Finding somebody take a long, long time. You been to the police?"

"The police are looking for him."

"He in some kind of trouble?"

"No. No, that's not what I meant. He's a cop himself, he disappeared while he was on a call. The police are looking for him but they haven't found him."

"And you think they won't."

"Yes. I mean no."

Yolanda is silent for a long time, just looking at Ellie and rubbing her chin. Ellie meets the gaze dead on. Finally Yolanda says, "You ain't telling me everything, but I believe that what you *are* telling me is true." She lifts a hand to check a tiny watch that is almost lost on the broad, brown expanse of her wrist. "I got no more appointments until four o'clock. Friday's always slow. You come on in back and we'll see what Yolanda can find out for you."

Ellie follows Yolanda through the curtain.

The rainbows dance a little pirouette.

This is impossible. The Wright Project burned to the ground twenty years ago. It burned so hot and so fast there was nothing left but piles of rubble and the smell of fire. Yet here it stands as it stood on Canal Street.

And it's still burning.

He isn't in the Project proper. The complex of five buildings is ringed by a circular sidewalk and he's on the outside of that. A five-foot strip of grass, incongruously lush and green, separates him from the sidewalk. But his eyes aren't for the grass, or the sidewalk, or even for the flag; they're for the fire. The flames scorch the sky, they burn the stars out of their sockets and set the cosmos ablaze. All the buildings are burning, it's volcanic, it's seismic; and the biggest plume of fire rises from the center of the complex, a twisting, dancing column of flame that shoots up so high it vanishes through the dome of smoke.

But despite the explosive strength of the flames, Nate doesn't hear a thing. Not a whisper.

He casts another glance at his prison. Beyond it the blasted asphalt stretches out and out until it is lost in a hazy distance. It's like the world has been leveled and paved. Nate considers his options: wander off into that lifeless tundra of rock and tar; head into the conflagration of the Wright Project; or wait here for the being who imprisoned him to return.

Tough choice.

He turns his back on the horizon and walks into the Project.

Beyond the bead curtain a narrow, dim hallway runs off to the right. The floorboards are bare beneath Ellie's feet, old and unvarnished, and the walls are unadorned by sheetrock or paneling. Directly in front of Ellie is a door that says *PRIVATE* in stern black letters, drawn in the same block style as the sign on the entrance. Yolanda trundles down the corridor. Ellie follows slowly, looking left and right. The horizontal beams that hold the two-by-fours in place serve as shelves for a plethora of small, strange objects. Some clearly mimic people or animals, little faceless dolls and statues and such; others are unidentifiable abstracts, little bits of feather and stone and crystal glued or tied or otherwise cobbled together. The single overhead bulb casts it all in sharp contrasts of light and shadow, giving even the more innocuous objects a vague aspect of the sinister. Ellie can easily imagine these strange baubles rising from their niches at midnight and dancing around the shop; or maybe they whisper to each other of the places they've been and the things they've seen, and murmur curses at those who pass by.

Yolanda pauses at the far end of the corridor and motions Ellie along. Then she vanishes through a second bead curtain, in the same wall as the *PRIVATE* door. Ellie hurries to catch up, but in her haste she somehow knocks a small figurine from its shelf. Ellie freezes at the sound of it hitting the floor.

She looks down slowly, afraid she's broken something. But she hasn't. The doll is lying right between her feet, looking up at her with small dark eyes, pencil-line mouth curled into a mysterious smile. Luckily it's made of twisted cloth with a head of wood, so it didn't break.

But the corridor is utterly silent now, as if all the other dolls and trinkets have taken a breath of horror and indignity and now hold it in as they await her next clumsy move.

Oh, stop being ridiculous. Being stared at by dolls—what'll she come up with next? Maybe they'll start spitting at her. She picks up the fallen item and returns it to its place, then hurries through the bead curtain. Beyond is a small room, perhaps half the size of the waiting room. In the center is a round table covered in purple velvet. Thick purple curtains swaddle the wall to Ellie's right and in front of her. To her left is a wide, tiered shelf that runs the length of the room and is packed with candles in various kinds of holders: glass and metal cups, flat tins, candelabra. Their steady flames provide the only light.

Yolanda is sitting at the table with her hands out and apart. Her eyes are closed. "About time," she says. "Come, sit with Yolanda."

Ellie chooses one of four chairs and sinks into its plush, overstuffed cushion. The tablecloth is soft and fuzzy. "What is your man's name?" Yolanda asks. Her voice has gotten all slow and dreamy, as if she's drifting off to sleep.

"Nate."

"Nate. . . ." Yolanda begins rocking her head slowly back and forth, back and forth. Ellie half expects her to begin crying *are the spirits present* or some other claptrap but she doesn't, she just keeps rocking her head and murmuring Nate's name again and again like it's a mantra.

This goes on and on and on.

Ellie glances at her wrist but the sleeve of her blouse obscures her watch. She begins surreptitiously moving her arm, trying to get the sleeve to ride up and reveal the face of her watch. How much time has she wasted on Yolanda?

But suddenly Yolanda speaks, in a voice as dry as a desert, cold as a glacier, older than both put together. A voice that narrates nightmares. "Put your timepiece away," it says. "I found him."

The grass only *looks* lush. It's dead and stiff, winter grass after it dries out in the spring. It crunches lightly beneath Nate's feet as he crosses the swath of lawn on his way to the sidewalk. He puts a foot down on the concrete, half expecting it to heave up and throw him back on his ass. It doesn't.

He takes another step. He's completely on the sidewalk now. Ahead of him, the wide path between buildings runs straight into the towering stalk of fire. He could close his eyes and just walk and the fire would eat him up.

He shuts his eyes.

Nate. . . .

And, opening them again, looks around for the source of a whisper that seems to say his name.

Nate. . . .

It comes from nowhere, it comes from everywhere. It rises from the ground like fog, descends from the sky like mist, drifts from the fire like smoke. He thinks of Nicholas Fenton. He must be here somewhere, he must hear this whisper.

Or maybe he's the whisperer himself.

Nate Watson. . . .

A sudden change in the plume of fire draws his attention. A *face* is forming in the middle of it, its eyes pits of blackness, its mouth a dark line surrounded by blazing lips. Its gaze is hollow and frigid, two chips of black ice in the middle of the fire; they seem to take everything in at once, suck everything into their obsidian gaze. The lips move as if the face is speaking, yet no sound emerges from its midnight mouth.

But the whisperer responds.

Nate Watson . . . is that you?

"Not him!" Nate shouts. "Not him!" Too late: the whisperer's attention has been caught by the face in the flames, the face that's masquerading as Nate Watson. He watches, sick and immobile, as the lips move again, spinning lies out of fire. And the whisperer listens; and the whisperer believes.

Someone here is looking for you, it says. *Will you speak to her through me?*

"Ellie," Nate says.

And the face in the fire smiles.

20

"WHERE IS HE?" ELLIE ASKS. "Is he all right?"

"He's here," Yolanda rumbles. Her eyes are open now, open and fixed on some spot four inches from Yolanda's face. The psychic's eyes have turned black like two cauldrons of pitch, and Ellie swears she can see little licks of fire inside them. Reflections of the candlelight. "He will speak to you through me."

Ellie stares at her. Can it be true? Did she contact Nate?

Does that mean he's dead?

"Ask him where he is," Ellie says. She has half-risen from her chair, letting herself be swept up in the possibility that Yolanda has really found Nate. "Ask him if he's all right."

But instead of answering, Yolanda smiles. It's a broad, toothy, mirthless smile, like someone put his fingers on the corners of her lips and pulled them back. She begins to laugh, smoky little hiccuping chuckles.

"Yolanda?"

Yolanda suddenly leans forward and tries to grab Ellie's collar. She jumps back into her chair, staying out of Yolanda's reach. *"I'm coming back!"* she booms.

"What?" Ellie says.

Yolanda starts bouncing up and down in her chair. *"Back back I'm coming back I'm coming back I'm coming back,"* she sings.

"Back from where?"

"Uh uh, not gonna tell, you'll have to wait and see, because *back back I'm coming back I'm coming back—*"

Yolanda stops short.

Her face goes still and slack.

Then she collapses face-down onto the purple velvet table.

"Yolanda?" Ellie says.

A terrific clatter issues from the hallway beyond the bead curtain. Yolanda doesn't stir, and doesn't seem likely to any time soon, so Ellie leaves her and rushes into the hallway.

The floor is covered with dolls and trinkets. They are cast every which-way, as if a petulant child came through and knocked them all down with random sweeps of his arms. Only one is left on its shelf: the little wooden-headed doll she had brushed to the floor earlier. She plucks it from the crossbeam and looks at it. Is this a message? Is there something significant about the sinister little figurine?

Holding it, she threads her way through the scattered knickknacks to the waiting room. Half the portraits of the zodiac are on the floor, the other half have been turned around to face the wall or hang at newly-crazy angles. Ellie stands in the doorway several seconds before noticing someone hiding under the table in the corner. "Are you all right?" she calls.

The hunched figure moves, producing a small head covered in curly, greying hair. A woman in her late fifties. She looks at Ellie from behind small blue glasses, then nods and says, "What happened?"

"Yolanda got suckered by a bad-ass spirit," Yolanda says.

Ellie looks behind her as Yolanda pushes through the bead curtain. Her eyes are back to their normal appearance but they're watering in rivers. Yolanda wipes them with the back of her hand, wipes them again. "I got cinders in my eyes. Cinders. What's your husband mixed up in, little Mrs. Watson?"

"I don't . . . I don't know."

"Hunh. What did Yolanda say during the trance?"

"You don't remember?"

"I go someplace else. What did I say? Tell me quick."

"You said you were coming back. I asked from where but you wouldn't tell me."

"Hunh." Yolanda wipes her eyes again. "That was not your husband who spoke to you," she says. "I don't know who it was but he was big and he was mean and he wanted to do more than talk."

"Do you remember anything about him? Do you know his name?"

"I told you, I go someplace else." She looks at Ellie with reddened eyes. "You ask that like there's an answer you expect, but Yolanda can't give that to you, no. All I can tell you about this situation is run from it fast as you can," Yolanda says. Then, looking at the woman who still cowers under the table, she says, "Ready for your appointment, dear?"

A bad-ass spirit. Yolanda's words seem to have hidden themselves away in Ellie's ears, to resurface again and again. Her Nate is mixed up with a *bad-ass spirit.*

What the hell does that *mean*, anyway? If she looks it up in an encyclopedia, will there be a picture of one grinning out at her?

Yolanda certainly wasted no time showing her the door after their session; she didn't even take any money. As she wanders down the sidewalk of a street she's never been on and whose name she doesn't know, Ellie finds herself unable to think coherently of much of anything except the *bad-ass spirit,* and it's only after she's gone several blocks that she realizes she's still clutching the little black-eyed doll. She stops walking and stares into its painted face. For the first time she notices a faint scorch mark that encompasses the top of its head, almost like a handprint. Somebody must have put it too close to a fire once.

She should probably bring it back to Yolanda; it may be significant to her in some way. Instead she tucks it into her pocket. Yolanda would probably be more than happy to trade the doll for Ellie's continued absence from the shop.

Ellie walks a little farther before stopping again, this time in front of a small, beaten-looking church. It's squeezed between two boxy neo-brutalist office buildings, hiding in their shadows, set back from the sidewalk by a rough, weedy-looking lawn in need of tending. Flagstones lead up to the front door, running alongside a narrow, rutted driveway that goes around to a parking lot behind the building. The lot looks empty. Church is not in session.

Well, what the hell. She trots up the flagstone walk and climbs the front stairs. The door creaks as she enters, the sound ripping through a sepulchral silence. She proceeds through a cramped vestibule stuffed with literature and bulletins and finds herself in the back of a long, dim, high-ceilinged room. The church isn't wide but extends back a good way. Glossy pews spread out left and right of the center aisle, which leads to an altar that somehow manages to be small and encompassing at the same time. The walls are lined with stained glass windows so dark as to give the impression that it's night outside.

Not many people here, just the backs of a few heads. The faithful, praying quietly, meditating. Sleeping maybe. She's surprised that the church has unlocked doors and no one to safeguard whatever treasures it may contain; but then she sees a grey video camera mounted on the left wall, sweeping back and forth, back and forth, and is reassured. She's still in present-day Island City, where churches and convenience stores have surveillance in common.

Beneath the camera are three curtained apertures. The middle one is drawn, the other two open. She can discern alcoves beyond the openings, alcoves with padded wooden benches and kneelers. This church must belong to that religion where you have to tell the priest all the bad things you did so God will forgive you, because God can't forgive you until you let somebody else know what an awful person you are.

Well, she's got a lot of stuff she'd like to get God's opinion on. She enters an alcove and closes the curtain and waits for the priest to say something.

Silence. Maybe she mistook the apparent invitation of the open curtain? But then she thinks maybe the priest is waiting for *her* to say something. So she does. "Hello?"

"Hello." A pleasant voice. Male, of course. "Is this your first confession?"

"I just came to talk," Ellie says. "To ask a question, actually."

"What about?"

"Is it possible for someone to . . . to come back?"

The voice stays pleasant. "From where?"

"You know, from being . . . uh, dead."

"Of course it's possible. Jesus came back from the dead, and so did Lazarus. And at the end of the world, all the faithful will be resurrected into the kingdom of—"

"I mean before the end of the world," Ellie interrupts. "I mean *now.*"

"Oh," says the priest. Disapprovingly, thinks Ellie.

"Is that possible?" she asks, when he doesn't answer right away.

"I'm afraid not," the priest says.

"Why?"

"That's just the way it is," he says.

"Do you believe in ghosts?" she asks.

After a pause the priest says, "Do you attend services here?"

"No," Ellie says.

"Where do you attend services?"

"Uh, nowhere."

"Well if you did," the priest says, "you would know the answer to your questions. And, I may add, many others. Now if you have nothing further to discuss beyond your outlandish questions, please make room in the confessional for someone who does."

"But—"

"Goodbye, miss."

She's getting brushed off by a *priest*. Unbelievable. She picks up her purse and leaves without a word; and as she goes down the front steps into the waning afternoon she mutters, "I'd like to see *you* tangle with a bad-ass spirit."

Yolanda closes the door behind the last customer. She looks at the wall clock and frowns; the glass face is smashed, the hands nearly unreadable behind it. How's she gonna put this down on her insurance claim? Vandalism by spirit or spirits unknown. Yes, sir, the adjustor will love that.

Her lovely little waiting room is more or less back in order, except for the clock and the picture of Aquarius which just won't hang straight anymore. She tries again to fix him, and he stays level for a few seconds then tips to an angle again. She stares at him a moment, then snatches him off the wall. One thing she can't stand, it's crooked pictures.

She trudges into the back of the shop, Aquarius tucked under her arm. Her dolls are still in disarray, though she swept them down into one end of the hallway so her customers wouldn't have to worry about stepping on them. She leans Aquarius up against the wall and starts sifting through the heap. She's got to at least find Mr. Knob and put him back where he belongs. He's—

The bell on the front door jingles.

Yolanda looks up, looks down the hallway. Stands. Walks to the bead curtain and through it and says, "Sorry, honey, Yolanda is closed for—"

Nobody's there. No old woman with a lost cat, no young man wondering about the contents of his father's will.

But the bell is still swinging slightly. Back and forth, back and forth. Somebody must have stuck his head in, looked around, left. Yeah, that's probably it. She crosses to the front door, scanning the seats and sofa. She turns the deadbolt quickly, locks away the outside world.

When she turns around, something's waiting for her.

It's a small creature, ugly, with a head like a lumpy football and eyes like tiny black mushrooms, the poisonous kind. Its skin, too, has a sort of fungal appearance, brown and white streaked over each other, smeared together. It perches on the arm of the sofa, using both hands and feet for balance, and it looks at her with its minuscule eyes while rocking slowly back and forth, left and right.

"Get out of my shop," Yolanda says, but her voice seems weak, she couldn't threaten a puppy with her voice and this is no puppy. "I didn't invite you. I didn't invite you."

The creature makes no sound. It just stares.

"You lied to me," Yolanda says. "You ain't who I was looking for. That don't count as an invitation."

It hops off the arm of the couch and approaches. Its arms hang down so far it can use its hands for movement, and it does, walking like some radiation-tainted simian. Its tread is utterly silent. Yolanda backs away from the thing until she bumps into the glass of her front door. "Stay away from me," she says.

It keeps walking. Its eyes begin to flicker.

Yolanda turns and scrabbles at the deadbolt. It won't budge for her, it's like it's glued in place.

Then the thing lands on her back, cold and rubbery and slightly damp. Its feet lock around her throat, its hand turns ethereal and shoots into the back of her neck. Yolanda gasps. It feels like the base of her skull is freezing.

She falls thunderously. The creature's little fingers reach inside her head. She feels them knifing around in her brain, carving up her consciousness. Trying to take away her mind.

She crawls across the floor of the waiting room, into the hallway, past Aquarius to the pile of dolls. The thing is still in her head, rides on her back like a child playing horsey. The hallway starts to darken, she's losing her grip on herself, her psyche. She shakes it off, this time. The thing breathes on her and her skin soaks it up and carries it to her brain. *Sleep*, says the breath. *Sleep.*

Got to find Mr. Knob.

Focus on Mr. Knob.

She paws through the dolls and baubles, knocking them all over, burrowing into the pile.

Where's Mr. Knob?

The creature on her back makes a little noise, a faint sigh of triumph, and it squeezes hard with its vaporous fingers.

Yolanda shrieks once, briefly.

And falls face-first into the pile of dolls.

21

ANDY SHOWS UP AT SEVEN on the dot, with a copy of *Tootsie* in one hand and some flowers in the other. Like he thinks this is a date or something. "Um, thanks," she says, taking the blossoms.

"You seen it?" he asks, waving the tape.

Hasn't everyone? "Yeah, but I'll watch it again." She goes into the kitchen, rummaging under the sink for a vase. She finds one that's chipped but serviceable and fills it up with warm water. She leaves vase and flowers on the kitchen table and goes back into the living room, where Andy is crouched in front of the television, examining the VCR. He has the TV on but muted.

"Thanks for the flowers," she says.

"You're welcome," Andy says. "I can't get your VCR to work."

"That is not your standard video cassette recorder." She goes over and sits on the floor beside him. "It's like one of those puzzle boxes. Gimme." She holds out her hand for the tape and he gives it to her. His fingers brush her hand. Deliberately, she thinks.

Uh-oh.

Maybe she can ignore it.

"Um, you have to put the tape in halfway, turn off the VCR, and turn it on again." She demonstrates. "Don't ask me why. It started doing it about six months ago."

"You should get a new one," Andy says.

"We never got around to budgeting the money," she says. "Sit?"

They go to the couch. He sits near her, but not touching her.

They watch the movie.

She actually laughs once or twice.

They pause it midway through to order pizza. To be delivered. They're just two people who don't want to go out, sitting home watching a movie. Except only one of them is home.

Pizza man comes. Pizza man goes. They eat on the floor in the living room. Dustin Hoffman parades onscreen in a red sequined dress. Andy steals glances at Ellie throughout the movie, like he thinks he's being surreptitious.

Near the end of the movie he says, "Ellie. . . ." He's blushing furiously, like he's just been scrubbed vigorously about the face and neck with a rough sponge. "Listen, there's something I need to talk to you about. . . ."

Oh boy, she thinks. Here it comes.

"You gotta promise not to tell anybody, though. Not Charlie. *Especially* not Captain Weiss."

Huh? "Okay, sure," she says, suddenly mystified.

"Because it's something I left out of my report because I couldn't explain it, it didn't make any sense." He won't look at her while he talks. "It's about when that kid disappeared from the hospital."

"You mean Billy?"

"Yeah, Billy. I couldn't tell you about it when I called you because, y'know, Charlie was standing right there. And I don't think it could have anything to do with Fenton. But . . . well . . . it sure was weird, anyway."

"*What* was weird, Andy?"

"Well, after he disappeared, I found his . . . uh, his . . . his skin. On the bed. Just his skin, nothing else." He finally meets her eyes. "And I went and threw up and when I came back it was gone. It disappeared." He laughs a forced little laugh. "Do you think I'm crazy?"

"No," Ellie says.

"Because it really hap—you don't?"

"No."

"But—"

"I met him."

"Who?"

"Billy. *After* you found his skin. It never did grow back."

"That's impossible. How could he live without his skin?"

"He did pretty well," Ellie says. "Well enough to try to rape me."

"But he had a broken pelvis."

"Apparently, he got better."

Andy stares at her like her head suddenly split open and popcorn spilled out. He says, "What happened?"

"I shot him," she says. Leaving Nate out of this. And the three dead boys. Andy's having enough trouble with the Billy thing.

"Where's the body?"

"It dissolved. Disappeared. Just like the skin."

"God," says Andy. "That's too weird."

"Thanks for telling me," she says.

"I guess it wasn't anything you didn't know already."

"I appreciate it anyway," Ellie says.

"There's something else." Andy runs a hand along the top of his head, ruffling his short, pale hair into a sort of crest. "It's a picture. A composite, actually, from a description we got from a guy at Marina Hospital. Danny Finch. He works in the morgue."

"A composite of who?"

Andy licks his lips nervously. "This hasn't been released yet. You gotta swear you won't tell anybody."

Does he think she's going to run out and talk to Bob Woodward? "Okay, I swear," she says. "Now spill it before I have to hurt you."

"It's a picture of somebody who went to the morgue claiming to be from the police department. He gave his name as Nick Talcott and he went in just before the bodies disappeared and then he vanished without a trace." Andy reaches into his pocket and pulls out a multiply folded piece of paper and slowly opens it as he speaks. "I don't think anybody noticed it but me, because I was poking around in the library not too long ago. Maybe I'm crazy. But you tell me."

He shows her the composite.

"What do you think?" he asks.

She knows this face. Moustache and beard, very neat. Hook nose. Weak lips. Cruel eyes.

Jesus.

"It's Fenton," she says. "God damn. It's Nicholas fucking Fenton."

He folds the paper back up and sticks it back in his pocket. "That's what I thought. But he's been dead for twenty years. So does he have a son? Is Finch nuts? I don't know what to think anymore, Ellie. This whole thing is just getting so weird—"

"I know," she says, taking his hand and squeezing it. "I know."

"I don't know what to do," he says, sounding even younger than he looks, like a little boy who lost his mother. "Do I tell Captain Weiss about the skin? Do I tell him his suspect is a ghost?"

"Don't tell him anything yet," Ellie says. "I doubt he's ready for this. I don't know what he'd do if you told him. But I know you'll do Nate and me and the city more good by staying on the force and out of the psych ward a little bit longer."

"Nate? Is he alive?"

"He's out there somewhere," she says vaguely, gesturing at the window. "Fenton . . . did something to him. We're working on it."

"Jeez, Ellie. I'm sorry. I didn't know."

"Shush. It's okay. I know."

They look at each other for a minute. Two.

On impulse, she leans across the pizza and gives him a kiss on the cheek. He smells just like she imagined he would.

Soap.

He turns an even darker shade of red. He puts his hand on her shoulder and squeezes.

Pulls her over and kisses her. On the mouth.

The next thing she knows, the tape has run out and the television's showing snow and Andy's above her and he's thrusting into her and she's running her nails from his neck to his ass and back up again, and his mouth is all over her, her neck and her chest and behind her ears, and then she's gasping and her hips are bucking and Andy's groaning her name and then he collapses down onto her, his body hot and sticky and hard.

He keeps saying, "Wow. Wow." Like he's never done it before.

Hell, maybe he hasn't. Ellie's not about to ask.

Sorry, Nate, she thinks. Needed somebody. Don't even really know how it happened. You understand, don't you?

Yeah, Nate understands.

Andy shifts around a little bit. He's still stiff. After a few minutes he begins to move again, but Ellie gasps, "Wait," and pushes him off and turns over onto her stomach and lets him come in from that angle, and for a few minutes more she can pretend there's nothing hiding outside in the darkness, she can pretend there are no bad-ass spirits and priests who don't care and dead men roaming the alleys of

Island City. She can pretend she never had a husband Nate who died and came back a zombie monster.

She can pretend there's nothing but her and a guy who smells like Ivory soap, fucking on the couch in her apartment.

Late night. Andy has long since gone. He offered to stay but sex is one thing, a sleep-over something else. Ellie sits on the couch staring blindly at the television, nothing but a box filled with colors and shapes and sounds, voices going back and forth, voices of people who live on the proper side of the dark divide that Ellie has only recently become aware of.

It gets later and later. She sits and watches the colorful blobs on the screen and listens to them bleat.

Nobody on TV is alone.

Exhaustion is catching up with her, making her eyes feel dry, making her limbs heavy and her head light. She pulls the afghan up farther, over her shoulders. The television blurs, the room darkens; and her head gets so light that it detaches and floats away.

Her eyes open to shadow and silence. The television is dark, though she doesn't remember shutting it off. It's sleeting outside, the tiny hard drops skittering against her window like a sandstorm. Ellie sits up. Her neck is stiff from sleeping sideways on the elevated arm of the sofa.

At her movement something stirs over near the door. Ellie freezes, but too late; she has been seen, her awakening has been noted. Something detaches itself from the other shadows and comes toddling toward her. Something small and dark and vague. It approaches slowly, rocking back and forth with an unsteady gait. Ellie brings up the afghan and holds it in front of her like a shield. Not much of a barrier against the creature from the park.

That's what's here, she knows it is. It tracked her down somehow. It's coming for her, like it did for Nate.

It gets closer, its progress silent. It might as well be floating through the air. Ellie slides to the far end of the couch, a matter of a few feet, a distance covered in seconds by the approaching apparition. "Who are you?" Ellie whispers. "What do you want?"

Silence.

Ellie tries to remember where she stashed her gun, but she can't seem to think, her mind is still half-foggy. A gun might not even hurt it, but she wants a weapon in her hand. "Keep away from me," she says.

She is ignored.

Ellie watches it come, waits for the inevitable.

The thing finally gets close enough for her to see it.

It's not the monster.

It's a child. Dressed in blue pajamas. A little boy with tan hair and a plump, sleepy face. His pajamas are covered with little Bugs Bunny heads in various poses.

And he's holding the little wooden-headed doll.

Okay, that's the explanation: she's dreaming.

The little boy stops right next to her, stares at her with great big eyes. His face is vaguely familiar but she can't place it. "Is that your doll?" Ellie asks.

The boy looks at it, then at her. He nods.

"What's your name?"

"Billy," the boy says. He has a lisp, it sounds like he said *Biwwy*. *Billy?*

"I want my mommy," Billy says, and he begins to cry. Ellie stares at him. Is it even possible that she's dreaming this? Billy, the skinless pig who tried to rape her, tried to—*did*—murder Nate?

"What . . . um, what's your doll's name?" she asks.

"Mr. Knob."

"Did your mommy give Mr. Knob to you?"

Billy shakes his head, still crying. "Uncle Peter made him for me."

"Is your mommy with Uncle Peter now?"

"No," says Billy.

"Where is she?"

"She's sleeping." *Sweeping.* "I can't wake her up."

"Why do you need to wake her up?"

"I smell something bad."

"What?"

"Smoke," he says.

"Where do you live, Billy?"

"'Partment."

"An apartment where?"

"Building."

"What's the *name* of the building, Billy?"

"Don't know. Big building."

"How many buildings are there at the place you live?"

He holds up one hand, all his fingers out.

She looks at him; he looks at her. His eyes are huge and imploring, begging her to somehow wake up a mother who burned to death twenty years ago.

What a charming little dream.

But is it *really* a dream? Was Mr. Knob indeed the possession of a child named Billy who lived in the Wright Project during the fire? She thinks of the scorch marks on the doll's head. Could that have been caused during the inferno? But if the doll was there, who rescued it?

Apparently the boy has given up on her, because he puts Mr. Knob down on the coffee table and turns away and runs to the apartment door. Ellie stumbles to her feet and calls after him, "Billy, wait!" She gets all tangled up in the afghan again, kicks free, stubs her toe on the table and says something unkind about it.

Billy's standing at the front door, one small hand on the knob. She starts to call to him again, hesitates; because maybe this scene is not something conjured by her dreaming mind, maybe it's something more, a film clip of the past. So she shuts her mouth, and watches.

Billy pulls open the door. Smoke billows into the apartment, black and choking. Cinders ride in on the bloom of hot air, tiny particles of soot, ashes levitated by the power of the inferno. People shoot past the doorway, blurs, fleeing the blaze like animals running from a forest fire. Billy takes a few steps out into the hallway, keeping one hand on the door to hold it open. He looks up at the ceiling. No sprinklers, no smoke alarms, thinks Ellie. Or are they just not working?

Suddenly someone plows into Billy and knocks him down. He lets go of the door. Without Billy holding it, the door swings shut.

And as it clicks into place Ellie sits up on the couch. The afghan falls away from her, letting the cold air gnaw into her flesh. But she's too busy blinking away cinders to care.

Ellie stumbles into the bathroom and inspects herself in the mirror. Her eyes are red and irritated, as if she had actually stood in the plume of smoke instead of just dreamed it. She thinks of what

Yolanda said after her channelling: *my eyes are full of cinders*. Did her impostor spirit come from the Wright Project too? What is it about that place that it intrudes on the present from so far in the past?

She puts drops in her eyes to soothe the burning. Too bad there's no such thing as mind drops.

The doll is still where she left it, on the table where she's shared so many meals with Nate over the last seven years. Its dark little face scowls up at the ceiling. How did Yolanda obtain the figurine? Is it really a relic from the vanished halls of the Project?

Only one way to know. She'll have to go back to the Yolanda's storefront tomorrow, apologize for returning with her truckload of bad karma, and find out what she needs to know.

For all the good it'll do her.

Ever since the face in the fire disappeared, things have been quiet in the Wright Project, sonically speaking. The burning of the buildings continues uninterrupted, but that doesn't make any noise and the only thing Nate hears as he wanders along the sidewalks of the Project is the sound of his feet crunching on the cement.

The face vanished suddenly, in mid-sentence it seemed, its features freezing and then melting back into the flames. Nate doesn't know what that signified. Maybe whoever Fenton was talking to realized their mistake and broke contact. That's the best explanation Nate can think of, anyway.

And since then, he's just been noodling around the Project. Checking things out. Wondering if and when Fenton will put in another appearance. He's sure Fenton knows where he is and what he's doing, but whether or not Fenton cares anymore is another question. Because he has an unpleasant suspicion that, however their initial contact ended, Fenton is up to something with the person who came looking for Nate.

A flicker of movement from the fire catches his attention.

He stops and scans the building on his right. It's heavily involved, most of the wall facing him is obscured by smoke and fire, billowing and flickering and. . . .

For the first time, he notices that the pattern of smoke and fire is repetitive. There's a big, distinctive puff of smoke that reappears every ten seconds or so, generated by some event he can't see inside the building. It starts to curl away from the main body of the conflagration, then dissipates and reappears.

Like time is cycling through the same ten-second interval again and again and again. But if that's what it's doing, why isn't the loop affecting him?

He sees the movement again. It isn't really from the fire, it's from one of the few windows still visible despite the inferno.

It's a face.

Grey and ghastly, the face comes up to the glass, its mouth gaping in a deafeningly silent scream, its hands splayed out across the window. It stays there only a second or two before vanishing, but that's long enough for Nate to get a good look at it. To see what it was.

A person.

It was a person.

Nate's eyes are fixed on the dark piece of glass.

A person.

A few seconds pass. The face reappears, exactly the way it did the first time he saw it. He can't seem to look away. He watches the face appear and disappear and appear and disappear. He wonders how many other people are still in the Project. Do they know they're living through the same few seconds again and again and again? What if they're looping through the moments before their deaths? Do they know each time how the story ends?

He hopes not.

How many times can you die before you go insane?

22

The sign on Yolanda's front door says *OPEN* but the door is solidly deadbolted. Ellie gives it one last tug and gives up. Shading her eyes from the sun, she tries to peer through the venetian blinds that block her view into the shop but they're turned too far towards closed. She can't see through the windows, either, for the same reason. But yesterday the blinds were all wide open, letting the sun blaze through. Now everything is closed up and secret.

Maybe Yolanda was so frazzled by the previous day's episode that she went home without turning her sign around; maybe she's home right now, safe, recuperating from all the excitement.

Yeah. Maybe.

She stands on the sidewalk and fingers Mr. Knob's smooth noggin. It's sitting in her pocket and she has somehow gotten into the habit of rubbing the thing's wooden head like it's a good luck charm or something. She backs off a few paces and looks at the floors above the storefront. The windows seem to belong to apartments; she sees faded curtains in some and stunted plants in others, glass suncatchers that gleam in the morning light and drawn shades that shut it out. Maybe Yolanda lives in one of those apartments. Maybe she wasn't coming from home when Ellie met her, but on her way back to it.

The door to the apartments is to the left of the shop door. It's made of glass reinforced with wire. Through the glass she sees darkly carpeted stairs rising up out of sight. A battered plastic runner describes the approved path to the staircase. On the left-hand wall is a row of empty black mailboxes with unreadable names. Ellie pulls on the door but it doesn't budge.

199

She's beginning to hate the faintly disapproving way a locked door won't move when you try to open it.

She circles the building. Maybe there's another way in. The place is right on a corner and the other street is busier. More cars, more pedestrians. Fewer windows, though. She finds one and peers through it but her gaze stops at thick purple curtains. This window must open onto the room where Yolanda does her thing.

Ellie remembers how dark it was in there, even with the candles. The curtains do a marvelous job of blocking outside light. She's not even going to try seeing through them.

Around back, in the alley between Yolanda's row of buildings and the next, there are three more windows and a fire escape overhead. Lawn chairs stand on the fire escape, covered with frost and a sprinkling of snow. Of the first floor windows, one is swaddled in impenetrable purple fabric, another opens onto a tiny, though immaculate, bathroom, and the third looks into Yolanda's office.

Yolanda has an office?

Yes, it's definitely hers, Ellie can tell by the junk inside, but it's a mess, a localized earthquake zone, with books shaken their shelves and papers from their folders. Esoteric knickknacks—more little dolls, incomprehensible bits of feathers and shells, that sort of thing—lie scattered about, perhaps thrown by the same force that smashed through the hallway yesterday. A computer system sits on a desk that rises like an island in the ocean of debris. The computer is turned on, Ellie can see the green power light on the front of the unit, but the monitor is turned toward Yolanda's chair and that's in the opposite direction.

Ellie wonders what's on that computer. Clues, maybe.

Only one way to find out.

She crooks her arm and smashes the window with her elbow and waits a few seconds for an alarm to go off.

Silence.

No alarm.

She clears away the broken glass, then shimmies through the window. Goes around and plops into Yolanda's chair. The screen is dark. She hits a key and a menu appears on the screen. Word processor, inventory program, catalog of spirits (*catalog of spirits?*), spreadsheet, financial software . . . diary?

She hits the key for the diary and is prompted for a password.

Oh boy. She gets to play hacker.

There are ways around this. A password on a menu program is nowhere near an airtight security system. She hits three keys and the computer reboots, and as it goes through its startup she begins hammering on the break key. She is rewarded with a series of ^Cs on the screen, along with the query *Terminate batch job (Y/N)?* She hits *Y* and ends up in the operating system.

Well, that was easy.

She types *tree* and gets a list of directories. There aren't many, and one is named *DIARY*. Gosh, what could be in there?

Files. Lots of them. She prints one to the monitor, experimentally, and it flashes by on the screen. Completely readable. Good. Yolanda's diary is all standard text. She takes another directory listing, finds the most recent file, and sends it to the printer.

It's good to be the office computer whiz.

The printer is a fast ink jet. Soon she has several pages of text. She flips through them, hoping to find something worth breaking and entering to get. Ellie reads about Yolanda's running feud with Maurice, about Yolanda's trip to the grocery store, and about her own visit to the shop and the Attack of the Bad-Ass Spirit.

But suddenly the tenor of the diary changes.

First is a long string of nonsense, of garbage—letters strung together into nonexistent words, nonexistent words forming huge and incomprehensible sentences.

Then, in the midst of the gibberish, a word. More precisely, a name: *wright project*.

She reads further and soon sees the words again. And again. Like a replicating virus they increase in frequency, and soon dominate the page, until finally all that appears is the words, over and over again: *wrightprojectwrightprojectwrightprojectwrightproject*.

End of file.

Ellie stares at the monitor, picturing Yolanda sitting in here banging away at the keys, all night maybe, typing the same words over and over and over. It's almost a mantra, the repetition of words, like she was trying to remember something.

Or maybe keep it at bay.

A thud from beyond the office door makes her jump. Yolanda,

coming home? Or something else? She turns off the computer, stands, takes the gun from her purse. Holding the pistol behind her back, she approaches the office door. She should call out, ask who's here, but she can't seem to find her voice to do so and that might be just as well.

Even if it's Yolanda, it might not be Yolanda.

It's all mechanical. The arms are pieces of the machine, *whir buzz click*, reaching into the purse to find money to pay the cabbie. The legs are part of the meat machine too, pushing her up from the seat and out of the taxi. The yellow cab drives away, leaving her standing before the blasted five acres of the place, the special place. Bums live here now, she can see them over near one of the buildings standing around a fire. Fire. She closes her eyes and sees the fire, high and bright and mighty. It ended all wrong, but now she can make it right. She has the power to bring it back. She can reach out to it and touch it in its exile, she can light a passage from there to here, light it with the glow that's in the head of the machine.

She walks out into the field, hardly noticing the unevenness of the ground, the overgrown lumps of brick and masonry. Illusory, all of it. She pays it no attention. She twists her ankle and it screams in pain, but it's just the machine and she doesn't mind it. She listens instead to the voice, the silky voice, that guides her to the most special spot in this special place. It's in the middle, surrounded by a low ring of rubble that now anchors plants—dandelions, plantains, broad-bladed grass. They are brown and bent by autumn and the early snows. They don't belong here anyway. She will see them go.

Inside the ring the ground is concrete, shattered into a hundred, a thousand, pieces. More vegetation pokes up through the cracks, twisted and stunted by the effort of breaking through the cement, or maybe just by growing here where the ground is poisoned with power.

In the center of the broken disk of cement is a copper plate, long since corroded from its original lustre to a feral green. Its taint spreads to its immediate surroundings, giving it the pale emerald corona of a glaucous sun in the midst of eclipse. This is the special spot where she must stand, where she must open the mind of the machine to light the way home.

She stands on it.

She feels the power.

"Come on, sir," she says. "Yolanda's calling."

Ellie slowly opens the office door. As she suspected, it's the one labeled *PRIVATE* on the side facing the shop. The hallway is dim, the dolls still missing from their appointed places. The shimmering bead curtain is dull and grey in the dimness. Gloom pervades the place, fills it up. It seems to be more than the absence of light, it seems to be an actual presence: darkness shining through the windows from some black star.

She stands a moment, listening. The wind has kicked up outside, she hears it rattling the windows and howling along the sidewalk. The alley, behind her, is sheltered from the squall. She can hear, faintly, the sound of traffic, the usual hum of the cars punctuated by the occasional horn.

But no sound comes from *inside* the shop. Whatever is *inside* the shop is silent as the dead.

As her eyes grow accustomed to the murky interior of the building, Ellie sees something down at the far end of the hall. Yolanda's dolls. They're piled up against the far wall, a jumble of little bodies, a mass grave of trinkets and figurines spread out in a heap. Yolanda never picked them up. Looks like someone's been pawing through them.

Ellie is suddenly uninterested in the source of the noise she heard. She begins to retreat into the office but something comes flying from the darkness, a small swarthy shape with arms like broomsticks and legs like iron. It wraps its limbs around her neck and pulls her out of the office and, shocked and unbalanced, she has no chance to resist. She stumbles through the bead curtain into the waiting room with the thing dangling from her throat.

Behind her, the office door quietly clicks shut.

Nate's feet have brought him back to where he started, the flagpole at the outskirts of the Project. The standard still hangs limp and exhausted, draped down against the battered stalk. Nothing has changed. Even the fire is the same, running through its allotted ten seconds before looping back and starting over.

Wait.

Something *has* changed.

The tar bubble is missing.

Nate goes to where it had stood. The only remnant is a black smudge on the ground, a stickiness on the asphalt surface of this blasted plain. He prods the smear with his foot and comes away with bits of rock stuck to his shoe. He sits down on the rocky plain, takes his shoe off, sniffs the sticky part. Faintly oily, with a hint of cheesy leather.

He puts his shoe back on. Trapped in an apartment complex that burned down twenty years ago, and the best he can think of is to smell his footwear. He stands, feeling vaguely embarrassed.

Use your head. Do better.

Something flickers in his mind, a candle flame blown in the wind.

And then a sound, a feeling, a suggestion of words. Emotions. Thoughts.

An invitation. Extended not to him, but to the thing in the fire. To Nicholas Fenton.

Nate recognizes the thoughts: it's the whisperer who had called for him not long ago. She is calling again, but now she actually *seeks* the being who misled her before. The tenor of the mind-call has changed, it's corrupted, flattened. He can sense her voice and it isn't the same. "What did you do?" he shouts. "What did you do to her?"

A chuckle, hollow and flickery as a fire, is the reply.

The homeless people in the field shiver as the wind turns hard and cold. It sends their fire into a crazy dance, snatches the sparks and the smoke and twists them out of all proportion and direction. Embers are driven into the grass, smoke is bent level and sent coursing across the street. Overhead, clouds gather, seeming to form from nothing, as if the air itself is coalescing into a bulbous plain of darkly majestic strata. The clouds swirl, rotating around an axis that is directly above Yolanda. As the veil over the sky spreads out from its center, a pinprick of a hole appears at the middle of the maelstrom, a tiny black spot like a passage running straight into the heart of a mountain.

White flakes start to fall.

The column of fire is changing. It no longer twists and dances randomly, it shoots straight up into the clouds. And the clouds are changing too, swirling around the point where the fire enters, contracting, condensing around the flaming plume. Their retreat reveals a liquid sky, brilliant with enormous stars and black as midnight in between. This is the sky Nate saw, when he first began his half-life and again when the disembodied voice made him promises in the dark.

The roiling disk overhead continues its rapid contraction, and now the Wright Project itself is beginning to shake, to twist and skid and deform upon itself. The flames stretch, reaching up toward the singularity where fire and cloud meet and circle like adversaries.

The buildings are not slow to follow the fire.

The brick and steel and concrete distend, writhe and ripple and form pseudopods that hold together while being pulled out of any semblance of structure. Nate stares, entranced, as solid becomes fluid and flows up into the vortex.

As the buildings twist out of his line of vision, he looks at the lonely flagpole that marks the spot of his entrance to this place. Its sorry banner is limp as a broken wrist. The undulations and contortions that fracture the Wright Project have reached it; it is swaying slowly, back and forth, back and forth, yards from where Nate stands. Momentarily it, too, will be sucked into the void.

He realizes suddenly, and far too late, what's happening.

The Wright Project is, somehow, returning to earth.

And it's leaving him behind.

Darkness pours from the sky in a syrupy stream. It gushes down over her and around her, it flows across the frozen grass, leaping and puddling like a thing alive. Yolanda raises up her arms and throws back her head and laughs. The white powder falling out of the sky sticks in the congealing gunk, sticks and accumulates and begins to grow. Through the stinging clouds of ash and debris she sees the homeless retreating from their overturned barrel, fleeing before the storm she has called down. The flaming oil drum rolls in the wind like some kind of firework, spewing sparks and fire and smoke as it tumbles across the field and into the street.

Already the blend of pitch and powder is taking shape, growing into five mounds around her. More continues to fall, hot, viscous liquid covers her from head to toe as it passes over her on its way to its appointed lot. Licks of fire accompany it now, small ones belching out of the black hole overhead, probing at the ground before dissipating. One courses over Yolanda and she smells her flesh burn, but it is only part of the meat machine and of no importance now. She doesn't flinch from it. Instead she seizes on the pain and sends it through the portal to speed the fire on its way.

The flames have taken her eyes, so she doesn't see the first police car when it arrives. She doesn't need to, anyway. Only one thing matters now.

Nicholas is coming home.

The first officers to the scene of the Wright Project are a man and a woman. "Looks like a grass fire," the man says as he gets out of the car.

"Yeah," his partner says, watching the flames lick across the grass.

"Fire in the barrel probably started it. See, *that's* why they shouldn't let these bums just have fires anywhere they want to."

"Yeah." The woman picks up the mike. "Dispatch, send a fire crew to Canal Street. We have a grass fire at the site of the Wright Project."

"Roger that," the radio says.

"What's that woman doing out there?" the man says, squinting at the distant, dark shape of Yolanda.

"Attention!"

The voice is enormous. Because her eyes are gone, Yolanda can't see the speaker. Doesn't matter anyway. She can't stop for anything, not now. Nicholas is almost here.

"Please clear the field! A fire crew is on its way!"

Come on, Nicholas.

Come.

On.

"This means you, ma'am!" the voice booms. "You, in the middle of the field!" It has a harsh, electronic quality imparted by the bullhorn the speaker is using. Sounds like he's getting pissed off.

Doesn't matter.

Here comes Nicholas.

He rides a plume of fire—no, no, he *is* a plume of fire—and he crashes into Yolanda's body, sweeps over her and consumes her. The fire reaches inside of her, burns her from the inside out, sears away what remains of her mind and replaces it with smoke and sparks.

And the field erupts in a mushroom cloud.

"Jesus!" The cop lowers his bullhorn, the little blasphemy echoing from the surrounding buildings, as the field goes up in a fireball the size of an apartment building. In the wake of the explosion the structures that border the vacant lot are alight, the sides facing the field lost under sheets of rippling fire; and the grass itself has become a solid plane of flame, burning over every square inch.

"Better call another fire crew," his partner says, reaching for the mike again.

<h1 style="text-align:center">23</h1>

"Get off me!" Ellie screams, shaking her body left and right. The creature hangs on tightly and swings with her, and like a child enjoying a ride it makes an odd, happy gurgling sound. *More, mommy, more!*

One of the swings carries it up near the couch and it grabs onto the furniture with its feet, its long and clever toes digging into the padded arm. Anchored now, it gives her a wrench that pulls her forward off her feet; she lands hard on her knees. A cold, spongy foot shoots out and closes on her wrist, her gun wrist. Before she even realizes what's happening the weapon is gone from her hand, sliding across the room and vanishing.

The thing's clammy paws run up and down her neck, squeezing and prodding. Then they seem to dissolve, they get all soft and goopy and they *enter her flesh* and ice radiates along her spine, into her head, across her chest and down her belly. She feels the thing's groping, grasping embrace questing through her, in search of *something*. She knows she must pull away, must break free of this infernal grip, but she's paralyzed by the ice and by a faint, faint *pleasure*.

It's going to take something away from her.

And, it promises, she'll be happier without it.

There's nothing recognizable in the Wright Project anymore, only swirls and eddies that were once buildings and earth and cement and fire. They all blend together into a muddy mess as they spin in helixes up to the sky. And then the last of the tendrils whips off the ground, and all that's left of the Project is a pendulous, amorphous teardrop dangling beneath the vortex. It slurps into the opening in fits and gulps. Nate's eyes follow the stuff up as it shrinks and shrinks and finally vanishes into a splotch of darkness against the starry sky.

Where the Project had stood the asphalt-covered ground is rippled and whorled. Nate takes a tentative step forward, then another, toward the center of the circle.

Toward the dark spot in the sky where everything disappeared.

But suddenly a shudder runs through the ground, almost a sigh, as if some painful process has finally ended. The shudder is quickly followed by a crack and then a rumble. The smooth surface splits into a network of cracks that quickly join and grow. The earth shakes Nate off his feet. Black goo oozes from the fissures, glistening in the pale starlight, flowing tarlike across the surface. Nate stumbles back before the advancing sludge, and watches as the former site of the Wright Project sinks into a caldera of bubbling pitch.

Then the ground itself begins to swell, rising like a gigantic festering boil toward the black disk, the hole in the panoply of stars. The apex of the tar dome distends like a finger, a finger pointing at the dark spot overhead. Stretches and stretches, almost touches the hole in the sky.

But before the swell quite reaches it, the hole winks out. The asphalt pimple holds motionless a moment, its surface quivering.

Then it pops.

And a black tide sweeps Nate off his feet.

Ellie feels the thing's icy fingers close on her heart. Cold sweeps over her, glacial, endless. The room flashes white in front of her and she thinks of the flesh of Nate's cheek when she touched it: so cold, so cold.

"No!" She wrenches herself upright, stumbles blindly away from the couch and the horribly tempting promise of the creature's embrace. But it doesn't let go so easily; despite the seeming ephemerality of its hands it still has a grip on her, and it comes with her. A chunk of the sofa tears off and dangles from its foot like some sort of prize.

It continues to worry at her as she staggers back into the corridor. Cold stabs into her legs, retreats, stabs again. She falls to the floor in front of the office, lifts her numb hands to the knob and fumbles to turn it.

Locked.

"No. . . ." She hasn't the strength to stand. With the thing perched on her back like an obscene monkey, she crawls down the hallway. Snow swims across her eyes. It could kill her now, but it doesn't, it lets her live. It's not her life it wants, it's something deeper.

She reaches the second bead curtain. The dangling, gaudy strands are made of battleship chain but she forces her way through them. The room beyond is dark, the candles extinguished or guttered out. *Their* light isn't what she needs anyway; the light she wants is beating on the other side of the thick purple drapes.

The creature seems to sense her intent, because it suddenly squeezes something inside her, squeezes it so tight she cries out and collapses. The thing makes a little noise, a sigh, like it just climaxed. She thinks of Nate and, belly on the floor, crawls the last few feet to the curtain. She reaches for it with a nerveless, trembling hand.

The creature's arm shoots out and encircles her wrist, holding her back from the fabric that dangles within inches of her fingers. But now only one of its hands is inside her, only one to strangle her spirit. And one is not enough. She slides forward another foot and grabs the curtain with her other hand and pulls with all the strength she has left to muster.

The creature lets go of her, its weight lifts from her back. She hears the bead curtain rustle, but not the footsteps that took the thing to it.

And the drapery still hangs thick and impenetrable over the window.

She almost laughs. The thing ran away from the sun, and the sun isn't even here. She pulls the curtain again, begins hauling herself upright using it for support; and at last the rod breaks from its moorings and the concealing fabric falls to let in the grey light. Ellie thuds to the floor with it, the sun on her back. It has no heat but it warms her anyway, warms her in the spot that the creature sought to freeze. She eyes the doorway but there is no sign of the deadly little creature. Trembling, she sinks to the floor and curls up on the purple velvet and lets the sun do its work.

When she opens her eyes again, the pool of sunlight has shrunk to a puddle around the window. She's still inside it, thank God, but it's barely big enough for her body now. She must have lain here for hours.

She looks around. Nobody's here. The creature is gone.

Then she realizes there's a small dim shape beyond the curtain. It paces back and forth, making little frustrated cries and chirps. The bead curtain rattles and the creature whines angrily.

Ellie gets to her feet. Only one way out of here, since she can't go through the store, and that's the window. She picks up one of the chairs around the wooden table and smashes the glass with it. Cold air gusts in, air that smells of gasoline and dust and garbage and smoke. The window is still too high to reach easily so she sets the chair down and stands on it.

The creature pounds angrily on the wall. *Bang, bang! Come back here!*

Fat chance.

She brushes away the broken glass and clambers out onto the street. She feels better, she feels *whole* again; whatever part of her the little monster was after, it has thawed or regenerated or whatever, though she still feels a faint little kernel of ice in her chest. That's probably just fear, though.

Perfectly natural.

Thank God the sun was out. If she'd come in the evening, or after dark . . . she imagines Yolanda sitting in her office with the beast on her back, hammering away at the keys in a hopeless struggle to hang on to her mind.

This is her fault. She got Yolanda involved in this mess. She has to find a way to bring Yolanda back from wherever the monster took her.

And Nate, too.

And while she's at it she should track down the devil in Hell and convince him to be nice.

Ellie looks at the sky. The morning's icy blue has been supplanted by a layer of thick, rumbling clouds. Lying senseless on the velvet, Ellie hadn't even noticed the change in the light. Lucky the clouds didn't get dense enough to permit the little creature to operate in the daylight. That doesn't mean they won't, though; they seem to be congealing, solidifying, even as she watches. Like skin on cooling soup.

She tries for a cab and the fourth one stops for her. She gets in and tells the driver, "Take me to the Wright Project."

He's an older guy, grizzled; he looks like the stereotype of a retired sea captain. He fixes her with a critical gaze and says: "Wright Project burned down twenty years ago."

"Take me to where it used to be."

He stares at her a moment longer, then shrugs, sets the meter, and guides the taxi away from the curb.

A mile from Yolanda's building, Ellie sinks back into the seat and relaxes. The little cretin, whatever it was, won't come after her in the daylight. She watches the sky, where the clouds rush and collide and pile up on top of each other. After they've gone a ways the cab driver says, "Big storm is coming, yes."

"That what they said?"

"They?"

"On the radio? The weather man?"

"No, look at the sky! Anybody could see."

He's right, anybody could see there's a storm coming. But what kind of storm? He's talking about wind and snow and sleet. Ellie hopes he's right and that's all this is, a sudden winter storm blowing up to slicken the sidewalks and bring out the plows. But she has the most awful feeling that the sudden gathering of clouds is not an atmospheric trick, but is somehow related to what's going on with Nate and Yolanda and Billy and Fenton. All tied in somehow. All part of Fenton's plan.

Maybe it really *is* just going to snow.

But she can't make herself believe it.

From the center arch of the bridge that links the old city to the new, Ellie gets her first glimpse of Chaos, in the form of the Wright Project. The inferno has returned with all the fury of the original. She can see the flames that sit astride the buildings like conquering giants jealously guarding their hoard. And from the center of the blazing complex a tower of fire shoots up into the whirling, roiling clouds, reaching so high it could scorch heaven itself.

Then they're down off the arch and all she can see is the twisting tower rising above the surrounding buildings. The rest of the fire is reduced to a red tinge on the bottom of the clouds.

The hellish spectacle of the Wright Project's return is not lost on the taxi driver. He twists in his seat to look at Ellie. "You don't want to go *there*, lady!" he says. "Mother of God, look at it burn!"

"No, I *do* want to go there, and I want you to take me."

"Lady—"

"Look where you're going!"

He turns around in his seat, veering left just in time to avoid scraping the guardrail. He says, "I am not taking my taxi to that place."

"Yes you are."

"No way, lady. Even if I wanted to the police will have the roads around it closed. You will have to walk to your fire."

"I'll walk, then. Stop the cab."

"As soon as we're off the bridge," agrees the cabbie.

"Now," says Ellie.

"What?"

She digs money out of her purse and shoves it through the slot in the plexiglas divider. "I said stop the taxi *now!*" The cabbie exclaims something in a foreign language and slams on his brakes so hard the tires squeal. The taxi bounces to a halt there on the bridge and she gets out. "I'll walk!" she shouts, slamming the door.

She barely has time to take a step backward before the tires spin on the slick pavement and the taxi takes off. She presses herself against the guard rail. Traffic is fairly light, a good two or three seconds between cars. She begins inching along the rail as vehicles whiz by.

Funny how fast thirty miles an hour looks when you're standing still. Much faster than it seems from inside a car.

Perhaps this wasn't such a good idea.

She is separated from the sidewalk by the guard rail and a high, sturdy chain link fence; and between the two barriers is a gap of perhaps a foot and a half, a gap through which she can see the cold grey water of the river far below. She never realized the pedestrian walkway was detached from the rest of the bridge. She rather wishes she hadn't seized this particular opportunity to find out.

The space between guardrail and traffic is about ten inches. Keeping herself pressed against the icy metal, she sidles along the bridge. She's more than halfway across, it isn't too far to the other side. She can make it.

Cars rumble by. Most give her as wide a berth as they can, though some seem to actually edge closer to her as they approach. The asshole patrol, represented as always. These vehicles zoom past inches away, so close that she could reach out and grab a mirror or a door handle if she wanted.

A siren gets her attention, and looking upstream into traffic she sees flashing lights crossing the bridge. Police car. It could be coming for her, or it could be coincidence. She scuttles onward, hoping for coincidence. But no; the black and white vehicle passes her and then stops, its lights whirling. Traffic stops in the right lane, people start honking their horns. Honking their horns! At the police!

The passenger door opens and one of the cops gets out.

"Andy," she says.

He stares at her a moment, then opens the back door on his side. "Get in, Ellie," he says. She slides in and lets him close it behind her. Charlie is driving. Andy drops into his seat and shuts the door and as Charlie puts the car into drive says, "For God's sake, Ellie, are you trying to get yourself killed?"

"Don't lecture her," Charlie says. "Like lecturing a cat. She looks but she don't listen."

"Should I say *thank you* for rescuing me from the bridge?" Ellie asks.

"You can say whatever you want to," Charlie says, "especially if it's an explanation."

"I was on my way to the Wright Project—"

"So were we!" Andy says.

"—and the guy driving the taxi saw the fire and decided he didn't want to go any farther, so—"

"So when browbeating him didn't work, you jumped out of the cab." Charlie slaps his partner on the shoulder. "Didn't I tell you, Andy? She's a tough cookie."

Ellie wonders if she should be pleased or offended that she has a reputation as a tough cookie. "What's going on down there, guys?" she asks.

"We'll find out in a minute," Charlie says. "Grass fire, is my understanding. What're *you* interested in it for?"

"Long story," Ellie says.

"Love to hear it some time," Charlie says. "Bet Andy knows the story, don't you, Andy?"

Ellie can see the back of Andy's neck turn bright red.

They turn off the bridge, tool down Harbor Road. Smoke from the fire at the Project spreads across the sky like a bruise, blotting out the high, thick clouds that preceded the inferno. Despite the cold there are people out on the sidewalk, staring up at the sky, hurrying away from Canal Street for their own safety or toward it for a better look. A fireman at the corner of Canal and Harbor is there to shoo the gawkers away. He waves the police car on through.

As they approach the site of the blaze, Ellie sees four police cars and three fire trucks jammed into the street. Crews blast water at the flames, uselessly; the conflagration doesn't dim, or even flicker, as the water pours onto it. Crowds have piled up at the cross streets that join Canal, held back only by barricades and the police officers who man them. Ellie watches the onlookers' faces as the car passes slowly by. The fire lights them up with reds and oranges, masks their eyes in darkness, plays shadow games with their features.

Charlie pulls up against the curb a few dozen yards from the Project. He stares, she stares, Andy stares. The inferno is before them, and it's like somebody lifted Hell's lid to let the fire out.

"Jesus," Charlie says. "Who thought grass could burn like that? Somebody must've spiked the ground with gasoline or something."

Grass?

Can't they see the buildings? The Wright Project has returned, larger than life and still burning. Ellie was half-prepared for this but she's still stunned, she didn't quite believe she would find this when she got here. This place was *destroyed*. She walked in its rubble just a few days ago.

Now it's back.

And she's the only one here who can see it.

"Jeez Louise," Andy says. "Grass fire. Sheesh."

"C'mon, we gotta man the barricades," Charlie says. He points at Ellie. "And you, tough cookie, stay in the jar."

Charlie gets out. Andy hesitates a minute, and looks at Ellie, his pink fingers twined in the steel mesh that separates the back seat from the front. She nods her head. No point telling him she sees apartment buildings where everybody else sees a vacant lot. He tumbles out of the car and goes to join Charlie.

She sits there until the two of them are far away, conferring with a person who apparently is directing the firefighters. Then she tries to open the door.

Locked. Charlie was taking no chances on his tough cookie getting loose.

She doesn't work too hard at opening the door before giving up; she's still too dazed by the situation to think about what she's doing. She'll get out of here, it'll just take a minute.

For now, she'll watch the Wright Project burn.

24

THICK, ACRID STEAM DRIFTS ACROSS the misshapen terrain, creeps like mist over the tiny bumps and ridges of the pudding-like lump of tar where the Wright Project stood. Like a cork being pulled, the removal of the Project released the pressured contents it had held in place; and now the congealing exudation of the earth has completely overrun any small traces of the Project which might have lingered after the departure of the flaming buildings.

Not that he thinks there was really anything left. The gate sucked the Project dry and left nothing behind.

Nothing, except him.

Nate stands motionless on the edge of the field of asphalt. He's covered in the stuff, and hates the way it feels. The sudden surge created by the disappearance of the gate knocked him off his feet and buried him in goo. It took hours of thrashing and clawing to work completely free of the liquid asphalt, and it got harder as it solidified. He's probably got burns all over his body from the hot tar, though with his pain centers switched off he can't feel anything. Thank God.

So now what does he do?

Well . . . he stands and he stares, and the sky lightens from black to a dusty pink as the tar cools toward solidity. There's no sunrise, nothing that can actually be called *dawn*, only a gradual supplanting of the darkness. He doesn't think there's actually a sun here at all. Whatever's causing the sky to lighten isn't anything so routine as a star.

Either way, there's something stranger in the sky than the pink sheen of the atmosphere: thousands of silver globes hang up there, in sizes ranging from pinhead to basketball. Their true diameters are impossible to guess; he has no idea how far away they really are, and they reflect the pink heavens and the grey earth to form a confounding fusion of sky and ground. His eyes slip off the spheres as soon as he tries to focus on them.

He sits down on the broken earth.

He thinks: What now, Night Watchman?

Overhead, the spheres begin to glow.

Ellie watches the Wright Project burn; and oh, what a spectacular burning it is! The fire seems alive, playful, leaping and frolicking from one building to another, arching into the sky and down again, like dolphins breaching as they gambol through the sea. The heavy clouds reflect the indignant glow of the inferno; their bottoms are red and volcanic and black as soot.

Stranger still, the buildings of the Wright Project survive the fires without crumbling, burn without being consumed. But maybe that's because they're not really here. Spirit buildings, ghost buildings. Is that possible?

Well, why not? She'd thought the Rules were written in stone, but the stone has turned to mud and taken the Rules with it and she has no idea anymore what's impossible and what isn't.

Suddenly a large dark shape swoops into view overhead. Ellie cranes her neck to see it through the window. It's a helicopter, a big one, circling the Wright Project out of reach of the flames. On its second pass begins dumping something, a powder or a liquid or some combination of the two, on one of the neighboring apartment buildings. This has no apparent effect on the blaze, no more than the streams of water coming from the fire trucks parked several dozen yards from her. The helicopter peels away and twists around again, graceful as a hummingbird, and levels off for another run.

Then a bolt of fire jumps from the tower and flashes through the air toward the helicopter. "Watch out!" Ellie gasps, as if they can hear her. But the pilot must see it, he banks away from the rogue tendril of flame.

Ellie laughs in relief, pounds the window with her fist.

Then the fireball changes course in mid-air to continue the pursuit.

Ellie's hand freezes on the glass, her laugh chokes in her throat.

The missile slams into the helicopter near the rear blade. In a burst of smoke and fire, the helicopter's stabilizer is severed. It twists out of control, out of sight, it crashes into the grounds of the Project, passing *through* one of the flaming buildings as if the structure isn't even there.

It isn't even there.

So how come she can see it?

The sweeping arm of the fire completely detaches from the tower and arcs down toward the knot of vehicles on Canal Street. It starts at the end opposite Ellie. She only watches for a second—long enough to see one police car erupt in a ball of red heat—and this is more than adequate to convince her it's time to get out of the car.

She slides down onto her back and begins kicking the window.

She hears the cars and trucks detonating one by one, a series of catastrophic *booms*. She keeps kicking. The glass keeps resisting. Maybe Andy or Charlie will think of her, realize her peril, come to let her out.

Maybe they won't.

Pain in her ankle, sharp and hot. She grits her teeth, kicks the window again. She puts both feet into it. Another explosion, louder than the others. Water sprays the windows of the police car.

The fire trucks!

She only has a few seconds now before the lightning reaches the car and blows it to pieces. She kicks again and finally the window cracks. She hits it once more and it breaks, and she's up and clambering through it fast as she can.

Her third broken window of the day. Must be a record.

She slips and a jagged piece of glass digs into her side. She cries out, her progress halted, half in the car and half out.

Boom!

Debris rains down, a hubcap, a tire, part of an axle.

She doesn't scream as she tears loose from the glass and falls onto the hot pavement. She gets all tangled up in her coat and has to slide out of it, leaving it hanging from the glass that tore into it. Her side is wet with blood. Without even bothering to stand, she scurries on hand and foot away from the car, and she hasn't gotten fifteen feet before it goes up in a ball of fire. The force of the explosion flattens her, knocks her head against the pavement. Pieces of the vehicle clatter to earth all around. The air stinks of smoke and gasoline and shakes with the roar of the explosion.

For a dazzling, dangerous second, darkness invades her head, oozes across her eyes. She wrenches herself away from it, tears a hole in the darkness and sees light behind it, firelight. Ellie shoves herself to her knees, then to her feet. Hot air swirls around her. She runs a few paces, stops, looks back at the wreckage. Three dozen yards of Canal Street have been transformed. Where water once rippled, flames.

And bodies.

Oh, God, and bodies. They lie everywhere, firefighters, police, many ablaze themselves, the corpses flaring and spitting like wet torches. And not all of them are in one piece. She has seen carnage like this on television, after bombings and missile strikes. She never thought to be one of the dazed survivors captured by the cameras— except there are no cameras, no one to see, no one to witness except the pressing throng of locals eager for a show. She looks for them; they're mostly gone now, and the ones who remain are on the ground, just beginning to look up, tentatively, as if a sniper with a rifle hides in the conflagration, ready to shoot the first to move.

The police who had manned the barricades are moving into the field of flaming wreckage; she sees them hunting among the vehicles, checking the bodies, looking for anyone still alive. She begins moving toward them but a sudden sound checks her, a sound she remembers from minutes before. A helicopter. This one is white, a news helicopter. Through the pall of smoke she sees the passengers in the enamel shell. They have the side door open, they're filming the catastrophe.

"Get that fucking 'copter out of here!" someone yells. The voice is hoarse, and barely audible over the fire, and who does he think is going to carry out the order anyhow? The helicopter zooms in closer. Ellie staggers away. She can no longer think why she came here, what she thought she would do. This is all beyond her, far beyond her. This is cosmic.

The farther she gets from the fire, the cooler the air becomes. She crosses Canal Street to the far end. There are emergency crews here manning a makeshift first aid center. Somebody drapes a blanket over her shoulders. She stares at the inferno. The copter is darting above the flames, the camera pointing here and there, entirely unmolested. Whatever shot down the other helicopter evidently doesn't mind this one. Maybe it *wants* to be on television. Maybe it wants everybody to see how the people of Island City fought it and died or ran away.

The retreat is underway: the beaten survivors of Island City's expeditionary force withdraw from the fire to the temporary safety of Harbor Road, they begin streaming into the first aid center. Reinforcements are coming already. From the corner of Canal and Harbor, Ellie can see the flashing lights of emergency vehicles on the bridge. One, two three ... she can't tell how many; her sight is impeded by the ash in the air and the tears in her eyes. Down where the bridge comes in there's a patrol car and a cop directing traffic away from the fire area, keeping Harbor Road clear. He wasn't there before. A good idea, but what'll they do when the entire city is burning?

She realizes she's standing in the road, in the way, and moves to the sidewalk. At the corner of Canal and Harbor a chill sweeps over her, like stepping from sun to shadow. It hits her hardest in the nape of her neck, it feels like clammy hands reaching into her. She whirls, flailing at her shoulders, but there's nothing on her, no lichenous little monster trying to freeze her soul. She looks around wildly. Is the beast near? Has the cloud cover gotten so thick that it can move around with impunity?

Nothing to see except people, not all of them intact.

Shivering, she pulls the blanket up higher, over the back of her head, wearing it like a hood. The blanket must be wool, it's hot and scratchy. But it doesn't touch the chill that has settled into her spine like frozen poison. The creature must be close. The only other explanation she can think of is that its damage is more durable than she had thought; kept at bay by daylight, maybe, and reasserting its presence now that daylight has been choked off.

Maybe *that's* why she can see the Wright Project when no one else can. She's been infected by the man who made it all possible.

What an honor.

One of the newly-arrived vehicles is an ambulance. Ellie stands away from it, letting the paramedics take those with worse injuries than hers. Using the blanket as a compress she has stanched the blood flowing from her side, and although she worries that she may have nicked something internal she doesn't think she's in imminent danger. Not from the wound, anyway.

She moves away from the building behind her, going out to the corner of the sidewalk. From here she can again see the cataclysm. Besides the Wright Project, fully five buildings have been engulfed by fire. The second wave of fire trucks pulls into position around the other side of the project, on Sutton Street. They're out of her field of vision. She hopes someone warned them about the fireball.

The television helicopter is still in the air, getting the fire from any angle it can manage. There are no ground reporters yet. Maybe the police are keeping them out. The news helicopter plunges into a great gust of smoke and after a moment emerges intact from the other side.

She limps to the person nearest her, a young, exhausted-looking firefighter who is watching the paramedics load people into the ambulance. She puts her hand on his shoulder and he starts, then looks at her. He says, "Can I help you, ma'am?" Still playing the role of defender, despite his obvious fatigue and the sweat that makes his dark face gleam.

"Just want to stand close to somebody," Ellie says. "That okay?"

"'Course it is." The fireman is quiet for a minute, then says, "This is the weirdest damn fire I ever seen, ma'am." He gestures at the burning wrecks of the fire trucks and police cars. "First time I ever got *attacked* by a fire." As he speaks, explosions erupt from Sutton Street, and his eyes leave her to look at the fireballs rising above the burning buildings. "Jesus God," he murmurs. Then, to Ellie: "Excuse me." And he joins the rush of people stampeding toward Sutton Street and the fresh disaster.

She wishes somebody would tell her what the hell is going on.

The ambulance whisks away its cargo of the injured, its tinny siren wailing a lament. She is left alone with a gaggle of refugees and two beleaguered cops, a man and a woman. She doesn't know them.

"You gotta get us out of here!" somebody cries. His demand is echoed by others in the crowd.

"More emergency vehicles are on the way," the guy says.

"Please try to stay calm," the woman adds.

Wrong thing to say.

Accusations, pleas, and arguments ensue. *If this was downtown . . . nobody cares if we all burn up . . . where are we gonna live. . . .* Ellie backs out of the crowd, toward the sidewalk. None of them know what's going on. None of them can even see the Wright Project. They think it's just another fire.

They can't stop it.

No one can stop it.

"Ellie!"

She looks around for the source of her name, and spies Andy—he's alive!—leaning up against the left front corner of the apartment building nearest her, where it abuts the overgrown tangle of plants that used to be the park.

The park.

"Get out of there, Andy!" she cries. She turns to the cops but they're besieged by the panicking locals, trying desperately to maintain a semblance of order in the chaos. She looks back at Andy. He's obviously badly hurt; even from where she stands, even with the mist in her eyes, Ellie can see his blackened skin, his singed clothing. He sags against the building like an empty robe hung from a hook.

"Help me," he croaks, all the vigor gone from his voice. "I can't walk anymore."

She starts to go to him, then thinks of the coldness in her neck and slows down. "What happened?" she asks.

"Wh . . . what?"

"What happened? How did you get there?"

"Charlie and me . . . got cut off by the fire . . . had to go around River Street and through the alley."

"Where's Charlie?"

"He couldn't . . . Couldn't make it. *Help* me, Ellie. Please."

Ellie glances back at the street. The scene is utter chaos; some of the wounded firefighters from the second brigade have returned, and those who are able, including even the spectators, are helping them get clear of the fire zone, which has by now spread to the other side of Sutton Street and east toward the heart of the old city.

"*Ellie*," Andy says, collapsing slowly down the wall.

"I need some help over here!" Ellie shouts, going to Andy. He has sunk to the ground and now lies on his side, unmoving. Smoke swaddles him, given off by the burned flesh of his body or his uniform, she can't tell which. She crouches down in front of him and rolls him onto his back.

Recoils with a gasp.

Because his face isn't just blackened, it's *charred*. His eyebrows and lashes are gone, his lips withered and split, his nose a sooty pulp. It's like someone held him down and dunked his face in the fire. How could he walk in this condition? How could he even *talk* in this condition? Unless. . . .

Trap.

She jerks away from Andy just as the thick, skeletal bushes behind him rattle and shake and then the beast explodes out of them, flabby arms outstretched. It plows into her chest and knocks her onto her back over the curb, stretching out her body. She feels a sharp pain in her side and the blood begins to flow again, to be drunk up by the blanket.

The thing's black eyes flicker, its pebbly skin ripples. It opens its slit of a mouth, revealing a gummy darkness inside its head. Fetid air washes over her, air that smells like dirt—not the rich black earth of a garden, but the foul and rancid dirt tossed over the offal of an abattoir.

No strength left to push the thing off. The world crumbles in from the edges.

Ellie's hand somehow finds its way into her pocket.

Where she carries Mr. Knob.

Her fingers touch the doll's wooden head and the beast shoots straight up into the air like she stuck a pin in its ass. Meeping softly, it retreats back into the bushes and stays there, staring balefully at her with its poisonous eyes.

But it's too late. She's too far gone. The world keeps crumbling, blurs into a smudge. The din in her ear reduces to a murmur.

Mr. Knob rolls from her hand.

And both smudge and murmur fade to black.

THE KING OF THE FIRE

25

THE TAR IS BEGINNING TO bubble again.

It's the globes, thinks Nate, as the air shivers with heat. They've grown incandescent, like gigantic light bulbs, cooking the air with their radiant warmth. No idea where they get it from. But if he doesn't find a way out of here soon, they're going to cook him good.

He gets up and moves to the edge of the tar swirl. Black goo oozes from the asphalt, no different from a street on a hot day, except that this street stretches off to the horizon in all directions.

Hellhole. No wonder Fenton wanted to leave.

He looks at the sky again, shading his eyes. The globes aren't even visible as individuals anymore, they've bled together into a single luminous sheet arching overhead.

He hears a distant rumble, like thunder. Stands to get a better look, even though there's nothing around to block his view.

Clouds of some kind are gathering at the horizon, encircling him. They loom high into the atmosphere, humping up into patterns he's never seen before in a cloud. They're liquid almost, running like hot chocolate through the blazing sky, staining it with their presence.

And beneath them, rain. Silver rain, it looks like.

A crash of thunder rockets through and nearly knocks him over. Then he plops down onto his ass anyway, and stares at the clouds.

Gonna be a hell of a storm.

Ellie opens her eyes.

She sits up, a shriek rising and dying in her throat. What's she doing here? What's going on? Then she remembers: the fungus creature jumped her, knocked her out. But now it's gone. Why did it run away? How did she drive it off?

She can't remember. Her mind feels like mud. Fighting the thing off must have claimed most of her energy. She gets wobbily to her feet and looks around.

She notices that the apartment building on the corner is engulfed, flames racing each other along its cornice and winking at her from its windows. This entire section of Island City seems to be on fire; as far as she can see, up and down Harbor Road, buildings are burning. The streets are deserted except for rubble and a few firestorms that may once have been vehicles. Smoke billows overhead, drifting across the river to darken the heart of Island City. There's no sign of fire on the island, not yet anyway.

Suddenly it registers on her that the fire crews, the police, even the gawking crowds are gone. She is alone on the sidewalk, alone with the sound of fire. She stumbles out into the street, where the emergency vehicles were parked. Nothing, except fresh oil stains like bruises on the pavement.

How could they leave her *alone*?

An explanation occurs to her, one that leaves her with a sick feeling in her stomach, like she swallowed a load of half-frozen Vaseline. Maybe she *hasn't* awakened after all.

She goes to the edge of the park. Andy's ill-used corpse is gone. The scrub trees are brown and barren, skeletal things raking scrawny fingers through the winter air. Brambles and underbrush stand thick and dormant, their former foliage forming a dense layer of decomposing leaves that covers the ground. Beyond this stunted barrier the contents of the park are invisible. It guards its relics with all the zealousness of the jungle.

And perhaps it guards something else.

Ellie walks into the brambles. Their branches clutch at her without touching her.

As soon as she crosses into the park, she feels a terrible, desiccating heat, as if she's stumbled into an oven. It oppresses her, it pushes her away with waves that crash and break against her, stopping her dead. She stands against the repulsion but can make no headway.

No wonder the inferno passed over the park. It's on fire already.

The park pushes against her, tries to throw her back. Ellie rocks back and forth as the emanations break over her. She times them. *Wave*, lull, *wave*, lull, *wave* . . . she takes a step forward into the lull, braces herself for the wave, takes a step into the lull. *Wave*, step, *wave*, step.

Each step is arduous. The waves are intense but the lulls have a prickly resistance of their own. Nevertheless, pace by pace she penetrates the thicket. She passes over the remains of asphalt walkways, walks beside scalloped red bricks, the decrepit remnants of flower bed borders that protrude from the ground like decaying teeth in a neglected mouth. She finds a trail of bent and broken twigs— perhaps the path Nate followed when they first invaded the park— and, turning, follows it into the heart of the little wilderness. The density of the vegetation astonishes her; she didn't really get a full appreciation of it the other night, but now, in the glow of the inferno, she does. She could almost think she had passed over to another dimension, a sinister, sylvan realm where Nature was sentient and hostile and waiting for her to get just a little closer. . . .

Okay, enough of that nonsense.

She reaches the clearing. It isn't large and it isn't remarkable, just a large ellipse of blacktop on the ground that hasn't quite fallen apart yet. Cracking at the edges, it's still solid in the center and at the far end of the oval, where the bronze statue of Nicholas Fenton stands looking gloomily over its overgrown demesnes. The statue is facing her and seems to be the source of the emanations that have been steadily resisting her forward progress. She can *see* it radiating swells of repulsion, feathery sweeps of oppugnation. Resisting them, she takes a laborious step forward, and another, and another.

She can see the statue's face in better detail now. The eyes have that deep, recessed quality common to statues, but on this one it takes on a sinister aspect, as if those black pits can actually *perceive* her, follow her movements and relay them back to some malign intelligence. The nose is small and unremarkable, the lips thin and rather weak, but the eyes make up for those impressions of frailty.

Closer.

The dark eyes watch.

The cruel mouth sneers.

The pulses intensify until it feels like they'll smash her to pieces. Even the respites are too strong for her now, they resist her like a nylon wall. She's not strong enough to make any more headway, she's reached the end of her expedition.

"You son of a bitch," she tells the statue, just in case it wants to know what she thinks of Nicholas Fenton.

A small dark shape—*the beast!*—leaps onto the icon's shoulders from behind and sits there, its flabby limbs dangling down over the statue's chest, its narrow arms locked around its neck, like a kid riding piggy-back on its father. It watches her.

It has the statue's eyes.

There is weathered writing on the pedestal. It says *Nicholas Fenton,* not that there was any doubt who this statue represents, and some smaller writing, the date the park was built maybe.

She sees something pink on the ground behind the pedestal, mostly obscured behind the rough granite dais. But she sees enough.

It's a hand, attached to an arm.

It's *her* hand. The arm is sheathed in *her* shirt. The firelight picks out *her* engagement and wedding rings on the fingers.

"Oh my God," Ellie whispers.

The statue's mouth twists into a leer. The crimson tint of the clouds seems to darken to vermilion, to fiery blood. The fungus creature opens its mouth in a little O, as if to inhale.

Ellie lets the repulsion sweep her away. It doesn't lift her up and it doesn't knock her down, it just pushes her back, away from the unholy statue and its hideous rider, through the trees and the bushes and the overgrown benches. She rides the wave until it peters out on the wide cracked sidewalk, depositing her—still standing—near the spot where she entered the park.

Expecting pursuit, she retreats across Harbor Road, to where the bank slopes sharply down to the grey river. The walls of the old lock beckon, only a few yards away. She can hide there while she thinks about what she's seen, what she's become.

What *has* she become? Disembodied, a ghost. The little monster stole her body . . . it killed her, but she's still here. *She's still here.* She rushes at the aged stone barrier, blunders into the wall and spends a second in utter darkness, cobwebs flecked with sand passing through her body, scraping at her spirit. Then she is stumbling across the surface of the river, where the lock forms a notch in the riverside. To her left the bank rises sharply from the weedy, slushy water.

She's standing *on* the river. It takes her a moment to come to grips with this. Then she notices an arm sticking out of the water. The arm is covered by a weathered blue shirt ending at its wrist.

Where there's a handcuff.

"Oh, Nate," she says.

This fire ain't doing nobody no good. Damned if she can stop it, though. She's crossed to the other side, she's joined the chorus of whispers outside the window in the night. Death ain't what she expected, not by a long shot; but then, Yolanda knows that what you expect is usually not even halfway close to what you get.

Damn little monster stole her body, stole her mind. Made her *do* things. Called that son-of-a-bitch Nicholas Fenton back from whatever hell he'd managed to get himself sent to. Can't think of anybody less deserving of a resurrection than Nicholas Fenton. Burned down the Wright Project. Nearly killed her then, did kill her now. Bastard.

Still, she's got one up on him. She wasn't supposed to make it through their little meeting intact, no sir. When Fenton came down out of the sky and they *connected* it was supposed to be the end of Yolanda. All gone, no more. But he didn't count on how tough Yolanda's little old mind was. Like other people exercise their bodies, she exercises her psyche—not just everybody can send their thoughts into the spirit world, oh, no, it takes *practice*. And the gift.

So now she stands at the edge of the Project, having survived Fenton's assault. Disembodied, but still together. And since the Wright Project and environs are rapidly turning into Fenton City, she figures it would be prudent to retreat. Which she starts to do, except she gets distracted.

There's this old building, see. Used to be a hotel. She knows that because it tells her; it's got its own identity, somehow, not like these other buildings that are just shells of brick.

And it's hot.

Red hot.

She hears it calling to her soon as she gets far enough away from Fenton for his own noise to stop drowning it out. He's a loud one, that Fenton, all right. Tornado, avalanche, earthquake loud. Don't know where he's getting his juice from, but he's definitely a bad-ass spirit if she's ever met one. And she has.

But this hotel . . . It's something else. It isn't just noise. It *calls* to her. So she goes.

A ghost always comes when you call it like you mean it.

Just ask Nicholas Fenton.

Ellie's reflex is to try to pull Nate out of the water before he drowns, so, still standing on the water, she bends over and tries to grab his hand.

Not surprisingly, she passes right through it.

But it *tingles*.

Not like the wall when she went through it. That was rough, abrasive. This is a faintly pleasant throb, an electric little buzz. She crouches down and brushes her fingers through his hand again.

Definite tingle.

She tries it again, slower this time. She wonders if Nate can feel her doing it. Is he unconscious? Is he dead? Is he in this body still, or somewhere else?

"I love you, Nate," she says. "Please wake up."

But he doesn't wake up. And when, a few seconds later, she tries to stand, she can't. Because her hand is stuck, like she thrust it into a pot of glue.

And the tingles are spreading up her arm.

Or rather, her arm is getting pulled inside Nate's body.

She struggles against it for a second, then stops. Why should she resist? If Nate's body wants her, why fight it? He doesn't belong to Fenton, he doesn't belong to the monster. He belongs to her, and she to him. Even if Nate isn't in residence anymore, the shell he left behind is hers, too.

So she lets it have her.

And climbs, gasping, from the frigid water of the Hunter River.

26

THE OLD HOTEL IS BURNING, like everything else around here, its upper floors all smoke and fire. Doesn't worry Yolanda none. It's just fire, *real* fire, clean. Can't hurt her on the other side.

There's a few stairs to the front door. She jaunts up them. Funny how you move like you're alive, even when you're dead. Maybe, after she's away from here, she'll try to figure out how to fly. She always wanted to fly. Maybe that was why she got into the drugs, way back when.

She stands in the doorway a minute, the fire at her back, soaking up the vibrations. It takes her a minute to adjust to what she's feeling.

Residue.

Kind of like the gummed interior of a blender that's never been washed. Everything that comes through leaves a little bit of itself stuck to the sides.

She feels murder. Old murder, yep. Gangland style—the old gangs, with the suits and the violin cases and the classical music, not the new ones that just drive by in cars spraying machine guns. She closes her eyes, psychically speaking, the better to hear the past. Several corpses lie in the lobby, a visiting crime lord and some of his entourage, including his mistress. His *moll*, they'd have called her. Sounds nicer than *whore*.

And she hears a voice, faint and weak, pleading with the mistress not to die. One of the gangster's people must've been screwing the girlfriend. His is an echo voice; the spirit that made it isn't here, didn't get killed in the shooting.

Residue. You don't have to die to leave it behind.

There's other things here too. That one's just the first, the oldest. She sees people coming and going, checking in, checking out. Mundane stuff. There's a hell of a lot of imprinting going on here, much, much more than usual. Even churches and funeral homes—places she's gone in search of spirits, places where death and strong emotions often meet and mix—don't accumulate so much psychic gunk. It's like everything that ever happened here got encrusted in the æther, just waiting for her to peel away the other layers and find it.

She catches a whiff of something familiar.

It's dangerous for her to open up here, so close to where Fenton is on his rampage, but she thinks she knows what she's got and she wants to make sure. Should be enough interference from all the other stuff going on here to mask her from Fenton's fiery eyes.

"Show Yolanda what you got," she whispers.

And she sees him. More to the point, she *feels* him.

Ellie Watson's lost husband. Nate Watson. He spent the night here not long ago. But oh, his imprint is cold! He's here in the flesh but he's been changed. Somebody's tampered with him. His spirit's gone out of him and come back half-frozen. He's got one foot on each side of the curtain.

Too bad she didn't know that when she first contacted him. She'd have known Fenton was an impostor. He's too *hot* to be half-dead.

She sees Nate Watson come in and he's wearing handcuffs with chains longer than his arms. The chains are probing around on the floor. He's controlling them somehow. Circling him are three *very* hot splotches, strong presences from the spirit world. They're juicing his chains, she can see them spraying something—she'd call it ectoplasm if she didn't think ectoplasm was bunk—to elongate and manipulate the things. The three blotches are probably invisible in the physical world, the man probably don't even know he's got them, but there you are. Yolanda sees what can't be seen.

She watches him wander around. He finds the ethereal corpses with his chains, then tries to touch them and evidently fails. Not surprising. He doesn't have any real clairvoyant ability, just the weird chains and the three blotches, which are nothing to sneeze at but aren't psychic in any traditional sense. Then he stands still for a while, then turns around and looks right at her.

And says, "Hello?"

Shocked, Yolanda opens her eyes and bounces back to the present. These are images, not spirits. There's no way he could have seen her. But obviously he did. No doubt about it, he was talking to her. He saw her standing in the doorway.

This has very definite *implications*.

Like, for instance, the web of time is all tangled up here in this burning hotel, so she can look across from one strand to another, see and be seen. She's heard of this phenomenon but never experienced it. Never expected to. Thought it, like so much of the other stuff she's heard about, was bunk.

She toddles into the lobby and stops by the decrepit remains of the desk. Closes her eyes. Peels off the layers, down to when the hotel was still open. Still ritzy. She says hello to the guy booking reservations. He doesn't even look up.

Hmph.

He's flipping through a reservation book, looking for the name of an impatient-looking man in a raincoat who stands on the other side of the counter. Yolanda stares at the book. Concentrates. If other ghosts can move things, she can too.

The man says something, his mouth moving but nothing reaching Yolanda's ears. He is pointing to the page with his finger. Yolanda concentrates, concentrates. . . .

. . . until something inside her head snaps and the pages begin flipping, like a high wind is blowing across them. The reservation clerk jumps back, eyes wide, shouting something.

Yolanda snaps back to the present. She can't believe what she just did.

She affected the past.

This is dangerous, very dangerous. She's not careful, she could start changing things even more than she has already just by riffling those papers. Even something little like that could become catastrophic. She knows the story about the butterfly in Hong Kong crashing a plane in Washington. This ain't like talking to the spirits, no sir. This is real.

She wanders away from the desk. Firelight flows through the windows, staining the decayed interior of the hotel crimson. She doesn't have long before the building is engulfed. She doesn't know what effect that'll have on the accrued images. Maybe a phantom hotel will remain, a book of the past for the knowledgeable to read; or maybe it'll just disappear.

She stops in the elevator nook. The doors open onto blank, black shafts. Between the two elevators is a tall mirror with gilded edges. Most of the gold has been scraped off, revealing tarnished silver metal beneath.

The mirror is hot too.

Red hot, if she dares to say it, just like the rest of this place. A volcano of psycho-spiritual activity.

The mirror calls to her. There's something behind it, some kind of presence, screaming in madness and rage and futility.

A gatekeeper.

It's younger than the hotel, younger than the early images she saw in the lobby; it was added some time after construction, though she can't tell when. And it's angry; oh, so angry. Hostility radiates from the silver surface of the mirror. She's standing dead in front of it but can't see herself. No surprise there. Mirror reflects light, she doesn't, what do you expect?

"Hey there," she says softly. Not that she thinks she can soothe the gatekeeper's fury, but it's worth a try. "Why don't you come outta there and let Yolanda take a look at you?"

No response.

Why put a gatekeeper on a mirror in a hotel? What's on the other side? She steps closer to the glass. A warning flicker passes through it, like a ripple. The guardian, telling her to back off.

"Well, I'm not leaving unless you come out," she tells it. "Yolanda's been hassled by better spirits than you."

Another ripple flips through the glass, in the opposite direction this time. Then two diagonals meet in the center, swirl around each other, reverse.

"Yolanda is duly impressed," she says.

She takes a step closer.

"But she ain't stopping."

And the guardian comes flying out of the glass.

The flesh is cold, the muscles are stiff. The body is half-frozen from its time immersed in the frigid water of the Hunter River. She spends a minute or so hacking up water from half-drowned lungs. But her arms and legs still moves when she tells them to, they still carry her up the rugged, muddy bank to the strip of grass above, where she stands in a *hot* winter wind a few yards away from an inferno.

Except it's not really her body, it's *Nate's* body. She's inside *Nate's* body. There are several immediate problems presented by this. Like, for instance, if she's in Nate's body, where's Nate? And now that she's in it, can she get out again? And what about her own body, there in the park, guarded by the little beast and the statue and the repulsion waves?

She looks at her wrists. Handcuffs. Just handcuffs. They're a little bit loose, they clank around when she moves, up to her wrist bones and down again. She wonders if she can do the thing with the chains, like Nate did. She concentrates on the cuffs, wills the chains to extend.

Nothing happens.

Not surprising. Wherever Nate went, he took his magic tentacles with him.

And that brings her back to the question, *where is Nate?*

Details. Details she can't afford to worry about. Not yet. Because the world is burning up around her, and the air is filled with smoke, and there's a monster coming at her from out of the park.

The gatekeeper is a child. Young, too, not more than five or six. Some evil bastard killed a little boy and stuck him in a hidden chamber behind a mirror in the elevator paddock of a hotel. Hundreds, thousands of people have stood here checking out their reflections, making sure their hair wasn't mussed, applying makeup, and all the while the corpse of a child moldered inches from their faces.

The thought is so appalling that it actually prevents Yolanda from defending herself, at least momentarily. Long enough for the spirit-child to get a grip on her, fasten onto her with plasmic hands and fix her with a gaze full of juvenile madness.

Of course the spirit went crazy, imprisoned here, doing nothing but watching people come and go and guarding the questionable treasures stashed on the other side of a mirror gate. That much Yolanda had expected.

But a child. . . .

So she's stunned, and the gatekeeper has his way with her, momentarily; he knocks her back and he slaps her around, in a psychic sense, quickly delivering enough punishment to discourage or destroy an untrained, unconditioned psyche. Somebody a little too sensitive and a little too nosy would be belly-up on the floor right now.

But Yolanda is neither untrained nor unconditioned, and she's having a bad day.

It's like wrestling, really. Work with what your opponent throws at you. Recovering enough of her composure to fight back, she takes the outward force the gatekeeper's exerting, bends with it, turns it over her head and uses it to pull and propel the child away from the mirror. Away from the corpse. If she's right, something was done to the child—either to its body or to the place where its body was stashed—to keep the spirit tethered, keep him from wandering too far, to keep him sufficiently juiced up to defend the mirror. So, she figures, the farther away from the mirror, the less powerful the spirit will be.

Sure enough, as she pushes the guardian back across the lobby, his struggles get weaker and his intensity gets lower. He's burning out like a candle running low on wax. And he seems to realize suddenly what's happening, that he's getting pushed to dissolution, because he stops struggling. Lets her shove him farther and farther away.

Not so mad, after all.

So she stops pushing. After a second the child begins to make a low, piteous mewling sound, like he's forgotten how to speak. Probably has, the poor thing.

She's going to hate herself for this, but this is war and she can't be concerned with niceties. "Tell me the name of your master," she says. The child must know it. The man's name must have been used in whatever binding ceremony locked the gatekeeper at his post. Can't bind a spirit without telling it your name, or getting its consent—and she doubts the child consented.

The guardian whines pathetically.

"I'll give you the gift but only if you give me the name of your master. You can talk, I know you can. What's your master's name?" She needs to have it confirmed, for herself. She needs to know who set up the hotel to fold back in on itself, layer on layer on layer. She also needs to know *why* but this poor, sad spirit can't tell her that. All he can tell her is *who*.

The apparition stares at her with huge, black, haunted eyes. His outline is a flickery glow, barely human-shaped. If she pushes him a little farther he'll be gone, he'll be released. But if she lets him go he'll snap back to his prison. She can feel the mirror struggling to pull him back. She knows he can feel it, too.

She's bluffing. She couldn't live with herself, so to speak, if she sent this boy back to the mirror. But there's no need to let the child know that. So she says, sternly, "You can nod your head for me. I'll say a name, and if it's your master's name you nod for me. Okay?"

He watches her, making no response. He'll probably nod to the first name she says, so she says one she knows is wrong: "Nate Watson."

No movement.

Well, well. A truthful child. Or else he doesn't understand what she's talking about. She says, "Giovanni Sanzone." One of her clients, an elderly man who likes to chat with his dead brothers.

No movement.

Being careful to keep her voice the same as before, she says, "Nicholas Fenton."

The child nods.

"That's what I thought," Yolanda says, and she gives the guardian a shove. He flies backward, turns into a fuzzy blob, vanishes as he nears the door. Released. Discorporated. He may have gone into oblivion, he may have gone to the other side. She doesn't really know. Either way, he's better off.

Yolanda turns back to the mirror, unguarded now. She can pass through it unmolested, see what's on the other side.

Make that The Other Side. Capitals. Because she suspects she's going to be leaving Island City far behind.

Oh well. If Fenton has his way, there won't be anything left of Island City anyway. And if he's got secrets on the other side of the mirror, they can only help her stop him.

Saying a prayer to St. Jude, she puts out a hand to touch the glass.

27

The fungus beast comes up short when it sees Ellie standing there, and it takes her a second to figure out why: whatever it was looking for—her own spirit, most likely—it didn't expect to run into Nate Watson. It thought it had already taken out Nate Watson.

Well, ha ha, thinks Ellie, you were wrong. Fuckhead.

It begins approaching again, warily, eyeing her like a hostile dog that's been hit with a stone. Ellie matches its pace, circling away from the river toward the sidewalk. She can't believe how big and clumsy Nate's body is. It lumbers like a wounded steer. Funny, she doesn't remember Nate being such a klutz.

She's up on the sidewalk now. The thing is in the street, just watching her. This is almost where she was when the monster got her the first time. She can tell because Mr. Knob is lying in the gutter, his little wooden head up against the curb. It hadn't even occurred to her that she'd lost him, but she's oddly relieved to have found him again. Keeping her eye on the creature, she kneels down and picks up the doll. His smooth, polished head is reassuringly cool and solid in her hand. Good to see you again, Mr. Knob.

Mr. Knob in hand, she backs up along the sidewalk toward Canal Street. The thing plods along after her. It seems to regard her as some sort of parlor amusement. Perhaps it can tell who she is underneath Nate's skin, perhaps it finds her jerky, uncoordinated movements diverting. How long its interest will keep it from striking is a question she wishes she didn't have to wonder about.

She reaches the corner of Canal Street and hesitates there, watching the thing. Its poisonous little eyes flicker dimly. It stops too,

243

sits back on its haunches, stares.

To hell with it.

She turns her back on the beast and starts running.

The mirror grabs Yolanda as soon as she touches it, seizes her and yanks her inside. The sensation is not unlike putting a hand on the business end of a vacuum cleaner hose, except that in this case the hose is nearly as wide as a garage door. The glass parts for her like a curtain and shoots her into some kind of wormhole, the path described by a series of consecutive glowing hollow rectangles with nothing between. The rectangles are not close together but she's moving through them so fast they form a nearly seamless wall of light.

At first the tube is straight and she can see the distant shapes distinctly, but then it begins to curve and twist and the ride becomes a stomach-wrenching exercise in cornering at insane speeds. If she still had a stomach, anyway, which she doesn't. Thank God.

Then, at last, the path straightens again, and she sees a brilliant light approaching, a light that blots out the glow of the rectangles. Her head is still spinning from her trip through the corkscrew. Apparently even spirit bodies can experience vertigo.

As she gets closer to the light it resolves itself into yet another rectangle; but beyond this one there is a silver void, a sheet of foil stretched tight over the opening.

The wormhole spits her out right at the trembling wall. She hits it and it shatters, pieces spinning all around her, clinging to her, evaporating. For a second there is darkness, and then she's lying on a hot, rocky surface. She can *feel* it under her body. But how can she feel anything when she's a spirit?

Answer: she's in a spirit realm. Everything is just as ethereal as she is and, consequently, just as solid.

She sits up, looks left and right. She's alone on a rocky plain of asphalt and tar, and a few hundred yards away a storm of silver rain is bearing down on her.

Then a voice from behind her says, "Where did *you* come from?"

Her head snaps around. Forgot to check her back. Yolanda is getting sloppy in her afterlife. Another one of Fenton's pets?

But then she sees who it is.

How about that.

"Well, hello there, Mr. Watson," she says.

An enormous, gaudily-dressed woman is definitely high on the list of things Nate never considered seeing here. "How do you know who I am?" he asks.

"Your wife hired me to find you."

"Really? You sure take your work seriously."

"Oh, this ain't for her. Right now I'm freelancing. You been here long?"

"About a day," Nate says. "I think. Hard to tell."

"Yolanda can see where that might be," she says. "That's me, by the way. Yolanda."

"How'd you get here?"

She shrugs, staring at the approaching storm. "I came through the mirror in the old hotel. Mr. Fenton cast a spell on it, made it a gate to the spirit world." She points at the looming wall of clouds and steam. "Mr. Watson, what is up with that storm coming this way?"

"Silver rain," he says.

"I think we don't want the silver rain to fall on us," says Yolanda. She gets to her feet with surprising ease. Nate stays on the ground. "Getting up?" she asks.

"Nope."

"Might Yolanda ask why?"

"No point. There's no way out of here. Nowhere to run to. The rain's coming from all around."

"There *got* to be a way out. We're in the spirit world, honey." She wrinkles her nose. "Kind of a low-rent section, but the spirit world nonetheless. There's a way out, sure as there was a way in."

"Well, you're welcome to try and find it," says Nate. The storm is bearing down on them, less than a hundred feet away now. They're in a rapidly-shrinking circle of tar and asphalt, and the rain steams in from every direction.

Yolanda eyes the encroaching storm. After a moment she says, "You've been here longer than Yolanda. Do you have any ideas you'd like to share?"

He remembers the tar that came out of the ground when the Wright Project disappeared. It came out like it was always just under the surface and something was keeping it down. Something like Nicholas Fenton. He controlled this place, he made the earth bubble and the sky cloud over. He controlled it but he couldn't leave it, not until somebody on the outside opened a way and helped guide him out.

How did Fenton get here? Why couldn't he leave? Questions he's been speculating on since the Wright Project disappeared, questions lent a new urgency as the storm looms close over them, as acrid mist billows at them like the spray of a waterfall. He can't see anything in the roiling cloud. It's the end of the world. It's coming toward him. Coming to eat him up.

Think faster.

Yolanda stands over him, but she isn't looking at him, she's staring at the storm.

"Everybody knows Fenton died in the Wright Project fire but nobody knows what he was doing there," Nate says. She lowers her gaze to him. "Maybe . . . maybe. . . ."

"Maybe he burned it down himself," says Yolanda. "You're right, that's what he did. I *know* he did. What about it?"

"He was here. Fenton and the Wright Project were both *right here* but they couldn't leave. Not until—"

"Until Yolanda showed him the way." She grimaces. "Don't remind me, honey. Not a happy chapter in Yolanda's career."

Nate stands up. The circle of tar has closed to fifty feet. "How did he get here?"

She shrugs. "Spell gone wrong somehow. He was gathering death energy from the tenants and it blew up in his face. Landed him here. He had this little place all prepared, he had access to it through the mirror in the old hotel where you spent the night."

"He was going to take his death energy across the street and into the mirror," Nate says, "but it backfired and he had to shift the whole place here, Wright Project and all."

"And then he couldn't leave because the way wasn't prepared right," Yolanda says.

"Or maybe this storm has been out there all this time, and Fenton was holding it back. Maybe that was why he couldn't leave. He couldn't hold back the storm and open a way back to earth at the same time. Or maybe he *could* have, but would've had to leave his . . .

uh, his death energy here."

"You could be right," Yolanda says. "What you tell me, the energy was manifesting as the Wright Project. Yolanda saw the Wright Project back where it used to be, even though nobody else could. Big old thing like the Wright Project would have taken a lot of time and juice to move. It needed to be *refined* but he didn't get a chance to do that. So he was stuck and he couldn't find his way back on his own, so he used Yolanda to do it for him."

The steaming rain is within ten feet of them now, steadily chewing up the asphalt plains. No more time for discussion. Got to do it now, or face the rain. "I think it's the . . . the spirit world reclaiming what Fenton made. I think we can punch through through the storm." He stands up. Not much time left now. "You made a gate once. Can you do it again?"

"I don't know. Fenton was pulling Yolanda's strings last time. But maybe Yolanda can get us through the rain. And what do you think is on the other side, Mr. Nate Watson?"

"Don't know."

"And what if you're wrong? What if it just burns us up?"

"Then we're already gone." He braces himself. "Tell me when."

"Yolanda hears and obeys."

Nate stares at the oncoming storm. It's the end of the world. It's eating the place up, munch munch munch. But *it's not a real storm*. It's just a facade. It's a two-dimensional image.

Two dimensions. Not enough to hold them. One pace ahead, once pace back, and the drawing disappears. The canvas is sundered.

One pace.

To break out of the drawing.

He draws a breath.

Yolanda takes his hand.

And says, "When."

They take a step forward, into the paper wall.

Ellie stumbles up the hot sidewalk with the beast in pursuit. It lopes after her on its hands and feet, running like a parody of a monkey, a pod-chimp from space. It's not pacing her now, oh no. Fun time is over and it's after her, it wants to jump on her and eat her up. And the God damn thing is faster than she is.

She flies through the intersection at Cross Street with the monster galloping behind. The Wright Project comes into view on the right, the dark buildings looming like gigantic charcoal briquets in the blaze of the fire. It's the belly of the beast, Fenton's domain—Nicholas Fenton, parent of the thing that hounds her heels.

As soon as she thinks of Fenton she hears a voice, a smooth, silken, luscious voice that she knows, she *knows*, is his. It says, *Why bother to run? Where are you going? This city belongs to the fire and it's going to burn it down and you might as well give up now and get it over with.*

What's sneaky about Fenton's voice is that, somehow, he makes it sound exactly like her own. Which it isn't.

Is it?

The beast leaps. Misses, because she puts on a burst of speed and darts right, into the street, to avoid it. It lands in a little brown heap on the sidewalk and handsprings back to its feet, immediately orienting on her again.

So now she has the Wright Project to her back, the flaming wreck of a fire truck to her right, the flaming wreck of a police car to her left, and the beast in front. Not a good strategic position.

The thing saunters toward her, taking its time. It knows it's got her now. It knows she has nowhere left to go.

Oh yeah?

She turns around and runs into the Wright Project.

28

THE SILVER RAIN IS LIKE a torrent of knives slicing through him. Tiny, razor-sharp knives that have been sitting in a bonfire for a few hours to get them nice and hot. They're cutting him to ribbons, slicing the ribbons into confetti, smaller and smaller pieces and each one, somehow, *containing* him, like the shards of a shattered mirror that continue to reflect the scene in front of them.

He screams but he has no voice, the knifing downpour has sectioned his throat and lungs and head. Something's wrong, something's terribly wrong. She was supposed to *protect* them from the silver rain but she's not, it's getting through, it's *getting through and it's eating him up!*

Because there's something in the rain that Yolanda didn't expect.

Images.

It's kind of like the old trick with Silly Putty, where you squash it down on the comics page and it comes up with the funnies imprinted on it. Except there's nothing funny about what the rain has to show her, and much as she'd like to she can't squeeze it back into a ball to make it go away.

She sees the Wright Project form, bubbling up like radioactive tar from the cracked and broken surface of the pocket world. The buildings take shape first, then burst into flame, culminating in a fiery plume that marks the arrival of Fenton himself. She sees the inhabitants in their death throes, the people killed in the fire dragged here instead of being set free like dead people should be. Even though Fenton's spell blew up in his face he still managed to bring the stolen spirits, the death energy, into his own little hell.

And he spends his death energy, when he needs to. Each time he uses the energy another spirit goes up like a match, consigned to oblivion instead of whatever afterlife may await them. She sees them in the rain, twisted shapes screaming soundlessly into the void, the residue left by their departure captured and utilized by the man in the middle, the king of the fire.

The bastard.

She sees Nate Watson. He arrives like the Project did, bubbling up from the tar, and Fenton does something to him—burns four souls to do it—and sends him back into the cracks.

She sees someone else, someone who looks kind of familiar, like she might have known him a long time ago. He doesn't bubble out of the ground, he falls out of the sky and lands outside the Project, and tongues of fire like hooks scrape over and through him, charring his bones, peeling away the layers of his flesh, then burn him up and make him disappear. Six more souls up in flames.

The images come randomly. Spirits burn in ones and twos and go screaming past her, and as if they can see her they reach out with tenebrous hands, clutching at her, begging her to save them. She can feel their passage, feel their grips, but only the way she feels the wind, there's nothing to hold on to because they're already gone and the storm is just sweeping up the husks. One passes right through her, cobwebs shooting through her heart, making it like to burst.

And a final indignity.

She sees herself.

She comes down out of the sky toward the Project, riding on a platform made of fire that carries her right into the scorching tower, right into Fenton's flaming embrace. A moment later a twisted soul, not even recognizable as her own, comes screeching out of the tower directly at her, hands curled like claws, trailing smoke and ashes behind.

She screams.

And the knives cut her to pieces.

The fire is a palpable presence on the grounds of the Project, suffusing the air, so that even in the wide, clear avenues between the buildings it feels like the molecules themselves are burning, pitting and scarring her flesh. Nate's flesh.

And the beast doesn't hesitate to plunge in after her, galumphing apelike along the sidewalk. She catches a glimpse of it when she looks back over her shoulder. Through the drifting, billowing smoke its squat and turgid form is visible as it toddles toward her.

It wants her.

The fire wants her.

Why not just let it take her and get it over with?

No, that's the voice that Fenton likes, the one that tells her to lie down and die like a good little girl. Not gonna do it. Gonna keep running.

Running where? She's on a straight track directly into the tower of fire, no way left or right, no way back except through the little monster and she doesn't have the strength to fight her way past it.

It's coming for her.

She starts running again, toward the middle of the Project, toward the pillar. When you're in this deep, the only thing to do is go in deeper.

Oh, Nate, where are you?

They're through the curtain and into a cacophony, into the sound of a thousand untuned woodwinds blasting a madman's symphony. The sonic assault leaves his ears numb, glazes his mind. Nate's eyes snap open; his vision is fuzzy but he can tell they're definitely not in the asphalt plain anymore. They're in the midst of what look like steam explosions, except the steam is made of incandescent numbers and it isn't coming from burst pipes but from three dark little spheres that seem to be orbiting him.

He reaches up and feels his head. All in one piece. She did it, she got them through! The trauma of the passage lingers, a network of burning spiderwebs all over and through him, but the sensation is fading quickly. As his vision clears he realizes the numbers aren't numbers, they're squiggles, tiny filaments that glow red and orange for a few seconds before fading to nothing. It's like the spray of a sparkler but more delicate, more complex.

He looks beyond the glowing squiggles and sees that the dark puddles of asphalt, the dusty pink sky, the thundering rain have been replaced by a vast mauve emptiness marbled with jagged, erratic veins of dark blue verging on black. Anemonoid encrustations dot the void, affixed with no apparent pattern or purpose. They pulse and glow at uneven intervals. As he studies the lucent, tentacled ornaments, he notices faint lines crisscrossing the scene, a shade of violet just slightly darker than their surroundings. Some run perpendicularly to his vision and some in line with it; some are twisted into bizarre geometry, eye-crushing and yet somehow orderly, as if with the proper equations you could plot the figures out. A mathematician's dream, but they give him a headache.

One of his satellites courses in front of his eyes, spitting its little squiggles and hissing faintly. The luminous snippets drift like smoke, twisting and twirling in the void. On impulse Nate tips his head forward into the dispersing cloud. He feels the filaments against his face, their touch soft and light as the wings of a dove. His face tingles, the small hairs standing on end, like he's bending down close to an electric field. He shakes his head back and forth, sweeping it through the black sphere's exhaust and twirling the squiggles into whorls and eddies that seem to stick to his hair, to lift it up with static electricity or some other force. He tries to catch one of the circling globes but it's far too quick for that, easily weaving a zigzag path between his groping hands. He tries again, with no more success, ending up clutching nothing but an armful of light. Through his ragged, dusty uniform he feels the electric flicker of contact and a faint outward pressure as the cloud expands against him.

He drops his arms and looks behind them. One pace back, an enormous bank of luminous fog curves away above and below, left and right, gauzy and soft yet hinting at iron beneath. A stone wall layered in cotton. Turning to his companion he says, "What do you make of this, Yolanda?"

Yolanda, beside him, still has her eyes scrunched shut.

He says, "We're through. You can look now."

She doesn't move.

"Yolanda?"

She opens her mouth and screams, clutching at her head. The scream is thin and high and piercing, shattering, more like the cry of some great injured bird than the cry of a person. After a few second the scream trails off but her mouth stays open and she pulls her knees up to her chest and locks her arms around them and floats there like a big gaudy cannonball.

Unable to think of anything helpful to do, Nate slaps her.

Her eyes open, but they're unfocused, the pupils big as dimes. "Yolanda!" he shouts, right in her ear. "It's okay! We're through! You did it!"

She finally seems to hear him, and looks at him like she sees him, though from the expression on her face he could be materializing crayfish from his nose. She turns away and says, in a tiny little voice, "That hurt."

"No kidding."

She slowly comes out of her curl. "The storm. . . ." She shudders. "Soaking up everything Fenton ever did in that little pocket place. And it all rubbed off on Yolanda when she came through. The knives were bad enough, but the images . . . he imprinted there in a big way. He polluted the whole place."

"I didn't notice," Nate says.

"You wouldn't," she says. "But Yolanda's got the gift. If that's what you want to call it." She looks at him. "I saw *you* there. What he did to you."

"When Fenton tried to con me out of my body?"

"No," she says. "When he put you back into it."

"What? *Fenton?*"

"Fenton," she says. "Fenton brought you back." She studies him a moment. "You didn't know."

"I . . . I didn't know *who* did it. But Fenton? *Fenton?*"

"Yolanda sees you are having trouble accepting this."

"Why on earth would Fenton have brought me back?"

"Wish I could tell you, honey, but all Yolanda sees is the imprint. It was Fenton who put you back in your body. With his death magic."

And suddenly it clicks. Why Fenton brought him back. The real purpose of his return to the mortal coil after having been so rudely shuffled off it.

He's been a stooge all along.

He was brought back to do exactly what he did: maim Billy and kill the boys, so Fenton could make Billy an offer he couldn't refuse. And after he did that, he played the stooge again, letting Fenton get his hooks into Yolanda when she came looking for him.

That son of a bitch.

"You all right, Mr. Watson?"

"Nate," he says. "Call me Nate. Yeah, I'm okay. Just getting used to being the Prince of Darkness's patsy."

"Oh, he ain't no Prince of Darkness," Yolanda sniffs.

"Close enough," Nate says.

"Don't you go giving him that kinda power. He got enough as it is." Nate says nothing. After a moment Yolanda pats him on the shoulder. "I know you ain't used to dealing with spirits and phantoms," she says. "That's all right, though. That's all right. You got Yolanda here to help you now. You ready to try and find the way back?"

He looks out across the deep mauve void and says, "Think we can do it?"

"Sure we can," Yolanda says. "Can't move that much death energy without leaving some kind of a trail. We just got to find it and follow it."

Nate looks at her. "That'll take us right to Fenton," he says.

She nods her head once, slowly. "Right to Fenton."

29

HE WAITS AS YOLANDA DOES some kind of psychic bloodhound shtick. She closes her eyes and throws out her arms and moves them around slowly while turning her head from side to side and tilting it up and down. Any second now Nate expects her to start sniffing the air and holding up a wet finger to catch the wind.

Tell me something good, he thinks. Good fortune for a change.

But after a minute she opens her eyes and says, "No good. We're too close to this thing—" She jerks her thumb at the wall of fog behind them. "—and there's too much interference."

"What'll we do?"

"Move away from it and try again." She begins drifting out into the void. Nate takes a step after her but instead of moving starts to spin in place, like an astronaut playing outside the capsule. "Yolanda!" he shouts, as the purple nothing and the misty curtain chase each other past his eyes. Around and around and around . . . and where's Yolanda? He can't see her anymore, he's spinning too fast. He needs her, she's his guide. He tries to slow his rotation by kicking out his other leg but it doesn't work, it only makes him spin faster.

"Yolanda!" he shouts again.

And round and round and—

Stop!

And, abruptly, he does. Just by thinking about it. He isn't sure his head and feet are pointing in the same direction they were when he started, but there's no gravity here so that's a moot point.

Yolanda, however, is most definitely gone.

He shouts her name a few more times and hovers there waiting for her to return, but she doesn't. How could she have disappeared so quickly? But this isn't Island City, this isn't earth, this isn't even Fenton's asphalt paradise. This is the spirit world, the void. The Great Purple Abyss. Who knows what twists and turns one step will take you through?

Yolanda isn't coming back. He's on his own, again, and he can't afford to hang around here any longer. Nate picks one of the nearby lines and decides to follow it. Tracing the path of the line will force some consistency to his travels and at the very least he'll be able to find his way back to where he started from.

Maybe.

He tries to get closer to the line. He almost moves his legs, attempting to walk again, as if he's standing on a city sidewalk. Old habits. But he catches himself before he does it, and thinks about moving instead. He's *here* and he wants to be *there*, and off he goes, drifting slowly toward the line. Immediately his perception of his surroundings changes. As if he's looking through a thick, curved glass, he sees the mauve backdrop twist and distort. Its dark blue veins shrink into shriveled ribbons, except one which balloons into a sea, a vast morass that compresses the other marbled colors into zebra stripes. The anenomes are carried along with the deformity, moving around like checkerboard pieces; and the lines move as well, the straight ones bending themselves into Gordian tangles and Moebius strips and the twisted ones becoming straight. He loses his own line as it becomes part of some geometric thicket he cannot hope to disentangle.

He stops and looks behind him for the great white wall, but although he's been traveling for only a few seconds his starting point is gone, swallowed up by the vast blue nothing. He searches for some frame of reference, some feature he recognizes, but everything has been rearranged. Nothing is static. Everything is changed.

He's lost in a sea of nullity.

And not only is his line all tangled out of shape; it isn't even any closer than when he started.

So he flings a chain at it.

The instant he decides to extend his chain, one of the black spheres zips around in front of him, faster than he can see, a blur. It vehemently spews its squiggles, not in a cloud but in a coherent stream beginning at his right wrist, and the filaments *make* his chain. The spray solidifies into the familiar silver metal as the stream of squiggles sweeps out from his hand. Stunned, he forgets snaring the line and simply watches as his chain snakes across the void, longer and longer, reaching far into the distance. The stream stretches thinner and thinner but doesn't stop; its focus steadily tightens until it's like a laser beam shooting through the æther.

He finally halts the process. Instantly the output of the sphere is transformed from a stream back to cloud, but it holds its position near his hand. The gleaming chain floats there like the tether of a spacewalker. He moves it now, curling it toward the line. The sphere emits a sheet of filaments, encompassing the entire length of the chain, making it obey Nate's will.

He retracts. The sphere's emission snaps back to a cloud. As the chain comes reeling back, glowing filaments fly from his silver bracelet like sparks. The dark globe hangs steady in the air until the retraction is complete; then it rejoins the other two in their orbit.

Huh. So that's where his chains come from. They seem to go a lot farther in the spirit world than they did back home, though. Maybe the effort of crossing over limits the range of the spheres.

He wonders what else they can do.

Well, nothing's going to happen if he just floats around like some piece of cosmic jetsam. He wills himself back into motion, on what he thinks is his previous heading. It doesn't really matter anyway; one direction's as good as another when you don't know where you're going.

As soon as he starts moving again, the void starts distorting around him. A pinprick of black appears in the middle of the dark blue abyss and quickly grows, pushing the field of navy into a narrowing ring. The anenomes slide merrily about. The lines hump and quiver orgiastically. Nate pays none of them any more than cursory attention.

He wants to see how fast he can go.

He judges his velocity by the rapidity of the changes around him, and they quickly become a blur of colliding colors and streaks of light. But through it all he doesn't feel like he's moving; he could be standing still while the world mutates around him, as the patterns curl and pile and hump and vanish.

But this isn't getting him anywhere.

He slams on the psychic brakes and the void stops changing shape and color, settles into a mishmash of mauve and blue and black all coiled up together in a grandiose backdrop.

Okay, think about this. He's in the spirit world and he's acting like he's floating in outer space. But he isn't. There's no direction here, no up or down, no left or right. No distance. He thinks of himself as moving forward but there's really nothing to move *through*. The concept of *forward* doesn't mean anything here. It's just in his head. What he has to do is stop thinking like a person and start thinking like a ghost.

Thinking like a ghost? As Ellie would say, what the hell does that mean?

God. If this is where ghosts go, how do they ever find their way back to the places they haunt?

She's reached the ring of concrete around the stalk of fire. It goes roaring up only yards from where she stands, a great roiling pillar of smoke and light. It seems to erupt right out of the ground. The inside edge of the sidewalk is cracked and blackened. Heat must've been too much for it. Which is kind of strange, actually, because she doesn't really feel the temperature. It's warm but nowhere near what you would expect this close to such an inferno.

And just think—nobody can see it but her. She's the only one left who knows what's going on. Nate and Yolanda are both gone, Andy's dead, the police and firefighters can't stop it because they don't know what it is.

She's all alone.

And then she's not all alone anymore. The thing waddles out of the smoke and plops down on its haunches in front of her, looking at her with those flickering mushroom eyes. *Go ahead*, it's saying. *Jump into the fire. End it all and save me the trouble.*

She feels something in her hand, looks at it. Mr. Knob. His twisted cloth body, old and worn, has taken a spark and caught fire. The heat is making the fabric flutter in her grip. Her last friend in the world, burning up.

She holds onto him far longer than she should. Her hand begins to blister. In a minute it'll burn. She's so dry inside the fire will just spread right up her arm, eat her up lickety-split.

And save Fenton the trouble.

"*No!*" she shrieks.

The beast tenses to spring.

She throws Mr. Knob at it.

She puts all her fear, her grief, her anger, her hate into Mr. Knob's round little head. And somehow, as his burning form flies the short distance to the creature, Mr. Knob grows into a fireball that just keeps growing and growing. It's a thin fire—she can still see Mr. Knob's head inside it like a pit or a seed—but when it slams into the fungus creature and envelops it in a translucent embrace, it makes the beast writhe and squeal and then fall down, squirming and screeching and clawing at the insubstantial flames.

Fenton's pride and joy withers and sizzles. The elastic arms and legs whip around wildly. The screaming continues unabated, until it suddenly stops and then the fungus beast explodes in a shower of hot, sticky bits, like gobbets of tar, splashing up and sideways and in every direction, hitting Ellie like flak, sticking and burning. She doesn't try to wipe them off, doesn't even move, just stares at the oily ring where the beast had been.

The monster is gone. Mr. Knob remains. All that's left of him is his head, smoldering on the sidewalk. Ellie finds herself laughing. It's a hysterical, lunatic laugh and she stops as soon as she realizes she's doing it.

She takes a step toward Mr. Knob.

But a sheet of fire roars out of the column and blocks her path. She stops short as the fire curves around to her left and then turns left again, rejoining the tower. It encircles her, she's fenced in by fire. And then a black void opens in the tower to her right, beckoning. A doorway. Fenton is inviting her to enter.

Thank you, no, she thinks. Can't come in today. Places to go, you know how it is. Except he's not giving her a choice. The fence is slowly tightening, giving her less and less room to move. She can either stand her ground and let it catch her, or she can go through the dark doorway.

She stays on the sidewalk as long as there's room, but ultimately the fire wall traps her in a space so small that if she shivered the fire would get her. And it keeps on shrinking.

Can't let it touch her. Got to go down fighting. She owes it to Nate, to Yolanda. To herself.

The door stands open.

Maybe if she accepts its invitation, she'll get close enough to Fenton to punch his lights out.

In a psychic sense, of course.

She turns her back on the encroaching fire and steps through the doorway.

30

NATE HAS LOST TRACK OF how long he's been floating in the void, motionless, just thinking. Trying to sort things out. Trying to figure out how he's going to get back to the real world. The mental movement he tried doesn't seem to work. Physical movement is out of the question. There may be a door to earth somewhere in this great purple nothing, but there's no way in hell he's going to find it just by wandering around. Might as well comb all the beaches of the earth looking for a specific grain of sand.

. . . Door . . .

One of his satellites goes fizzing by. He watches it, stares at it.

Door.

The globes project energy into the physical world, energy that powers his chains and probably his regeneration, perhaps even energy that animates his dead flesh.

He's disembodied now. Maybe that makes him energy. So if he's energy, and the spheres project energy across dimensional barriers, maybe he can arrange things so they'll project *him*.

What he needs is a door. Come on, satellites, he thinks. Make a door.

They just keep circling him, hissing faintly. Door? What's a door?

Come *on*. Visualize. A gateway right here, to take him back.

A sphere floats serenely past his face. *Fizzzzzzz.*

"Damn it, I don't care who made you," Nate says. "You're *mine* now and you'll do what I want. Make a door!"

Nothing.

Okay. Maybe he needs to visualize more. He closes his eyes. Three spheres can make a triangle. So he wants a triangle-shaped door. Right in front of him. The orbs can make a triangle and they can use their squiggles to pry open the wall keeping him out of the physical world and he can step through the opening. That wouldn't be so hard, would it?

When he opens his eyes again, he sees his three satellites sitting in front of him, describing a triangle, base down. The space between them is filling up with squiggles. As he watches, the glowing filaments interlock with each other, pile up and melt together like pieces of glass in a furnace. And when they pile up the top of the triangle, a shudder sweeps through the glowing shape and it disappears, leaving the three black orbs and empty purple void between them.

Shit. It didn't work.

He reaches out slowly and puts his hand among the spheres. And sees the tips of his fingers disappear, then his hand. He pulls his arm back and hand and fingers return.

He did it. He made a door.

But where does it go?

One way to find out. He sticks his head through it. But all he sees is a series of dull blue-grey triangles, evenly spaced and separated by stretches of void. The string is growing as he watches, stretching farther into the distance—oops, he forgot, there is no *distance* here. Got to keep that in mind if he's ever going to figure this place out.

So where does the tunnel go?

He wills himself through the portal and now he's floating in between the triangles. He drifts to the first of the luminous geometric shapes and reaches out to touch it, but there's a resistance that increases as he gets closer; he gets within a foot or so of it and no matter how hard he pushes he can't move his hand forward another inch. It's like trying to push two magnets together.

And then, suddenly, the triangles come to life.

They light up in sequence like fluorescent bulbs, starting with the ones farther away from him, shining a luminous bluish white. It takes maybe two seconds for all the triangles to illuminate, and when the last one—the one nearest him—goes on he feels a sudden tremendous suction on his body, like somebody threw a switch to turn on a gigantic vacuum. It yanks him away from the gate and shoots him down the wormhole, and he can only hope it takes him somewhere he wants to go.

Ellie steps through the doorway and instantly things change. She's not standing in the middle of a tower of fire; she's in a little round building with brick walls and a bare concrete floor. Pipes and wires run everywhere, they snake across the ceiling and rise up from the ground and hang from the walls. On the wall next to the door is some sort of electrical panel, with a great big lever and a light that glows red like eyes reflecting light.

A metal door stands behind her, shut up tight. She must have walked *through* it somehow, or else it closed after she came in and she didn't hear it. Then she takes a closer look at it and decides that this door hasn't opened in quite a while. The metal is scorched and partially melted and it looks like it's fused with the jamb into a single sheet of iron.

Well, that settles that. Didn't come in that way, not getting out that way.

Next question: Where's Fenton? If he's here, she can't see him.

She walks forward slowly. The place is a mess. Many of the wires, detached from their moorings, hang down in loops and rock slowly back and forth, back and forth. The pipes glisten in the flickery light. Condensation, making them look like the slick guts of some enormous creature. Can't imagine where it's coming from; the air is dry and brittle with winter. At least, it was outside. In here it's kind of lurid and steamy.

She moves a handful of dangling cables near the wall, revealing a thick vertical pipe, hugely jointed like an arthritic finger, made of black iron streaked with rust. She squeezes between the pipe and the wall and finds herself at the edge of a more open part of the building, where the floor slopes concavely down to a metal lid. A drain or something. Maintenance hatch. Sewer access.

A way out?

Yeah, right.

She approaches the hatch, gets down on the floor and creeps over to look at it. Drawn to it. It's got some sort of design on it, a circle and four triangles, like a compass rose that isn't finished.

She's seen this pattern before. Where?

She remembers it had moss growing on it. . . .

Knife point.

That's where it was. Chiseled into the rock. Knife Point, which Fenton was planning to develop. Develop into what?

Touch it, Ellie. Lift it up. See what's underneath.

That voice again. Telling her what to do. Well she's not going to listen to it. She stands up, not taking her eyes off the metal hatch. What *is* underneath it, anyway?

Suddenly the lid bumps up, like someone poked it from below. Ellie jumps back a pace. The lid goes again, and this time when it falls back into place it lands on a set of blood-red, black-nailed fingers steepled on the concrete floor.

Something's coming to get her.

Look at the fingers.

Billy.

Her reaction is instinctive: she leaps forward, onto the lid, slamming it back into place, smashing the fingers. Except now that she's on it she doesn't see any fingers. In fact, now that she's on it, the metal plate doesn't look much like a hatch at all. The hinges seem to be all one piece, immobile.

And now that she's on the hatch, she can't get off it. Her feet are welded in place just like the front door. Her whole body—Nate's body —feels like it's on fire, hot acid racing up and down, up and down, toes to skull and back again.

She's been suckered. Again.

That son of a bitch.

Getting light-headed now . . . too hot, lava gathering at the base of her brain . . . pushing her up, up . . . pushing her *out.* . . .

And Ellie loses her grip as Nate's body begins to burn.

After a series of twists and turns and gut-wrenching drops and loops and switchbacks and spirals that would give a roller coaster designer enough ideas to build a thousand rides, the wormhole finally levels out again. Nate shoots along on his back, hardly noticing the triangles as they flash by. It's moving so fast that it's all a blur and he left most of his brain at the bottom of a corkscrew quite a ways back anyway.

The wormhole spits him out and he smashes into something, he can't see what, but it shatters like candy glass and pieces go spinning off in every direction. Some of the shards shoot through him, slice him up like ice knives, like when they went through the rain. But this time it only lasts a second, and then he's through the barrier and out of the void and back into the physical world.

On top of the tenement where he died, actually.

It's on fire, heavily involved in flames and heaving smoke. He's near the big ventilation unit, though it's partially fallen through the roof and big gusts of fire billow out of the narrow, jagged cleft this has created. Beyond that he can see the stubby shed where the stairs come out. Smoke dribbles from under the eaves. Fire in the stairwell. Place looks like it's been transplanted to Hell. All that's missing are little demons with pitchforks.

Doesn't matter, though. He would recognize this rooftop no matter what happened to it. He walks through the fire—it doesn't touch him, *can't* touch him, he's nothing but a ghost—toward where the pentagram was, where he died and came back as Fenton's puppet. It's not burning yet, though the heat has melted the black candles into puddles. Like tar.

He can see the Wright Project from here.

He goes to the edge of the roof. Through the blowing licks of flame he can see the edge of the nearest building of the complex. It looks just the way it did back in asphalt land, still cycling through ten seconds of eternity and then starting over again.

It seems like the whole world is on fire. Everywhere he looks, he sees burning buildings. The old hotel. The decrepit apartment buildings. Urban renewal, Fenton-style. Canal Street and Sutton Street are both choked by the burning wrecks of vehicles. Some are too big to be cars.

Fire trucks.

The city brought its resources to bear against the fire and they were destroyed. And now, apparently, the fire has free rein. *Fenton* has free rein.

"No you don't," Nate whispers. "No you don't, you son of a bitch."

Unimpressed, the fire burns on.

The gathering energy builds up inside her, shoots her out of Nate's body Roman candle style. She crashes through the roof of the roundhouse, bursts into the fiery sky. The buildings of the Wright Project loom around her until the flames snatch her and send her still higher, up and up and up, over the tops of the structures, higher than any of the buildings nearby. Eddies of superheated air swirl around her, buffet her, spin her around like a drifting cinder. She's becoming part of the inferno, a wisp of fire lost in the maelstrom.

And higher.

And higher.

And she's almost to the clouds now, they float overhead like congealed lumps of dark, greasy fat. The buildings of the Project are laid out beneath her, the five buildings huddled in a circle as if for protection from the chaotic streets around them.

But the attack came from the inside, and the Project never had a chance.

It seems she's gone as high as she's going to. The rising heat keeps her just beneath the smoky clouds, not pushing her higher but not letting her fall either. She can see much of Island City from her lofty, precarious perch. The old city is dark beneath her, dark and squat and rancid, no lights anywhere—the fire must have taken out the power—and it's burning, so much of it is burning. Only the width of the river has kept the fire from reaching the island and the rest of Island City.

Although it looks like the Hunter River Bridge is burning.

It must be the pavement. What else is on the bridge to burn? Whatever it is it's not the best fuel in the world, the fire is low and blue, like a gas flame turned down low. Ghost fire.

Flashing lights swirl on the far side of the central arch of the bridge. They've got the drawbridge up for the first time she can remember, trying to keep the fire on the mainland, away from the population center. She wonders if they're evacuating the inhabitants of the island using the other three bridges, or if they're sitting tight and hoping they can check the fire on the mainland.

They can't, but they don't know that.

She watches the fire ooze along the bridge, staying low and blue, until suddenly an orange arc of it swings down and ignites something beneath the bridge, something she never noticed before. The fire quickly spreads across this thing and she sees it's a room or building or something, clinging to the underside of the bridge like a monkey to a tree.

It burns for a while, then there's an explosion and a shower of sparks that cascade down to the river in a blinding sequence of flares.

And the drawbridge slowly begins to grind shut. The flashing lights back quickly away from the closing gap. Ellie stares, aghast, at the cancerous fire growing on the belly of the bridge.

Fenton just took out the drawbridge control center.

The barbarian is opening the gates.

Nate jumps off the roof and lets himself glide to the ground. He falls slowly, as slowly as he wants to, because he's a ghost and gravity doesn't have any more claim on him than he wants to give it.

He lands where Billy landed after Ellie killed him. In the grass. At the edge of the Wright Project. The nearest building is only about ten yards away, wrapped in fire, windows dark as the void he just escaped from.

Dark.

Why are the windows dark?

He looks behind him. The entire western wall of the tenement is ablaze. Surely that should be reflected in the windows of the Wright Project, but it's not. They're like little pools of pitch, and they don't change as he gets closer to them.

Maybe he should go inside and find out what's there.

He stops next to the building. The windows, even the first floor windows, are too high up for him to see through. He could float up to them but there's no point, they're not transparent like normal windows are. So it's just a matter of getting in. He's a ghost, so it shouldn't be too hard.

But he hesitates. Because on the other side of this wall, it's Fenton's world. Fenton's rules. Whatever spell he laid down on the Wright Project is still in effect, and if Nate crosses the boundary, will it catch him too? Or will he, as a latecomer to the party, not be invited?

He bets *not invited*.

And if he's wrong?

Well, at least he'll only have ten seconds to think about it.

31

He can walk through walls.

He finds this out by attempting to touch the building. Instead of feeling a solid surface, his hand sinks into the structure like it's made of warm gelatin. He pulls back, startled, but there isn't any brick or concrete dripping off his hand and it appears to be still intact so he pushes it in again. The side of the building sort of curves in on his arm, the way a balloon does when you poke your finger into it. It's like the building is *almost* as solid as he is, but not quite. Or would it be the other way around?

Doesn't matter, and there's nothing to it, really. He just takes a few steps forward and he's on the other side, like when he and Yolanda crossed the storm into the spirit world. It's a bit of a slog, but nothing worse than walking through deep mud.

As soon as he's in the building, Nate wishes he had stayed outside.

He's in somebody's apartment. In the living room. It's small and kind of cramped, with a threadbare couch and chair crowded together against the outside wall facing a television—an old one, huge, bulky, with a knob for changing channels—that sits across the room. To his right is a tiny kitchen nook, to his left two doors. Bathroom and bedroom, maybe. Behind him is a teensy window. Can't see anything through it. It's black as ink on this side, too, like light gets lost on its way through the glass.

The television is on, replaying ten seconds of a show that hasn't aired in fifteen years. Someone's sacked out on the couch watching it. A guy. He seems to be asleep. The guy grunts and rolls over, every ten seconds. And every ten seconds the ceiling collapses in flames, smashing television and sleeper, crashing through Nate's spirit form and leaving an unpleasant abraded feeling in its wake.

But that's not what makes Nate wish he weren't here.

The place has an atmosphere.

Not just that. It's a presence. Pervasive, invasive, lurking coiled in the air like an invisible serpent. It feels, it hears, it sees, it senses. Nate has blundered into its domain and it knows he doesn't belong here so it tries to incorporate him into the ten-second regime. Tries to pull him in. When the ceiling goes back into place, when the scene on the television starts over, Nate feels time folding in on itself, doubling back. He feels it as a tug, no other way to describe it, a tug on his gut like somebody's trying to turn him inside out. And it would do it, too, if he didn't react in time—not really turn him inside out but turn him around, yank him back and make him start the last ten seconds over again.

In fact, how does he know it didn't? Would his thoughts be exactly the same for each ten-second sweep? How could he tell what was new and what was recycled?

Crash goes the ceiling, a falling, crumbling, flaming wreck.

Other bodies in the rubble, carried down from upstairs. Nate didn't notice them before.

Loop.

Ceiling overhead. Television playing. Guy sleeping. Nate feeling like he's been shot in the stomach with a forty-five.

The place has an atmosphere.

Void.

Yolanda's sick of the void. Getting into the spirit world was a lot easier than getting out seems to be. Maybe that's why there aren't more ghosts running around: everybody's lost.

Like her.

Enough of the whining. Got to find a way back. There's a bad-ass spirit whose butt needs kicking. "You can't hold Yolanda, no sir," she says. Say it out loud, that'll make it true. Her voice seems muted even though there's nothing around to absorb it. Or maybe it sounds that way *because* there's nothing here. It just goes and goes and goes and disappears into the purple stuff. If you tried to talk in outer space, what would you hear?

Getting silly, Yolanda, she thinks. This ain't gonna do her reputation any good, no sir. Go tracking down dead fathers and mothers and sisters and brothers, go speaking with the spirits, and now she's stuck in their world and she's helpless as a baby on an Interstate. Don't think so.

She needs to find something to hang onto, something in the real world she can use as an anchor. Something she can use to reel herself in. Got to be something strong. Something she can get a fix on, something she won't lose. Can't use the hotel, the timelines are all messed up there and God only knows where she'll end up. Got to be something else.

Like the Wright Project, and Nicholas Fenton.

Sure it's crazy. It's walking right up to the lion and putting your head in its mouth and inviting it to please bite down.

But what's the point of being dead if you can't take a few risks?

The ceiling crashes down, smashes everything. Then it's back where it started, and so is Nate.

The place has an atmosphere.

Got him.

It's tougher reaching into the physical world from the spiritual than vice versa. Maybe she's lacking something now, some *vitality*, that she had before Fenton and the beast worked her over. So it was tough, sure, but now she's got him. Two points on a line, Fenton and Yolanda. A line out of the void and straight into the fire.

Because that's what her contact with Fenton's energy brings into her mind: fire. The flickering light, the smoke, the acrid tang in the air that makes your eyes water and closes up your throat. But none of that matters.

Because she's got him, and she's going to use him to haul her ass out of here.

"Hang on tight, Mr. Fenton," she whispers. "This time Yolanda's coming to you."

She's got to get out of here.

Ellie tries to kick her way free of the fire tower, like she's swimming or something. Doesn't work. She moves a little bit but not nearly as much as she needs to. The fire seems to have some kind of a grip on her, hangs onto her like deep, sticky mud. Suction. Doesn't want to let her out.

Can't go down, either. It's like trying to swim against a geyser. The rising current of the flames keeps her at her present level, won't let her get any closer to the ground. Like it or not, she's staying where she is.

Don't like it.

Can't do much about it.

She stops trying to move and lets herself hang, gives herself a few seconds to rest, to think, and that's when she notices that something's in the fire with her. She can see it in the flames, a distortion, like a lens of some kind tricking the light into circles. It hovers not far from her, hiding in the licks of flame, keeping its distance; but as she floats there it shows itself more, like it's getting bolder. Like it's concluded she has no tricks up her sleeve.

Safe conclusion.

Can't be Fenton. Fenton wouldn't hide. If he wanted something from her, he would just come roaring right at her, take it if he could and demand it if he couldn't. But even though it's not Fenton, it's probably nobody else she wants to talk to either.

Then it says, *Who are you?*

The voice isn't audible, not in the traditional sense of being heard with the ears. No, this is more of a visual thing: communication by fire, changes in shape and intensity conveying meaning. And, somehow, she understands it. And not only that, she *recognizes* the voice.

It's Andy.

She doesn't know how she knows him. Certainly there's nothing left of the man she knew. The scrubbed face, the short blonde hair, the wide ingenuous eyes are gone, but there's no doubt who it is. And somehow he recognizes her, too. She says his name and tells him hers and he explodes into a string of babble, one panicky question following another with no pause for an answer. Just as well, since she has none.

Finally he runs dry, and after a moment asks one more question. *What are we going to do?*

Wish I knew, says Ellie.

~~~

Crash! The ceiling caves in. Then it's back overhead.

The place has an—

No! How many times has he recycled that thought? How many times has the ceiling fallen through him? How many precious minutes has he wasted in here?

Crash!

The place has—

Stop it!

He's not part of this scene. He's got to stay above it. Come on, start moving toward the door. . . .

The ceiling comes smashing down. Nate keeps moving. The door is getting closer. The living room is small, it doesn't take long for him to cross it and reach the hallway. It's shrouded in a pall of black smoke that blots out anything more than a few feet distant.

He feels a sudden pain in his gut, like somebody jabbing him with a spear. It passes momentarily with a wrenching sensation, as if the spear has a hook on the end and is being used to turn him inside out. Then it's gone. But it'll come back in ten seconds. It's the displacement, hitting him hard because he resists it. If he flows with it, there'll be no pain, just a *blink* and then everything starts over again.

Can't think like that. Weakens him. It'll make him Fenton's prisoner if he isn't careful. That's what Fenton wants: more souls to stoke the fire. And Nate has no intention of burning in *that* furnace.

So why doesn't he do the smart thing, and get out of here?

Because he still doesn't know how to stop Fenton, that's why.

Blink.

Ouch.

Can you help me get out of here, Andy?

How? he asks. *I tried, I can hardly move.*

Me either, says a new voice. It's coming from above them somewhere, but she can't find the source. Andy's a refraction and so is she, presumably, but this voice seems to come right of the fire.

And its sentiments are echoed. A multitude of voices, up and down the column of flame. A chorus of lament. *Trapped, we're trapped . . . Can't move . . . my baby, where's my baby . . . I want my mother . . .* A
~~~

hundred cries, a thousand, all tied up in the fire.

And then she realizes that it's not fire at all.

It's the spirits of the Wright Project.

She and Andy are different. They're afterthoughts. They weren't captured like the others were. Maybe that's why they cling to the fire like wads of gum, stuck to it but not incorporated into it. At least, not yet. Maybe there are other spirits here too, like them. Hiding.

The voices keep babbling until a rumble sweeps through the tower, instantly silencing them. All of them.

Fenton.

The rumble is a command of silence, even though it carries no words, and the spirits in the fire—the spirits that *are* the fire—heed it. Their master orders, and they obey.

Where are you, Fenton? she asks. *Where are you hiding?*

Who are you talking to? Andy says.

Come out, Fenton! Let me see you! Are you gonna go on hiding forever?

A murmur rises from the other spirits. *What are you doing? Are you crazy? Quiet, be quiet, you heard him!*

Yeah, she heard him. And she's damn sick of him.

Come on out, you fat bastard! she cries. *Show your face!*

"You want to see my face?" His voice rises up from somewhere below, smoky and oddly familiar. It drains the anger out of her, sucks in her courage and spits out the kernel of fear at its core. She sees something moving down there, though she can't see what it is until it shoots up into the air. It rises up to her level and hovers there, flames dribbling from it, dripping to the ground like burning fat. It's a humanoid figure wrapped in a mantle of fire.

It's Fenton.

He lets her see his face.

And his face is Nate's.

32

HE WALKS UP THE SMOKE-filled corridor, the ghost of a man moving through the ghost of a building, no idea where he's going or what he'll do when he gets there. But he keeps moving, because it's better than standing still. Nobody else seems to have the same idea, though. The hallway's dark and quiet as the inside of a coffin. Where are the alarms? Where are the people? Where—

Blink.

That was a bad one. It doubles him over like a sledgehammer to the solar plexus. But it's good, in a way. It brings him back to reality. He is not in a burning building. He is in the spectre of the Wright Project and it's however Fenton wants it to be. No alarms. No sprinklers. No people. Just death. Death in the smoke, death in the fire, death in the very structure of the place. And all of it going to feed Fenton.

Keep going. Because Fenton's here somewhere. He suspects, actually, that Fenton is in the tower of fire. Or else he *is* the tower of fire.

So what's he doing in here instead of going right to the source?

Nate would like to think he's exploring Fenton's territory, trying to find something to use against him. Trying to find a way to stop him.

Yeah, he'd like to think that.

It feels a lot better than thinking he's gone chickenshit.

The link is a glistening thread from her mind to his, Yolanda at one end and Fenton on the other, getting closer together every second. The distance between them isn't physical, oh no, Yolanda's not going to make that mistake and get herself lost in a paradox of infinite distances separating places that are really right next to each other. Bad enough she tried physical movement and misplaced Nate Watson. He's probably still lost back there in the void. She'll find him and bring him out, after she's out herself.

Won't be long now. The link is getting hotter every second (though she really shouldn't think in terms of *seconds* either, because seconds are an illusion, time is seamless, especially here)—hotter and, concurrently, more dangerous. The closer she gets, the greater the chance Fenton will notice she's coming and blow her away.

She can only hope he's too busy to be paying any attention to her.

Fenton has stolen her husband's body.

His uniform is gone, burned away and replaced by a cloak of fire draped over him like a mantle. The handcuffs are gone too, replaced by bracelets of white-hot light—though maybe they *are* the cuffs, actually, superheated by the presence of Fenton's flame spirit.

The fire doesn't cover Nate's body completely. It leaves the front of his torso bare, so Ellie can see the huge Y-shaped cut where the kids cut him open. It's enormous and jagged, a crudely performed imitation of an autopsy incision. Sloppy but effective. Ellie suspects it is being revealed for her benefit. *See what happened to your husband?*

His face has changed. It's obvious that the spirit animating the flesh is not benign. Even leaving aside the eyes, which are dark and smoldering with little sparklike flashes deep inside, Fenton has made Nate's face cruel. The smile is a sneer, the brows are twisted, the posture of the head conveys arrogance and a cool upper-crust brutality.

"A body," Fenton coos, checking himself out. Holding up his hands and turning them one way then another. He shows them to her. Nate's wedding ring is gone, melted off his finger. "A good body. At last. Thank you." His voice is like molasses, sharp and sweet and black as a pirate's heart.

Andy says, *Nate . . . is that you?*

Fenton laughs.

It's not Nate, Ellie says. *It's Nicholas fucking Fenton.*

"Nicholas fucking Fenton!" He holds up his arms. Liquid fire spurts from his hands, twirls into rings and bizarre patterns. Like Nate's chains, only much more precise, much more dangerous. "I'm back and I'm going to finish what I started. The power of life and death, the power of fire, all for me! I shouldn't be so fortunate."

You got *that* right, Ellie thinks.

She looks at his hand again. The wedding band is gone. The ring Nate scrimped and saved for, during those first years when they had loans to pay, when they were just barely getting by. The symbol of their marriage, gone in an instant.

Something inside of her snaps.

You son of a bitch, get out of my husband's body! she shouts.

"Okay," Fenton says.

The fire leaves Nate's body, streams out of his ears, his nose, his mouth. His features go slack, like a rubber Halloween mask on a styrofoam head. The streams of flame swirl around above him, forming a manlike glob in the air above his head; then it splits back into fragments and darts back into him, lighting him up with malign intent. "There! How was that?" Fenton giggles, then suddenly his face goes all dark and mottled and dangerous. "This flesh is *mine* now, and I'll come and go as I please. Not as you please. Don't command me again." And then he giggles again. "Unless we're in bed together and I ask you to."

He roars away in a plume of fire and smoke, like a torch flying through the air. He heads northwest, toward the little park. *In your dreams, pal*, Ellie says.

Big talk, now that he's too far away to hear.

He's out of his mind. Psychotic. Maybe he was like this before, maybe he got this way while he was . . . wherever he was during the twenty years of his absence. Either way, he's nuts. Does this make him less dangerous, or more?

Was he serious about them being in bed together?

That bastard, Andy says. *He can't talk to you like that.*

More big talk. *Yes he can*, she says. *Until we figure a way out of this, he can talk to us any way he wants to.*

The son of a bitch.

Nate walks through stretches where the corridor is engulfed in a swirling corkscrew of flames. He walks past curious burn marks on the walls, marks that spark and smolder as if about to birth new sheets of fire themselves. The hallway goes on and on, straight from one end of the building to the other, closed doors on each side passing slowly by as he walks.

Blink.

Nate grits his teeth and keeps going.

Through a cloud of smoke, he sees the hallway's end.

There's a metal door ahead, with a square little window lined with chicken wire. The window's partially smashed but it hasn't been broken. Take a lot of force to get through reinforced glass.

Then he sees the pile at the foot of the door. Hesitates and keeps going. He gives the pile only cursory attention.

Bodies.

A whole heap of bodies, children and women and men jammed up against the metal door. One of the men still clutches a blue aluminum baseball bat. The weapon that smashed the glass. Nate can imagine them pounding away at the door, beating on it, cursing it, all the while breathing in the toxic smoke that fills up the hallway, pushes out the air.

They must've come out of their apartments and tried to get out through the front door, but it wouldn't open. He isn't naive enough to think it was stuck. Fenton locked it. Maybe he locked all the doors, some kind of automatic mechanism designed to keep the tenants trapped in the burning buildings. Maybe the only way out was through the tiny little windows in the apartments.

Blink.

Can't take the loopbacks anymore. He takes a blind step forward, through the door. There's a concrete landing outside. Nate walks out onto it, then onto the grass. The grass feels funny now, kind of like soft butter, like he could sink into it if he wasn't careful. It's not solid like the floor of the Wright Project. The difference between phantom ground and real ground, he supposes. Phantom ground is harder.

A few yards in front of him is the burning wreckage of fire and police vehicles.

A few yards to his left is a sidewalk leading into the center of the Project. Leading to Fenton.

The temptation to walk forward through the debris, and to keep walking, is so strong as to be disgusting. He turns away from the spectacle of the flaming machine carcasses, and sees something flash across the sky from the fire tower. A streak of light, a fireball, a comet. It arches over the buildings at an angle toward the river, leaving a trail that hangs and fades like a fragmenting ribbon. He follows the trail to where it begins but there's nothing to see in the tower, just coils of fire twining and curling around each other.

He looks again at where the projectile disappeared from view. Maybe he should go that way and see if he can find where it landed, if it landed at all. Find out what it is, where it came from.

Hah.

He knows where it came from.

He's just trying to postpone his trip to the center of the Project. The center of hell. The place and person where all the destruction began. Nicholas Fenton.

Nate turns away from Canal Street and walks slowly down the sidewalk, into the Project.

Yolanda can feel Fenton's movement, but it doesn't affect the link. She's too close, his emanations are too strong, for her to lose him. Still, the feedback she's getting from him dips a little, like he's moving away from a weak spot—the Wright Project grounds, probably—and then shoots up again. He's gone to another aneurysm in the dimensional wall. Maybe the hotel.

She'll find out soon. She's almost there. And she thinks, God willing, that Fenton still hasn't noticed her approach.

Won't be long now. The void is starting to fuzz out around her and the physical world is coming into view. It starts as an outline, trees and bushes pencilled in over the mottled purple emptiness of the spirit world and gradually growing thicker, denser. The abyss at her feet solidifies into lumpy ground, the abyss overhead thickens into a sullen, cloudy sky the color of used-up iron.

She lets the link go. She can guide herself in from here. She just needs to *attune,* get herself completely in sync with the physical world again. She lets herself feel the trees and the shrubs and the ground, lets their essence flow through her. Yes, this is real, this is good, it's bringing her back. All the way back.

She's in a park. An ugly, overgrown little park with trees like gnarled grey fingers and bushes like withered hair, ground covered with slick leaves decaying into a mulmy film over earth that's rotted from the inside out.

"Yolanda takes it back," she says softly. "This is *not* good, no sir."

Where's Fenton? Close, he's close, the air reeks of him, his power fills it like cheap cologne. This is another one of his places. Through the wilderness of brambles she sees a white light and she heads for it. Slowly. She feels something pushing against her, abjuring her. Repulsion hex. Hard to stand against, but she quickly catches its rhythm and moves forward in its lulls. Not a very good hex, actually. Not strong enough to keep somebody out if they're determined to come in.

She's almost to the light before she suddenly thinks that maybe the hex isn't about keeping something out. Maybe it's about keeping something *in*.

Maybe she doesn't really want to be here.

Too close to stop now, though. She pushes the final few steps to the edge of the brambles, the edge of the light. It's a garden in the middle of the park, a little garden with asphalt on the ground and spent flowers sagging in decrepit beds. Cracked and crumbling benches are scattered about like grazing sheep. And near her vantage point there's a bronze statue of a man, and in front of the statue is Nate Watson's body, though it's obvious that Nate Watson isn't in there, no sir. The aura is all wrong. The aura is all smoke and fire and heat and hate.

Fenton.

He's jacking off, staring up at the statue, and Yolanda would swear it's staring back at him, its head bent down to meet his eyes. If the statue had any available openings he would probably be hammering away at it, humping the bronze. Pathetic, in a sick kind of way.

It's the statue that's pulsing. There's something inside it trying to get out. That's what's generating the repulsion, that's why it rises and falls, rises and falls. It rises as the trapped thing exerts itself and falls as it rests. Not a hex at all. Something trapped, that should stay trapped but doesn't want to.

What could it be?

And what'll it do when Fenton breaks it loose?

33

Nate stops at the ring of concrete surrounding the fire tower. There's a doll's head lying on the sidewalk. It's round, mostly, and it's intact, mostly. A bit scorched, but otherwise undamaged. It sits in a charred smear that looks like somebody dumped out crematory ashes and then spread them around with his shoe.

The doll is facing upward and smiling like it knows the most amusing secret. Nate stoops to pick it up before remembering he can't. He's just a ghost, right? But then he thinks, the Wright Project is a ghost too. So maybe he can.

Nope. His hand passes through it. Makes him tingle though. Like electricity. He wonders what it means. How it got here. Where it came from. What it could tell him, if it could talk.

Nate straightens up and looks at the scorching column. He had half-expected Fenton to come roaring out of it and try to burn him up, but that's apparently not going to happen.

So does he dare go in after him?

The fire is all around him. Except for the doll's head with its enigmatic smile, he's totally alone. No help. No advice. No backup. Nothing. He wishes Ellie were here so he could kiss her one last time. He wishes Yolanda were here so he could pick up some of her self-confidence. He wishes Frank were here to watch his back.

They're not. And they're not going to be.

Okay.

Do it.

Eyes on the fire, he slowly walks forward.

~~~

</div>
~~~

Nate.

Oh, God, Nate, thinks Ellie. Stop.

She spotted him as he came down the sidewalk and she and Andy have been hollering at him but it's no good, he can't hear them, he doesn't communicate the way they do as part of the fire. He's not sensitive to what they're saying.

And now he's about to step into the fire, like he can't see it or thinks it won't hurt him.

Suicide.

Nate! she screams.

Stop, Nate! Andy shouts.

No flicker of notice from Nate.

Come on! she calls. *The rest of you—help me! Yell to him, tell him to stop!*

For a second there's no response, and then a small voice says, *He told us to be quiet.*

He's not here now, Ellie says.

He's everywhere, a different one says. Soft, like it's afraid Fenton is listening.

That's just bullshit, Ellie says. *Fenton is not God.*

Nate can help us, Andy says. *He's special. Right, Ellie?*

Yes! she says. *Yes, he's special! Fenton keeps trying to stop him but he keeps coming back. Fenton's afraid of him.*

Fenton's not afraid of anything, the second speaker says.

But he's the one we saw, a third voice says. It sounds confused. *Remember? Back in the . . . other place.*

That's right, we saw him in the other place.

The spirits take up the murmur about the "other place," whatever the hell that is—where the Wright Project went when it was gone, she guesses. So Nate found his way there somehow, and then found his way back again, and he's still on Fenton's ass.

She becomes aware of a warm feeling swelling within her, pushing out the fear that's been coiled like a poisonous snake in her stomach. It takes her a moment to realize what it is: Pride. In Nate.

That's her husband down there, and he won't be stopped by the likes of Nicholas Fenton.

The murmur of the other spirits increases in intensity, and now Nate has taken a step back from the column and is looking around as if trying to figure out where a strange, half-audible sound is coming from.

I think he hears us, Andy says.

I hope you're right, Ellie says.

While Yolanda watches, the guy in Nate Watson's body is getting awfully worked up. And the air seems to be tightening, like it's solidifying and constricting around her. The swells of repulsion have faded into a seamless low-level pressure, but behind the pressure a crescendo is building, the way water piles up behind a dam and makes it burst.

This is not going to be the place to be when the captured energy busts loose.

Fenton grits his teeth. Holding back the orgasm. Building up the pressure inside, so it'll have greater power when it finally explodes. That's what'll free the trapped thing: not the inevitable spurt of semen, but the pent-up tension about to be released.

She gonna stand here and let it happen?

No, sir.

Yolanda steps out of the bushes, strides over between Fenton and the statue. His eyes are closed.

She says, "*Excuse* me."

Fenton's eyes flick open, unfocused, staring up at the sky. Then they come down and light on her. He's got flames in his gaze, way at the back, the color of a forest fire glowing over a ridge. Then he closes his eyes again, like she's too trivial even to waste a raised eyebrow on.

The indignity. *Dissed.* By a hunk of stolen meat.

Nobody disses Yolanda.

Unfortunately she can't think of anything to do about it. Too bad she's not solid, she'd whack him one with her handbag.

Fenton grunts, once.

Uh oh.

Yolanda dives out of the way as Fenton's stolen penis erupts, not in white liquid but in fire, like he's pissing gasoline and somebody struck a match or he's got a wicked case of the clap. The burning stream breaks against the statue, curling over and around it, bathing it, heating it. The bronze starts to glow.

A few seconds later, it explodes.

The blast enters the physical and the spiritual worlds and savages them both. Yolanda sees the pavement crack and run beneath her insubstantial hands, sees the pebbled benches and the brick-lined flowerbeds erased, turned into long trails of fine rubble. The shockwave flattens her like a steamroller, makes her feel like a piece of paper somebody scribbled on. She starts to sink into the elastic earth, but then a terrible force seizes her and pulls her out again, drags her back toward Fenton and the statue. Groggy, she struggles to resist the pull and manages to slow her backward progress. She looks over her shoulder. Where the statue had stood there's now an erratic, pulsing ring of fire, but it's a different kind of fire, it burns *in* instead of out, sucking and feeding on itself.

Another gate.

Where the hell is Fenton going now?

Then the air over the park lights up. Bands of fire come arching in from every which-way, the children of Fenton's inferno coming home to their father. He stands in front of the roaring vortex, arms upraised, flames pouring from his body. The incoming streams crash into him, snaking down his arms like lightning down a rod and then erupting from his body to go swirling down the wormhole.

Slipping . . . Can't hold on. . . .

She loses her grip and the vortex stretches her out, pulls her in, eats her up.

The last thing she hears is Fenton laughing.

An explosive shudder shakes the air, a shudder Nate remembers. He felt the same thing after the Wright Project got ripped from its foundations and sucked into the gate back in Fenton's pocket world. He looks up at the fire tower, wondering if the voices he heard from it —faint voices crying for him to stay away—were all in his head. He's lost everything else, why not his mind too? But no, he thinks they were real. The voices of the souls Fenton captured in his scheme. The souls of the Wright Project.

And as he watches the tower begins to bend, while all around him the smaller flames roar into the air like streamers, arching away overhead toward the park.

Fenton's park.

Maybe he should have followed the comet after all.

~~~
~~~

Ellie sees the light gather off to the northwest, where the park is, but there's nothing she can do about it except wonder what it is. Can't go there, can't tell Nate about it. So when it climaxes in a liquid burst of illumination, gobbets of glow splashing around like radioactive milk, all she can do is stare. Well, stare and ignore Andy's questions. He keeps insisting on asking her things. Like she knows what's going on any better than he does.

All around, the fires are leaving the gloomy seared city, shooting into the air, bending, converging and cascading into the park. Even the ghostly blue fire from the Hunter River Bridge retracts, lifting up from the pavement and swirling southward to the park like wayward neon.

And after all the other fires are gone, the suction comes for them. The tug becomes inescapable. The tower leans into it, whips around as if in a high wind, making it look like the earth is shaking in crazy spasms.

Then the earth lets go, and they go screaming into the air. The dark buildings rush past below them in a blurred parade. The flight lasts only a few seconds before they bank down toward the park, into the clearing in the middle where Fenton's statue stands, and the world is just a black and grey smear except for the park and the clearing and the ring of inward-burning fire and Fenton, in Nate's body, standing in front of it with his arms raised up like he's being mugged.

They go *through* Fenton on their way into the ring.

They're out again in a second but Fenton's odious aura clings to Ellie like filthy mud; clings to her spirit in clumps and she doesn't think it'll ever come off, not ever. Little bits of Fenton attached to her like cancers.

Then they shoot into the dark ellipse of the ring, and all her thoughts are left behind, and Fenton's cackle rings like crystal in her ears.

Nate feels the pull too, the pull from the park, and though it isn't strong enough to drag him in it does make him a bit light-headed. Or maybe it's just vertigo caused by the sudden dispersion of the Wright Project. It simply collapses, like it was nothing but a picture drawn on a balloon and somebody stuck it with a pin. Its erasure leaves him standing in an empty field that looks almost exactly like it did before

Fenton brought the Project back.

Well, almost exactly. A grass fire of some significant proportion seems to have swept through the place. And the surrounding buildings are looking even more burned-out and decrepit than they used to, though every trace of the inferno is gone and the wreckage isn't even smoldering. Not even in Canal Street, where the twisted metal of destroyed vehicles sit like expensive New Age statuary.

He doesn't spare much time checking them out as he races past.

He has to get to the park.

He's afraid he'll be too late to see or stop what's happening, and he is. The park is dead again, whatever animated it is gone. He rushes into it, straight for the clearing. That's the focal point of the power that was here. The garden, the statue.

And when he steps out onto the asphalt, it's immediately obvious that whatever happened here was catastrophic. The pavement is blasted, bombed out, scraped down to nothing. The benches have been blown off their bases and now describe lines of rubble like rays from where the statue stood. The area has been scoured clean of the scraggly brown vegetation that had been starting to emerge from the pavement.

He walks slowly to the shattered pedestal where the statue stood. Twisted pieces of bronze are scattered around like seeds. In front of the pedestal is a body, lying on its back, its features blasted into unrecognizability. Its arms are stretched out over its head and ashes nestle in the crooked embrace of its blackened ribs. It seems almost to have *melted* into the asphalt, merged with the pavement.

Nate steps over the carcass, not looking at it too closely. The ruined pedestal is in front of him now. Its top is cracked and scarred by fire. The stump of a core of some kind protrudes a few inches from the cement. It takes him a moment to realize the core is made of bone and not iron.

Human bone, by the looks of it. He bends down, looks at it more closely, and when he does he notices something on the ground behind the pedestal. More bodies. The blast must have radiated out from the front of the statue, because these bodies are in better shape than one that's been melted; they're hardly damaged at all. Well, one of them, a guy lying on his stomach, looks a bit cooked, like a hot dog left on the grill too long; but the other is intact and therefore he can see quite plainly that it is Ellie.

Ellie.

He rushes to the corpse, kneels down beside it. Ellie. Her eyes are open and glassy, her mouth twisted into a frightened grimace. Her skin has a faint, waxy, cyanotic cast. Her right side, not far from her kidney area, is a mass of crusted blood. There, an injury. Maybe somebody stabbed her. Maybe it wasn't Fenton's monstrous offspring.

It's a sad day when you have to hope your wife was stabbed to death.

Oh, Ellie.

He leans down to kiss her, even though he can't possibly touch her. His lips brush hers.

And stick to them.

His face tingles. Vertigo swirls in on him again, spins him around and around and then dissipates, leaving him lying on his back staring up at the stars.

He sits up, feeling strangely heavy, limbs like icicles. He looks down at himself and sees the curve of breasts and two slim, slightly bluish arms ending in small hands. He slowly lifts his arms up and looks at his wrists. Bare. But then the skin bubbles and splits, and a clear viscous liquid bubbles out and solidifies into silver bands.

He's inside Ellie's body. The body that Fenton stole from her.

He looks at the pedestal.

No matter what Fenton did, no matter where he went, it won't be far enough to save him from the Night Watchman.

NIGHT
WATCHMAN

34

Nate wanders through the empty streets, not sure where he's going. His senses, in Ellie's body, are shockingly acute after the days he spent in his own deadened shell. There's pain from Ellie's wound, for one thing, a dull throb that occasionally flares into a hot, stabbing agony shooting across his back. She probably needs medical attention but he's not going to find a doctor in this neighborhood, not tonight. He'll be lucky if he can find a working phone. All the street lamps are dead, and no lights shine from any of the buildings.

Fenton's knocked the Canal District back to the stone age.

He can smell the burned odor that lingers in the air, sharp as the crack of a whip. He can feel the chilly bite of the late autumn air. Ellie's body quickly begins to shiver with the cold. He needs to find heat and shelter. And, later, a doctor. He can't find Fenton if he dies in the street.

Nate looks around. He's managed to end up on River Street, one block up from Cross Street and the park, two blocks from the river. Overhead, the removal of the thick, sordid clouds and the absence of the streetlights allows the slivered moon to cast a pallid illumination over the city. Its cold, grey light shines on the burned-out field where the Wright Project stood; Nate's got a view straight down River Street to the abandoned, burned-out lot. Looks like scar tissue. In the moonlight the damaged buildings around him are hulking, cartilaginous things decorated with shadowlike patterns left by the fire.

He notices he casts a faint, elongated shadow. Turning around, he sees a glow from up the street. Electric lights. He goes that way, shivering like crazy. Won't it be a pisser if he dies of hypothermia? Get killed, come back as a zombie, get killed again, come back as a ghost, reanimate your wife's body, then die of exposure. Oh, yeah. That'd be hilarious.

He stops at the corner of Bayshore. Across the way is a huge warehouse, lit up with a string of pale sodium lights that must run off a generator. A big loop of a driveway goes up to the warehouse, guarded by chain link gates. To the right of the driveway is the backside of a garage, with big black glass doors facing the street. Neither structure looks particularly bad off. The inferno must've missed it. Kitty corner to it, though, there's an apartment building that was hit pretty hard.

Choosy fire.

It's probably too much to hope that the heating system in the warehouse runs off emergency power, but maybe he can find a space heater or something. The fence would be a simple climb even if he didn't have his chains, except that it's topped with a barbed wire crest that sticks out at forty-five degrees; but that comes down with a couple good tugs and then it's up one side and down the other. He drops to the pavement on the other side and sprints up the driveway. Ellie's body limbers up the more he uses it, the more he works out the kinks and the stiffness.

He'll have to take care of this body. He owes it to Ellie.

He reaches the warehouse and stands there a moment panting slightly. *Panting!* As in breathing. Been a while since he's done that. He puts his hand between his ... to his chest and feels his heart hammering.

Feels good. Feels like a privilege. But after a moment of basking in the heat of exertion, he feels a tingle in his side and remembers his injury. Better not push himself too much. His old regenerative powers don't seem as effective on Ellie's body as they were on his.

The warehouse looms in front of him, a blank wall three stories high. The driveway ends in two enormous overhead doors; to their right is a human-sized door. It's made of metal and is painted bright green. Nate tries the knob. It turns, but the door doesn't move. Deadbolted. There's a narrow gap between door and pavement and Nate sends a chain through this gap and up the other side, and after a few seconds of feeling around he finds the deadbolt knob and gives it a turn.

He tries again to open the door, and this time it swings inward before stopping at the end of a thick chain.

Yeah, yeah.

Nate shuts the door, finds the chain, and undoes it. Then he pushes the door open and goes inside. The place is cavernous. The ceiling is so far up Nate can imagine clouds forming beneath it. The concrete floor is slightly damp, as if those imaginary clouds had been raining recently, leaving a thin sheen of water to reflect the three big lights arranged in a triangle on the ceiling. There are more lights but the rest are dark. The warehouse is crowded with crates and pallets, a forest of merchandise, but partway up the wall Nate can see a catwalk that rings the warehouse on three sides. Glass doors and picture windows are spaced along the catwalk. Offices and such, most likely.

To his left, a spidery metal stairway ascends to the catwalk. He climbs up and tries one door after another until he finds one that opens. Beyond the door is a break room. In the dim light filtering through the venetian blinds on the window, he can see a big formica-topped table in the center and cabinets and a counter along the right-hand wall. There's a toaster, a microwave oven, and a radio on the counter, and a deep metal-basin sink. A refrigerator stands against the back wall.

And there's a quartz heater on the floor, unplugged.

Heat!

Nate plugs the heater into an outlet and turns it on, but nothing happens. Shit. The generator isn't powering the electrical system. Maybe there's a special plug. . . . Nate looks around and spots another outlet near the door. This one is colored red. He wonders if that's significant, and drags the heater over there and plugs it in.

The power switch on the heater lights up. The fan whirs to life. A few seconds later, warmth billows out through the shiny wire grill. Nate stands in front of it, puts out his arms, lets himself thaw out.

He feels another stab of pain, and this time realizes it's *hunger*. It's been so long since he was hungry . . . amazing how fast he forgot what it was like to be alive. Reluctantly leaving the warmth of the heater, he goes to the fridge and opens it. Not much in the way of pickings. Well, it's not like he's in a deli or something. He grabs somebody's half-eaten sandwich, pulls a chair over in front of the heater, and sits down getting warm and munching on the first food he's tasted in days.

Ah, what luxuries.

After he finishes the sandwich he gets the radio and plugs it into the other socket of the generator-powered outlet. He tunes past commercials and snippets of music until he finds news.

He's not surprised to find them talking about the fire.

". . . Roads leading into the affected area remain closed to traffic, and as I said before, the Hunter River Bridge was damaged by the fire and is reportedly unusable. Emergency crews are returning to the scene of the disaster. Any listeners in the Canal District are urged to remain calm and find shelter in any available, undamaged building until rescuers arrive. As of now the official death toll is thirty-seven, including fourteen firefighters and police. That estimate is expected to rise as rescue crews begin going through the area. No word as yet as to what atmospheric conditions may have caused the fire to suddenly go out—"

Nate switches off the radio. *Atmospheric conditions.* Yeah, that's a good one. Due to atmospheric conditions, this inferno has been temporarily disconnected.

Where did Fenton and his fire go?

Into the hills.

Knife Point, to be exact.

Ellie recognized it at once. She and the other bound spirits remain caged in the tower of fire, but now the column erupts from the rocky spine of the hilltop. From the circle she noticed when she was here with Andy those days ago, the glyph she had taken for somebody's scrawled, half-finished compass.

The fire has changed. It's got more spirits in it, spirits of people killed by the inferno Fenton triggered, called into the fire by whatever ritual he pulled off in the park. The column is slowly rotating counterclockwise. Right now she has a view into the city but she's being turned toward the lake, and before long she'll be looking up the hill toward the road where she and Andy parked when they visited Knife Point those days ago.

Speaking of Andy, he appears to have lost it. He keeps mumbling *son of a bitch*, over and over and over. Ellie isn't sure if this is an epithet against Fenton or just an expression of disbelief, and she isn't inclined to ask because she's watching *him*, down at the edge of Knife Point. He isn't in Nate's body anymore. Now he's human fire, legs and arms and torso and head shaped from crystal flames.

No wonder he wanted to build up here. It was another one of his special places, like the park and the Project. He seems to have had power points scattered around the city. She supposes that's easy to do when you're a land baron.

So there Fenton is at the tip of Knife Point, and he's looking down toward the darkling city beneath them, and off to the southwest the lake sparkles in the moonlight. What's he doing? Sightseeing?

What's he waiting for?

Yolanda feels like a piece of taffy fresh off the machine. She tries not to show it, even though there's nobody around to see. The hills are deserted except for her, the souls in the tower, and Fenton, who's down at the tip of Knife Point looking off to the horizon like she and his other victims don't even exist.

She can see the trapped spirits plain as day. They cling to the blazing column, fruit waiting to be picked and eaten. They're hard to recognize as people, they're all twisted and misshapen and scarred, except for the new ones who remain discrete from the fire. Like Ellie Watson, for instance, hanging there like the figurehead on an old-style boat.

There must be people in the tower she knows. Neighbors from the Project who didn't escape the blaze. But if there are she can't pick them out, they're too far blended into the tower for her to recognize them.

She wonders if *they* recognize *her*.

That was the worst thing about the spell Fenton's little monster laid on her: making her go back to the Project, using her to drag it and its destroyer back from oblivion. She barely escaped from it the first time, and she escaped alone. To be brought back to the site, and worse, to be used as the instrument of Nicholas Fenton's return, was an insult of monstrous proportions.

It all comes back like lightning, the way it always does, usually late at night when she's alone in her room, not when she's out in some forest in the middle of the night and operating in disaster mode. But Fenton is here, and her old neighbors, and maybe even, somewhere in the fire, her lost little boy. How could she *not* remember?

How could she not remember coming out of her haze? She smelled smoke, acrid and pungent. She tried to stand up but missed the floor the first time, knocked her head on the coffee table. The shock of the blow helped jar her to some semblance of lucidity, enough at least to see that the room was on fire. The entire wall opposite the sofa was burning, including the door to the bedroom she shared with her boy.

And his doll, his little Mr. Knob, was over near the fire, starting to burn.

She screamed for William and stumbled over to the bedroom door. She grabbed Mr. Knob and pounded his flames out against her own breast. The door was a rippling sheet of fire but she kicked at it anyway and it fell in, letting oxygen rush into the bedroom, triggering a fiery explosion that knocked her on her ass. Charles, over on the couch, grunted. She stumbled back and tried to wake him up but he kept shoving her away, he wouldn't move, and she had to leave him. She *had* to. She couldn't move him herself, and the fire was shimmying up the walls, across the ceiling, curling down over the door to the hallway. There was only one way out. She went to to the window and opened it and looked out and the other buildings were burning too, all of them, everywhere she could see.

Even though she was on the third floor, she jumped out the window. Broke her leg and her tailbone. But Charles and little William, they burned right up, nothing to find but ashes, and all she had left was Mr. Knob.

She went straight after that, laid off the junk that had been suppressing her psychic gifts. The junk had nearly killed her by letting the fire take her while she stupored. The junk had killed Charles and, indirectly, her boy.

And oh, how she clutched Mr. Knob's little wooden head, during the withdrawal, when her mind was left wide open and all manner of ghosts and spirits and wandering haunts blew through it, matching the shivering agony of her body with a cold, dead wind that withered her mind. Mr. Knob became a sort of totem, the most special of her artifacts. She used him as a focus, used him as a guardian, used him as a receptacle for whatever energy needed dispersing.

If she'd only had Mr. Knob, she could've fought off Fenton's little wombat. But Fenton stole Mr. Knob when he came to her and lied to her and then ran away, yes he did, stole him so she'd have nothing but her own self to fight with.

"You son of a bitch," she whispers.

Nothing but her own self, and her own righteous anger.

Carrying her anger like a sword, she drifts toward the tip of the promontory.

His stomach full and his body warmed, Nate leaves the warehouse the way he came, out the front door and over the fence, and goes quick as he can down River Street toward the old hotel on Canal Street. It's the tallest building in the immediate vicinity, it'll give him a good view of his surroundings, which will maybe help him assess the situation. And Yolanda said Fenton had put a spell on it. It's one of *his* places. Maybe there'll be something to see.

The streets are still deserted. The emergency crews the radio announcer talked about are nowhere to be seen, though Nate does hear a distant helicopter thumping the air. Surveying the damage by air first, maybe. Prudent cowardice.

He turns left on Canal Street. The barren property of the Project is across from him, dark and crusted like a scab. Cursed ground. One block up is the hotel, scarred and pitted by the fire. He looks at it in the moonlight, judging whether or not it really is still sound; and concluding that it is, he darts inside.

It's even blacker than it was the first time he came here. He tries to remember the layout. Elevators were straight in from the front door . . . where were the stairs?

He picks his way forward, using his chains to probe a clear path across the floor. Last time he did this he ended up feeling corpses that weren't there. Ghost corpses. Not this time, though. The place is bare. He thinks of the columns of fire roaring into the park and wonders if, like a vacuum, Fenton sucked the spirits out of this place too.

Maybe.

And maybe it's just his own nervousness making him feel like the hotel is watching him, that the floor and walls and ceiling and columns report his progress to some cold gelatinous brain somewhere in the depths of the building.

All in his head.

He's gotta be crazy. He should go across the street to Mrs. Barrett's building and climb up to *that* roof. At least he knows his way around there. But that roof isn't safe, it was falling to pieces when he was there as a spirit. He glances over his shoulder. Can't see out the front door. Moon must have gone behind a cloud, he thinks. It's as dark out there as it is in here.

Yeah.

That's it.

A cloud.

And if the darkness feels sticky, if it clings to him like tar paper, it's all in his head. *Come in*, says the old hotel, in his head because there's nothing here to speak. *I've got a room prepared for you.*

He shouldn't have come here. Before, the place seemed haunted, but now it's positively *alive* with malign intent. It doesn't want him here. It's awake and aware and angry.

Fuck it. He's angry too.

He walks, and walks, and walks. His chains scrape across the floor, finally touching a wall, and he stops. Looks around. Shadows cover everything like a layer of flies, except something on his left that glimmers faintly, like a glow-in-the-dark toy that's lost most of its luminescence. He reaches out and touches it. Cold and smooth. Glass. A mirror, maybe.

The mirror he and Yolanda both came through, maybe.

He stands there with one hand on the glass, staring straight ahead at the darkness. Why can't he see anything? Why does the mirror glow when nothing else has any light?

Yolanda said the mirror was a gate. Is that what makes it shine?

The glass starts to get warm under his fingers. Then it starts to get sticky, like syrup, like it could flow down off the wall and envelop him in a film of gooey crystal; but it doesn't, it stays vertical. So he puts his other hand on it. Light radiates between his two hands, rippling in sinuous waves. He can see himself in the glass, almost. It's a vague image, it might or might not be him. Could be someone else entirely. But it's definitely human, definitely a man.

Oh. Right. Can't be him, then. He's in Ellie's body. Funny, that doesn't seem like something he would forget, but he does. It doesn't feel that different from what he's used to.

But who's this he sees looking out at him?

He pushes harder on the yielding glass. The flickers of light intensify, flashing back and forth more rapidly, painting the face in the mirror with bands of greenish-blue light.

He draws a sharp breath.

It's a face he's seen before, though only in bronze. And then again, reflected in the inhuman features of the fungus creature.

It's the face he can't get away from.

It's Nicholas Fenton.

35

Yolanda wonders how close she can get before Fenton notices she's coming. It's not a question of noise; she's a spirit and a spirit makes no sound, unless it wants to. Groaning, thumping, even rattling chains sometimes. All very inappropriate when you're being stealthy. So he won't hear her. But Fenton's got his death magic, he'll probably detect her presence if he isn't too preoccupied with whatever it is he's doing out there.

She keeps getting closer. She needs to see him face to face. Tell him what he did to her boy. She can't make him care, but she can make him regret it. She steps out onto the broad, flat base of Knife Point's blade. Stops.

Whoa.

Lotta static coming up from the ground. She feels three separate lines of energy in the stone beneath her feet, coming into the rock and feeding the tower of souls. So that's why Fenton came here. This is ground zero, the nerve center, the place where all his energy comes together. Three streams. The Project, the park . . . the hotel? What kind of energy could he be getting from that old, broken-down hotel?

Something to do with the time-layering effect, she thinks. Tapping into something that happened there long ago, or will happen in the future. Or maybe something else entirely. Yolanda just doesn't know. Can't figure it out. This is all like nothing else she's ever run into.

She looks at Fenton. He blazes at the tip of the point like a bonfire. Does she dare confront him when she knows so little about him? Does she have a hope of stopping him? Can she even slow him down?

She thinks of her boy.

She'll try, for her boy.

She gets within five feet before Fenton turns around.

"You again," he says after a moment. His voice comes from all around her. He speaks in crackles and roars and flutters, his words animate the brush and the trees and fall from the sky and rumble up from the stone at her feet. "I thought you would know better, being a psychic and all."

"Yolanda ain't afraid of a two-bit land shark like you," she says.

He laughs. The ground shivers. "You're not afraid of me? You should be. You've never seen anything like me."

"I've seen your kind," she says. "Other spirits who liked to go around strutting and boasting. You all go to the same place in the end."

"Threatening me with hell?" Fenton asks. "But I'm not ever going to die. I'm going to go on and on and on, forever."

"That what you think?"

"What I *know*," he says. "I've got a place all ready."

"I've been there," Yolanda says. "It's gone now."

"It wasn't right anyway. I didn't have time to prepare it properly, what with the explosion and all. But this time I will. It'll be our paradise."

Paradise for Fenton, maybe, but hardly for his captured victims. "They won't last forever," Yolanda says.

"My spirits? No, they won't. But I can always get more." He laughs softly. "I'll come out and harvest, when I need to."

"People are not a crop for you to pick!"

Fenton shrugs. "That's not up to you, is it? Unless you'd care to stop me."

She stands there, watching him.

"Uh-huh," Fenton says. "That's what I thought." He turns his back on her. "I named Knife Point, y'know. Everybody thought it was because of the way it looks, but actually, I was going to make it a blade at the throat of the city. Nobody even remembers what it used to be called." He raises a blazing arm to gesture at Island City. There's an answering flash from the distant darkness, a pulse of pale white light like a candle behind frosted glass. "The Project is out there. Straight line from here. The park is over there." *Flash.* "Also a straight line."

"Yolanda is duly impressed," she says, "by your ability to connect two places with straight lines."

"And the hotel," he continues, ignoring her, "where I'll go after everything is all prepared. Right there. Dead on straight line."

Flash.

The image in the mirror doesn't show any animation. It's cold and grey and inanimate. Might as well be a reflection of a corpse.

Now isn't that a nice thought. Fenton, a corpse.

But what's he doing in the mirror?

Nate extends his chains at the glass. The surface bows inward, then snaps back into place and his chains are *inside* the mirror, snaking down toward the inert spectre of Nicholas Fenton. No feedback comes from them, they're numb, totally numb, like hands that have been in icewater—but he can see them moving through the mirror and directs them through sight.

Toward the man he's come to think of as the devil personified.

Toward the inert form of Nicholas Fenton.

But suddenly Fenton's eyes open, and his entire body gives off a wave of light that sweeps out and over Nate, that suffuses the interior of the hotel and flows out through the windows and the doorways and the cracks in the walls. It's over in a second and it leaves Nate feeling sticky and unclean.

He slowly lowers his arm from his face. He hadn't even realized until now that he'd covered his eyes. The mirror has faded back to its original dim intensity; Fenton's image has vanished. Nate's chains dangle to the floor, severed at the point they had entered the glass. The lengths that had been inside the glass have vanished.

Okay.

Putting things inside the mirror is a bad idea.

"You understand now?" Fenton says, turning back to her. "I told you. You've never seen anything like me. I'm not somebody's dead Uncle Herman. I'm Nicholas Fenton and I pull all the strings."

Yolanda says: "Why?"

"Why? *Why?*" Fenton raises his arms. "*Because I can!*"

Fire surrounds her and lifts her up, sears her though she has no flesh, blinds her though she has no eyes. *"Everything is ready and you have to go away now,"* Fenton roars, in a voice like a forest fire. *"You're too much of a nuisance. You don't know when you should just leave something alone!"*

Yolanda was never sure a ghost could feel pain. Sure, sometimes people would say *Is he in pain?* and she would always say *No, dear, the suffering is behind him now,* even if the ghost was screaming and moaning in her ear. She did it out of kindness to the living; who wants to hear that their dead loved one is wailing in torment, howling just beyond the great grey wall between life and death? But she was never positive if the spirit was in pain, or was angry, or frustrated, or what; she never knew if they told the truth, or just played for sympathy.

Now Yolanda knows for sure that a spirit can suffer, because Fenton is roasting her, boiling her, withering her soul, and God oh God it feels worse than the burns and the broken bones and all the aches and pains she's ever had. Tapping into his death magic and sending it through her. He could snuff her out easy as a candle but he's not, he wants to make her hurt first. He wants to hear her scream.

So she screams for him.

But while she's screaming, she's also probing. Probing the link between Fenton and the soul tower. Probing Fenton himself. Trying to figure out how much power he's using, how much he really has stored up. What she finds is not encouraging. He's tapping a fraction of a fraction of what he's got. He's got enough power in the tower to level the city. But he's not doing it, that isn't what he wants.

What does he want?

Fenton was right. He's like nothing she's ever seen before. He's certainly too strong for her to stop. She knows spirits; she's summoned them, she's cast them out. None of them were this powerful. This is beyond them all.

She has to try anyway. Bite him the way a dying animal bites at the hunter.

Since he's too strong to attack directly, Yolanda opens up her own mind and lets Fenton come rushing in, whether he wants to or not; he can't stop himself, he's falling into a pit that suddenly opened right beneath his feet. A pit lined with spikes. Poisoned spikes. Stabbing into him. Toxic. Kill you dead.

But he just laughs, and turns up the heat. Toying with her. No fear there. He's got the power, he's got the magic. All she's got is the rage that led her to challenge him, and that's not enough.

Not even close.

The rotating tower returns Ellie to where she can see Fenton down at Knife Point's edge. But he's not alone anymore. Somebody else is with him—it's *Yolanda*—and it looks like they're fighting or, more accurately, it looks like Fenton is kicking the shit out of her.

The two of them are standing very close to each other. Fenton's got his arms up like a scarecrow, enveloping Yolanda in a mushroom of yellow fire that cascades from him in sheets and rivers. Yolanda's screaming, her head thrown back and her mouth wide open, but Ellie can't hear her over the roar of the flames.

She wonders if the others can feel their vitality being drained off to power Fenton's insanity. After twenty years in the tower they're probably not feeling much of anything at all, but she can, he's siphoning away the energy she and the others give off as they float in the fire. Makes perfect sense, actually: burning fuel makes it release its energy and the faster it burns, the more energy it gives off in a shorter time. Apparently this even applies when spirits are the fuel.

Right now Fenton's not burning them up; he's just using the routine energy they give off, like an idling engine.

So what if. . . .

What if she goes to him *voluntarily*?

Not like trying to leave the fire, that didn't work at all, but just going with the power flow. Could she ride it into Fenton and through him and come out in one piece?

The idea is lunacy. But it's better than waiting around to get burned up.

She tells Andy her plan, but he isn't listening, he just keeps mumbling to himself. She doesn't waste the time it would take to tell the others what she's thinking. She just does it.

She feels their energy flowing down the link between them and Fenton. Reaches into it. And it accepts her entry, it lifts her out of the fire and sends her down the conduit, down a one-way path to Nicholas Fenton.

Nate touches the glass and it lights up again, the spectre of Fenton reappearing exactly as before, its eyes once again shut. This time Nate examines it minutely. The flesh is an ash blue color. The hair is a greyish-red. The shoulders are narrow, the face pinched. Like somebody stuck a hose in him and drained out all the soft stuff. He's wearing a pressed yellow suit, one that looks dusty, like it and its wearer have been lying around for a long time.

So what does it mean? Did he leave just a tiny little piece of himself here? Something that, in the mirror, looks like the whole man, with only one thing missing: animation?

"You've got your fingers everywhere, don't you?" Nate says to the image. The mirror fogs where his breath touches it. Just like glass. The haze quickly dissipates, but Nate stares at the mirror where it was, stares and stares as if he could break the mirror just by looking at it.

He has the most awful feeling that the image is waiting for *something*. That when this *something* happens, its eyes will open like they did before, only this time it'll wake up and come flying out of the glass like a vengeful banshee, come flying right at him. . . .

He pushes harder on the glass. If he could just get his hands on Fenton, just one more time . . . just wrap his chains around Fenton's little neck. . . .

Then the mirror opens beneath his hands, the surface suddenly splitting to admit them. He loses his balance and stumbles against the mirror and the glass parts for him, and he crashes through the shimmering membrane into the darkness beyond.

Ellie drifts down Knife Point, angling toward the ground. The trees pass by to her right and left, the bare grey stone scrolls by beneath her. Ahead, Fenton's fire illuminates the night. Ghost light. She wonders if anyone else can see it or if, like the Wright Project, it's only visible if you've been touched by spirits.

Touched. Molested. Whatever.

Getting closer. Light's getting brighter. She tries once to get out of the current but it holds her in place, she's locked into it, might as well be bolted down. She tries again anyway, struggling to break free. No good. She's going to ride the link right into Fenton's fire.

She expected this.

But please, God, let her be guessing right.

She emerges from the trees onto Knife Point's serrated edge. Yolanda is broiling, Fenton is laughing. She doesn't think they see her coming.

Please don't let Fenton see her coming.

He's not paying any attention to her. He's reveling in Yolanda's destruction. The tap takes Ellie right through the Yolanda's body and she comes away with the barest hint of her agony and even that's enough to nearly make her pass out. Feels like being dragged through a pit of white-hot nails. Got to stay conscious, though, can't let herself black out. She's almost to Fenton. Almost. . . .

. . . Blacked out. Where is she? It's dark, it hurts, it. . . .

No. She didn't black out.

She just passed through the barrier.

She's inside the fire, inside Fenton.

36

Nate tumbles out of the mirror and lands on his back on the cold, hard floor. He lies there a moment staring up at the ceiling. It's made of plaster done into swirls, supported by walls with marble facing that gleams in the subdued light, so finely polished that it appears wet. Right in front of him is the wide gilded mirror, and to either side of that are the elevators. They have ornate wrought iron doors, the metal twisted into flowers and vines and sunburst faces that look serenely out at the elevator paddock that, a few seconds ago, had been stripped of all its finery and was in addition black as pitch.

Nate starts to pick himself up, then somebody appears to help him, a *bellhop* for God's sake, complete with the red shirt and the little red pillbox. "Are you all right, ma'am?" the bellhop asks as he helps him to his feet.

"Yes, fine," Nate says. "I, um, slipped."

"We just waxed the floors," the bellhop says. He looks to be Billy's age, maybe a little younger. "There you are, good as new."

"Thank you," Nate says. The kid touches the front of his hat, smiles, and walks back to his position near the registration desk. Nate walks along behind the kid, out of the elevator paddock and into the lobby.

Jesus. The lobby.

Talk about urban renewal. In less than five minutes they've replaced the marble tiles on the floor, resheathed the pillars, brought in couches and chairs and plants in pots big enough to bathe in. The front desk has been polished to a lustrous brown, and behind it a bored-looking man in a tuxedo looks out at the lobby with red-lidded eyes. And they've even brought in people to play the part of hotel guests, sitting here in there, alone and in groups, reading the paper or chatting or just staring off into space.

The front door opens and four men and a woman enter. Nate glances at them, looks back at the lobby, then snaps back to look at the newcomers again.

He doesn't know three of the men, and he doesn't know the woman.

But isn't that fourth one Nicholas Fenton?

Being inside Fenton's body is just as unpleasant as it was the first time. Like being dragged through manure that's been festering in the sun. But it's different now, worse, because he's trying to digest her. He might not know she's there, but he's still using her as fuel. She might as well be a sandwich Fenton ate without realizing it.

But unlike a sandwich, she's able to move. She forces herself up the path taken by the energy that resides within him. It's more difficult than she expected; there doesn't seem to be one major conduit, the energy just kind of sloshes around inside him, permeates him and emerges wherever it happens to be. She fights to keep moving in a single direction as the random waves of power try to push her first this way, then that. Pushes through the boiling clouds, the heat, the swirling eddies that batter her, shove her back. But as she moves Fenton is stripping away her coherence layer by layer. He'll flay her down to nothing and never even know he's done it.

A wall of fire rises up in front of her, thick and impenetrable. She kicks and claws into it anyway and it tortures her, sets her ablaze, turns her from a spirit into a brand.

And then she bursts out of him, limp and spent, unable even to move any farther. The fire billowing out of Fenton pushes her along, through the field of death magic that envelops Yolanda, past her and back toward the tufted ridge. Exhausted. Feeling like a log that's been whittled to a toothpick.

But free.

She guessed right, barely.

And she has another idea.

She crawls back to the fire column. The other spirits are still there, roiling and burning. She screams until she gets their attention. It takes a lot more screaming than she wants it to.

She tells them her idea.

Predictably, they want no part of it. What will Fenton say? What will Fenton do? He'll *hurt* them.

If Ellie had physical teeth, she would grind them. But she doesn't. So instead she yells some more.

While she's yelling, Fenton finishes up with Yolanda.

Yolanda has learned a couple of things in the last few minutes.

She's learned that Nicholas Fenton's techniques for inflicting pain are not imaginative, but they're brutal. She's learned that a spirit's capacity for agony is at least as great as a body's.

She's learned that when fury confronts power, power wins.

"Had enough?" he says, throwing more fire at her, making it rise up around her, over her, enveloping her. Burning her up. Burning her away. When it's over she'll be gone, like she never existed at all, vanished like a dry cobweb.

She thinks of her boy. Now she'll never see her boy, there on the other side. She'll never see God. She'll never see anything.

But suddenly Fenton stops.

Looks over his shoulder.

Screams, "Get out of my hotel!"

And leaps over Yolanda's head, trailing fire like a comet, bounding up Knife Point to the fire tower. The tattered wisps that were Yolanda slowly sag and contract, pulling back together into something coherent. Something that looks like it *might* have been a person.

Once.

A long, long time ago.

Fenton roars past Ellie without even pausing. She doesn't see him coming and hardly knows when he's gone, he moves so fast, plunging headlong into his fire tower; then as she watches the thing collapses into the rock like a volcanic implosion. The psychic eddy he creates spins her around, pulls her forward into the sigil carved into Knife Point, the circle with the four triangles. She feels the aftereffect of whatever Fenton did, a faint tugging that holds her in place, tries to pull her into the stone herself.

Behind her, a fiery lance slices from the promontory's edge through the night toward Island City.

When she at last yanks herself free of the circle's attraction, she goes out to the edge of Knife Point. Yolanda is there in a heap on the ground like a pile of old laundry. Ellie steps past her, to the very tip of the knife, and looks out at the darkness. The island part of the city is all lit up, the skyline shining against the broad expanse of the lake, but the mainland section is the same color as the night.

Except for one spot.

A spot that glows like the heart of a nuclear explosion.

Fenton's destination.

"Whas . . . whas you see?" Yolanda says.

"I don't know," Ellie says. "But it's wicked."

Nate quickly turns away from the newcomers as they approach the desk, but he keeps a surreptitious eye on the one who looks like Fenton. It *is* him, Nate would swear it's him, but a younger version, in his twenties maybe. He hangs in the back of the group, walking next to the woman. The two of them stand close together and are discussing something, and Fenton looks happy and animated and thoroughly harmless. He smiles and there's no insanity. He laughs and there's no malice, only mirth.

What in God's name is going on here?

They're at the front desk now, the guy in front talking to the clerk, getting their rooms.

Through the wide glass doors, Nate sees a long black car glide to a halt beside the curb. A man gets out the passenger side. He's wearing a trenchcoat and a fedora.

A trenchcoat? It's summer in this place, everybody else is in short sleeves.

Nate moves his attention off Fenton and to the guy approaching the hotel. The doorman does his job, letting the guy in. As he enters, he reaches into his trenchcoat.

Fenton turns to look at the door.

The trenchcoat guy pulls out a small black handgun, looks like a revolver. Fenton shouts a warning and grabs the woman's hand and starts pulling her away from the desk, seeking cover behind a pillar.

Trenchcoat opens fire.

Bang, bang, bang!

Three shots drop three men even as their own hands head for their own jackets. Screams split the air. The clerk ducks under the counter, the bellhop dives behind a plant, the guests scramble out of their seats and sofas, crawl across the floor.

Trenchcoat aims for Fenton and the woman. Fenton's almost made it to the pillar. The woman is wide open.

Nate flings a chain across the lobby and snares Trenchcoat's wrist.

Simultaneously, the Fenton Nate remembers comes roaring out of the mirror in the elevator paddock.

Nate jerks Trenchcoat's arm and his shot goes wide, blows away a chunk of the pillar inches from the woman's head. The bullet ricochets. Young Fenton goes down. Wrapped in fire, Fenton blows into the lobby and seizes the woman's hand. *"Bastard!"* Fenton shouts. *"I wasn't ready yet!"*

Trenchcoat drops the gun and starts gibbering. Nate lets go and the assassin turns and runs out of the hotel and jumps into the black car. Its tires screech as it roars away.

The woman screams. Little rivulets of fire dribble down her arm. Young Fenton mumbles something and rolls over. His eyes are closed.

The Fenton in the fire starts dragging the woman back toward the elevators, and the mirror. She screams some more. The fire reaches her torso, creeps up her neck and down to her waist. Her eyes roll up in her head, she sags down like a sack filled with rocks. Fire Fenton doesn't appear to notice. He keeps dragging her toward the mirror, even though she's gone all limp and motionless.

Nate flings a chain, snares her right ankle and pulls. Fire Fenton finally gets a clue and pauses to look behind him, his eyes moving from the woman to the unconscious young Fenton to Nate and back to the woman again. "You don't understand," he says to his sagging captive. "I have to save you. It's all right. It's me. Nicky."

She just hangs there, eyes wide open, staring up at the ceiling.

Fenton lets go of the woman's hand as if it suddenly bit him. Arm and hand slap limply against the marble floor.

He looks at Nate.

"You," he says. "You, you bastard, *you* did this!"

"Why don't you just reanimate her?" Nate says. "You seem to get off on that."

"This is all your fault," Fenton rages.

"*My* fault? I saved her *and* you before *you* showed up and killed her." He looks at the woman. She lies curled up on the floor. The fire that covered her body and, presumably, killed her has dissipated. "This is what it was all about, huh? You burned down the Wright Project, you killed all those people, you gathered all that death magic, just so you could come back here and save this woman. But *I* already did. And now you screwed it up."

"Don't—" Fenton says.

"You fucking idiot," Nate says.

Fenton screeches and leaps at Nate in a rush of fire and air. Nate ducks under him, scuttles beneath the inferno to the elevator nook. Fenton comes roaring in after him. Nate stands his ground in front of the mirror as Fenton comes rushing toward him, but just before they meet he kicks back and pushes through the glass.

Fenton comes through after him, a fireball with a face, but Nate is already falling, falling, falling through the darkness, leaving Fenton and the mirror behind.

"I'll kill you!" Fenton shouts, his threat echoing from the invisible walls to reach Nate, far below. "You hear me? *I'll kill you!*"

And Nate thinks, so what else is new?

It doesn't take long for Nate to reach the next stop on the Mirror Express. This time it dumps him out onto grass. Soft summer grass, not the crisp grass of winter. He stands up, bewildered. It's still dark, but he's definitely out of the mirror. So where is he?

He starts walking.

The sky changes from ink to indigo. Stars come into being, and the moon appears as if from a bank of dark clouds. The silence gives way to the chirping of crickets and the sound of running water, and some strange hooting call which might be an owl, and a chorus of frogs singing for mates.

Nate stops again. A cool breeze blows crosswise to him, stirring his hair. He listens to it whisper. He listens to the faint, fluttering crash of fully-leafed trees waving in a wind that blows above his head.

This doesn't sound like Island City. And it's *definitely* not inside the old hotel.

The sky becomes an inflamed red over his shoulder, pink streaks shooting through the dome and obscuring the stars. He can see the silhouette of hills outline by an approaching dawn. But it was early night when he entered the hotel, dawn shouldn't be coming for hours.

Without regard for this fact, the engorged sun has begun to clear the hills, showing just a sliver of itself over the low, rambling summits. Nate stands and stares as the infectious light of sunrise breaks over him. In the gathering light he can see what he has been hearing. He is looking up a gentle, verdant slope studded with trees that grow singly and in copses. To his right, the placid water of a narrow canal ripples in the morning light. The sound of running water comes from behind him, and though he does not turn to look he knows that if he does, he'll see the Hunter River.

As for the sun, it looks strange, vaguely artificial. It takes him a moment to realize this is because it's shaped like a Valentine heart. It's almost enough to make him laugh. Nicholas Fenton, the killer magician, created this whole place as a love offering to a woman who died forty years ago. This must be the way Fenton's pocket dimension was originally intended to be, a lush replica of the Island City basin rather than a field of blasted asphalt. He recreated it when his rituals were complete, and he made the sun look like a heart. Nate doesn't know if he should guffaw at the mawkishness of it all or weep for the creature young Nick Fenton became.

The heart-shaped sun continues rising above the Grey Hills, the hills that ring the city to the east and north, the hills featured in half the postcards put out for the tourists and travelers.

Fenton will be coming soon. Hoping this fake sun won't have the same effect as the real one, Nate tosses a chain at a nearby tree.

It works.

"Thank God," Nate says.

He is looking at the tree and not at the mirror that hangs in mid-air a few yards away, and so when he gets knocked off his feet it comes as a complete surprise.

He looks up and the devil is standing right in front of him. A devil made of fire. The grass withers around him, the earth dries, the flowers blacken. And behind the devil the tower of flame reaches up into the pallid sky. The sounds of nature are subsumed in the roar of the holocaust.

"You miserable little bug," Fenton spits. "You ruined everything! I was going to bring Carol here. We were going to be happy forever.

Now she's *dead* and it's *your* fault!"

"You're the one who killed her," Nate says.

"You forced me to play my hand too early. I wasn't ready! But you set everything in motion by going through the mirror. I had to come when I did. I had to save her."

It sounds like Fenton is talking to himself. Nate says, "*I* saved her. *You* killed her. Understand?"

"I didn't know that. How could I know that?"

"You could have paid attention."

For a moment, Fenton just stares at Nate. Then he howls and raises his arms, fire gathering around his hands. Nate doesn't bother to get up. He flings both his chains at Fenton from where he lies on the ground, catches him around the waist and around one arm. His chains carry *heat* back to him but he doesn't care, he's got Fenton in his grip now and he squeezes, squeezes hard. Somehow his chains keep a grip on him, even though Fenton is made of fire.

The devil with Fenton's voice squirms and struggles, obviously shocked that Nate's chains can touch him. The advantage will be momentary at best. Nate tries to yank Fenton off his feet, but as he does Fenton disappears and Nate pulls back empty chains. He snaps them back quickly.

Except for the harsh, hissy rumbling of the fire tower, it's quiet.

Nate stands up, eyes on the tower. No sign of Fenton, and no trace of him except the patch of burned grass where he stood. Nate slowly turns in a circle. Ready. Waiting.

He sees the canal where it reaches the river. The old lock isn't so old here. It's bigger than he imagined it.

He sees the Hunter River, broad and calm, but broken here and there by foaming white water as it breaks over rocks. It's shallow, and wider than he remembers, and doesn't seem quite as straight. Across it is the island. No buildings there, only trees.

It's like they're in the past somehow, except the past wasn't like this. When there was a canal, there were buildings. Now there are no buildings.

He keeps turning.

Keeps turning.

Facing the fire tower again.

Fenton's standing there waiting for him.

"I wanted you to see it coming," the devil with Fenton's voice says. Then he raises an arm and blows Nate away.

37

FENTON THROWS FIRE THE WAY other people throw baseballs. The missile hits Nate in the chest and lifts him up and carries him back across the grass. Fenton keeps pouring it on, keeping up the pressure, dropping Nate's burning corpse into the river.

Except Nate's body is neither a corpse nor burning.

Because Nate has three satellites, and in the seconds before Fenton's attack he brought one of them around as an interceptor. He didn't know if it would be able to block Fenton's firepower, but it seemed like it should; psychic fire versus psychic sphere. Energy versus energy. And the sphere took the brunt of the assault, the fire breaking over it into a corona surrounding Nate's body, singeing it, doing some damage but not enough to seriously injure him.

Blew out the sphere, though. By the time Nate hits the water, he feels weaker, like he had three legs and somebody just kicked one out from under him. But hey, Fenton probably thinks he's dead.

Silly man.

Doing the dead man's float, Nate lets the river carry him to the lock, paddling as discreetly as possible beneath the water to steer himself into its open mouth. The current pushes him up against the southern wall of the lock and he turns his head to the grey stone to catch some surreptitious breaths. Rusty iron rungs set into the wall form a ladder leading up.

He hears the whispery chuckle of flames behind him.

Fenton.

Nate rolls over in the water, flings a chain without even looking for a target. Fenton's there, all right, on the edge of the wall, looking down at him. The chain catches him around his fiery neck.

Nate yanks him into the water. Lets go quickly, grabs the ladder, starts to climb.

The water begins to bubble and steam and hiss when Fenton hits it. Nate climbs the ladder quickly. Got to get out of the river before it boils. He doesn't quite manage it; superheated water scalds his legs beneath the knees. He grits his teeth and keeps climbing. Steam billows from behind him.

He can hear Fenton thrashing. He hopes it hurts.

Nate reaches the lip of the wall and rolls off the ladder onto it, gasping for breath. Vapor wafts overhead. The hissing is like a hundred steam pipes bursting.

Then, abruptly, it stops.

Nate rolls over and looks down into the lock. The water still churns, but there's no sign of Fenton. The steam is already beginning to clear.

Then, with an explosive roar, the wall of the lock crumbles beneath him; and Fenton's harsh, mocking laughter rains down. "You're a fool!" Fenton shouts.

Nate rolls with the motion of the wall, tries to jump free of it. It's not easy when it's crashing down like an avalanche beneath him. He manages to clear the bulk of the debris, lands partway up the bank in a heap of shattered grey stone. The upper door of the lock sags outward then bursts. The water in the canal comes rushing out in a roaring, frothing gush to join the river.

Fenton is standing at the top of the bank. He doesn't look quite as fiery as before, but Nate can see the tower pulsing in the background, can see things—spirits—popping like firecrackers to feed Fenton and bring him back to the power level he wants.

"You think you can stop me just by *getting me wet?*" Fenton roars. "What an *insult!*"

Pop. Pop. Pop.

"You'll just be a smudge on the ground when I'm through with you!"

Pop. Pop. Pop.

Then the popping stops.

And Fenton raises his arms.

And to Fenton's apparent chagrin, the popping starts again.

~~~

What Ellie told them was, *Go through the tap. All of you at once. Not even Fenton can handle that much power.*

They wouldn't do it, then. They were too afraid, too long in thrall to Nicholas Fenton to contemplate rebellion, or like Andy too new to the tower to be able to put a coherent thought together. So they just watched, and waited to be plucked.

As Yolanda burned.

As they came into the coil.

As Nate Watson fought Nicholas Fenton and *injured* him.

Except they didn't see Nate Watson. They saw *Ellie* Watson, who had been in the tower with them and escaped. *Ellie* Watson, embattled. Knocked around like a cue ball but refusing to stay down.

It was the sight of Ellie fighting to free them that brought Andy back to a semblance of sanity, that brought Ellie's last words back to him.

Go through the tap.

Come on! he cried to the others. *Don't make her fight him all alone! Come with me!* And this time, when murmurs swept up and down the tower, they were uncertain. Hesitant.

But not flat dismissals.

And they started to turn into assents when Fenton got dunked in the river.

Look, he's vulnerable! Andy shouted. *Ellie can hurt him—so can we!* And some of the trapped spirits said *Yes! Into the tap!*

Most still hesitated.

But that was before Fenton started eating them up like so many pieces of candy. Every *pop* was a father, a mother, a child, a lover. And the next *pop* could be any of the ones who were left.

And the charge of the spirits began.

Nate backs off a pace. The fire tower is a mass of eruptions and the effect on Fenton is not a beneficial one. In fact, he's beginning to swell into a grossly distorted fire balloon. "What . . . are they doing?" Fenton whispers, his voice like a bank of candles guttering in the wind.

Nate backs off farther. Ten paces. Fifteen. Fenton continues to bloat.
~~~

"You can't do this to me," he protests.

The tower has become a fireworks display.

"I *command* you to stop," Fenton says, in a voice drained of all power to command. "Get back . . . into . . . the circle."

Suddenly Nate realizes what's happening.

The spirits are *willingly* going into Fenton, supercharging him, and he can't handle it and he can't stop it.

Gonna be one hell of an explosion.

Nate turns and runs for the shattered wall of the lock. He clambers over the debris to the channel. The water from the canal still rushes by in a frenzied surge to freedom. Nate wraps one of his chains around a big chunk of stone and then climbs into the flood up to his neck.

Fenton has swollen to the size of a house. Desperately he begins releasing energy. He thinks he's squandering his power, Nate realizes, even though his alternative is to burst like an overfilled blimp. Power means more to him than anything, even the girl he was trying to save. He would risk destruction rather than give any up.

Nicholas Fenton is a stupid, stupid man.

Fire washes out from Fenton, scorching the grass down to black earth, roaring into the sky, sweeping down the bank toward the broken lock. Nate sinks deeper into the flood. God, he wishes he didn't have to breathe anymore. Being dead had its advantages.

Here it comes.

Nate ducks under the water as the fire scours the rocks. He feels its heat on his exposed chain, even though the water is cold. It goes on and on and on.

And on.

Nate's lungs start to feel like he's inhaled some of that fire, but he can't come up for air, not yet, his head will be scorched to a cinder in a second.

Finally the fire disappears. Nate surfaces immediately.

Fenton's still there. He's the size of a tank, but still there. Concentrating. Getting himself under control. Nate looks at the tower. It's just a shred of itself, a thin, pale, flickering wisp of flame, a vine stripped of leaves and fruit. The spirits are gone, all of them, sacrificing their existence to destroy Fenton.

And he has the gall to *still be there.*

Nate climbs out of the flood. Fenton's twenty, thirty feet away. No sign that he's aware of Nate's presence.

Nate flings both chains, straight on. Wraps them around Fenton's bloated guts. Fenton makes a noise like a wolf howling.

"*Pop*, you son of a bitch!" Nate says.

He squeezes hard enough to crush stone.

And Fenton ruptures with a sound like breaking wind.

Ellie stands on Knife Point, alone. Yolanda is gone. Ellie thought the psychic would be able to pull herself together again, but the damage Fenton wrought was too great and she slowly lost coherence until she finally evaporated. And with Yolanda's discorporation goes Ellie's hope of ever sorting out the details of the disaster called Nicholas Fenton.

So now, alone, she watches the hotel. Yolanda said that was where the final action would be, that was the place that glowed red hot. It's dark now. Ellie stares at where it was and wonders what's happening there.

She's still watching as it blows into the sky.

The blast knocks Nate off his feet and into the flood, and the flood sweeps him out into the river. He struggles to keep his head above water, because he doesn't want to drown and also because he wants to see.

See the outer shell of Fenton's spirit form peel back like the rind of a rotten fruit.

See the internal fires, the dozens of tiny bright spots that are the lost souls of the Wright Project. See them erupt in the wake of the first gush of energy, shoot off through the air, luminous rockets leaving glowing streaks that slowly fade behind them.

Fenton's still howling.

Sick white light flows out of him now, viscous, gangrenous light. The light Nate remembers from the park. It oozes out of his ruptured body and soaks into the earth, and Fenton sinks with it, his howl transformed first to a gurgle, then to silence.

Gone, and good fucking riddance.

Nate struggles against the current. Kicks toward shore.

Things begin to change around him. The world seems to be curling up at the edges like old paper. He reaches the riverbank. No grass left anywhere, just scored and blackened earth. He pulls himself from the water and crawls up the slope. The ground feels like dry canvas. It comes apart in his hands, and below it there's nothing but deep blue-black void. It calls out to him.

The other side.

Fenton's world is crumbling, his kingdom dissolving, and it was just a palimpsest painted across the void. Nate reaches into the holes in the ground. He feels invisible hands taking hold of him. Ellie's flesh slips away, he sheds it like a robe and swirls down, and down, and down.

Out of the meat machine.

Into the blue.

Epilogue

It's a long walk back to the hotel, but Ellie makes it. She's a ghost, she has nothing better to do. As the first streaks of dawn lighten the air, she reaches the devastated remains of the Canal Street area. Rescue workers are everywhere, sifting through the rubble.

It's worse than she remembers. Like the hotel was ground zero of a bomb blast, it and the buildings around it have been leveled, transformed from ordered structures into random jumbles of masonry and brick and wood and steel.

She stands a while, watching them work, extricating survivors and corpses alike from the wreckage. She drifts over to the old hotel, checking things out. It looks like a regular, albeit ruined, building. Nothing to mark it as ground zero of the last battle between Nate and Nicholas.

"I see something!" a fireman shouts. He's leading a battered, blackened child from the remains of Mrs. Barrett's tenement, but he's looking across the street, toward where Ellie stands. "In the hotel!"

Others come to care for the kid. The fireman and a couple of other workers cross the street to the wreckage of the hotel. Ellie follows them into the rubble. She quickly spots what the fireman must have seen: an arm, a female arm, protruding from a lean-to of rubble near what was once the front door of the hotel.

"Alive?" one of the workers asks.

"Help me clear some of this shit away," the fireman says.

Ellie drifts closer to the arm. She can go through the junk, she doesn't have to wait for them to move it.

"She's dead," the worker says.

"Damn it all," the fireman says.

Ellie looks at the hand. It's the left hand. It's wearing a ring. It's wearing *her* ring. How'd her body get here?

She touches the hand and doesn't resist as the empty body pulls her inside. The shell isn't *dead*, it's just vacant. Ellie has learned there's a difference, though she doesn't know for sure what the difference is.

It's quick and it's smooth and she's back inside herself. Where she belongs. But there's the lingering traces of somebody else in here, too. Somebody . . . familiar.

She wiggles her fingers. Tries to move, but can't. She's pinned by debris. Her ears are clogged with dust and dirt but she hears the fireman exclaim, "She's alive!"

Hard as it is to believe, she is.

It takes them a very long time to dig her out. By the time she's free, she knows all their names, whether or not they have families, where they live.

And she knows that the traces she feels inside her belong to Nate. He found his way into her body somehow. She wishes she could know what he did, if he stopped Fenton, how he did it. Maybe she'll find another Yolanda some day. Somebody who can reach Nate, wherever it is he's gone, and ask him what happened in the old hotel.

They put her on a stretcher and load her into a big ambulance. There are other people in here too. Some are groaning, most are quiet. Soon some people jump into the back and the ambulance begins to move. One of them, a woman, asks her how she feels and she says not too bad, a little numb. The woman nods and tells her to rest.

Rest sounds good. She closes her eyes.

Through the fuzz in her ears, she hears the driver switch on the siren. The ambulance lurches as it picks up speed.

She sees Nate's face in the darkness and smiles.

And they drive off into the night.

About the Author

James V. Viscosi is the author of several horror and fantasy novels. An expatriate New Yorker, he currently resides with his wife and various finned and furry animals in sunny Southern California, where he spends most of his time hiding beneath a very large hat. Visit him at www.jamesviscosi.com.